Forgive me FATHER

KATERINA ST CLAIR

Forgive Me Father

Author: Katerina St Clair

Edited by: Caitlin Cook

Copyright © 2024 by Katerina St Clair

All rights reserved.

Printed in: United States of America

Contents

A Message to my Readers:

This work is by no means a reflection of how I view Catholicism, Christianity, or any religion in general. This work is merely a piece of fiction and not meant to be taken literally in any sense. If you are sensitive to stories relating to the use of religion in a negative context, please do not proceed with reading. Please look over the trigger warning list carefully before diving into the story.

Now, enjoy the read.

Trigger Warning List

**Read this list of triggers carefully before proceeding
with the story:**

- Self-harm

- Mentions of child SA (Insinuated never shown on paper)

- Abuse

- Child Trafficking

- Drugs/Alcohol abuse/Addiction

- Stalking/Harassment

- Graphic violence/Death on page

- Dom/Sub play

- Non-consensual sex

- Non-consensual sexual actions

- Bloodplay

- Bondage

Playlist

Trouble (Stripped)- Halsey

God Must Hate Me- Catie Turner

Arsonist's Lullabye- Hozier

The Fruits- Paris Paloma

Do It For Me- Rosenfeld

Unholy- Sam Smith & Kim Petras

You're Somebody Else- Flora Cash

Daylight- David Kushner

In Your Arms- SOMBR

Love Is A Bitch- Two Feet

Hotel- Montell Fish

Black Out Days- Phantogram

Older- Isabel LaRosa

Universe- David Kushner

Dedication

For all of those who spent a little too much time daydreaming in Sunday mass.

Forgive me, Father-

Chapter 1

EDEN

S unday.

    The Lord's Day.

"It's the day we have gratitude for family and faith," My Mother's reverent voice echoes down the hall, "let's be thankful that we can gather together as a family and go to church. Not everyone has that blessing." It's hard to tell whether she's trying to convince us or herself more that we're anything but dysfunctional.

One day a week, this family acts as if Dad isn't cheating on Mom, I am not a screw-up, and Aiden isn't a massive pothead.

What a shame my pitiful ass had to come home indefinitely from college and ruin it for all of them.

On paper, we look like a picture-perfect family. A son, set to get a full-ride scholarship for his accomplishments on the high school football team, a husband running one of the most successful law firms in this small, good-for-nothing town, and a wife always the first to participate in all of the neighborhood socials.

To anyone not looking too closely, our lives reflect the epitome of a loving and stable nuclear family. Even down to the goddamn white picket fence home in the middle of who fucking cares, suburbia.

But there are cracks in the veneer. I see them when I look at my mother. I'm not sure how burying her sorrows in a bottle of wine every Saturday night and watching reruns of The Office fixes a life devoid of love from the man who stole away her twenties. I suppose I too might be able to drown out my pain over Friday martinis with the girls in the backyard, pretending as if all husbands don't get a rise out of seeing who can pin down the girl still young enough to get mistaken for a teenager in the bar.

They were perfectly happy living in denial, laying their sins to rest before breakfast each day under a framed picture of the Ten Commandments.

Honour thy father and thy mother.
Thou shalt not commit acts of adultery.
Thou shalt not bear false witness against thy neighbor.
What fucking hypocrites.

But, for one day a week, we can act like everything is fine. We can pretend like we show face in the cathedral as role models in faith instead of the vain need to present to everyone else that we are perfectly normal.

"Mom says you have five minutes," Aiden sighs, looking over at the boxes stacked haphazardly in the corner of my room. I still hadn't gotten around to unpacking them since throwing everything in my car and fleeing from my dorm to come home.

"I can drive myself," I mutter, messing with the settings on my camera, feeling unsettled the longer Aiden watches me from the doorway.

Aiden's brown hair is tousled effortlessly. His freshly ironed dress shirt and slacks have a slightly disheveled look — his tie loosened, shirt untucked, and his blazer is nonchalantly draped over his shoulders. The stereotypical catholic schoolboy attitude is a threat to any girl's chastity, which I'm sure he takes advantage of.

"Good for you. Mom wants to make sure you actually show," He yawns, nudging one of the lighter boxes down from the stack next to him.

Toiletries and other non-essentials spill out of the box and roll under my barely made bed. I look up to see a shit-eating grin plastered across his face.

"Oops."

Slamming my camera down on my desk, I snag my car keys from my bed, ready to kick my brother so hard in the ass that he walks funny during Communion.

"Get the fuck out, so help me God-" I start, ready to slam his smug face right into the door.

"Language, Eden!" Mom yells, scolding me as if I haven't heard considerably worse coming from her each time she dresses up for my father, doing whatever she can to get an ounce of his affection. "We are leaving now!" She continues, slamming the door with a great deal of anger.

"You're not seriously wearing that?" He questions, my eyes following his down to my oversized dark blue sweater and worn black sweats.

"I'm going to be sitting, kneeling, and holding hands with a fuck ton of strangers for an hour and a half, and you want me to dress like it's my goddamn wedding?" I question, nudging Aiden out of the way. "Piss off."

"Wedding?" He laughs. "I forgot you believe in unrealistic things. Weddings, becoming a photographer, making it through a year of college-"

Drowning out my brother's incessant need to bring me down in any way he can, I cover my ears, letting the jangle of my keys clacking together become my primary focus. A deep-rooted craving to dull the tidal wave of emotions rolling through me threatens to consume me as I walk out of the room. I bite back the urge to grab the cloth-wrapped blade I keep hidden in my room, my mind already conjuring images of me dragging the fine metal edge across my skin until the red drowns out the pain. Double-checking to ensure all parts of my body are concealed in the mirror closest to the front door, I hold up my middle finger to my brother, praying that for once God hears my message and flips my car before I can make it to the church parking lot.

As much as I dread being surrounded by unfamiliar faces demanding to know why I've come home, the cathedral has never ceased to amaze me.

In the grand expanse of the cathedral, a vast pool of holy water glistens under the soft, filtered light streaming through the stained-glass windows. The water, undoubtedly tainted by the dirty hands of sinners creeping idly into the space, occupies a central place in the nave, its surface reflecting the intricate mosaics and ornate arches above. The pool's edges are framed with elegant stonework that's similar to the intricately carved birch pillars adorning the space.

Centered at the altar on a raised platform, the priest's and deacon's chairs are positioned before the Eucharist. Small seats and kneeling pads for the altar servers are arranged towards the back of the large podium, which is used for reading Scripture.

The choir sits toward the back wall, hidden and meant to be out of the disciples' line of sight. Positioned to the left of the grand space, a separate room meant for confession remains un- bothered. Its door will be unlocked and opened thirty minutes before Mass for people to cleanse their heavy souls. Unlike many catholic churches, Saint Michael's chose a more direct approach to confession, positioning the priest's chair in front of the pen- itent, forcing you to look the man in the eyes while confessing your sins.

Over the years, confession has felt more like a game than an actual act of repentance. Lying to Father Kevin about my sins has become easier. He's old and frail, his best years behind him. Sometimes, I wonder if he looks forward to hearing my wild sins, eager to learn what temptations Satan has led me to.

Last week, I told him I tried meth for the first time, which was hilarious given the one time I tried pot, I vomited so much that I swore I'd never touch drugs again after that day.

The week before that, I told him I took part in an orgy, telling him it might be best if I didn't drink from the communal chalice when receiving the blood of Christ.

Playing these games with the old man has given me something to look forward to while I avoid the real demons at play inside my soul.

My mom thinks confession will eventually give me the courage to tell her why I came home.

My father could care less that I dropped out. Less money for him to spend on a deadbeat child. He's barely spoken twenty words to me since I made my way back to this small woodland town.

Shame.

I see Aiden talking to a few of his friends from the football team. Aiden has always been popular at school, but I'm not sure anyone knows the real him.

Drinking my third cup of complimentary lemonade, I isolate myself from the gaggle of overdressed members of the congregation, keeping to myself on one of the couches in the gathering space meant to be utilized before Mass.

Scrolling through social media on my phone, I nervously skim the posts from my friends back at college, turning my phone off entirely when I see *his* face in one of the group photos posted over Spring Break.

Downing what's left of my drink, I toss the cup into a nearby trashcan, frowning when it misses the rim.

"She shoots, she misses," Her familiar voice chimes. The couch shifts under the added weight as she joins me with a wide grin on her face.

With dark curled hair, golden honey eyes, and rich olive skin, Zoey Lee is the epitome of human perfection. Unlike my unmanaged brown locks, murky hazel eyes, and freckled pale skin, she always looks full of life, kissed by the sun, her teeth as white as snow.

If she weren't a childhood friend who hated organized religion as much as me, I'm not sure we'd have anything in common.

"How many women have gossiped about my mom today?" I question, leaning into her. Her curvy body and full breasts are accentuated by the beautiful, flower-printed dress she's wearing.

"Six. Dahlia always has something to say after your dad gives her the flirty eyes," She hisses, pointing to the young woman my dad stands uncomfortably close to.

"And what's Aiden been saying?"

I know damn well he's already led the charge on starting rumors about me, in the church and out of it.

"Apparently, your meth joke has gained some traction," She says contritely, patting me on the back. "But I know it's not true," She whispers, giving her cross necklace a small kiss. "As does the big man," She smiles. I feel the cold metal of my own cross pressed to the center of my chest nagging for attention.

Rolling my fingers over the rosary in my pocket, I use the sacramental meant for prayer as a distraction, keeping my thoughts away from the scars on my wrists.

"I should go light a candle," I mutter, the feeling of people's searing gazes suddenly much more apparent.

"I meant to tell you something," Zoey smiles, shifting her eyes around the room. Tugging my arm, she gets me to sit back down, her lips pressing to my ear. "Father Kevin is retiring."

"Father Kevin? The man who said he would "die at the altar before leaving" is retiring?"

Zoey nods her head excitedly.

"He went forward to the clergy, requesting an early retirement to enjoy some time in Jerusalem. They approved his request and appointed a new priest. The announcement is supposed to happen today-"

"Hey, Eden," One of Aiden's friends, an altar server, yells from across the room. His evil little grin is more than enough to tell me where this is going. "You think the Lord would approve of you using meth?" I see my brother's elbow drive into his side.

So much for respecting thy neighbor.

Hearing the whispers in the room escalate, my dad looks over to where I'm standing, his eyes set in the same rigid and cold way that I used to fear as a child. Hearing the sound of his belt buckle in the back of my mind, I clear my throat and leave Zoey behind in the crowded gathering space.

I shove past the large oak doors, dipping my finger into the pool of holy water.

"In the name of the Father, the Son, and the-" I pause, looking to the empty pews, wondering what the point is if no one was watching.

"Fuck this," I hiss, stopping myself mid-blessing. My eyes peer toward the vacant confession room, deciding to confront Father Kevin.

Making my way toward the room, I throw back my shoulders, raise my head, and prepare to face the old man with as much courage as I can muster. Forcing the door wide open, I start to speak but pause, perplexed by the sight in front of me.

Ten minutes till Mass.

He should still be here.

He's always here.

But instead, I find someone else here.

Dressed in sleek black from head to toe, his tailored shirt and pants cling to a broad, imposing frame. Arms crossed over his chest, he towers above most of the men in the congregation, standing around 6'4. His dark hair, cut into a faded undercut, frames intense hazel eyes that lock onto mine, the green irises almost swallowing me whole. A chill runs through me—lying to Father Kevin is one thing, but I could never deceive this man. Black ink traces up the side of his neck, a silver cross glinting at his throat. Youthful yet hardened, he leans into the doorway, his gaze piercing until I'm forced to look away. Beautiful and haunting all at once, the man isn't someone I've seen in the cathedral before. His mouth moves, but I can't hear a sound.

"W-What?" I question, struggling to find my words, the large sweater hugging my body now considerably warmer.

As he pushes away from the wall, a gold wedding band flashes on his finger before he tucks his hands into his pockets.

"I asked if I can help you?" He reiterates, glancing toward Father Kevin's empty chair.

"Where is Father Kevin?" I question, keeping my focus on anything but the man's painfully striking eyes.

"Father Kevin wrapped up early today. Between you and me, I think he's despondent about today being his final Mass," He sighs, pausing before me. "Was there something you needed from him?" The man's jaw tenses the longer he watches me. "You looked fairly livid coming in here."

I try to catch my breath, but the man's presence is suffocating. His deep voice and large frame are enough to make anyone second guess their actions in the house of the Lord.

"I came here for confession," I lie, forcing my face into a neutral expression. "But I don't plan to have a stranger absolve me of my sins," I snap, a small smirk spreading across the man's alluring face.

"Have a list of sins to share, do you?" He questions, almost as if he's mocking me.

"Not as many as his altar servers," I grumble. "Do you suppose God knows how frequently Father Kevin has felt the need to share my confessions with his bottom-feeding sycophants?" I question, the man's brows raise at the comment.

"Sycophant?"

"Perfect little disciples, all dressed in white, kneeling at the man's feet as if he's a deity, just begging to lick his feet and follow his every command. What would you call them if not servants?"

"I would call them children of God. Subservient to their Father," He whispers, taking a step closer. I feel the heat trapped behind my cheeks, my nails viciously clawing at my palms in my clenched hands.

"I've never been one to submit so blindly to anyone or anything," I hiss, not letting up on my position. "Perhaps that's why Father chooses to spill my secrets."

He surveys me, letting his eyes linger on my neck much longer than I'd like.

"Yet, you wear that cross?" He questions.

"Nominal faith is better than nothing."

Nodding, he glances behind me, the busy chatter of those beginning to funnel into the space breaching the quiet air between us.

"Eden Faulkner, I'm guessing?" He questions.

The way he says my name awakens every nerve in my body. My stomach rolls with anxiety, my skin flush with heat.

"So, I was right. He's spoken about me?" I question. "You ready to judge me too?"

His head cocks to the side at the accusation in my tone.

"How could I have anything but empathy for an orgy-loving, meth junkie?" He asks sarcastically. "Although I can't say any of that fits the girl I see before me," He says, as if he has me entirely figured out.

"Then what do you see..." I trail off, giving him space to reveal his identity.

"Roman," He clarifies, his canines flashing as his lips curl into a smirk.

The low hum of the choir singing in praise catches my ear, the first warning to take a seat before Mass begins.

Wishing now more than ever I could escape and hide in the bathroom, I shake my head, letting my fingers touch my temples. The last thing I have the patience to do is stand next to Aiden for an hour and a half and play nice.

"I suppose that's your queue to leave," Roman says, extending his arm toward the open door.

I shoot him an annoyed glance, then slowly step back, letting out a dismissive scoff.

"And what about you?" I question, narrowing my focus.

"I'll be participating, just in a different way," He shrugs, giving me little clarity on who he is.

"Right," I hiss, rolling my eyes at how relaxed and indifferent he seems.

Turning on my heels, I make my way toward the door, startled as an arm blocks my way. His body leans into the doorway, stopping me from going any farther.

"To answer your question, Eden," He whispers, his voice low as his breath brushes the back of my neck. "What I see is a girl who opens her mouth before thinking far too much," He snaps, his lips inches away from the back of my neck. "You'd benefit from learning how to close those lips of yours. Maybe try focusing all that emotional energy you're spitting out on something more rewarding."

As I turn my head, he remains unmoved, his nose just inches from mine and his body towering over me in the doorway.

"Yeah?" I question, malicious thoughts toward this man festering in my mind. "Well, maybe you can come up with something for me to focus on, then."

I shake my head at him. Watching his eyes follow me as I walk away, his body creeps backward into the confession room until he's no longer visible.

I make my way through the pews, ignoring the fire under my flesh, keeping my head lowered until I've locked eyes with my family who'll forever be disappointed in me.

Forty-five minutes of scripture, thirty minutes of hymn, and twenty minutes of kneeling later, Father Kevin finally pulls his focus away from the altar servers. Clearing his throat, people begin to quiet as he moves toward the front of the room.

"Before we receive the Holy Spirit, take in the blood of Christ, and say our goodbyes for the evening, I want to address the elephant in the room," The old man says with a smile, as whispers ripple through the pews.

He clasps his hands together in front of him as he looks solemnly over each section of the altar area, waiting for the excited chatter to die down.

"I'm sure many of you have heard a rumor revolving around my departure from the church-"

"Hey," Aiden snaps, grabbing my hair to get my attention, his mouth inches away from my ear. "I promised a few of my buddies I could smoke with them after Mass. You mind driving me to The Overlook?"

"Why the hell would I do that?" I swat his hand away from my hair, responding quietly enough to avoid my parent's listening ears.

"Wouldn't hurt to have me backing you when Mom and Dad decide to scream at you when we get home," He hisses, holding his position with my parents over my head like a fucking gold sticker. "Agree, or I will tell them all the rumors are true."

Jerking back, I make sure he can feel the iciness in my glare. "Fuck you."

"I'll take that as a yes," He snaps, swatting the back of my head before returning his focus back to Father Kevin.

Keeping my head down, a nagging presence begins to eat away at me. Unable to ignore it for long, I look around, turning to find Roman leaning against a wall at the back of the room, his eyes locking with mine instantly.

Glaring at the man, I tug at one of the sleeves of my sweater, thinking of Roman's gold wedding band, wondering where his wife could be.

How long has he been looking this way?

"I have sadly decided to move on from my time here and take a leap toward my next adventure brought by faith," Father Kevin exclaims. My focus is pulled away from Roman. "But do not think I have left you empty-handed."

Finding Zoey in the crowd, she gives me an "I told you so" look.

People around me begin clapping and sobbing in shock. A few even leave the room dramatically to hide their intense emotions after hearing the news.

Who the hell would want to take over-

"Father Briar," Father Kevin motions to the back of the room, my body going rigid as Roman pushes away from the wall and confidently makes his way to the front of the altar.

Zoey's jaw drops as she takes in the sight of Roman, her eyes wide with awe. It's clear that his striking looks have left her and the other women in the pews breathless. As he shakes hands with Father Kevin, the women's attention is riveted on him, their gazes lingering with undisguised hunger. Meanwhile, their husbands sit seething with barely contained frustration, their hands clenched tightly in a mix of jealousy and anger as they watch their wives' obvious fascination with him. "This is Father

Briar," Father Kevin smiles. "He's just finished his duties at a previous church and is thrilled to step into my shoes-"

"Is he not a little young for the role, Father Kevin?" My father questions, nudging my mother, whose eyes are glued to Roman.

Father Kevin's eyes sparkle with pride as he introduces the new priest. "Father Briar has shown extraordinary promise from a young age," He begins, his voice tinged with admiration. "His brilliance in seminary was matched only by his unwavering faith and dedication. He overcame significant personal trials, including the loss of his family at a young age, which deepened his compassion and resolve. Despite his youth, he has already demonstrated a profound understanding of God's will and a rare gift for guiding others. His journey has been one of remarkable resilience and divine purpose, and he is uniquely prepared to lead this congregation with wisdom beyond his years."

In this light, Roman looks much more approachable than he did in the confession room, feeding the audience his warm smile and soft, welcoming eyes.

Taking the mic from Father Kevin, he clears his throat, the low rumble of his voice making my stomach somersault.

"Thank you, Father," Roman smiles, taking in a deep breath. "I know what you all must be thinking right now. Who the hell is this kid standing up here?" Audible gasps slip out from some of the more traditional congregation members at the crude language.

Feeling a smile creep along my lips, I force the expression back down, eyeing the gold band wrapped around his finger.

So, it's not a woman he's devoted to, but rather God.

"I know I have big shoes to fill following in Father Kevin's footsteps, and I cannot hope to match the legacy he has built. However, I promise to lead this congregation with unwavering faith and dedication. I am committed to getting to know each of you personally and guiding you with sincerity and compassion. Together, we will seek to follow God's path and strengthen our faith." His eyes linger on mine as he surveys the room.

Feeling as if the last part was a personal attack, I react without thinking, holding up my middle finger in the center of my chest.

Seeing a smirk spread across his lips moments after the gesture, I quickly lower my hand, feeling more exposed under his gaze than I have all evening, despite the lingering stares I've faced throughout the service. Lowering my head, I stare at my feet, keeping my focus far away from Father Briar and his aggravating, cocky attitude.

"With that," Father Kevin interjects, "I suppose it's time to begin Communion."

Our family is one of the last to funnel our way to the altar. Trailing behind Aiden, I step on his heels every chance I get. Biting back the need to scream at me out of frustration, he continues to follow our father dutifully without saying a word. Meanwhile, I watch as the congregation passes baskets around, the church persistently collecting donations as if it were still in need despite the apparent wealth displayed all around us.

Stepping on his heel so hard he nearly loses his shoe, Aiden finally turns around, raising his fist. I point my finger to the large cross hanging above the altar.

"What would Christ say?" I question, forcing a sympathetic tone.

"That you should have been aborted," He hisses, his insult doing nothing to pierce my hollow insides. When it's finally our turn to receive Communion, Aiden quickly puts on a kind smile as our parents take their places before the altar servers holding the chalice. My brother steps up to Father Kevin, who gently places a piece of bread on his tongue. I move to the one empty spot, intentionally avoiding the chalice due to my complex relationship with alcohol. When I stand before the altar server, I open my mouth to receive the Eucharist, only to be startled when a hand, commanding and impressive, with long, strong fingers that taper to firm, square tips, unexpectedly grasps the shoulder of the young altar server beside him.

"I'll take over." Roman smiles, grabbing the metal bowl filled with bread. He moves to stand in front of me, and I'm only slightly aware that I might be gaping up at him.

"Not one for the blood?" He questions, my mouth snapping shut.

Saying nothing, I don't feed into his teasing remark. At that, I'm ready to reject all of Christ's sacrifices. At this point, it feels like I'm already damned.

As I begin to step down from the altar, a sudden, unexpected pressure on my bottom lip makes me freeze. His hand finds my face, his thumb slipping between my lips with a commanding touch. He gently but firmly drags my lower jaw downward, forcing my mouth open. As he maintains a steady pressure on my jaw, his gaze lowers, studying me intently. I stare back at him, my eyes wide with a mixture of confusion and intrigue. "Stick out your tongue," He demands. My family is too focused on receiving Communion to realize what's happening.

Hesitantly, I do as he says. Roman places the bread on my tongue, his thumb slightly tugging on my lower lip before his hand slowly moves away. A dizzy haze creeps over my senses, pressure coiling between my thighs at the gesture.

"The body of Christ," Roman whispers, my mouth quickly closing.

"Amen," I say instinctively, still shocked by the feel of his finger on my lip.

"Good girl. See, you can submit. Try to remember that the next time you feel inclined to open that pretty mouth out of anger," He whispers, his lowered eyes quickly lightening the moment my mother approaches him.

Backing away, I touch the parts of my face he'd touched, unsettled by how easily he was able to get me to do what he wanted.

Unable to shake my nerves, I take a deep breath, making the executive decision to leave the building and spend the rest of Mass overthinking in my car.

Chapter 2

ROMAN

I make my way into the vestibule. The women of the church linger, taking extra time to prod me on my life story, lust and hunger dripping from every word they say to me. Watching several husbands congregate toward the back of the gathering space, I see many eye me with disgust, too insecure with their fragile masculine egos to address how livid they are to see their wives are capable of whoring themselves out for someone.

Forcing on an appreciative smile, I glance around the gathering space, wondering at what point I'll stop trying to pinpoint her brown locks and underdressed figure in the wave of overly tight dresses and ironed dress shirts. Father Kevin looks peaceful, leaning into fond farewells and kind words from his loyal followers. I catch him glancing at me every time someone mentions how dearly he will be missed.

"I hate to see you go," One of the women in the choir bellows, her arms wrapping around the old man, while eying me down in the corner of her vision.

Patting her a few times, the old man excuses her and leans into me to shield his words.

"You'd think they could at least be truthful in two priests' presence," He jokes, raising a brow.

"She seemed genuine," I tease, smiling a little deeper once the man rolls his eyes.

"I don't think I even knew this many women were in the congregation prior to today," He smiles, doing his best to avoid the disciples using him as a way to get a closer look at me. "I may have devoted my life to God, as have you, but holy hell, a confidence boost like this would have been nice once or twice."

Patting him on the back, I try to ease his discomfort.

"I hope you're not worried. I've never had an issue with temptation," I say with full honesty, kicking myself for the lack of control I had earlier with Eden. Her defiant attitude had done something to me that I wasn't willing to explore yet.

Most of the time, looking past women has been simple, my mind always reverting back to my promise to God, my sinful and depraved thoughts locked away in the depths of my mind.

So why the hell can't I shake how much her recalcitrant behavior rattles something loose inside of me?

Waving a large white paper in the air, one of the younger altar servers, Nathan, waltzes over with a smug look on his face.

"Is that the list?" Father Kevin asks, the boy's response merely a slight nod.

"You won't believe who signed up to serve this fall," The boy scoffs, looking me up and down.

Taking a deep breath, I catch the lingering scent of pot and let a smirk play across my lips.

"Big fan of medicinals?" I question, his smug look quickly fading.

"Eden Faulkner?" Father Kevin sounds surprised, but her name immediately sparks my interest quicker than any interaction I've had since ending Mass.

Still feeling the ghost of her lips wrapped around my thumb, I shift uncomfortably in place, clenching my jaw as I sense the increased blood flow making its way between my legs.

Shit. Maybe it's time for a divine reset. Images of deep-rooted, evil sins make their way to the forefront of my mind, reminding me of the parts of myself I left behind after I was ordained.

I devoted my life to God to scathe my demons, not waltz right into their grasp.

Trying to figure out why she has been on my mind since our interaction in the confession room is better left unsolved.

Or maybe it's the fact that I know exactly why she is on my mind that's eating me alive.

"She willingly signed up?" Father Kevin questions, his feelings toward Eden something he didn't hold back sharing with me.

Having been large contributors to the church's remodel, the Faulkners are well-known in this town. Her father, David, and mother, Morgan, are both some of the most devoted Catholics to the church. Their son, Aiden, is an engaged and effective youth coordinator and is one of the favorites here. Eden, however, is "Satan's greatest creation," according to Kevin.

"Not exactly-"

"I signed her up," A middle-aged man chimes. Both he and Kevin smile at each other, a woman similar in looks to Eden trails behind the man. The two men are clearly familiar, and my presence seems to be no consequence to whatever relationship these two have with each other.

"Your last attempt to help her find redemption?" Father Kevin jokes, my mouth opening before I've had the time to process my words.

"Is your grip on your daughter so weak that you had to enlist a priest to teach her some moral guidance?" I ask, watching as the man's eyes widen in surprise.

"Sorry, I can't recall your name, Father," The man hisses, his hand outstretched between us.

I grin, taking his hand and clamping down as hard as I can. He winces as his face reddens with anger.

"Roman Briar, but here you will know me as Father Briar," I boast, watching the man scoff.

"David Faulkner," He snaps, glancing back at his wife. "This is Morgan." The woman's head barely raises to acknowledge me.

It would seem she probably received an earful for her unabashed stare towards me during Mass.

"Eden and Aiden are yours?" I question, his head glancing around the space.

"Aiden, yes. Eden, regrettably," He sighs, his words making me squeeze his hand just a little tighter.

"And where is the golden boy?" I question, ready to meet the golden child of the Faulkner family.

"He's spending time with his sister at The Overlook. She wasn't feeling too good after Communion," David says, seeming unbothered by the state his daughter might be in or why.

Dropping his hand, I slowly nod, grabbing the list from the altar server. Her name is scrawled at the very bottom of the page.

"And she knows she's been signed up?" I question, his eyes rolling.

"As if getting her to do anything altruistic is possible. This was the only way," He snaps. His ego is suffocating me.

"Okay, so, she'll be made aware that serving requires hours outside of Sunday Mass, correct?" I question, his eyes narrowing.

"She won't have a choice in what she does. Father Kevin was hardly able to keep her in line. I'd like to see what you're capable of."

"I assure you, David," Father Kevin smiles, sensing the tension, "Father Briar will turn your daughter into a woman deserving of being in the Lord's house."

Looking nowhere in particular, I find the sign to the office and politely excuse myself from the conversation.

"I have to finish filling out housing paperwork," I smile, still unsure how eager I am to live on the same grounds as the church.

With a slight nod, Father Kevin dismisses me, continuing to indulge in conversation with the Faulkners.

Tucking the sign-up paper in my pocket, I work my way through the crowd, ignoring people's attempts to speak to me, giving them a large enough smile to satiate their need to be recognized.

When I reach the office, I quickly close and lock the door. Sighing, I make my way to the desk, taking a seat in the polished leather chair behind it.

I flatten the paper on the desk. Feeling for my flask still tucked away in my pocket, I bite back the urge to have a drink as I take notice of the mandatory hours of training written after each server's name.

Having been in the church for years, Eden has the fewest hours.

Looking at the painting of Mary Magdeline hanging on the wall across from me, I grab a pen, tapping it against the corner of the desk.

"Well, since they think she's irredeemable," I say, pointing the pen toward the painting, "What's a few more hours?"

Scrawling the most hours required for a server next to Edens's name, I tuck the paper back in my pocket, typing up an email for the church's newsletter to announce the altar server's commitments.

Matthew 6:11-13: "Give us today the food we need, and forgive us our sins, as we have forgiven those who sin against us. And don't let us yield to temptation, but rescue us from the evil one."

Chapter 3

EDEN

Tapping my fingers along my steering wheel, I follow the rhythmic tune of The Lumineers, drowning out my spiraling thoughts. The events that unfolded during Mass replay in my mind, the memory of feeling Roman's hand on my face regrettably causing more excitement than it does anger.

Being touched by someone throws me back to that night in *his* dorm. The haze from the alcohol blurs his figure, my wrists are raw from restraint, my screams painfully muffled-

Aiden slams his hand on my passenger-side window, startling me out of the memory. His two friends, Nathan and Zack, wait impatiently behind him. He gestures curtly for me to unlock the car. I press the unlock button, and after a soft click, the boys pile into my Kia, kicking my chair as they all clamor inside. Stealing the passenger's seat, Aiden nudges my arm, trying to get my attention.

"You didn't stay the whole Mass? Now you'll really need me to vouch for you," He snaps, the pungent smell of weed emitting from Nathans's backpack.

"Can you just shut the fuck up and let me get this over with?" I question, gripping the steering wheel.

"Whatever, Eden," He sighs, tugging the aux chord free from my phone. "We're not listening to this shit while being forced to deal with your moody ass."

Twenty-five minutes of mind-numbing rap music later, I pull into The Overlook, getting a bird's eye view of our house and the church from up here. Slapping each other on the backs as they leave the car, Zack lingers, his eyes watching his friends before looking at me in the rearview mirror.

"Do you need something-"

"Come out and join us," He says with a grin, his tone much kinder than any of my brother's other friends.

Dragging my knees to my chest, I look back at him with a raised brow.

"I'm not a fan of pot," I snap, startled to see him smile deeper.

"I'm not asking you to smoke. Clearly you're not feeling great, and your brother can be a mega dick. Just get some fresh air. It's probably going to rain, and that's the best time to get a good inhale," He says, slinging his arms across the back of my chair, his chestnut hair falling into his eyes.

Shaking the front of my car, Aiden throws up a middle finger to Zack, mouthing "What the fuck" as Nathan vigorously digs in his bag for his homemade bong. He ignores my brother's taunts as he waits for me to respond.

"Say yes so I don't have to look at Aiden pretend to jack off anymore," He pushes, my eyes rolling at the sight of my brother doing just that.

"Fine," I hiss. "But I'll leave you here if you try and force me to smoke." I smile, and there's satisfaction lining his face.

"Pinky promise I won't," He says playfully.

Opening my door, Zack follows.

Impatiently waiting for Nathan to light up the bowl, I take a seat on the hood of the car, twirling the keys on my finger and watching as my brother greedily takes a massive drag. Aiden passes Zack the bong, and he takes a small hit, blowing the smoke in the air. He passes it back to Aiden before joining me on the hood.

"That was a weak ass hit, man," Aiden scoffs, watching Zack shrug his shoulders as he laughs at his friends.

They continue to pass the bong back and forth, burning through their shitty, overpriced stash pretty quickly.

"Who's my brother's dealer anyway?" I question Zack, his hand rubbing the back of his neck.

"Zack is," Aiden laughs. "Did you forget you guys were in the same class before you graduated?"

Racking my brain, I finally pinpoint why his features were so familiar to me.

"Wait. Zack *Lerman*?" I question, smiling like an idiot. "No fucking way, I thought you went off to college?'

"I did for a little," He sighs, his face growing a faint shade of pink. "Wasn't really my thing. Now I'm working for my dad, selling Teslas to the rich assholes in this town."

Putting the pieces together, I scold myself for being so forgetful.

"I never knew you were-"

"Your age? It's cool. We only ever saw each other in passing, and even then, our friend groups never really mingled."

Laughing at his statement, I shake my head.

"What friend group?" I question. "I barely had any friends. Still don't."

"Shocker," Aiden murmurs.

"Why don't you keep inhaling that shit Sativa and stop being a dick?" Zack snaps. Nathan laughs at the shocked look of embarrassment on Aiden's face.

I rub my arms, taking in the scent of the looming clouds.

"College wasn't really my thing either," I sigh.

"You still taking pictures?"

"Trying to," I admit. "Feeling a bit uninspired these days."

Smiling once again, I tug at the sleeve of my sweater, nervously trying to focus on something other than Zack's gaze.

"I have a question," Nathan exclaims, his eyes bloodshot. "Why the hell did you come home?"

Feeling the drop in my stomach, I shrug my shoulders, keeping my features as nonchalant as possible.

"Like I said, college really just wasn't my thing-"

"She had a psychotic break," Aiden interjects.

"Aiden, I don't think-"

"Come on, Eden. You might as well share it since the rest of your little secrets are all over town. You both should've seen how fucking messed up she looked when she got home. Bruises all over her, bloodshot eyes. My dad's theory is drugs, but I guess now it's less of a valid theory-"

"Aiden-"

"Or maybe it was a crippling sex addiction. You always were a prude. Maybe she met the wrong kinky fuck and-"

"Aiden," Zack yells. Nathan's smile drops instantly as my brother's focus finally drifts back to me.

Unsure when the tears started slipping free from my eyes, I feel them roll down my cheeks. I take in a shaky breath, my jaw clenched; my nails dug into my palms. I slide off the hood of my car, gasping as I take in a breath, the looming presence of a panic attack breathing down my neck, close to the surface. I move to the back of the car and lie back against the trunk, grateful for a little space to calm down.

Listening to the sounds of Nathan and Aiden bickering, I press my head to the cool glass of my back window, hoping the panic will subside. Footsteps approach me, my hand ready to wave off my brother and his string of insincere apologies.

"I'm fine, Aiden-"

"Like I said, your brother is a dick," Zack reiterates, remorse etched into his features.

Leaning into the back of my car, he crosses his arms, watching me closely as I wipe away my tears on the sleeve of my sweater.

"I didn't mean to have that reaction," I sob, scolding myself for being so vulnerable around a group of potheads.

Zack hoists himself onto the ledge of the trunk, grabbing my hand and urging me to slide down and sit next to him.

I allow my hand to stay in his as he cranes his head up to the rolling clouds above.

"Your brother has had to deal with your dad's anger a lot more since you got home. I think he resents you for that."

I laugh in disbelief. "Aiden has never liked me." I shake my head, somewhat wishing it wasn't this way between us. "He was so happy when I left for college, and miserable when I came back."

Shaking his head, Zack rolls his shoulders back.

"Your brother, as much as I love him, is an idiot in disguise who doesn't think about anyone but himself. He's got shit he needs to figure out," Zack admits. "But really, between you and me, why did you come home? Seems like you need to talk about it."

Closing my eyes, I bury the images trying to resurface from that night, biting my inner cheek to focus on pain rather than what happened.

"It's not worth talking about," I mutter. "Just know I had a good reason for coming home."

Zack rubs his hand along my back, but I lean away. He stops the movement but doesn't lift his hand while he looks over my face. I settle back into the touch, letting his fingers run circles along my spine, his eyes still searching my face for something more.

"Well, whatever the reason, I'm sure it was justified," He smiles.

Giving me some comfort, I smile back, taking in a breath of relief.

Tugging at the sleeve of my sweater again out of habit, he observes the thick material, giving it a long look.

"It's kind of warm for this, don't you think?" He questions, pulling at the sleeve.

"It's about to rain," I say, a few droplets hitting the hood of the car. "It's fine."

I try to tug my sleeve back, but he keeps the material between his fingers as something floods his expression.

There's a shift in his eyes, the same shift I saw in *his* eyes the night everything changed. A pit of fear settles in my stomach.

"Now that I think about it, maybe we did interact in high school," Zack whispers. "Was it junior or senior year when you rejected my prom proposal because I was a 'washed up druggie'?" He asks, holding up quotations with his free hand.

"Zack, let go-"

I tense as he forces his hand under my sweater, the feeling of his hand touching my skin close to unbearable. I want to yell out to my brother, but I'm frozen. His hand viciously tugs at my sweater, trying to force it off of me.

"Aiden-"

"You know, everyone is curious why you were so bundled up all summer." I try to move away but can't without risking him seeing everything. "You guys were fucking right! She is hiding something!" Zack yells to the others, my eyes seeing red as the sweater is forced up around my neck. I scramble to get away from him, slipping out of the sweater as my feet hit the ground.

Stumbling away from Zack, I see my sweater clutched in his hand. I cross my arms immediately. The sheer white tank top is clung to my chest as the cool night air stings my exposed skin. Wide-eyed and confused, the boys move toward the back of the car towards Zack, watching me with varying expressions. Without the sweater, I'm unable to hide the mangled flesh working up and down my arms, some cuts newer than others. Zack and Nathan cover their mouths as they shake uncontrollably with silent laughter. Aiden remains still, his eyes wide with shock.

"Would you fucking look at that? Eden Faulkner, the once perfect little princess in high school, now comparable to a fucking beat-up chopping board," Zack laughs, my eyes peering down at the horrendous cuts spanning up and down my arms.

Shakily reaching into my pocket for my keys, I'm startled when I don't feel them.

Twirling the keys on his finger, Zack smirks at me, his hand extended out toward Aiden and Nathan.

"I believe you both owe me twenty. Told you I could get that sweater off with one conversation."

Slapping a twenty in Zack's hand, Nathan laughs, my throat concealing a sob as Aiden reaches for his wallet.

"Y-You," I start, moving toward them, my vision lined with red. "You fucking assholes-"

Aiden shoves my chest, and I plummet to the ground, my ass scraping against the dirt and gravel.

"Thanks for the ride," He sneers, glancing at his friends for approval. "Find your own way home if you can. It's not like you hold much value on your life," He spits.

Suicide was selfish and any act of self-harm was just as bad according to our parents, so while I wasn't surprised by the look of disgust on Aiden's face, the pain of his betrayal in the moment crushed me. Ignoring my quiet sobs, they get into the car as I struggle to stand on shaky legs.

"God damn it, Aiden," I yell, tugging at the driver's door handle, but he'd locked all the doors by the time I was able to get to the car. I slapped my hand against the window, my palm stinging from the impact.

Opening the driver-side window ever so slightly, Zack tosses something out towards me. I recognized the frayed cloth just as the razor blade nestled in the fabric falls loose and skips across the ground.

"Have fun with that. You probably still have some clean skin somewhere," Zack laughs, latching his hand around my forearm, shoving me back down to the ground as he backs the car up to leave. The small droplets of water that once kissed the ground were now dense enough to soak through my thin shirt.

I watch as my car turns on the main road and they drive away, my scream muffled as water and dirt seep into some of my newer cuts. Forcing myself off the ground, I wrap my arms around my torso, glancing up toward the sky, as my hand fumbles to grab the cross around my neck.

Running my hands through my hair, I tug at the necklace as hard as I can, furious when I realize it's not going to break. I feel around for my phone before realizing I'd left it in the fucking cupholder.

"Is this you?" I question, peering up toward the sky. "When will it end? Do I not deserve your grace?"

As usual, there's no answer, leaving me to feel utterly alone. But what's new?

Chapter 4

EDEN

Each drop of pounding rain against my skin is like tiny needles. My shirt, soaked through, clings to me, leaving nothing to the imagination. I hug myself tightly, feeling their eyes on me again, the shame burning hotter than the cold that's making me shiver uncontrollably. Mud cakes my legs, stinging the fresh scabs that line my arms, each one a harsh reminder of what was exposed. Every step is a struggle, each one pulling me further from the safety of home and deeper into the realization that my parents will believe whatever lies Aiden feeds them.

They always do.

The anger in my chest tightens, making it harder to breathe, harder to think of anything but getting away from this night-mare.

"I fucking hate him," I hiss, wondering how I can go home and not kill my brother.

For as long as I can remember, Aiden has made it his life's mission to torment me. He was always second best before I left for college. Since I got back, he's twisted their disappointment in me into something vile, turning them against me at a time I needed them most.

Slipping on mud as I walk, I try and think of something positive.

Nothing but negativity festers within me.

"I am going to fucking murder-"

Seeing headlights up ahead, I stop in my tracks, weighing out the pros and cons of the situation.

Either I stop this car and risk getting murdered, or I somehow try and find another way home before nightfall.

Seems like my odds are 50/50.

Running out into the middle of the road, I wave my scarred arms, no doubt looking like a crazed lunatic or some sort of swamp monster covered head-to-toe in mud and grime. The black 4Runner rolls to a stop before me, but the windows are too tinted for me to see inside. I stumble haphazardly toward the driver's side door which is now opening.

Grabbing the door, I gasp, unable to think up a valid excuse believable enough for the situation I'm currently in.

"I'm sorry-" I begin, but my words catch in my throat. Roman's wide eyes meet mine, both of us stuck in a state of surprise.

When I asked God for grace earlier, this is not what I'd meant. At that moment, divine intervention seemed so cruel.

Wishing now, more than ever, that I could crawl into a hole. Becoming much more aware of my exposed body, I can feel my nipples peeking through the soaking wet material of my top. I immediately move to wrap my arms around my middle.

"Father-"

Without a word, he steps away from the running vehicle, ignoring the rain that soaks through his clothes. The flannel and black shirt instantly begin to cling to his muscular frame. His large hand grips my elbow and firmly guides me toward the passenger side door.

"Father, wait-"

"Get in, Eden," He snaps, his tone rigid as he flings the passenger side door open. Rain rolls down his face.

I swallow hard, deciding not to argue as I slide into the passenger seat. The scent of car leather and a hint of spice fills the interior. I watch him move around to the driver's side, his anger palpable. He slams his door shut and grips the steering wheel tightly, his frustration evident even without words

Shaking from the cold, I run my hands through my hair, mortified by how indecent I am in his presence.

"Who did that?" He questions, keeping his focus out the window, the rain slamming down on the glass. He moves his hand to the center of the dash and turns on the heat.

Feeling the gust of warm air, I settle into the seat. Keeping a safe distance from him, I angle my legs toward the window, staying silent as I try to come up with a lie to cover this up.

"I'm not asking again. Who did it?" He moves his eyes to me, staying focused on my face. I can sense his rage is palpable enough to keep him from glancing down at the cuts I know he's seen on my arms by now.

"No one-"

He grabs the bottom of my shirt, his warm fingers brushing against my skin. My eyes widen as he points to the nail marks on my side, dark pink and rough scars beginning to form as my body still works to heal from the night I'd prefer to forget.

Looking him over, warmth floods my cheeks, traveling down my body, inconveniently settling between my legs as much as I wish it didn't.

"Who did that? Was it your brother's friends-"

"That wasn't from today," I mutter, fighting back the urge to cry.

Clenching his jaw, he yanks his hand away, pressing his fingertips over his closed eyelids.

"Why the hell are you even up here?"

"Why are you?" I push, pissed by the authority in his tone.

"Your father said you were going to some lookout spot with your brother. I like being alone with my thoughts after Mass and wanted to see if it was worth the drive. Your turn," He hisses.

"Aiden... I drove Aiden and two of his friends up here to... smoke, after Mass."

"Who were the other two?" He questions, not letting me finish.

"Zack and Nathan."

"From the congregation?" He bites out.

Nodding, I force myself to continue.

"They placed a bet to see if Zack could see what was under my sweater," I sob, opening and closing my hands. "He was being kind, and ripped it off when I least expected it-"

"Stop talking," Roman hisses, his knuckles white from how hard he's gripping the steering wheel.

Several seconds pass, his focus on anything but me.

Eventually, his gaze finds its way to my arms. I expect to see judgment written across his face, but his expression is something I can't quite decipher. Something like understanding mixed with sorrow.

"How long?"

"Three months," I admit, feeling as if this is the first time I've actually been honest with a confession.

"And the nail marks?" He questions. "When did you get those?"

I bite my lip as I swallow down my pride.

"Three months, two weeks, and one day," I say coldly.

He looks back out the window before putting the 4Runner in drive and pulling away from The Overlook.

The sound of the rain drowns out the silence between us.

I didn't have to give Roman too much direction to get me home. My family name is well-known enough in this town, making it common knowledge where we lived. As we enter the gated community, I give him the pin, and the gate swings open. He parks the car a few blocks away from my house. The heavy rain makes it impossible for anyone to be out. He turns off the ignition and shifts his focus towards me.

"Thank you, but I need to clarify, my brother-"

"Should tread carefully," Roman hisses, my excuse silenced.

Shaking my head, I narrow my eyes.

"Aiden is easily influenced-"

"Is that not who the Devil preys on most?" Roman questions, the divide between the two of us prevalent in these moments.

He believes faith is the only path. I believe –well, I don't even know what I believe in but it hasn't been anything since that night.

"You can't blame the Devil when everyone has free will. Everyone has a choice in the sins they commit," I hiss, waving my arm in his face. "The Devil didn't make me cut my skin to cope with –"

"Do you enjoy pain?" Roman asks, his hand curling around my wrist. Watching him study the cuts, I shake my head.

"I enjoy forgetting."

He glances up, his eyes piercing through me for a moment before he responds.

"You think this will make you forget?" He drags his finger down my wrist. My breath catches in my lungs, my body betraying me with a dull throb between my legs.

Fuck, what am I doing?

My house is just a few blocks away, I could just leave-

"I'll take other suggestions," I blurt out. His expression turns dark, something that sounds like a low growl rumbles in his throat.

Unlike Zack, Roman doesn't treat me like I'm his prey. The way he looks at me comes from some other place.

Perhaps desire?

Maybe hate?

He glances down at my pants pocket, the small blade wrapped in thin cloth sticking out. When I see that he's noticed it, I quickly reach down to conceal it.

"You keep it with you?" He questions.

"No I-"

Grabbing the cloth, he unfolds it before me. He nestles the blade in his palm, pinching its dull side while keeping my wrist firmly at my side with his free hand.

"Pain can be released from the body in many different ways. Some see pain as God's greatest test for strength," He pushes, holding the blade close to my wrist, my eyes growing wide.

"What are you doing-"

"Your plan was to lock yourself in your room and do this to yourself wasn't it?" He asks. "Tell me, do you feel relief in this moment?"

Watching him gravitate the blade closer, I turn my head away. He grabs my chin between his fingers, forcing me to look back.

"Watch," He urges, touching the point to my wrist. "If this is really how you think your pain should be handled, you won't mind watching."

I yank the blade away from him and lean over the center console, my anger wrapping around me like a protective blanket as I get in Rowan's face.

"Fuck you," I hiss. "You're no better than them-"

His voice cuts me off in a low growl.

"Lay back," He snaps, no gentleness in his command.

"What?"

Pushing me back down into the seat, he reaches over me and grabs the lever to move the backrest towards the back seat. His face is inches from mine as I lay back, almost completely horizontal by the time he releases the lever.

"Relax, Eden," He snaps, looking me over up and down. "You asked for a suggestion, now I'm giving you one."

Feeling his body loom over me, I wait for the sudden urge to run away, but my body loosens instead, desire unraveling the tightness that had been constricting the center of my chest for far too long.

What the hell is happening?

"Give me your hand," He demands, my head already shaking.

"I'm not-"

Grabbing my hand gently, he moves it toward my stomach, letting it settle above my waistband. He cups the side of my face, elbow resting on the center console for support.

"Some think pain helps the soul heal," He whispers. "Others like me think this is a better approach."

With his free hand, he urges my hand below my waistband. My heart beats out of my chest as my fingers graze my underwear, the feeling of his breath brushing my face only adding to the growing need between my legs.

"You committed a sin, you confessed, now recite your Hail Mary to me as part of your penance," He demands.

"What are you doing, Roman?' I question, his hand continuing to guide mine.

"You need relief," He whispers. "So touch yourself while telling me your prayer."

Startled by his words, I stop myself from pulling away, wondering if this is some cruel joke.

"I'm not-"

"Do it, or I will do it for you."

Feeling another wave of desire course through my center, I bite my bottom lip hard, feeling the blood seep into my mouth. Roman focuses on the red painting my lips. Reaching his free hand up, he uses his thumb to untuck my lip from between my teeth. My morals fade away as his hand and mine slip beneath my underwear and touch soft skin.

"Start here," He growls, grazing my clit with his fingers that are still wrapped around my own. My center drips with anticipation from the single touch.

His breath brushes the side of my face as he pulls his lips to my ear. My face becomes scolding hot from the touch.

"Now, say your prayer."

I try and rationalize what's happening. I turn my head so I can meet his eyes and find his expression void of playfulness. Slickness coats my inner thighs, the need to feel his touch breaking all the resolve I have left.

"H-Hail Mary, full of grace, the Lord is with thee; blessed art thou among women and blessed is the fruit of thy womb, Jesus-"

His hand guides my shaky fingers toward the sensitive bundle of nerves, exploring the area in small, circular motions. A breathless moan escapes me as his body inches closer to me.

"Just like that," He praises, looking over my bleeding lip. "Keep going."

"Holy Mary, Mother of God, pray for us sinners-"

"You'll need all the prayers she can provide so long as you are with me-"

His words stop short as he pushes his fingers inside me. Another heady moan falls from my lips, the feel of him undeniably pleasurable. I clutch his flannel shirt as he slips in and out with ease, the sound of my wetness adding to my arousal. As he moves, so do I, focusing on my swollen clit as he continues to pump his fingers deeper and faster. I squeeze my eyes shut as I try to control the sounds threatening to escape from me. Something warm and wet brushes across my lips. My eyes shoot open as Roman licks my bloodied bottom lip clean.

"Finish your prayer while my fingers are buried inside you," He demands.

How the fuck am I going to do that?

How do I ever stand a chance to move past this?

Why do I not want to forget this?

"Now and at the hour of our death, a-amen-"

He moves faster, curling his fingers, touching a spot inside me that sends ripples of pleasure through my lower stomach. I spread my legs wider, feeling the brush of his knuckle at my entrance as he buries his fingers even deeper. He grabs my chin, getting me to focus on him.

"I want to hear it," He urges. "I want to hear your pleasure," He pushes, pumping in and out of me, demanding my release.

Tugging on his flannel to get him closer to me, I can't help but let a soft cry of pleasure slip past my lips. My hips buck up into his touch. That night with *him* is the last thing on my mind.

Feeling his nose touch mine, I'm guided by lust as my hand reaches out to touch the impressive bulge between his legs, wanting to bring him the same pleasure I'm feeling now.

I gently graze the part of him straining against his pants, but he quickly grabs my wrist, slowly easing his fingers free from me.

"Lesson over," He whispers, putting my hand back in my lap. Speechless, I watch as he brings his glistening fingers coated in my wetness to his mouth.

He takes in every drop of me, letting his eyes close as he devours the taste. I remain awestruck, somewhat seduced by how erotically captivating I find him to be in this moment.

The cross pressed to my chest feels like it's burning my skin as he lowers his hand away from his mouth. Feeling empty and needy, I consider grabbing his hand and putting it back where it was. A throbbing ache tells me this hunger for more of him won't go away anytime soon.

Roman helps me get the car seat upright before creating some space between us. My cheeks are flush, my gaze catching on the large bulge still threatening to burst from his pants. A spark of satisfaction zaps through me knowing he was just as affected by this as I was.

"I-I."

"You're *my* altar server," He says, changing the subject as if he didn't just finger fuck me seconds ago. "You start your service hours tomorrow." He shamelessly readjusts the strain in his pants, keeping his eyes locked on mine the entire time.

"You just-"

"And I'll do it again. That's the last time that blade is touching your skin," He seethes, something sinful creeping into my mind.

"You swore an oath to God-"

"I am no stranger to temptation, Eden," He says. "And while my devotion to God is unwavering, I fear you just might become my greatest sin."

Still trying to process everything that just happened, my body yearns to feel his touch again, needing more. The last thing on my mind is cutting. The craving to release myself in a different way awakens something hungry inside me I've never felt before. But it feels delicious and sinful, and I want to let it out to play with Roman.

"And if I refuse?" I question.

A smirk curls along his lips, his words send a wave of pleasure through me.

"I suppose that will make it more fun for me."

Turning toward me, he lowers his eyes. "I'm sure you know I can keep a secret?" He questions. "Because no one else other than me is touching you like that again."

Saying nothing else, he moves the 4Runner from where we were parked and drives towards my house. My center is still warm and throbbing with need, barely satiated.

For the first time in months, the desire for pleasure has outweighed the need for pain.

How the hell do I come back from this?

1 Corinthians 10:13: "No temptation has overtaken you except what is common to mankind. And God is faithful; he will not let you be tempted beyond what you can bear. But when you are tempted, he will also provide a way out so that you can endure it."

Chapter 5

ROMAN

As I help her out of the car, she seems lost, her cheeks flushed with the remnants of the sinful pleasure we just shared. The memory of my fingers relentlessly moving inside her, the way her body responded despite her futile attempts to resist, is still fresh. Recalling each time I pushed deeper, seeing her eyes rolled back, her gasps brushing against my face, sends a shiver down my spine. The tension in my pants is undeniable, driven by a feral need to bring her pleasure—a need so overwhelming that no amount of repentance could ever erase it.

Seeing her in the middle of the road, so vulnerable and broken, staggering toward my car like that, her arms covered in those cuts... and those *nail* marks –brought me nothing but rage.

A rage I thought I had successfully suffocated long ago.

I'm no idiot.

The marks on her side tell a story of a fight she barely survived.

She masks the pain of what happened well, maintaining a detached exterior while retreating into the chaos of her mind, shutting everyone out.

As she steps out, her legs trembling, she holds onto me for support. The moment her flushed cheeks and plump lips purse into a scowl, I feel the blood rushing back between my legs. Her nervous gaze meets mine, and I can't help but imagine how she'd look with my hand wrapped around her throat, those pretty lips gasping for air –

"I c-can't go in there like this," She stutters, clearly still affected by what happened between us in the car.

The moment she touched the bulge of my cock above my pants, the line we'd crossed struck me like a frosty splash, and clarity washed over me. I'd broken the principles I vowed to uphold during seminary. This girl is a test from God, challenging me to see if the demons I thought I'd buried still linger. She ignites a fire in me, one I thought had long since burned out. As I look at her now, I see the sweet innocence others have already sought to exploit, their selfish desires threatening to consume her.

"My arms," She continues, "If my dad sees the cuts, he'll kill me."

From the brief interaction I had with David Faulkner earlier today, I know she's not exaggerating.

You'd think most parents would be able to uphold the virtue of empathy when seeing how mangled she is, drawing obvious conclusions as to why she'd ended up like that. But I guess the Faulkners weren't all that observant or just didn't give a fuck.

I remove my flannel and drape it over her shoulders, guiding her arms through the sleeves. As I do, I can't help but linger on the sight of her perfect breasts visible through the sheer fabric of her top. The thought of her hands tugging at my hair while I explore her further tempts me intensely. I wonder how much longer I can endure this frustration before giving in to my desires. I notice her scent clinging to my fingers as I button up the front of my shirt, making the urge to touch myself with that same hand later overwhelmingly enticing.

"I'll walk you to your door-"

"No," She yelps, shaking her head frantically. "Aiden has no doubt spun them a story-"

"I'm sure your parents would prefer the truth from their priest over whatever story your pothead of a brother has come up with," I snap, her eyes squinting at the sudden reminder of my title.

A priest is what I am to this girl.

"Priest," She scoffs. "I thought the general cup of tea for priests was blowjobs from young boys behind closed doors?" She jokes, the stereotype one I find abhorrent but sadly true for some within the church.

Touching a child that way is not just sinful. It's demonic.

There are few things I would risk going the Hell for, but killing child abusers might be one of them. I'd never repent for something like that.

"Not my thing," I smirk.

"So what is your thing, then? Finding impressionable young women, doing as you please with them?" She questions, digging for something else.

She wants to know if she's the only one I've allowed this to happen with.

Leaning in closer, I whisper, "Eden, if you're wondering how often I've let this happen, you might be surprised to learn I've always resisted the lure of touching a woman." My voice softens as I add, "So you can imagine my astonishment, finding your taste lingering on my tongue at this very moment. It's just as surprising for me as it is for you."

Her cheeks grow red, and I see her confidence to push me further drop. I'm not sure if she's satisfied with my answer, but there's no reason to be anything but truthful with her. She seems to accept what I've said for now as she turns her head toward the front door of her house.

"Well, it won't happen again," She snaps, a lick of anger rolling through me at the idea of this being a one-time instance.

She's right.

I can't allow it to happen again.

"Can we just get this over with?" She questions, clearly exhausted.

Nodding, I allow her to pass, letting her lead the way. I bury my hands in my pockets, readjusting my dick as we walk forward, my erection refusing to be ignored.

Up until this point, I'd been so consumed by Eden that I hadn't really taken in the house in front of me. It's a towering symbol of wealth. The white exterior gleams under the accent light; massive windows with dark shutters and an imposing black front door give it an air of controlled perfection. The wrap-around porch, with tall columns and immaculate steps leading up to the front door, exudes an unsettling calm. A large second-floor balcony with French doors overlooks the pristine, emerald lawn, dotted with regal shrubs and trees. Everything here is meticulously crafted to project an image, but the silence around it hints at something darker beneath the surface.

As we walk up the steps to the front porch, I have to stop myself from touching her lower back. Her hand shakes as she reaches up to ring the doorbell.

Shouts escalate from inside the house, and Eden flinches at the sound of what I can only assume is her father's voice. His exact words are muffled, but the force behind them is unmistakable—a booming, thunderous sound that reverberates off the walls, making the air feel tense and heavy.

The door swings open, and the rage plastered across her father's face is palpable. He shifts his expression the second he notices me behind Eden.

Creeping up behind her husband, Morgan looks relieved. My eyes gravitate to the staircase behind them where Aiden sits. We lock eyes before he bows his head, shame leeching the color from his face.

"Eden," David sighs, pretending as if he wasn't about to scream at her. Stepping through the door and onto the porch, he pulls her into an embrace. Her hands barely touch his sides as she stands there, stiff and unemotional. "Father Briar?" He gently nudges Eden over to her mother. "Is everything okay?"

"No, I don't think so, David," I sigh, looking toward Aiden again. "You think you can get your boy to come over here for a second?"

"Aiden?" Morgan questions, her voice scratchy as if she'd been crying. "He's been worried sick about his sister-"

"It's fine, Mom," Aiden snaps, making his way to the front door.

"Eden, what the hell happened?" David asks. Aiden looks at his sister, a warning in the way he glares at her from the doorway.

Shameful but amusing, urging her to lie in the presence of a priest.

He's got balls.

"I can answer that," I smile, Aiden's hands already shaking.

"No need, Father Briar. Thank you for bringing her home-"

"She drove your boy and his friends to a lookout spot at their request. It would seem Aiden and his companions wanted to get high. Then they left Eden up there in the middle of a rainstorm. I went to explore the area after you'd mentioned it during our conversation after Mass. Imagine my surprise when I found your daughter staggering down the muddy road soaking wet, with no phone and no car."

Looking toward the driveway, I see her muddied Kia.

"I'd struggle to get home too if my brother allowed his friends to steal my car and go on a joy ride."

Snapping his mouth shut, David looks at his daughter, his eyes wide.

"Is that true, Eden?" She nods slowly, and Aiden begins to shift his weight nervously from one foot to the other. Morgan's hand goes over her mouth to hide the shock.

David inhales a sharp breath, touching his belt. I watch as both Aiden and Eden flinch. Anger boils the blood beneath my skin at what I see, imagining the very limited list of things that could illicit such a response from them. My nails dig into my palms through clenched fists as I do my best to stay focused on the current situation.

David turns to Aiden, his hand moving swiftly, the sound of the slap sharp and jarring as it makes contact with skin. The boy stumbles back into the house from the doorway. As he steadies himself, he turns back to face us, spitting blood onto the porch. His bottom lip is split open, and a red mark is starting to form on his cheek.

A part of me is gratified seeing Aiden punished, making it harder to control the smile that threatens to make its way across my face.

"Morgan, take Eden inside and get her cleaned up. Her brother will be in to apologize to her once we're done talking," David hisses. "Father Briar?" He questions. "Do you have time for an at-home confession?"

Glancing at the porch furniture, I eye two chairs.

"Absolutely."

Aiden makes his way over to the chairs I'd spotted earlier, crossing his arms over his chest as he slumps his body down into the cushion. His eyes are red and puffy, his jaw taut with irritation. I sit down next to him, aware that David lingers just inside and is probably watching and listening.

"Listen, I didn't do anything, it was all Zack's idea-"

The need to strangle him with my bare hands flares to life. The thought of him gasping for air excites me more than it should. Something primal influencing my desire for retribution.

"Tell me, why do you hate your sister so much?"

I saw the look on her face in the headlights of my car.

Aiden allowed his friends to hurt her.

He dared them to.

"I don't hate my sister," Aiden says, shifting uncomfortably in the seat. "I don't hate Eden."

"Then why allow your friends to do what they did? Why participate in a bet like that at all?"

The little prick narrows his eyes at me and scoffs.

"She wasn't wearing that flannel when we left her, Father. You saw the cuts, too. You and I both know how the Church feels about the act of self-harm. It goes against the fundamental belief in the sanctity and dignity of human life. She should be ashamed of herself."

"And allowing your sister to be harmed by others is any better?"

Aiden goes still, his lips pressed thinly together. The look on his face tells me he's lost to some memory. I can't help but think of David and the way Aiden and Eden had flinched as he reached for his belt.

"What sins do you wish to unburden yourself of tonight?"

"I don't expect you to understand me or my family. The way they treat Eden now, the way they resent her, was how I lived my whole life before she went to college. She was their golden child. A true child of the Lord. So you can look at me like that, pretending like you haven't already judged me, but I promise you, what I did to Eden was light work in comparison to what my punishments were growing up," He whispers, purposefully keeping his voice down. "I don't resent my sister for what she's done to herself. I resent her for coming home and throwing me back into Hell, which is exactly what this situation is. Sure, they act like I'm their new favorite, but that doesn't mean the punishments go away. Every time she's around, it only gets worse. And wanna know the best part? She has no fucking idea how bad it gets because he always left her alone."

"Left her alone?" I question. "He hit you both," I assume, Aiden's head slowly nodding.

"Yeah, he did, still does-"

I stay silent for a moment, quieting the rage that's currently urging me to rip David's arms from his body.

"His punishments for me were always hands-on."

"Aiden," David snaps, tapping his foot impatiently from the doorway, watching his son with a threat beneath his gaze.

"I'm sorry to interrupt, Father Briar, but dinner is ready. Is he free to go for now? Has he received his prayers?"

As I glance back to Aiden, he swallows harshly, and I see a deep-rooted fear etched into his taut face.

"Nearly," I smile. "Give us five?"

David nods and moves back inside the house.

"I suppose my greatest sin is hoping she'd screw up big enough and he'd turn his attention to her for once," Aiden says, his selfish need to be free of his father obscuring his ability to see just how fucked up his strategy for freedom was. "Now, I've only made it worse for both of us," He sighs, getting up to go inside.

Grabbing his hand, I stop him before David can see.

"Is your father... hurting you now, Aiden?"

"Does it matter? Father Kevin helped him unburden himself of his sins regularly, so all's forgiven, right? He gets to meet God, regardless."

I stand in his way, blocking him from moving closer to the front door.

"Has he touched you?" I push, his eyes narrowing at me.

Has he touched Eden?

"Have a good night, Father Briar."

Nudging past me, he slips inside the house, his head lowered as he passes his father. Watching her brother, Eden looks petrified, her eyes shifting from Aiden to me, before landing on her father who'd made his way outside to me.

As he walks closer, I see him in an entirely new light. His existence to me is a cruel mockery of God's goodwill. His nature is corrupted and deeply entwined with the malevolence of Satan's influence. Something dark and thick, like tar, lodges in my throat when I look at him.

"I'm sorry my kids dragged you out here, Father Briar," David says, almost playfully as if bemused.

How many times have you touched Aiden?

Have you touched Eden?

Why hasn't Aiden told anyone?

How could Father Kevin allow such sins without contacting authorities?

Or killing the man himself.

"No bother, it seems to have been a misunderstanding-"

"Regardless, I will see to it Aiden recites his prayers and is properly punished."

My blood runs cold.

"I don't think punishment is necessary-"

"Nonsense. It's my duty as a father to remind them that actions have consequences. He committed a grave sin, and it pains me deeply to see either of them stray from the path God has set for them. I won't let this go without consequence. He'll face punishment, not just from me, but more importantly, he should seek forgiveness from God through confession and penance. Only by truly repenting can they begin to make amends and return to God's grace."

"You plan on delivering Eden a punishment as well?"

"All in good time," He sighs. "I thought she had outgrown the need for me to discipline her, but it would seem the Devil has found his way back into her life-"

Taking a step closer, I get in the man's face, my nose inches away from his as I look down several inches at him. Throwing on a false smile, I pat the front of his shirt.

"God is always watching, David," I whisper. "I am always watching, too." Pulling my lips to his ear, I don't hold my tongue. "I've always felt the need to offer punishment to the sinners who need extra motivation to return to God's path, be that mothers or fathers, sons or daughters. I'm not sure what your brand of punishment is but," I push, theorizing this man is a glorified fucking pedophile. "You can deal with Eden by your own hand, or you could allow me the opportunity to give her some new insight," I smile, watching something shift in his expression.

"So, you saw the list?" He questions, a devilish grin spanning across his face. "I wondered if Kevin had invited another enthusiast into the church. It would seem he has."

I draw a blank, knowing the altar servers' signup sheet isn't the list he's referring to. My intuition wrenched a tightness in my chest as he grinned.

"Of course," I smile, doing my best to be agreeable, despite having no idea what this fucking means.

"Quite the lineup this year," He smiles. "Tell you what, you can do as you please with her. Punishments are all yours," He smiles. "My son, however, is off limits."

My stomach twists at his words. Reaching my hand out, I smile at the man.

"Let her feel God's wrath, Father."

Holding onto the man's hand, I stop him from retreating inside.

"And what about the list? Where can I get clarity on my role in all of this?" I question.

Patting me on the shoulder, the man looks gleeful.

"I thought Kevin would've told you everything?"

"He did, mostly," I lie. "It's been a long day."

The last thing I need is David discovering I'm not part of his inner circle. I need to know what's going on here.

I fear David Faulkner's position in the church is far more influential than anything I could've imagined.

"I should get inside. You have a blessed night, Father."

Watching him slip inside, I remain standing on the porch as I try to unravel the sticky web of details that are far too vague for me to untangle.

I'd been accepted into the church, taking an oath to serve under God.

But what was Father Kevin's role in all of this?

Why did the man really leave?

What does that mean for my role in all of this?

Glancing over my shoulder, I meet Eden's gaze through the window before she bows her head as her father takes a seat at the table.

One thing's for sure.

David Faulkner will be hauled off in a body bag if he ever lays a hand on her again.

Chapter 6

EDEN

I get a sick feeling as I watch Roman descend the steps of our home.

"You mind if I see Father Briar off and say thank you for bringing me home?"

"Go for it," My dad says with a wave. "Your mother can reheat your food," He adds with a smile. Though the lifeless look in his eyes whenever he glances at her is always unsettling.

Aiden pokes his potatoes, his eyes following me as I make my way outside.

Roman has barely made it to his 4Runner as I step outside. As I move towards him, he seems lost in thought, his eyes staring blankly at the driver's side door.

"Hey, I'm sorry my dad made you-"

"Give me your phone," He snaps, holding out his hand.

"Why would I do that?" I question, tugging the device free from my pocket.

At dinner, Aiden had silently handed it over to me under the table, avoiding my father's watchful eyes.

"Hand it to me, or I'll get it myself," He warns, keeping his hand out in front of me.

I hesitate before unlocking the phone and handing it over to him. He snatches it quickly, his fingers fumbling around on the screen.

"Do you need help finding something? I assumed you knew how to use it since you asked for it. Unless..."

"Unless what?"

"Unless your looks have deceived me, and you're too ancient to know how to work a smartphone."

He shoots me a playful smirk as he finishes and locks the phone.

"So not ancient, huh? You can't be my age. From what I know, priests start seminary around twenty-two."

"Tack on seven years. I'll be twenty-nine in October." He hands my phone back to me, our fingers touching during the exchange.

"I added my number in there. I want you to call me in the morning once you're up. You'll be starting your service hours bright and early."

"Service hours?" I question. "My dad really did sign me up?"

"That he did," He mutters, leaning into the side of his car. "You've got the most service hours, actually."

"I can't," I stutter, the idea of being isolated with Roman both terrifying and exciting. "I had to pick up a job. My parents are making me pay rent while I'm living at home. I work at Idlewood Coffee in the mornings, the cafe downtown-"

"Then you'll come find me after that."

"And what if I already have plans?" I snap. "It's Monday-"

"You'll make time," He shrugs, looking toward the house. Taking a step closer, he pushes a strand of stray hair behind my ear. I close my eyes, hating how much I love the feeling of his touch, biting back the urge to step a little closer.

"Lock your door tonight."

"Why?" I question, his head cocking.

"Do it. I don't like it when you don't listen."

His hand falls from my face as he backs away, leaving my skin yearning for his touch. Dazed and confused, I watch him as he retreats to his car. I make my way back to the house, and as I make my way up the stairs to the front porch, I look over my shoulder to see him still waiting in the driveway. He doesn't leave until I close the front door behind me.

Tossing myself on my bed, I shoot Zoey a quick text, asking if she's working at the cafe in the morning. Quickly getting a "yes" back, I scroll through my contacts, rolling my eyes at the sight of Roman's name now in my phone. Clicking my phone off, I look down to see dirt still caked on my skin in places. My one prerogative for the rest of the night is to thoroughly cleanse my body in hopes of washing away the remains of the day, both physically and mentally.

The collar of Roman's flannel shirt touches my face, and I take in his scent. I think of the way his hands explored between my thighs, wondering if he resented me even though I had no intention of tempting him on any level tonight. But now I'm the one tempted to explore this connection between us.

"Eden," Aiden's hoarse voice calls, his body lingering in my doorway. "Can I talk to you?"

I glance at the clock on my nightstand. It's late, almost midnight. I'm surprised he's still up. Surely his apology could wait until the morning.

"Sure."

He enters the room, turning to quietly shut the door until it meets the frame. As he turns back to me and makes his way to where I'm sitting, I notice how exhausted he looks. He runs his hands through his hair as he takes a seat beside me on the bed.

"Did talking to Father Briar take that much energy out of you-"

"Dad's hurting me," Aiden blurts out, the compulsion to goad him about today's events dies out completely the moment those words leave his mouth.

Staring at Aiden, I swallow nothing, my hand clutching my phone.

"What do you mean-"

"You remember how it was growing up? Yea, you got your share of shit, but you were always their favorite, and I could never do anything to please them," He says, his head bowed as he speaks. "Dad was always keen on using that damn belt on you, but when he took me into his room for my punishments, I never saw the belt," Aiden sobs, a million thoughts running through my mind. "I would have fucking loved for it to have been the belt."

"Aiden-"

"When you went away, I had an opportunity to please him to the point he felt that his punishments weren't needed anymore. Then you came home, and for some reason, he never felt the need to take his frustrations out on you like he used to. Once again, I was his outlet when he was angry. I don't hate you, Eden. I envy the fact he never went after you the same way he comes after me. I hate myself for expecting you to have done something about a problem you didn't even know about. I thought that you fucking up would make his focus go somewhere else. I was wrong," Aiden continues, tears dropping from his jaw and blotching his jeans.

I rub his back, but he flinches and jerks away.

"If he isn't using the belt, Aiden, what is he-"

"Kids," My father snaps, both of us jolting at the sound.

Nudging the door all the way open, he stands with his belt in hand. My mother lingers behind him, a sheen over her dilated eyes, not doubt from the handful of Xanax she'd probably taken after dinner.

"Aiden, let's go," He urges. "Morgan, you go enjoy your shows. Eden, get some rest-"

"No," I snap, standing in between my father and Aiden, staring him down.

"He's already apologized and confessed. We are far too old for physical punishment, Dad," I hiss. "Aiden is-"

My mother gasps as my father's hand coils around my neck. He uses his body to force me back into the dresser. Aiden moves quickly from the bed, clawing at my father's shirt, trying to get him off of me.

"It's disrespect like that which made it easy for me to let Father Briar take charge of cleansing your sinful mind," He hisses, the thought of them agreeing on anything seeming absurd.

As my airways tighten, I'm thrown back to my childhood, recalling every time my father's drunken beatings went too far. His grip tightens slightly, and suddenly, I'm in my dorm room again, with *Eric's* drunken eyes watching me as he–

Aiden kicks my dad square in the crotch from behind. He releases my throat, and I crumple to the floor, gasping for air. My mother's cold hand touches my face, a broken look in her eyes as I look up at her, my vision blotchy. I hear my father's footsteps move quickly to Aiden as he tries to get beyond his reach.

"Wait-"

"You'll make it worse," My mother whispers, her lips pressed to my ear, my neck throbbing with pain from my father's grip. She holds me still as I look over to see Aiden trembling, the kind of fear written across his face something I'm intimately familiar with.

He's been hurt like me.

By our own fucking father.

And my mother knows.

Grabbing Aiden's collar, he begins tugging him towards the door as my brother struggles to resist him. Nudging my mother off of me, I follow after them.

I don't care if this is a dumb idea. I have to do something.

"I told Aiden to smoke the weed," I hiss, watching as my dad pauses his steps. "I told him to smoke the weed and dared Zack to take my car on a joy ride to scare Aiden while he was still high. None of it was his idea." My breaths are quick and shallow as my mind works to come up with a way out of this. Fuck the consequences.

"You believe in God's divine faith, as well as truth. Don't punish Aiden for my sins," I beg.

He releases Aiden, a mixture of confusion and irritation written across his brow.

"You allowed your brother to take the fall for your own immoral behavior?"

Looking at Aiden, I know what needs to be done.

The focus has to shift.

Forcing on a smile, I lower my head.

"Happily."

Like a feral animal with an instinct to kill, my father grabs me by the hair, dragging me into my bedroom. A scream is ripped from my throat as pain sears over my scalp.

"Go to your rooms, now!" My father yells to my mom and brother. I can hear their sobs from the hallway, my mother's soft voice saying something to my brother I can't make out.

Slamming my bedroom door shut, my dad tugs me to my bed. Panic washes over me as he forces me down on my stomach, bending me over the mattress. He pulls my wrists behind my back, wrapping them with his belt. My body goes rigid when he grabs the back of my head to keep me down.

No.

He wouldn't. Yeah, his punishments were physical, but they'd never been like this. Shock paralyzes me, images of Eric flashing through my mind. This can't happen again. I can't let it happen again.

Wailing into my mattress, I feel him drag down my sweats, my ass fully exposed to him, nothing but a thin layer of underwear concealing the most vulnerable parts of my body. Clicking his tongue, he looks over my exposed skin, the cuts on the front of my thighs hidden from his vision. I squirm, but I'm unable to get free, his hold on my neck pushing me further into the mattress.

Fuck.

Aiden wasn't lying.

"While your punishment will be much different than Aiden's," He hisses, his lips close to my ear. "Believe me when I say that I look forward to seeing Father Briar and the church show you what real discipline looks like."

"What are you doing to Aiden-"

"Shhh," He coos. "Aiden is confused, as are you. You both have no idea what it's like to be a parent. Your mother and I have given you everything," He mutters, his hand touching my ass. The necklace of my cross digs into the skin around my neck as I continue to struggle against him.

Dear God, if you are listening, please-

"Dad, get your fucking hands off of me-"

I yell out in pain as his open palm connects to the bare skin of my ass, the sound of the contact echoing through my room.

"Just like when you were a little girl," My father hisses. "I thought you'd learned your lesson, but –"

His hand comes down again, this slap more painful than the first.

"I suppose not."

Seconds turned into minutes. His hand repeatedly drove down on my ass, my legs threatening to give out each time his hand met the already raw flesh. When he tugs the belt from my wrists, I swing my arms out, ready to start a fight I probably won't win.

As I try to pull myself up from the bed, I feel the metal from the belt buckle slap against my skin, my back arching as I plummet to the floor. Dragging my pants up before he can see the front of my thighs. I fall onto my side, my body in unbearable pain, a small sob exiting my lips. Standing over me, my father staggers, and I can smell the alcohol leeching from his pores.

Crouching down, he watches me, regret spanning across his face.

"I never wanted to hurt my little girl, Lord," He whispers. "Please forgive me." His fingers graze my cheek.

I remain on the bedroom floor, shaking uncontrollably

Standing up slowly, my dad glances toward my door.

"I expect respect from you and your brother moving forward."

Swinging open the door, he exits my room, leaving me alone in the silent aftermath of his drunken fit of rage. I want to go to Aiden, to my mother, but the pain is almost unbearable. I roll over to the edge of my bed, placing a hand on my mattress to hoist myself up. When I get to my feet, Roman's command echoes through my mind.

Lock your door.

So I do.

What does he know that I don't?

Does he know about my father's violent tendencies?

What did Aiden really tell him during confession?

Stumbling my way to my bathroom, I grab my phone from my dresser on the way in, being sure to lock the door behind me.

Outbursts like this from my father are always fueled by alcohol and a horrible week at work.

He's never touched me like this.

Do I really know how far he's willing to go?

He already seems to think Roman is going to turn me into the perfect, god-fearing woman he's always wanted me to be.

I need to find a way out of this.

I need to find a way to get Aiden out of this.

My mother might be able to turn a blind eye to what my father is capable of, but I won't.

Aiden does not deserve this.

I don't deserve this.

I turn the dial on the tub, letting the warm water fill with as many bubbles as I can, desperate to feel something other than the burning pain scraping like glass across my ass cheeks. Slowly dragging myself to my feet, I face the mirror and begin peeling off my clothes, layer by layer. I examine my body, a mosaic of scars and fresh cuts tracing up my arms, thighs, and sides, stopping near my breasts. Shades of purple and blue cloud my skin, with a nasty bruise already blooming around my neck from the vice grip my father had me in earlier.

Glancing at my phone on the countertop, I know how foolish it would be to call the police.

If they never believed my mother the few times she did call when my dad took it too far, they'd never believe me.

Sheriff Acosta locks hands with my father every Sunday.

Aiden and I are alone in this.

"What the fuck has my life become?" I mutter, no longer able to look at my reflection.

Crawling into the bathtub, I bite back the pain of the warm water touching my inflamed skin. Feeling the bubbles surrounding me, I settle into a soapy sense of relief. My mind begins to wander.

My father had taken his anger out on me.

Is that all I'm good for?

An outlet for men's pain.

The pain from that night tries to cloud my mind.

I feel his nails digging into my thighs as he tries to pry my legs open. His voice has a rough, uneven edge. Like sandpaper as he leans down to whisper in my ear. The smell of alcohol is heavy as he opens his mouth.

"I'll take it slow for you, Eden," He whispers. "I'll take it so slow, you'll be fine," He mutters, my eyes barely open, my arms next to my body, like dead weight.

"Eric," I sob, the farthest thing from ready to feel anyone's touch as I try to figure out why I can't move.

Only moments ago, I'd been drinking with my roommate, and now, I lay sprawled across Eric's bed, his phone in hand, the light from his camera blinding me.

Just weeks ago, I'd broken down to Eric in this very room, spilling my life story to him, detailing everything my father had done to me, the feeling of his belt and fist permanently seared in my body.

"Eric, please-"

"Quiet, Eden," He growls, covering my mouth as he forces his fingers into me, my body tight and unwelcoming to their intrusion.

"God baby, I can barely get them in-"

Dragging my head out from under the water, I gasp for air, the ringing sound from my phone pulling me away from the memories of that night. Blinking back the pain, I glance around, reminding myself that I wasn't really back in that dorm room.

As my vision clears, I see my phone screen light up again, the ringtone blaring on its second loop. I quickly wipe my hands on the towel next to the tub before swiping the screen to answer and holding it up to my ear. My hair drips water down my face and into my eyes and mouth as I sit back into the warm water again, almost dropping the phone down my front between my breasts.

"H-Hello?"

"Eden?" He questions, his voice low.

Roman.

"Oh. Hey, sorry I didn't answer sooner," I turn my head away from the phone speaker, hiding my sob, as another wave of pain rips up my spine from my backside.

"Did you need something?" I question.

"Have you been crying?"

"No," I choke, gasping for air. "I'm fine."

"Where are you now?" He questions.

I laugh, hoping it will hide the sobs that escape me. "Well, I'm actually soaking in my bathtub, easing some aches and pains." That's believable, right? Technically, it was the truth.

"Do you have any other suggestions for easing my aches and pains, Father?" I question, resting my head on the rim of the tub, expecting nothing from the man.

A low growl comes through the phone's speaker before he answers.

"Are you alone?"

"Yes, why-"

"Put me on speaker," He demands. "And listen to me carefully."

Proverbs 6:20-22: "My son, keep your father's commands and do not forsake your mother's teaching."

Chapter 7

ROMAN

A s I make my way down the corridor to the office space Father Kevin left behind, I can't help but notice the eeriness of the cathedral this late at night. I peer through the open blinds that hang over the glass window that is embedded into the heavy wooden door. I see the picture of Mary Magdalene guarding the room as I fumble around in my pocket for the keys Father Kevin left for me. I step inside, David's words still resonating long after our conversation ended.

I thought Kevin would've told you everything.

Trying to figure out what David could've meant, I start rummaging through the cabinets, eventually finding a folder full of bank statements and invoice slips for Saint Michael's. Laying the bank statements across the desk, the name on the signatory line next to Kevin Dowe's immediately grabs my attention.

David Faulkner

Managing Partner | Faulkner & Associates

Every expenditure statement and invoice includes his signature next to Father Kevin's. Tapping my fingers along the desk, I take a closer look at the computer before me, Father Kevin's profile still set up on the device. All I need is the fucking password.

I look around and see what appears to be an old, leather-bound Bible tucked under a stack of other books on the edge of the desk. I push the other books aside and begin flipping through the pages. It's written in Latin, probably older than the Vatican's first secret.

I pause when I see a page with color that shouldn't be there, one word sticking out to me, its letters highlighted in bright yellow.

"Satanas," I whisper.

Satan, in Latin.

Slowly trailing my fingers over the keyboard, I type in the seven letters, saying a prayer to Jesus that this password works. Slamming my finger down on the enter key, the screen loads. I tap my foot vigorously under the desk as I wait.

Several seconds pass.

You're being delusional Roman-

Father Kevin's desktop pops up on the screen, a single application for email set up from what I can see. I run the mouse over the application icon, hesitating before double-clicking.

Looking up at the picture of Mary Magdalene, she seems to watch me, judging me for sticking my nose where I know it shouldn't be.

"You'd think having you here would've done something to keep the man honest," I scoff.

The email application is empty. I move the cursor to the left over the 'Trash' folder. Opening it, there's one email. The subject line reads 'Inventory'.

Holding my breath, I click to open it. Attached to the email is a furniture inventory sheet with ridiculous prices listed by each item. Some pieces with retail dates from roughly eleven years ago were priced around twenty thousand dollars, all set to deliver to this church three months from now. The list continues, with twenty items in total. Scrolling down to the bottom of the order form, I see David Faulkner's signature again.

What the hell kind of furniture is worth spending nearly four hundred thousand dollars on?

Was it hand crafted by the descendants of Apostle?

The bottle of bourbon on the bar cart in the corner of the room calls to me. My eyes grow heavy, exhaustion from the day finally setting in. This mystery is getting close to becoming too much of a mental burden to bear without sleep.

Looking over the list a final time, one of the furniture pieces stands out to me. Its age is much older than the rest, and its description is eerie.

Twenty-year-old vintage sofa, mint condition, premium brown leather, great for family events.

Enlarging the image of the sofa, I find that it's nothing more than ordinary, like something you'd pick up in a department store or a yard sale, frankly. But it's got the highest asking price of all the pieces, nearly double the cost of the other furniture.

"What the fuck-"

My head snaps up, and my heart thunders as the quiet of the office is pierced by the deep, resonant toll of the massive church bell. The sound is jarring, cutting through the air like a thunderclap, its vibrations reverberating off the stone walls. The darkness of the midnight hour makes the sound feel more ominous as if the bell is warning of something unseen.

I log out of Kevin's profile, giving Mother Mary one last look before leaving the office.

Thirty minutes have passed since I left the cathedral and made my way home. My eyes have stayed glued to my phone. Two glasses of scotch are not enough to stop me from wondering what she's doing right now.

Did she listen to me when I told her to lock her door?

What the hell was David like when I wasn't around?

Was Aiden telling the truth?

Pacing around my home, the space is barely unpacked, boxes still sealed shut, my bed one of the few things I prioritized getting in order. After showering to clear my thoughts, I walk around the room in a pair of sweats, the damp fabric clinging to my skin. The tattoo that begins around my neck and spirals down my side and along my back is exposed. If anyone looked closely enough, they'd see the intricate designs skillfully concealing the array of scars that weave across my skin. Twisting thorns and vines, beautiful and dark, wrap around my body like a living entity. The memory of the needle's sting against my scarred flesh lingers. The pain was oddly soothing—a welcome distraction compared to other torments I've endured. The hours spent under the needle were a blend of agony and solace, offering a strange, cathartic relief.

Throwing myself back to that moment in the car with Eden, my cock stiffens with deep longing. I try to think of anything but the idea of pleasuring myself to the memory of what she felt like wrapped around my fingers. The brief taste of her I got was more addicting than any of the harder substances I tried in my youth. I can't get the feeling of her hand grazing my hard length out of my mind.

I thought this fucking overpriced bourbon was supposed to make it harder to get it up.

Running my hand through my hair, I glance over at my phone again, quickly snagging it from my nightstand.

I never should have looked up her number on the altar servers' information form.

I should have kept my distance.

Tensing my jaw, I unclasp the cross from my neck, setting it on my nightstand.

One call won't hurt.

Checking on her after what happened isn't out of the ordinary.

If I call once and she doesn't pick up, I'll leave it at that.

Its thirty minutes past midnight, I doubt she's still awake.

Leaning back into my headboard, I tap her number, placing my phone on my chest, letting the ringing noise from the speaker distract me from the strain between my legs.

After ringing four times, I start to lose hope. The idea of bothering her like this is so foolish-

"H-Hello?"

Hearing her soft voice, the memory of her gasps of pleasure enters my mind. My hand finds its way beneath the waistband of my sweats, wrapping around the base of my cock, giving it the attention it's been begging for all night.

This is fine.

Once I'm off the phone with her, I can ease my sexual frustrations and be done with it.

"Eden?" I question, the way her name sounds as it caresses my tongue adds to the throb beneath my hand.

"Hey, sorry I didn't answer sooner," She mutters, a small sound of pain leaving her scratchy throat.

Has she been crying?

"Do you need something?" She questions, the sound of water splashing in the background throwing me off.

"Have you been crying?" I question, suddenly more concerned than frustrated.

"No," She chokes, but I know she's lying.

If only I could punish her for that one.

"I'm fine," She forces out, a dull sob concealed on the other line.

Fuck.

She has been crying.

And what am I doing?

Getting harder to the sound of her voice.

"Where are you now?" I question, doing my best to stay neutral.

She laughs, but it's hollow, laced with defeat. "Well, I'm actually soaking in my bathtub, easing some aches and pains...Do you have any other suggestions for easing my aches and pains, Father?"

Father. She bites out the title like it's a wall between us, and she's the battering ram. Tension wraps itself around my inside like a vice. Slowly, I start to stroke myself again, hoping to ease the pain. I'm assaulted by the image of her in the bath, her body wet and warm, her beautiful breasts bouncing as her pretty lips scream out my name –

"Eden," I snap. "Are you alone?" I question, a solution forming in my mind.

"Yes, why-"

"Put me on speaker," I demand. "And listen to me carefully."

The sound of water moving comes through the speaker, followed by a soft thud.

"I set you on the edge of the tub," She whispers. "So what's your solution?"

Tugging my sweats further down, my throbbing cock springs free. I wrap my hand around the hard length of it, taking my time as I work up and down the base in painfully slow drags.

"Do you want pain, Eden, or do you want pleasure?"

Waiting several seconds, her voice comes in a whisper.

"Pleasure, Father."

My ears devour her words. I close my eyes to revel in the possibilities of what comes next, the ache of my release already threatening to end this before it begins.

"Then go ahead and do something for me, beautiful. Take your right hand and run it down your body," I whisper. "Go all the way until you've reached that pretty pussy of yours, and listen to my voice while you slip inside yourself."

A brief pause precedes the sound of movement and a small gasp of pleasure that makes me bite my bottom lip in anticipation.

Stroking myself faster, I continue coaxing her for more.

"Now take your left hand and massage those perfect breasts of yours while imagining those are my fingers fucking you," I groan, a bead of liquid gathering at the head of my stiff cock.

Her voice cracks trying to stifle another moan. "And w-what are you doing right now, Father Briar?" She questions. "Remember, it's a sin to lie."

Smiling at her wittiness, I lower my voice.

"You want to know, Angel?" I purr. "Right now, I'm stroking my cock to the idea of you pleasuring yourself," I continue, "and imagining what it would feel like to have those pretty lips wrapped around me, struggling to take all of me in." I groan, stroking harder as her gasps become deeper and heavier. "Now be a good girl for me and put in another finger."

"I can't, Roman-"

"Do it," I snap.

The sound of movement escalates, my hand working the pre-cum vigorously up and down my length, the wetness adding to my frenzied obsession with the woman on the other end of the line. For a few moments, we become nothing but a mix of sinful sounds.

"Do you know how desperately I want to taste you, Eden? Do you know how much I want that pretty little pussy of yours? To slip my fat cock inside you, stretching you out until you scream –"

"Roman-"

"Father," I hiss. "You say prayers in my name. Now recite yours while you cum all over your fingers."

She forces herself to try and say the prayer.

"Our father-"

"Your father," I moan. "Only yours, Eden."

"M-My father, who art in heaven, hallowed be thy name-"

"Good girl. Let me hear that dirty mouth finish."

"Thy kingdom come; thy will be-"

Her moan of release echoes through the speaker, and I'm unable to hold mine off any longer. Biting my bottom lip, my own release sends cum jetting towards my lower stomach in violent spurts. I keep my hand wrapped around my length, coaxing wave after wave of pleasure from my flesh. A warm, peaceful sensation courses through my body as I work to control my ragged breathing. I can hear Eden through the speaker still, the sounds coming out of her leading me to believe she's experiencing something similar.

I grab a tissue from my nightstand, cleaning up my release, my cock still somewhat hard. I imagine it wouldn't take much to get me going again.

"You were right," She whispers after a few moments. "Your suggestion did help ease the pain, Father. Sleep well."

She ends the call abruptly. I stare down at the black screen on my phone, wondering if I should call her back. I wasn't completely convinced that there wasn't more she needed to talk about.

Before I can place my phone back on the nightstand, the screen lights up with a notification.

One unread notification from: Eden Faulkner

Tapping on the notification, I sit up in my bed, nearly dropping my phone, my eyes plastered on the image in front of me.

It's a picture of Eden, wet hair and all. She's licking the side of one of her glistening fingers, her eyes lowered as she looks at the camera. The peaks of her perfectly round tits and delicate light pink nipples are cut off at the edge of my screen. My mouth begins to water as I trace a finger over the image of her curves.

A single line of text appears after the photo.

Following up with the single text, she gains the upper hand.

> Your move Father.

The screen fades back to black moments later.

Eden Faulkner.

Has the devil himself sent you to test me?

1 Peter 5:8: "Be sober-minded; be watchful. Your adversary the devil prowls around like a roaring lion, seeking someone to devour."

Chapter 8

EDEN

W hat have I done?

What sane person has phone sex with a priest? As if letting him listen to me finger fuck myself wasn't enough, I poured gasoline on an already out-of-control fire with that photo.

Can I blame the Devil for this unyielding desire to tempt him more, or do I thank God for the unexpected reprieve Roman grants me from the torment of trauma threatening to break me almost every day? I bend at the sound of his voice, falling into a consuming pit of lust and hunger anytime I think of him.

This isn't like me.

I barely sent Eric anything erotic, even when he'd begged for them.

Why in the fuck would I tempt my goddamn priest with a photo of myself licking my own cum off of my fingers?

Roman never responded after my raunchy photo or the text that could be interpreted in a million different ways. In the heat of the moment, I'd felt in control.

I wanted to know how far Roman was willing to go.

Now, one climax and zero new texts later, I'm wondering if he'd already reached that limit.

The pain from my father's special brand of punishment lingers, and with Father Briar now paying closer attention to me, cutting isn't an option to relieve the tension building in my chest and radiating through the rest of my tired body.

Glaring at the jewelry box where I hide the blades, I count to ten in my head.

They will always be there.

There is no need to add more wounds to an already mangled body. If you don't stop, you won't have any clean skin left.

Not today.

Fastening the tie to my apron, I work several layers of concealer onto the bruised skin around my neck. The best I could do was to make it look like someone had a great time sucking on my neck in a fit of passion.

I deliberately take my time getting ready, trying to avoid any chance of my dad insisting I sit down for breakfast. I move to the floor-leaning mirror in my bedroom, smoothing down the form-fitting, long-sleeved black turtleneck dress, making sure it covers the front of my thighs under the apron. In my hurry to make it back home a few months ago, I'd left most of my clothes in my dorm room. I knew they'd get thrown out after I left, but I couldn't care less at the time. I was frustrated to find the four pairs of pants that I had to my name all in the wash this morning, leaving me with this or a pair of pajama shorts to wear to work today.

I moved to the closet, pulling out a pair of knee-high boots to hopefully combat the chilly air on my otherwise bare legs. Glancing at my phone, I grab my bag and hurry out of my room before I'm late.

The smell of eggs wafts through my nose as I creep downstairs. I catch sight of my brother slumped over the dining room table with his head resting in his palm as he pushes food around on his plate. His skin is dull, and the bags under his eyes tell me he got about as much sleep as I did last night. Grabbing my keys from the hanger by the front door, I'm stopped by the sound of my father's voice before I can make my escape.

"Eden," My dad chirps happily as if he didn't smack my ass raw last night. "Aren't you going to say goodbye?"

Poking my head into the dining room area, all three members of my family look at me. The only one smiling out of the group is my father. He looks considerably less disheveled than he did last night, his neat appearance and tailored suit fitting for someone who runs a law firm.

"Goodbye?"

"You're aware that your service hours begin today with Father Briar, correct?" He eyes me as he takes a drink from his mug.

"David, she has a long shift, maybe-"

He cuts my mother off before she can finish. "You're to be at the church directly after work, Eden. Am I clear?"

"Of course," I smile, glancing at Aiden. "On one condition," I push, my father's eyes widening.

"Let Aiden come with me to work. There's free Wi-Fi, and he can get some of his college entry work done," I smile. "We can go over scripture on my lunch." His expression softens with a smirk of satisfaction. I can let him think he's won if it means getting Aiden out of here.

"Aiden-"

"I'll grab my bag," Aiden says, almost jumping up from the table. Nodding in approval, my dad watches us as we leave, wagging his finger in the air.

"Eden?"

My body stiffens as I clutch the doorknob. "Yes?"

"See to it that you're on time for Father Briar today," He snaps, a warning hidden in his words.

Without a word, I turn the doorknob and leave, looking forward to spending half my day lost in espresso pulls and overpriced macchiatos.

Aiden's head stays pressed against the glass as he blankly stares out the passenger-side window of my car. The gnawing sound of whatever alternative band he was playing blared loudly through the speakers, reminding me of something my college roommate would've liked. We'd been quiet up to this point, the silence between us somewhat comforting.

"You didn't have to offer to take me with you today."

Looking his way, I shrug.

"It's whatever. I'll be busy most of my shift. Probably won't even notice you're there," I tease, forcing myself to pretend everything can be normal.

I have to believe it will be.

"Are we going to do that? Are we going to pretend like nothing happened last night? Just like we pretend everything is okay each time he hits Mom a little too hard? Or what about how we pretended that he didn't slap me so hard one time that I had to miss picture day? I heard your screams last night, Eden-"

"And will talking about it change anything?" I grip the wheel tighter. "My ass is so sore I can barely walk, and you want me to dwell on it right before work? Ignoring this messed-up family is a hell of a lot easier than facing the fact that I have nowhere else to go. College is your way out, Aiden. I fucked up, but you still have a chance to get out. So instead of wasting your summer getting high with your washed-up friends, do what I should have done—find a way to stay the hell away."

He's silent for a moment, staring at his feet before looking over to me and clearing his throat.

"Why did you come back if you knew how bad it was here?" I can hear the genuine concern in his voice. He's not asking to hold it against me, but because he wants to help, which is a much harder reality to face. It'd be easier if he was truly a dick.

I want to tell him to ask Eric.

This family loved his evangelical, God-fearing ass so much. I'm surprised no one has reached out to him after we split.

"There was something worse at college than this family," I whisper.

I slowly regain consciousness in the hospital bed. The room is dimly lit, with the soft hum of medical equipment in the background. I blink, disoriented, trying to make sense of my surroundings. My vagina throbbed with horrendous pain, feeling as if it had been ripped apart and sewn back together again.

A woman in a white coat looms over me, smiling gently before taking a seat at the edge of the bed. Her expression is soft, her eyes filled with compassion.

"Where... Where am I?"

"You may still feel groggy from the pain medication," She says, placing her hand on my forearm. "Do you have any idea how you got here, sweetheart? How's your pain level?"

I try to pull forward any recollection of what might've happened that resulted in me lying in the hospital, but my memory is foggy. Fear tightens the muscles in my chest.

"No... my head... and my stomach. And my...I-I feel sore. Everything's blurry." I touch my head slowly.

"My name is Dr. Moore. It seems you were given something... a drug, likely without your knowledge. We're running some tests, but the important thing is that you're safe now."

"A drug? What do you mean? Did someone..." My voice falters in realization.

"We tried to track down your I.D. to phone someone but couldn't find it in any of your clothing. It looks like someone tried to hurt you. You were found unconscious. But you're in good hands now, and we're going to help you through this. The wounds you came in with were extensive in some areas," She sighs, glancing to the door; a man and woman in police uniforms stand in the entryway of the

room, one with a clipboard in his hand. The look they give me tells me they're waiting for permission to step in.

I close my eyes for a moment, feeling the tears slipping down my cheeks. The pain and fear mix with confusion as I try to process what she's saying. I take a shaky breath and open my eyes again.

Dr. Moore squeezes my arm. "It's going to take time, but you're going to be okay. You have people here who care about you. The police are going to want to talk to you just to understand what happened and help find out who did this. The rape kit we'll administer is very straightforward..."

"Eden!" Aiden yells, pulling me away from my thoughts, my foot slamming on the brakes, narrowly avoiding blowing through a red light.

Gasping, I extend my arm out over my brother's chest.

"Where did you just go?"

Shaking my head, I roll my fingers over my eyes, trying to calm myself down, focusing on reality rather than the memory of that night.

"Nowhere, Aiden," I sigh. "I'm just tired."

Hit with the comforting smell of roasted coffee beans, I point to a couch isolated in the corner of the room, texting Aiden the Wi-Fi password, letting him go and do his own thing.

"Want anything?"

"Anything that will keep me up. I barely slept last night," He sighs, narrowing his eyes at my neck.

"Right," I smile, my throat still swollen.

Zoey waves at me from the counter, ignoring the customer in front of her.

Making my way around the counter, I playfully nudge her to the side, clocking in on the register's tablet.

"Can you make Aiden a double shot of espresso?" I ask, her mouth stuck in a pout as she looks at my brother. He gives her his best doe eyes in hopes she'll eventually cave.

"Fine," She sighs, rolling her eyes. "I was going to make one for myself anyways."

I don't find it hard to smile at Zoey as she giggles and makes her way over to the espresso machine. Her apron is covered in pins representing different organizations and causes that some might argue compete with the large, silver cross hanging from her neck. She's never struggled to have an open mind, which drew me to her instantly. I never felt less than or judged when I was around her.

Back at college, I never had anyone I'd consider a friend. Sure, there were people I saw regularly, but everything always seemed so superficial. It reminded me a lot of my family, which was ironic since I left for college to get as far away from them as possible.

My roommate spent most of her free time shacking up with frat boys any chance she could get, sometimes even bringing them back to our room, locking me out until she was finished. I spent more nights than I care to admit sleeping in the hallway of our dorm. I'm not sure she cared.

I can't picture Zoey doing anything like that, which is why I'd consider her a friend. And although she makes an effort to go to church with her parents every Sunday, I know if she had a choice, she'd say fuck it to organized religion entirely.

Finding her own relationship with God outside the church has always been her mindset.

I'm snapped out of my thoughts by the sound of a man's voice. "I'm looking for recommendations. Anything on the menu you'd recommend?"

The sound of coffee beans spilling on the floor draws my attention to Zoey. She does this almost every shift I have with her, but I'm still surprised.

"Sorry!"

The man in front of me is at least six feet tall, with light brown curls and a sweaty, flushed face. A hockey jersey covers his large frame. Freckles like mine dance across his face adding to the charm of his dark blue eyes and friendly smile.

This is exactly the type of boy I would've fawned after in high school if I wasn't busy planning a perfect Catholic wedding with Eric.

"Depends. Did you just run a marathon?" I joke, as he pushes his wet hair out of his face.

He laughs. "Close. I just got done with hockey practice, and I'm in serious need of some caffeine before I hit the shower and start studying... So, what do you recommend..." He stops, looking at my name tag. "Eden? Pretty, like the garden," He smirks, my cheeks growing hot at the comment.

"What about, um, a d-dirty chai latte?" I stutter out like an idiot.

He leans closer to me over the counter. "Just how dirty is it?"

The confused look on my face makes him belt out another laugh.

"I'm messing with you. That sounds perfect. How much-"

"It's on the house," Zoey interjects, pushing me out of the way of the register. "Eden here can make your drink. Just wait for it at the end of the counter."

"Are you sure? I don't mind paying-"

"Super sure. Move along, blue eyes," She waves as the man drops the ten-dollar bill he meant to pay with straight into our tip jar.

"Zo, what are you doing-"

"He's hot and has come in here multiple times and never asked for a suggestion. He always gets the same thing. So go and make that sexy man's drink and strike up a convo while I make Martha a decaf latte and listen to her bitch about her heart problems."

She nudges my shoulder, and I can't help but shake my head. Making my way through the station, even though I've made the drink dozens of times before, I take a little extra time making it today. Topping it off with a layer of cinnamon foam, I slide the mug across the counter, proud of myself for the near-perfect leaf design swirled on the top of the drink.

"Wow, I would order this every time if I knew this was the presentation I'd get," He grins, looking at me.

"Oh shit," I whisper, pinching the bridge of my nose. "I didn't ask if you wanted that to go-"

"I usually get it to go, but I think I'll drink it here today."

He picks up the coffee cup before extending his free hand out between us. "I'm Luca," He says, and I take his hand in mine.

I point to my name tag playfully. "Eden. Just in case you already forgot."

He shakes his head at me before releasing my hand. "Humor me, Luca," I whisper, leaning my elbows into the counter, getting a closer look at the man. "What inspired you to switch up your drink order?"

"Full honesty," He whispers, leaning into the counter, too. "You caught my attention the minute I walked in. I've never seen you here before. Now, I'm crossing my fingers hoping you're not a high schooler and this entire meet and greet turns into a disaster."

I smile at his charm.

Maybe getting to know this man wouldn't be the worst idea.

At least this is appropriate. It's not like I can shamelessly flirt with a priest in public. Ever.

Taking a closer look at Luca, I see a cross is settled under his jersey. I raise my arm and point to his chest.

"Are you religious, or is that just a fashion statement?"

"Definitely Catholic," He smiles. "Although, never been huge on the idea of going to church."

"Trust me," I sigh. "I get it."

Grabbing one of the pens and empty customer survey forms next to the register, Luca quickly writes something out and slides the piece of paper across the counter.

"I have practice in the mornings most days and work every other day at my dad's outdoor gear store. Evenings are totally free. Normally, I'd say it's time for me to go," He whispers, grabbing the drink again, "But since you made this for here," He sighs. "I guess I'll have to sit down and do my studying here."

"I guess you will –"

"Father Briar," Zoey chimes, my attention immediately stolen from the conversation with Luca.

Whipping my head around, there he stands, in black joggers and a grey hoodie, the tattoo on his neck peeking out from the neckline. I don't think anyone would guess he was a priest.

"Did she just say, Father?" Luca questions. "As in, that man's a priest?"

"Yeah," I mutter. "That's exactly what she said."

Locking eyes with me, Roman raises his brows once he notices Luca. A wave of arousal washes over me, pooling in my lower stomach. Crossing my legs, I bite my cheek, trying to focus on something else.

Why the fuck is he here?

Tugging at my collar, the material feels tighter

Turning back to Luca, I try to pick up where we left off.

"Do you want to sit with me while I take my break?"

Luca nods, his eyes burrowing into mine with a look of curiosity and satisfaction. "Sure-"

Taking a step out from behind the counter, I keep my back facing Roman, blocking out the sound of his voice as he relays his order to Zoey.

"Zoey, I'm taking fifteen," I yell, making my way outside and away from Father Briar.

Chapter 9

EDEN

Aiden doesn't even look up as I exit the coffee shop with Luca. He is too lost in his studies as music blares from his headphones. I quickly guide Luca to one of the many tables positioned on the side of the cafe. We take a seat across from each other, his drink nearly spilling.

"Note to self: when you mean now, you mean now," Luca laughs, taking a long drink from the cup.

"I hate seeing people from church outside the cathedral," I say with full honesty. My reasons for avoiding Roman are not something I want to explain to anyone.

"I get it. My parents tried the whole Sunday Mass thing for a while. Then, they got dragged into Bible study sessions and prayer groups. Eventually, they got sick of having to be involved in so many different activities to be fully accepted into the church. That's kinda when they broke off."

The veneration in his tone as he tells me about his parents is obvious. My intuition tells me that they're close, that there's a lot of love there. The concept of having a choice when it comes to faith is foreign to me.

"I wish my parents were capable of giving their all to something other than the Church. My whole life has been centered around the Catholic faith and serving God. Not to mention, my dad's interpretation of scripture is literal. It's the ultimate authority for him, and it has a major influence on how he wants us to live."

"Jesus, when you say literal, you mean-"

"If you looked up 'Crazy Catholics' on Urban Dictionary, my parent's pictures would no doubt pop up," I sigh, leaning my face into my hands, my ass still throbbing from the punishment my dad probably spent the morning justifying to himself was necessary.

"Well," Luca sighs, "I've never minded a little crazy in my life."

I smile. If I wasn't trapped by just how much my parents being 'Crazy Catholics' affected my life, I'd probably have a chance of developing a truly healthy relationship with someone for once. The weight of the realization that my home life was something I'd never be able to share with someone like Luca hits me, shame and longing distorting my features as I dip my head, unable to look at him any longer.

His fingers wrap around my chin, lifting my head up so that our eyes meet again. His touch is warm and gentle, and I feel my face grow hot from the attention.

I can't help but give him a smile, even if it's an awkward one.

"What are you doing?"

"Hoping to see that again-"

"Eden?" A deep voice questions from somewhere in my periphery, the familiar way it sounded coming through my phone last night sending warmth through my body.

Oh no.

Craning my head up, I see Roman glaring at us, his fingers clinching tightly around his paper to-go cup as Luca's hand falls from my face.

"Rom-Father Briar," I correct.

"Faulkner," He smirks, throwing on a pleasant front despite the anger lingering in his stare.

Is he jealous?

My texts from the night before were still unanswered. Maybe it's just my mind whispering deceitful thoughts to that more logical part of me, but I chalked up yesterday's love affair with the priest as some sort of one-night stand fantasy he'd been dying to fulfill after being abstinent for so long.

"Who's your friend?" Roman points at Luca.

"We actually just met, Father," Luca smiles, holding his hand out to Roman. "Luca Thorn."

"Roman Briar," He says flatly as he eyes the empty seat next to me.

"Well, Father, as you can see, we're busy," I bite out, pleading to Roman with my eyes to just walk away.

"I don't think Luca would mind if I sat here while I finished my drink, would you, Luca?"

Luca gives Roman a tight smile, gesturing for him to join us.

I'm sure, in most cases, any devout Catholic would welcome the presence of a priest if they were in this situation, probably fearful of God's wrath if they denied such a holy figure.

But most priests aren't Roman, nor do they look like him, either.

Roman had removed the sweatshirt I'd seen him in earlier, standing in front of us now in a plain, form-fitting t-shirt, the same shade of black as his pants. His figure stands taller and more imposing than Luca's, his older age adding to the fullness of his frame. As he moves closer to us, I notice the defined muscles beneath his shirt, drawing attention to his physical strength. My gaze lingers on the tattoo snaking up his neck, catching a glimpse of its intricate design—a complex pattern of black vines and thorns twisting together.

"Not at all, Father," Luca smiles.

"Great. Eden, do you mind?"

He knows damn well that I do. But giving Roman any sort of attitude in front of Luca would raise questions that I didn't want lingering between us. I'll have to play nice.

"Not at all, Father," I grin. "Be my guest."

Taking a seat directly next to me, Roman's scent fills my nose. His leg brushes mine as he adjusts himself to get comfortable in the chair, but instead of moving it away, he keeps the contact between us. He settles his left hand in his lap and leans back, widening the space between his legs.

"So Luca, I see you're wearing a cross. What faith do you follow?" Roman questions, acting like he really gives a shit.

What's his move here?

"Catholicism, actually. Forgive me, Father, but you seem pretty young to be a priest." Luca's tone is cautious, but I catch the skepticism etched in his expression as he waits for Roman to respond.

"Perhaps young in age, but not in mind," Roman sighs. "You should come by the church sometime. Eden's family are very active members."

"He doesn't go to church-"

"I might, actually. I haven't had the opportunity to see this town's cathedral since I moved here. I suppose it never hurts to try something out," Luca challenges, feeding into the charged air I feel between them.

"You a hockey fan?" Roman eyes Luca's jersey.

"Fan, player. Pretty much my only hobby," Luca beams as they go back and forth on the topic, my own thoughts drowning out their conversation.

Roman's fingers graze the side of my leg, and my mind wanders back to last night.

"-She's my altar server," Roman says, my ears tuning back into the conversation.

"You serve?" Luca questions with surprise.

"Not willingly," I snap, looking over Roman. "My father signed me up-"

Beneath the table, Roman subtly slips his hand under the part of my apron resting on my lap. He inches slowly up my exposed leg, pushing up my dress as his hand settles in the groove where my thigh meets my abdomen. I stiffen as he hooks his pinky around the fabric of my underwear and presses his other fingers flush against my center. I feel his long fingers begin to move between the folds of my flesh, spreading me open as his thumb teases close to my entrance. The sensation threatens to dislodge a moan from my throat.

"You okay?" Luca questions. Roman's fingers continue gliding through my wetness. I bite back a yelp when he pinches my clit, his way of warning me not to expose what's happening under the table.

All it would take is for Luca to lean over a bit too far to see Roman's hand is somewhere it shouldn't be.

"Yeah, I'm fine-"

I smile as I reach below the table, pressing my hand to the material of my dress between my thighs, feeling his hand nestled in my underwear, continuing the slow, up-down motions between my folds. His pointer finger swirls around my entrance, and I try to cross my legs. The slickness from my desire for him soaks my thighs as I work to keep my focus on Luca.

God, please give me strength right now.

"What do you do for fun, Luca? Big on playing games?"

"Some. You, Father?" Luca asks, casually sipping from his drink, still unaware of the game Father Briar is playing with me below the table.

Fuck.

I hate how much I love this.

Anyone could come around the corner of the coffee shop and see Roman's hand under my apron from behind.

"I love a good game of spades," Roman smirks. "I rarely lose at cards. In fact, I'd probably say I rarely lose any game I—"

With my elbow, I nudge some stray napkins off the table down to the ground between us. Roman's legs are tilted towards me, his inner thigh being the perfect place for me to place my hand as an anchor point while I lean down to pick them up off the concrete. He continues making idle conversation with Luca.

While he's distracted, I move my hand further up between his legs, wrapping my hand around the thick bulge of his cock and squeezing before sitting up completely and placing the napkins back on the table. I move my hand back to my lap until it's flush over his. I spread my legs wider for him and press down firmly through my dress so he's forced to still his movements.

I plan to show him that this is a game he won't win.

The man stifles a groan, his right hand shaking around the empty coffee cup.

"You mind tossing that behind you in the trashcan around the corner, kid?" Roman hands Luca his cup while he's still tucked between my thighs.

Glancing behind him, Luca shrugs, swinging his legs over the bench and turning away to walk back towards the front entrance where the trashcan sits.

Pulling his hand away from my throbbing center, Roman grabs the back of my neck with his free hand and pulls me closer. His left elbow sits on the table as he holds his glistening fingers in the air between us. Seeing my slickness coat his fingers elicits a needy groan from some deeply hungry place inside of me. Unable to stop myself, I look down at the strain between his legs. I push out my lower lip in a pout, moving closer to him, our noses almost touching.

"Forgive me, Father-"

Squeezing the back of my neck to silence me, Roman slides his fingers into my mouth, the taste of me coating my tongue. He presses further into my mouth, grabbing my face as I nearly choke on his fingers that hit the back of my throat.

"You want so desperately to feel my cock, Eden?" He growls, referencing not only now, but last night when I reached into his lap briefly before he'd brought me to my house.

"Then learn how to take it," He hisses, coaxing his fingers further down my throat, a gag trying to force its way out. "You can barely handle my fingers. How do you think my cock would feel pounding into that pretty pussy?" He brushes his cheek against mine. "We both know that fucking glorified frat boy isn't the reason you're nearly soaked through your underwear," He whispers, his lip grazing my ear, nipping at my earlobe. "You said it's "my move" Eden?" He questions, throwing my words back at me. "This is only a taste of what kind of moves I'll make after you sent me that fucking picture last night."

Pulling his fingers free from my mouth, I gasp, finally able to take a breath before seeing Luca's head of curls emerge from around the corner. Roman looks up at him and smiles, reaching down in his lap to adjust his very prominent erection before Luca reaches the table.

"Is that your brother in there?" Luca questions. "The one studying?"

I slide away from Roman to put some space between us so I can think straight.

"Yeah," I admit. "Why?"

"I did a few summer athletic camps with him," Luca shrugs. "We got to chatting while I was tossing away the cup..."

Trailing off, Luca turns to Roman.

If the tension was visible, it would be thick enough to cut right now.

"Father Briar, aren't you leaving? You said you're still settling into your new place, right?"

The last thing I need is Roman anywhere near me right now while I try to recover from the feeling of his fingers in my mouth.

His words of taunt are echoing through the chambers of my mind.

How do you think my cock would feel pounding into that pretty pussy?

I clear my throat, crossing my legs to ease the ache at my center.

"You're right, Eden," Roman sighs, dragging his hoodie over his head and down his torso before standing. His hand is in one pocket, barely concealing the bulge that still lingers in his joggers.

"I'll see you at the church at five," He moves past me, his eyes latching to mine. "Don't be late," He whispers.

Causally brushing past Luca, he ignores the man's attempt to shake his hand, turning the corner, disappearing, and leaving me here in a lusty haze.

Touching my cross, I try and think.

How much more of this can I allow?

"I wasn't really keen on speaking in front of your priest, he's a bit-"

"Intimidating?" I question, answering for him.

"Just a bit."

How the hell could I have let Roman do that to me right in front of Luca?

A boy actually my fucking age? That I might actually grow to like? That might actually be good for me?

One who has not devoted his entire life to the church.

"So, Aiden. I got to talking to him. A few of my buddies and I plan on heading to the meadows and having some drinks, maybe lighting a fire. I invited your brother and the spunky girl at the counter to come. She said you two are friends. You care to join?"

I lower my head. The idea of being alone with any group of men again after what happened with my brother and his friends yesterday was not on my bucket list.

"I promise you don't have to drink to have a good time. I can pick you up from the church later. Aiden said he planned on dropping you off-"

"My relationship with alcohol is not the best," I admit. "It's even worse when it comes to social settings."

"I swear to stay sober so you don't feel alone," Luca smiles. "You seem like a cool girl, and honestly, it would be nice to associate with people other than my teammates," He shrugs. "So, what do you say?"

Going to a party in the middle of nowhere with people I don't know is the last thing I should be doing, but locking myself in my room, hiding from my dad will only open up the possibility that I'll reach out to Roman again, and that can't happen.

"Okay. I'll plan to come with Aiden," I sigh. "What should I bring?"

Smiling, Luca raises his brows.

"Got a swimsuit?"

Chapter 10

ROMAN

A few lingering patrons, mostly the elderly and those with a bit too much free time during the weekdays, are scattered throughout the church, quietly immersed in their daily prayers. I save my over-the-top outfits for weekend Mass, opting instead for a more professional look today—a dark dress shirt neatly tucked into my overpriced slacks.

Father Kevin had been kind enough to leave behind the funds for a new wardrobe, not to mention the monthly salary was already extremely generous. Even for some of the more well-off congregations made up of mega-rich assholes, this salary seemed a bit outlandish.

Peering over at my office, I'm filled with a flurry of emotions. I've kept the door shut, unnerved by what I found on the computer and ashamed that I satiated my physical desires there earlier today after returning to the church from the coffee shop. The pressure in my throbbing cock wouldn't subside after seeing Eden earlier at the coffee shop. I couldn't stop thinking about that black dress that hugged her curves and how smooth her skin was. The smell of her pussy and mouth lingered on my fingers, and I wanted to think of her as I came.

At this point, I've got a one-way ticket straight to hell.

Glancing at my watch, twenty minutes are left till five. Eden hadn't messaged me, but I don't have any reason to think she won't show up tonight for her service hours.

A small smile tries to pull across my lips as I think about our interaction at the coffee shop; the look of her so flustered by my words is indescribably satisfying.

Unable to avoid his image in my mind, I grow angry at the idea of Luca being there today.

Showing up to the coffee shop was idiotic.

Inserting myself into her conversation just to keep the man from being alone with her was damn right foolish.

He said maybe one sentence to her at that counter, and I reacted like that?

What the hell would I have done if he had touched her?

Why am I reacting like this?

I've been with women in the past.

For me, it's always been simple.

Sex was just sex. Nothing more.

So why the hell am I consumed by thoughts of having my cock buried deep inside Eden?

Why do I wonder what she would look like with her hands tied up, her knees bowed in prayer to me as she-

"Father Briar," David's unsettling voice pierces the quiet, pulling me away from my sick reveries of his daughter.

"David?" I question, glancing around, unsure when the man walked in. "I'm sorry, I was lost in thought," I admit, narrowing my eyes at the man.

"Did we have a meeting?"

He moves to stand in front of me, a portfolio tucked between his arm and side.

"No, not scheduled, but I did just talk to Kevin," He admits. "I spoke with him on the phone, and it would seem he was unaware how much you really knew about our... ideologies in this church. He didn't know you held the same beliefs that he and I share," David sighs, my mind still drawing blanks. "Your position was supposed to be temporary, correct?"

I nod my head. "Only a few months-"

"Kevin would like that to change," David snaps, taking a step closer. "It's not very often we find individuals who can be brought into our circle here, and given your age, you could be a great asset to this congregation for a good long while." David smiles, glancing toward the open doors leading into the confessional space.

"Kevin saw a login on his account. I assume it was you?"

No point in lying.

"Creative password," I smirk. "Inside joke?" I continue to play into whatever the hell is going on here.

"More like a dance with God," David smirks, lowering his voice.

"You saw the inventory, then?"

"Some expensive furniture," I shrug. "Any reason why?" I probe.

Anyone willing to pay any of those prices for old and outdated furniture is delusional.

"Our operation maintains Saint Michael's opulence and keeps your paychecks coming. In exchange, we utilize the space for inventory." He looks around the space. "It was one hell of a remodel our work funded," He smiles, tapping his foot on the floor. "Underground tunnels make for more discrete transportation."

Laughing, I try to hide my confusion and suspicion.

"Can never have too much furniture, I suppose," I tease, winking at the man.

Giving me a casual nod, David glances at his watch.

"My daughter should be here soon," He sighs, grabbing my shoulder. "I meant what I said at my house. Eden is a sinner. I want her to feel God's wrath through you. Her rebellious nature is blasphemous, and she must be set back on the path to God."

Smiling, I pat his shoulder.

"Of course, David. I plan to fulfill your wishes in the name of the Lord to the best of my ability."

It's becoming more obvious as the days go by that David Faulkner is not someone to fuck with. So, if I have to feed into his extremist religious ideologies in order to avoid whatever psychotic brand of retribution he's dishing out, so be it.

I'm not sure how Kevin managed it here for so long. He seemed like a decent man.

"You know, Roman, I was unsure about you at first," David points out. "I had my men look into you at the DA's office. We never want any sticky fingers in our work here. You served before you took seminary?" He questions, clawing at the grave of my past.

"A few tours," I shrug. "Saw enough that even God has struggled to steer me away from the bottle," I admit, torturous screams trying to force their way into the back of my mind.

Shut it out.

Don't let it in.

"A background like that could be very useful to us," He smiles, extending the portfolio out to me, shaking it in front of me like it's my birthday present.

"Kevin and the others gave me the green light to show you this. We're excited to welcome you into the real brotherhood of this congregation," He pats me on the back as I take the portfolio from him. "I'll leave you to it," He turns, dipping his finger in the holy water, saying a silent prayer.

"Our first meeting is after Mass this Sunday," David exclaims. "That's where you can place your preference on inventory before the buyers do."

"Meeting?" I look down at the portfolio, turning it over in my hand.

"Here, at ten. Doors lock at nine-thirty," He smirks. "Have a good night, Father," He waves. "Oh. And mind certain areas of Eden's skin. She should have known when to shut her mouth."

Mind Eden's skin.

What the fuck does that mean?

The doors shut behind David, those lingering in the pews for their own worship outside of Mass leave, and the only face in sight is my reflection in the pool of holy water.

Setting the portfolio on the rim of the stoup, I flip it open, wondering if there's still any scotch left in my –

Backing away from the binder, my heart beats out of my chest, my stomach rolling, ready to throw up that shitty overpriced coffee Eden's friend made me. Clutching my cross, I take a shaky breath, filled to the brim with feral rage, my vision going fuzzy, clouded with adrenaline.

Like I'm back in the pits of war, violence tugs at my heart, the bloodthirsty need to rip someone apart escalating with every image touching my vision.

The descriptions.

They weren't descriptions and pricing details for furniture. They were for fucking *children*.

I flip page after page, each child dirtied and petrified, some holding up their hands, squinting at the flash from the camera.

Item: Leather Futon

Age: Seven Years

Description: Brown with blue accents and decorative fringe.

Status: New

Price: $10,000.000

Name: Molly Jackson

Age: Seven Years

Description: Female, Brown hair, blue eyes

Status: Virgin

Price: $10,000.00

There are twenty children, all matching the twenty pieces of furniture I'd seen listed in the email saved on Father Kevin's computer yesterday. Invoices, paid in full, were attached to each image, all except one on the last page of the portfolio.

Name: X

Age: Twenty Years

Description: X

Status: Non-Virgin (ideal for breeding)

Price: $50,000.00

No name. No face. The highest listing price.

"What the fuck," I whisper, reflecting on what David had said.

What Aiden told me back at his house.

His father is hurting him.

His father is hurting so many others too.

And now, he thinks I'm just like him.

I slam the portfolio shut, suffocating on the oppressive air in the cathedral. I need to get out of here.

The police.

I have to take this to the police-

"I had my men look into you at the DA's office. Never want any sticky fingers in our work here."

They already know.

This whole God's damned town is run by these sick fucks.

And I'm at the center of all of it.

Every violent memory that I've kept suppressed comes rushing in, my hands shaking as I try to take a deep breath.

Reload.

He's bleeding out, Briar!

Kill them.

Fucking shoot him.

"Father?"

Slowly looking up, I see a boy with light brown hair and bloodshot eyes headed towards me. The stench of pot hits my nostrils.

Zack.

Fucking Hell.

Is God testing me again?

"I just came by to drop off my stuff before my buddy's party," He sighs, holding up a worn old robe. "I figured I'd be able to use the washing machine to get it ready before Mass..." He trails off, my chest rising and falling in rapid breaths.

"Are you alright?"

I see Eden standing in the rain, her expression of pain and sorrow.

David has hurt her.

Zack has hurt her.

"Come here, Zack," I calmly coax him forward. "You forgot to bless yourself before entering the Lord's house," I hiss.

Swallowing nervously, Zack sets his things down, taking a cautious step toward me.

"Is something wrong, Father Briar?"

"Bless yourself, Zack," I snap, "And then we can speak."

Nodding his head, he creeps closer to the pool of holy water, peering down at our reflections in the large basin.

Reaching his hand toward the water, he taps his middle finger against its surface.

"Now, Zack, don't be shy," I smile, grabbing his wrist and pushing his hand a little further down. "You didn't hold back when you stripped Eden and left her on the side of the road, so why show restraint now?"

His eyes snap to my face. "How did you-"

"God knows all," I seethe.

"I meant to confess-"

"Well, I'm listening now. Here's how you can repent."

Motivated by feral rage, I grab the back of his head, shoving it into the water and forcing it to the bottom of the bowl. His arms flare, and I tighten my grip. His muffled screams bubble up to the surface of the water as I hold him there for a few seconds before yanking him back up. His head falls back, and his mouth hangs open as he sucks in air.

"How does it feel to be defenseless, Zack?" I yell, my teeth nearly snapping like a rabid dog. "Repent!"

"Forgive me, Father-" His voice trembles as he gets the words out, and I'm satisfied by the way he trembles against my chest.

I drive his head back into the water one more time for good measure, clawing his scalp as I drag him back up once I'm convinced he's spent enough time breathless at the bottom of the bowl.

"If you ever fucking touch her again," I yell, slamming his head into the concrete rim of the basin. A deep gash forms across his forehead from the impact, dripping blood down the holy relic. "I will fucking send your ass straight to Hell. Swear to God you will never touch her again!"

Curling in on himself, he starts to sob like a small child, snot oozing from his nostrils down onto his lips before reaching his chin. His eyes are wide with fear.

Good. He should fear me.

I close my eyes, inhaling deeply as I recite Luke 10:19 to myself.

I have given you authority to trample on snakes and scorpions and to overcome all the power of the enemy; nothing will harm you.

And that's what Zack is —a snake.

"Swear to him," I command, my mouth gravitating to his ear. "Swear to me."

"I s-swear, Lord," He sobs. "I swear, Father-"

I look down to see his blood on the hand I have fisted into the neckline of his shirt. A familiar feeling threatens to bring my past to life. I take another deep breath, trying to calm my nerves. Shoving him to the floor, I take a step back, grabbing the portfolio that had fallen to the ground a few feet away.

"Get the fuck out of this cathedral, and take your dirty ass clothes with you. I'll be seeing you on Sunday. Open your mouth about any of this, and I'll say you attacked me first. I'm sure your track record will make that story pretty fucking believable."

Clutching his bloodied head, Zack stumbles to his feet, bending over to grab his clothes and backpack without saying anything else.

As he straightens his back and turns to face me, his whole body freezes. The muscles in his face go taut. "E-Eden."

Shit.

Turning around, I see her standing in a white robe in the doorway to the altar room. Her fists are clenched around the rope at her waist. Her hair spills over her shoulders and down her back, a few locks falling in front of the eyes that are currently locked on the two of us.

Lowering his head, Zack pushes past her, brushing her shoulder on the way out. I can still hear him sobbing as he makes his way down the corridor.

Eden remains in the doorway, shaking as she surveys the room, the blood on the floor, and the portfolio under my arm.

She creeps closer, her skin flushed with a fierce, uneven heat, patches of red blooming across her face and neck, while a cold sweat clung to her brow.

Words caught in my throat as she stood before me.

I watch as she dips her finger delicately into the holy water.

"In the name of the Father, the Son, and the Holy Spirit," She whispers, nudging past me without another word.

Chapter 11

EDEN

I was able to make it home just in time to change after my shift at the coffee shop. Thankfully, Mom finished the laundry, which meant I had a few warmer, and frankly way more comfortable, clothing options to pick from to get me through the rest of the night. I'd found her in the house, already drunk off a bottle of wine, tuning out the world around her in front of the TV.

I prop my feet up on the dash, blasting the heat in Aiden's car as I wait for him. I look over to see my father's car isn't in the driveway.

Odd.

He's typically home from work by now, ready to get my drunk mother to bed before enjoying a glass of scotch for himself.

Where the hell could he be-

Sliding into the driver's side door, Aiden slings his bag into the backseat, its contents clacking together, clearly filled with a few swiped bottles from our parents' wine cellar.

"Do you know where Dad is?"

"Who gives a shit. I'm sure he's still at work, or at a bar some-where with his coworkers." Aiden scoffs, backing out of the driveway.

"I need to tell you something about the party tonight. Zack was hanging around Nathan earlier and saw some texts about it on his phone. He invited himself to Luca's bonfire since he knows one or two of Luca's friends. I told Luca you probably wouldn't show up if Zack is there-"

"It's fine," I say coldly, cramming my hands into the pocket of my hoodie. "It's not like I can avoid him forever."

"Trust me, I'm trying to," Aiden sighs, looking over at me.

"You know you could ditch this whole service hour thing. We could go grab some food, talk about how shitty this semester is going to be for me. I know you love pointless high school drama."

"As much as I want to say yes, I think it's best that I go. I don't want to disappoint Dad, now do I?

Or Roman, for that matter. Although skipping out on altar server services hours after what happened at the coffee shop might be needed to douse the flames still burning under my skin every time I think about his stupid hands on my body. I'm not willing to risk the outcome of rebelling against him or my father so boldly.

Getting these service hours done will be one step closer to never having to be alone with him again.

God, I forgot about confession. The idea of becoming per-fectly pious crosses my mind. I'll never sin again. That will be the plan.

"Is that Dad's car? And look, isn't that Zack's Toyota?" Aiden pulls into the Saint Michael's parking lot, heading in the direction of our dad's black Mercedes sedan.

Aiden comes to a stop, parking next to my father, the man barely noticing we're here as he continues to talk on the phone.

Getting out of the car, I slam my door shut behind me.

Jolting, my dad lowers his phone, his eyebrows raising as he rolls down the window.

"Cutting it close on time, Eden."

Looking back at Aiden, I roll my eyes.

"I made it, didn't I?" I cross my arms over my chest.

"I suppose so," My dad scoffs, craning his head to look at Aiden. "I'll see you both later tonight."

Leaving the conversation at that, he rolls up his window and gets back to his phone call as he pulls out of the parking lot and onto the road –going in the opposite direction of our house.

"I can walk you in, Eden-"

"It's fine," I smile, cramming my hands into my pockets. "I'll see you at seven. Go help Luca set up for tonight."

As I make my way to the front doors of Saint Michael's, I reread Luca's texts from earlier.

> Looking forward to seeing you tonight! Haven't had a proper social in months. Feel free to feed me all the exciting details of your training with Father Briar!
> (PS tell Aiden I would love some extra help setting up)

I make my way to the quiet space designated for altar servers to change. I close the door, turning the lock, pulling the handle a few times to make sure no one can get in.

Turning around, I see a freshly ironed, white server's robe on one of the benches, a note placed on top.

Eden Faulkner

Glaring at the virgin white material of the robe, I roll my eyes.

"Of course you want me in this," I hiss to myself, biting back a slew of vile curses.

Growing up, every aspect of my life was controlled by my parents, down to the clothes I wore. Sundays were a parade of pristine dresses and polished shoes, symbols of a family cloaked in piety and perfection. But beneath the surface, the tight seams of my perfectly pressed clothes mirrored the suffocating grip my parents had on my identity. Each outfit they forced me into was a constant reminder of the freedom I never had.

During her first week of college, my roommate, Ivy, invited me out for drinks. I found myself at a dimly lit bar, a place my parents would never approve of. The air buzzed with laughter, clinking glasses, and a freedom I hadn't known before. As the night wore on, the tight grip of my past began to loosen.

The neatly pressed blouse I had worn out of habit felt out of place in a college setting. My hair was tousled, my lipstick slightly smudged, but for the first time, I didn't care. In a spontaneous act of defiance, I borrowed my friend's oversized jacket, embracing its comfort. After that night, I threw away almost all the shirts my mom had bought me before leaving home.

Glaring at the mirror, a thought passes over my mind.

There aren't any rules for what can be worn *under* the robe.

If he wants me to dress like one of his perfect little virgin servers, fine, I will.

Tearing off my hoodie, I stare at the black lace bra Zoey convinced me to buy, my breasts strangled in its overpriced material. Usually, I would never wear something like this under my clothes. But since I'll see both Roman and Luca tonight, the idea of being a little scandalous for one, or maybe both of them, gave me the courage I needed to get out of my comfort zone. I felt like I was taking a little control back of my body.

The light from the setting sun filters through the blinds, casting shadows across my scarred skin. I take off my pants, bundling them with the rest of my clothes, and throw them in a wad in the closest empty locker.

Going back to the mirror, I look at the bruising along my neck where the makeup has started to wear off. My fingers drift to the chain with my cross, adjusting it carefully so I don't irritate the sensitive skin. Swallowing my nerves, I pull on the white robe, kicking off my shoes as I pull my arms through the sleeves, the cold tile floor on my bare feet grounding me as I work to stifle the tension in my chest.

"Nothing's going to happen. It's just a few hours. You can do this."

Shaking my head, I tighten the rope around my waist and leave the changing room. As I make my way to the altar room, loud shouting breaks my train of thought.

"How does it feel to be defenseless, Zack?" Roman's voice shouts, my body seizing up at the sound of anger in his tone.

Peering at the double doors, I spot water seeping out, with strange swirls of red mixing into it. The color twists through the water as it spreads across the floor, making me pause, unsure of what I'm really seeing.

Taking a cautious step forward, I realize that I forgot to put my shoes back on as I walk across the tile and closer to whatever is spilling out from the doorway.

"Swear to him-" I hear Roman continue, a muffled voice sobbing uncontrollably.

With a shaky hand, I grab the handle of one of the large double doors and gently nudge it open. When I'm able to stand fully in the doorway, I look up towards the altar, my hand coming up to cover my mouth to hide the shock of what's in front of me.

Bleeding from his head, Zack cowers before Roman, whose eyes are clouded with rage. Trembling on the floor, Zack looks utterly defeated—his head wet, clothes drenched, and a thin trail of blood smearing the side of the holy water pool. Roman, looking anything but godly, steps closer, his gaze locked on Zack, too consumed by his fury to even notice me standing there. Despite the fear and shock gripping me, a dark sense of satisfaction stirs underneath, watching Zack reduced to this.

"Get the fuck out of this cathedral and take your dirty ass clothes with you. I'll be seeing you on Sunday. Open your mouth about any of this, and I'll say you attacked me first. I'm sure your track record will make that story pretty fucking believable." Roman snaps, pointing to the bag of clothes resting behind Zack.

Gripping his head as he snags his stuff, he stumbles as he turns to make his way out of the room. His eyes lock with mine, my hand dropping from my mouth as I try to find the words to say.

Zack swallows, his body frozen in place.

"E-Eden," He stutters, Roman quickly stepping aside, finally taking notice of my presence in the doorway.

Roman stands before me, like a dark angel, teetering on the edge of heaven and hell. His face is drained of color, making him look almost ethereal as if he's been touched by something beyond this world. His chest rises and falls with a raw intensity, his fists clenched at his sides, the sight of blood staining his fingers only adding to the dangerous allure that radiates from him. There's something undeniably magnetic about him in this moment—both terrifying and irresistible—that sends a thrill through me, leaving me captivated by his every breath.

This is the man he truly is, concealed by his sacred vows.

This is the man I let touch me.

Unpredictable. Rageful. Vengeful. Dangerous.

Yet, here I am.

I could turn around and leave. I could go to the police.

My legs moved on their own, as if guided by a force greater than myself, pulling me forward, closer to him. I hadn't told them to move, but it was like something divine had taken over, leading me toward what I needed to face. It felt like the very ground beneath me was drawing me closer, beyond my control, like I was being called.

My fingers dipped into the cool water within the font, without hesitation. The sensation of the cold liquid sent a shiver up my spine, the holy water clinging to the tip of my finger like a whispered prayer.

I stare up at Roman.

"In the name of the Father," I murmur, my fingers tracing from my forehead to my shoulders. "The Son," I continue, letting my hand rest briefly over my heart. "And the Holy Spirit," I whisper, the words barely audible as I finish the sign of the cross.

Without another word, I nudge past the man, moving forward with a quiet resolve.

May my silence unsettle him.

Micah 3:8: "But as for me, I am filled with power, with the Spirit of the Lord, and with justice and might."

Chapter 12

EDEN

I step onto the altar, my heart racing, as my fingers trace the cool metal of the chalice. It feels both forbidden and strangely comforting, like I'm grounding myself in something familiar. I move to the paten, running my hand over its smooth surface, trying to escape the chaos in my mind. The soft linen of the corporal brushes against my skin, offering a small sense of calm. I linger near the candles, drawn to their warmth, letting the flickering light steady my breath. Gripping the ciborium, I focus on its weight, trying to anchor myself as my thoughts continue to swirl.

I can feel Roman creeping up behind me, his breathing audible.

"Eden-"

"Where should I sit?" I ignore his need to talk about what I walked in on. "Still to your left?" I point to the wooden seat.

Glaring at the chairs, Roman shakes his head.

"Eden, what you saw-"

"Or will you have me kneel at your feet during Mass?" I toy with the knotted rope at my waist, pulling at the frayed ends.

Stepping in front of me, he holds up his hands. His brow furrows as he opens his mouth to speak, but I quickly cut him off.

"Let me see you in it," I snap, glancing back at the chair. "Take a seat," I urge. "Then we can talk."

Looking back at his chair, I can see the tension crackling in the air between us. The power play I've set in motion clearly frustrates him, his eyes narrowing into a glare that threatens to cut me into a thousand pieces. The attraction simmering beneath our conflict only heightens the stakes, making his struggle to maintain control all the more intense.

"I'm not doing this with you."

"You're going to have to," I hiss, "or else I'm going straight to the police-"

"And what do you think they will do?" He takes a step toward me, his hand coiling around the rope at my waist, tugging me just a bit closer to him. "You think they'll care what happened inside the walls of this church?" He snaps angrily. "That little fuck deserved what I did to him. Don't act like you disagree. Don't stand there and act like you're going to open your mouth about what you saw."

"What makes you think I won't?" I let my eyes travel up and down his body, making sure he knew I was sizing him up, daring him to underestimate me.

Tensing his jaw, Roman eyes the chair, his hand coiling tighter around the rope around my waist.

"Fine, you want me in the chair, Eden?" He challenges, his voice laced with tension as he grabs hold of me. I try to push him away, but his grip is firm as he drags me along with him. He drops into the chair with a deliberate sprawl, pulling me between his legs. I can feel the heat of his body pressing against mine, even through the clothes that separate us. His chin tilts up, eyes locking onto mine. The air between us is thick with a mix of desire and defiance. My hands press against his chest, resisting, but the magnetic pull between us is impossible to ignore.

Looking down at him, I cock my head to the side as his hands move from the rope to my hips.

"Your turn," He hisses. "Take a seat."

I try to move away, eyeing the deacon's chair beside him.

"Not there, Eden."

Looking toward his lap, I bite back the smirk tugging at my lips, shaking my head at him with mock disapproval. My eyes flick upward to the massive cross hanging above the altar, and I can't help but find the situation almost comedic. "You really think this is a good idea in his presence?" I tease, my voice laced with playful defiance, letting the weight of the moment settle between us.

He grabs me, pulling me toward him with a firm, insistent grip. My body instinctively leans into his, his hand sliding up my thigh, urging me onto his lap. His other hand quickly finds my opposite leg, guiding me with an urgency that sends a shiver through me. As I straddle him, the thin fabric of my underwear brushes against the hardness beneath his robes, a dangerous sensation that heightens the tension between us. My hands grip the back of the chair for support as I settle into his lap, his eyes widening when he realizes I'm wearing nothing beneath the robe but my panties. He leans in closer, his voice low and filled with playful authority as he murmurs, "God will forgive me. After all, he created temptation for a reason, didn't he?"

"Maybe, but even temptation has its limits. Think you can handle it, or should I remind you of what happens to sinners?" I rock my hips gently, feeling the hard length of his cock under the fabric of his robe rub against my bare thigh. His hands tighten around my hips,

"Sit still, Eden," He growls. Adrenaline courses through me at an all-time high. "We need to talk about Zack."

"Is that your secret? You get off on punishing your altar servers?" I look down at him, my hands wrapping around the back of his head, burying into his locks.

"Maybe that's why you and my father get along so well."

Grabbing the back of my neck, Roman tugs my hair hard, exposing my neck to him. A small yelp makes its way out of me, my body aching from the pressure.

Leaning into me, he drags his cheek along my exposed neck, grazing his nose along my jawline.

"I will never be like your piece of shit father," He snaps, more forceful than usual. "I'd much rather have you here like this, walking the line of my faith to God, than anywhere near him."

"And if God were to turn his back on you for this?"

"I can always worship someone else." His eyes trace over my body, slow and deliberate, as if he's trying to memorize every detail. The intensity of his gaze sends a thrill through me, and when our eyes lock, the desire in his expression is impossible to miss. He looks at me like he's barely holding back, and it's enough to make my breath catch.

The warmth between my legs grows as his cock continues to press against my center through our robes, and I decide to test just how far he's willing to go.

"Why was Zack deserving of your punishment, Father?" I rock my hips again, his hand tightens around the hair at the nape of my neck.

"Eden-"

"Confess," I snap, feeding into the pain from his touch. "Confess your sins to me, Father Briar."

He lets go of my hair and I see his jaw tighten, the muscles flexing just beneath his skin.

"Take off the robe, Eden," He growls.

I shake my head, and his hand moves to my ass.

Unaware that the skin there is still sensitive, he delivers it a harsh slap, my body slumping forward into him as I hide a sob.

He moves his lips to my ear. "I said take it off. Right. Fucking. Now."

I lean back to glare at him as I fumble with the material. Growing impatient, he reaches down between us and tugs at the rope around my waist, slipping it off and tossing it to the floor. "Thanks for the help," I say dryly.

Leaning back in the chair, he looks satisfied.

"My pleasure. Now take it off."

It feels as if every celestial eye is upon me, the weight of unseen judgment heavy in the air. My cheeks burn with a deep flush as my fingers nervously toy with the hem of my robe. Slowly, I reach down to the bunched fabric in my lap and drag the material up my body and over my head, exposing my skin to the warm, dim light. The robe finally slips from my grasp, cascading to the floor, leaving me standing there, vulnerable and exposed, the anticipation thickening with every breath I take.

Bared before him, in nothing but my undergarments, Roman takes all of me in, his hands trailing up my sides before running down my front.

"Black lace?"

I could feel the words forming on my tongue, sharp and cutting, designed to slip right under his skin. He had no idea what was coming, but I was about to make sure he felt every ounce of the sting.

"I thought Luca might like to see it later tonight."

Roman's eyes widen, sparks of rage flicker in his dilated pupils. He jerks me closer until my breasts are flush with his chest, my knees hitting the back of the chair.

"He won't see a fucking thing, Eden. If you let him touch you —"

"Why do you care? Maybe I want him to touch me."

He bares his teeth, hissing out his response.

"Why do I care?" He almost growls. "Because every time I see you, it's like you're pulling me further away from everything I've sworn to uphold. You make me question everything—my vows, my dedication, even my faith. I crave you in ways I'm not supposed to, and it's driving me mad. I can't stand the thought of anyone else touching you, because, God help me, I want you for myself, despite everything I've been taught, despite everything I believe. You've gotten under my skin, and now I can't get you out, no matter how hard I try." My breath catches as his confession sinks in. My heart pounds in my chest, the tension between us palpable, electrifying. My eyes flicker down to his hand, resting on my thigh, and there it is—the ring. A simple band of gold, worn smooth from years of devotion, a constant reminder of the vows he's taken. The same ring I thought was a wedding band when we first met. It gleams softly in the dim light, symbolizing everything he's dedicated his life to—everything that stands between us.

I reach out, my hand hovering just above his, my fingers trembling as they brush against the ring. Slowly, deliberately, I trace the band with my fingertip, feeling the weight of what it represents and the intensity of the moment. Our eyes lock, and the room seems to shrink around us, the world narrowing down to just this—the tension, the longing, and the unspoken promise of what might come next.

"Is this what's holding you back?" I whisper, my voice barely audible, laced with desire. The ring feels like a barrier, but as I glance back into his eyes, I see the crack in his resolve, the part of him that wants to forget it all, if only for a moment.

"Take it off," I mutter. "And touch me."

"Eden-"

"Your demons want me, Father?" I tap the ring. "Then take off the ring...and sin. You can ask for forgiveness later."

His eyes meet mine, searching for something— reassurance, maybe absolution. But all I offer him is the intensity of my gaze, the silent understanding that this moment could change everything.

Slowly, deliberately, he begins to slide the ring off his finger. It's not a quick motion; it's hesitant, almost reverent as if he's peeling away a layer of his soul. The ring slips off, and for a moment, it rests in his palm, heavy with the weight of what it means. His eyes darken, the last vestige of resistance melting away as he places the ring on the arm of the chair, the sound of metal against wood echoing in the stillness.

His hand, now bare, finds its way back to my thigh, and this time, there's nothing holding him back. The touch is different now—bolder, more assured. It's as if the removal of that ring has unleashed something within him, something raw and powerful.

He pulls me closer, his fingers digging into my skin with a newfound intensity, his breath hot against my neck. There's no more hesitation, no more barriers. His eyes devour me as I grind my nearly naked body against him, craving the friction.

A sense of euphoria pulses through me, the light that filters through the stained-glass windows casting a rainbow of colors that dance along my flesh.

Roman's body is tense as he groans, resisting the urge to thrust his hips into me.

"Give me a reason to praise God, Father."

Like a starved man, his lips latch onto my front. My fingers curl into his hair as he guides my hips, dragging my center over his length. I let out a moan of pleasure, needing more. He curses under his breath, moving his hands to my back and to the clasp of my bra.

"My turn to confess," I smile, running my lips along the edge of his jaw. "I lied. I wore this for you, hoping you'd touch me again."

"You want me to touch you, Eden?" His words cascade through my body like a rockslide; the rough, gravely tone tearing me apart as they clamber down to rest between my legs.

"Yes, Father. Please."

Roman stands, lifting me with him, his hands cupping my ass. I gasp, wrapping my legs tightly around his middle as he turns us around and lowers me to where he'd just been sitting. My legs loosen from around him as he kneels to the floor. Gently, he latches on to the backs of my knees, and drapes my legs over the chair's armrests, leaving me in front of him, spread wide open.

"What are you-"

"Giving you a reason to renew your faith, Eden," He whispers. "Feel free to praise God while I worship you."

He lowers his head, pressing his lips to my inner thigh. The sensation of his warm lips on my skin is enough to ruin me. I lean my head back into the chair as his hands move to my underwear, feeling his fingers rub the dip between my folds over the fabric. With his free hand, he pulls my hips closer to him, his mouth still exploring my skin.

His kisses turn painful as he latches his teeth to me. I slam my mouth shut, biting my cheeks to try and muffle my moans. I look down to see his face hovering above my center, the warmth of his breath caressing me, adding to my already out-of-control desire for him. He watches his fingers as they slide over the material of my underwear, a look of hunger etched into his features.

"Roman-"

With a violent yank, he rips the lace underwear from my body.

"Keep saying my name," He whispers. "And don't fucking stop until you cum."

Plunging his fingers into me, I release the moan of pleasure I'd been holding back. He dips forward, and I watch as his mouth opens and his tongue begins to lap up the wetness between my folds. The evidence of my desire drips down onto the chair under me as he continues to pump his fingers in and out, feasting on me, devouring me.

I rock my hips against his face, already teetering on the edge of release.

He drags his tongue up once more and settles on the bundle of nerves, making me ache with the need to feel him deeper inside me. I tuck my lips between my teeth, praying to God that I last just a little longer so he can give me more.

And then he does the most delicious thing. He sucks.

An overwhelming burst of pin-pricking pleasure bubbles up into my stomach. The pain from the raw skin on my ass is gone. All I can feel is him, and he holds my clit in his mouth and flicks his tongue back and forth, trapping me in a warm, wet vice. He lets out a groan that vibrates through to the very depths of my Godforsaken soul.

"Roman," I whisper, the stimulation hitting a tipping point, his fingers curling every so often, hitting the spot that makes me lose all sense of control.

"Roman," I moan, his mouth working harder, the wet sound of his tongue lapping at me, his fingers plunging in and out as I gush for him. All of it is my new addiction. It is too much and yet not enough.

A tight coil of warmth unravels inside me, and pleasure explodes through my core. My muscles spasm around his fingers and a growl of approval encourages me to rock against his mouth. He pulls his wicked fingers from me as I ride out the rest of my orgasm with his tongue. When I go to move away from him, he places a hand on my stomach to hold me in place.

"Roman, I can't take anymore-"

He swirls his tongue over my too-sensitive clit, shoving his mouth deeper into my flesh the more I try to resist.

My legs shake as another orgasm threatens to rip through me, the sensation almost painful.

"Roman!" I yell, trying to hold it together. "Please," I hiss. "Please, I can't take anymore-"

He slowly pulls his head away from my center, his chin glistening with my release. He rubs a thumb over his skin, collecting the wetness before placing it in his mouth and licking it clean.

I watch as Roman gets to his feet, the strain of his cock still there under his robe.

"Stand up."

Not sure where this is going, I begin to stand, my legs shaking. Roman takes my arm, turning me so he can take back his seat.

"Time to repent, Angel." He dips his chin, looking up at me through his long lashes. "Turn around and bend over."

Swallowing hard, I panic. I don't want him to see the raw, reddened skin on my backside.

Glancing down at his fingers, I decide to lower myself to my knees. His brow furrows in confusion as I take his hand in mine.

"What are you –?"

I place his fingers in my mouth, holding his wrist with one hand as I place the other on his knee. I keep my eyes locked on his as I did as he'd done earlier and begin to lick him clean.

His eyes grow wide with lust, cupping the side of my face as I work, watching me as I work. I give his fingertips one final swirl of my tongue before slowly dragging them out of my mouth.

"Do you taste how fucking sweet that pretty pussy is?" He drops his hands to my waist, standing me up in front of him.

"Now let me see that pretty ass-"

Before I can stop him, Roman pivots me until I'm no longer facing him. As his voice trails off, my cheeks grow hot. I close my eyes, readying myself for the pain of his touch.

I flinch at the unexpected feeling of his fingertips gently caressing the sensitive skin.

"I didn't do this," He whispers, his thumb rolling over the cut still healing from the contact with my father's belt buckle.

"Just get it over with, Roman," I hiss, knowing damn well the man values pain just as much as pleasure.

All of this is fun and games, but at the end of the day, I know I'm just a body for him to –

Something warm and soft touches my skin, the feeling gentle and welcoming. I stiffen as he presses tender kisses along my sensitive flesh, his fingers caressing the small of my back.

"Who did this, Eden?"

The truth gets lodged in my throat. I can't tell him.

"Eden?" he growls in between kisses.

All a sudden the room becomes too small, and I begin to suffocate. I pull away, wanting more space between us. I don't owe him an explanation. And I can't trust him. He might have said he's nothing like my father, but I barely know Roman. Letting him in isn't an option. The last person I let in was Eric, and that turned out far worse than I ever could've imagined.

I swipe my discarded robe from the floor, forcing it over my head, shimmying quickly to get the fabric in place to cover my body.

"What's your game here, Roman?" I cross my arms across my chest protectively. "It's clear you get off on being in a position of authority. That you enjoy making me submit to you. It's even clearer you have suppressed sexual desires, which I've regrettably enjoyed exploring, but none of that matters. You don't even know me. And I sure as hell don't owe you anything."

Standing up, he shakes his head.

His expression goes blank. Taking in a deep breath, he shakes his head. "I think we might have taken things too far."

I laugh, knowing the regret must be settling in for him. "You're embarrassed, aren't you? For turning away from your commitment to God with me of all people."

"Eden, that's not-"

"How do you think this plays out? Do you think I'll continue being your altar server, letting you touch me in private while listening to you preach to this congregation about the importance of upholding sound morals and virtues? I thought allowing this to happen would bring me some relief, but instead, it's just added to the pain I carry with me every single second of every single day," I snap, tears flooding from my eyes.

"You think hurting Zack makes things easier for me, Roman? It doesn't. What do you think will happen when you're not around, and he and I are alone again?" I yell, his eyes lowering. "I don't know what the hell you think is happening here, but it's done. I know my father was here. I know you two spoke. And I've seen that fucking binder in our home. You may say you're nothing like him, but having anything to do with him is just as bad," I sob, wiping away the tears from my cheeks.

Roman takes a step towards me, but I move around him to the altar, swiping his gold ring from the arm of his chair. I turn around and close the space between us, grabbing his hand and placing the ring in his palm.

"Take your fucking ring. Repent to God and leave me the hell alone."

I brush past him down the altar steps towards the doorway leading out into the vestibule.

This had been a mistake.

I was sad and vulnerable.

He was horny and powerful.

And now, it's over.

I barrel through the double doors, nearly slipping on the mix of blood and holy water. Running into the altar servers' changing area, I quickly remove the robe and put on my clothes from earlier. I gather the rest of my things and make my way back to the front of the church, luckily making it to the front doors without seeing Roman again. I spot my Kia in the parking lot, Aiden waiting in the driver's seat.

As I get to the car, I throw my things in the backseat before opening the passenger door. I don't know why I did it, but I looked up to the front of the church as I moved to get in the car. I pause, seeing Roman standing under the portico just outside the entryway, his hands balled into fists at his side, the fading light of the day catching on the gold ring on his finger.

Glaring at him, I hold up my middle finger as I slide into the car.

"What was that about?" Aiden closes the book in his lap and reaches to turn down the music he'd been blasting before I got in the car.

"Nothing. Let's go."

Roman Briar.

My priest.

My secret.

The biggest sin I've ever committed.

Chapter 13

ROMAN

Six Weeks Prior

Welcome to Idlewood.

Population: Twelve thousand.

Nestled in the Rocky Mountains, this small town feels like it's been swallowed whole by the forest—thick, unyielding trees that make it damn near impossible to remember there's a world out there beyond the pines. The mountains are beautiful, sure, but they're also a trap, locking you in with no way out. Life here drags on, slow and suffocating, like you're stuck in some kind of purgatory.

The people here are friendly enough, but they've got a taste for gossip that never quits. Every little secret is like gold, and they'll dig until they've unearthed every bit. It's strange, really—I've been in some hellish places, seen things that would turn most people inside out, but there's something about this quiet, stagnant life that feels like its own kind of hell. Like I've traded one war for another, only this time, the battles with the silence, the sameness, and the ghosts of what I left behind.

But this is my home for the foreseeable future.

Enjoying the piping hot cup of dark roast, I watch the people of Idlewood roam the streets, each face giving me some new insight into the people here.

There's a woman who glides out of the boutique across the way, her blonde hair perfectly styled, not a strand out of place. She's got a purse that probably costs more than most people's rent, and she's walking like she's got somewhere important to be, even if it's just the café for a latte. She's one of those who'll show up at church dressed to the nines, all smiles and grace, but I can see it in her eyes—there's something darker underneath, something she's trying to bury under all that polish.

As I take another sip of my coffee, I notice a man in a worn denim jacket, boots scuffed from hard work. He stops to chat with an older woman, probably a neighbor, tipping his cap, his smile warm and genuine. There's a kindness in his face, the kind you don't see much these days—a real, honest warmth that comes from living a life grounded in something real. This is the kind of man who doesn't need to flaunt his faith; it's written in the way he lives.

In Seminary, no one tells you how hard it is to truly stay judgment-free.

Kevin warned me not to explore Idlewood, saying the charm of living here would grow on me through my service in the church.

Bullshit.

The best way to understand this town is to see it for what it is, not just through sermons and sacraments. Tolerating the fake smiles and questioning looks is easier when I feel like I've figured these people out.

In a month, I'm supposed to start my work, proving my worth through the followers I can gather. But sitting here now, I wonder what made me step into this line of work. My relationship with religion was always shaky at best, never fully committed.

If it weren't for the church at basic training, I'm sure I'd have turned away from religion entirely.

Initially, the idea of giving myself up to any religion felt odd.

Snorting coke off my barracks coffee table while learning how to kill a man as efficiently as possible seemed like the way to go.

Fuck women, go to work, and pummel a man bloody for looking at me the wrong way.

You tell me, does that seem like it would end well for a man with urges as violent as mine?

There's something about watching your fellow soldiers bleed out in front of you that makes it hard to believe God is real. I strayed from His light, ventured into the darkest parts of my soul, and indulged every sinful urge. Facing death forced reflection I didn't know I needed.

When there's nothing left, you reach out to the big man upstairs—it's instinct. But pretending I'm a man void of sin? That's almost laughable. Listening to confessions, offering absolution as if it can erase the burden of evil—it's always felt a bit ridiculous to me.

Yet, here I am, ready to cleanse the conscience of anyone willing to waltz into Saint Michael's.

In Seminary, they made it sound so easy.

Serve God.

Repent Sin.

Lead a life of virtue.

Spinning the gold ring around my finger, I'm reminded that the weight of my promise to God can be suffocating at times.

A life void of sin.

Is any man capable of turning a blind eye to their deepest desires?

Does Kevin struggle with his own temptations? He never lets it show, always presenting a calm, unwavering front. I wonder if behind closed doors, he battles the same demons I do. If he's found a way to quiet them, or if he's just better at hiding the fight.

I almost wish someone would sin right in front of me just to prove they're human.

It's really all an act if you look at it from my perspective.

I play the role of God's hand while struggling with my own demons behind closed doors. They come to me for absolution, only to fall back into the Devil's grasp by next week. It's all one big game.

The prize? Hopefully, an afterlife.

Many would think it's odd how I choose to view my own religion.

I see Catholicism as a tool to find peace, nothing more, nothing less.

If I die and there is nothing, at least I lived trying to be a better person.

Tried being the distinguishing word.

Pretending that I'm perfect, like some of these rich assholes, is impossible.

I lower my head as someone walks by the table I'm sitting at, trying my best not to be seen.

A new face like mine in a town this small?

They'd have my whole life story figured out from a few phone calls, I'm sure.

It's almost hypocritical for a war veteran like me to preach about God's will.

I stand at the pulpit, condemning death and sin, all while knowing what it feels like to take a life with my own hands.

What kind of man does that make me?

Am I as fake as the rest of the people of this town?

Taking in a sharp breath, the chill air hits my lungs, signaling the oncoming Autumn season.

I fidget with the cross around my necklace, feeling the areas where my skin has begun to rash from the friction.

Pain is good.

It's a reminder I feel anything at all.

Watching the leaves blow across the road, I lean back in my chair, stretching my legs out as I can, rolling my neck to try and ease the soreness from the long drive here. Everything I owned was packed in my 4Runner at the hotel.

Rolling my finger over the circular burn marks up my arm, I scoff at the look of them.

If my dad were alive, what would he say now?

Would he scold me for leaving the Army? For choosing a religious path instead of the one he forced on me?

It's hard to say. Knowing him, he'd probably beat me either way.

That's the sick part. A man like my father—vile to his core—could beat his son and his wife and still show up in church every Sunday, somehow convincing himself he'd make it to heaven because of God's grace.

That's the flaw in the system.

No matter how awful you are, I'm supposed to believe if you give your life to God, you deserve forgiveness.

Bullshit.

Evil people deserve to be punished.

Maybe that's why I chose to become His hand.

Staring into the bottom of my cup, I feel a surge of frustration. The drink's empty, just like this moment. I toss the cup in the bin and decide a walk might clear my head.

Shoving my hands in my pockets, I veer toward the park in the middle of town. I'm still lost in thought when I hear a whimper, faint but unmistakable. It stops me in my tracks.

The noise grows louder, a mix of gasping and sniffling that sets my senses on high alert. I glance around the empty park, trying to locate the source.

There, in a more isolated part of the park, I spot a figure on a bench, hood pulled up, back turned. The whimpering is high-pitched, the body too small to be male.

Walk away Roman.

I keep moving forward on the path, but the stifled cries escalate, causing the hair on the back of my neck to rise.

The sound pulls at something deep inside me—it's just like my mother's voice when my father had gotten too rough with her. The pain in the woman's sobs is unmistakable, her voice trembling as her body shakes.

Biting my cheek, I close my eyes, taking several deep breaths.

Just walk away Roman.

The cries get worse.

Just walk-

Before I know it, I'm veering off toward the bench, my feet carrying me across the dying grass. The sobs drown out the sound of my footsteps, and I find myself creeping closer, stopping just short of her. I lean against a nearby tree, keeping a safe distance, close enough to observe without intruding.

Observing is fine.

We're in a public space after all.

"Ivy, that's not what I'm saying," The woman sobs, her phone pressed to her ear, her face angled away from me.

She's wearing a dark hoodie, too thick for the warm weather, with a backpack slumped next to her. Her foot taps rapidly, a clear sign of her anxiety.

"Who the fuck cares what Eric said. I'm telling you that's not what happened," She cries, her voice trembling. "How many fucking times did you meet him? Maybe three times when he happened to come to our dorm room when you weren't busy fucking some random guy? I knew you for months, and not once did you ask me my side-"

Stopping her tangent, she looks at her phone, tapping the screen.

"Ivy?" she yells. "You did not just fucking hang up!"

She tosses her phone across the grass. Her hands cover her face. Her screams become muffled by the sleeves of her hoodie. Her sobs are strangled, her voice ragged from crying for so long.

"None of you were fucking there," She sobs. "No one but me and him were there," She cries. "And now I'm alone in all of this."

I take a step closer, and she shifts slightly, just enough for me to get a full view of her face.

Beautiful, rich eyes swollen from tears, rosy cheeks, dark brown hair framing her face, and a full pout that looks almost angelic. She's too focused on rummaging through her bag to notice me, pulling out a small cloth with trembling hands.

This is none of my business.

I should just leave her alone-

But then I see it, the glint of sunlight reflecting off the blade, and my stomach drops as she rolls up her sleeve, revealing fresh lesions on her skin.

All straight cuts.

All by her hand.

I watch in shock as she slides the blade across her wrist, the cut leaving a trail of red, the pain silencing her sobs.

She adds another set of marks, her face twisted in pain. The sight of someone so beautiful choosing to hurt herself ignites a deep anger within me.

"Do you fucking hear me now?" She hisses, yanking a necklace from her throat and tossing it to the grass.

She stares at her bloodied wrist, her fingers slowly turning the blade, and my heart pounds as I realize she's no longer holding it horizontally.

"D-Do you," She chokes out, "hear me—"

"Stop," I hiss as I press myself against her back, my hand closing around her bleeding wrist, my other hand grabbing the blade, ignoring the sting as it cuts into my fingers. I toss it away, watching it land next to her cross and phone.

"Oh my God, don't-" She sobs, her voice trembling with fear. "Please don't tell anyone."

She almost killed herself, and she's worried about what people will think?

How fucked up is this town?

I continue to hold her in place, her body trembling beneath my touch.

"I'm not going to hurt you," I whisper, trying to keep my voice calm. "But you were going to hurt yourself." She shifts her weight from one foot to the other. "What kind of person would I have been to let that happen?"

She laughs, but it sounds defeated. "Either you're from the church, trying to kiss my dad's ass," She sobs, "or you're not from here. Anyone else would've let me do it," she hisses, the self-hate in her voice cutting deeper than any blade.

I hold her tighter, feeling the blood sliding down her wrists coat my fingers.

"Yeah? And what if you did it? Then what?" I ask, trying to redirect her thoughts.

"They always told me in Catholic school that suicide's a mortal sin. So, I guess a spot in Hell would be it for me."

She's Catholic.

The only Catholic church in Idlewood is mine.

Perfect.

I stopped one of my future disciples from committing god-damn suicide.

"I call bullshit on that," I sigh, keeping her still. "There are far worse people than you deserving of a spot in Hell," I joke, trying to lighten the mood.

"Yeah?" She questions. "You don't even know me."

"Why are you crying?" Her bottom lip starts to tremble.

"What is this, fucking confession?" She snaps, her anger flaring.

"Here's how I see it: you've got two options. Tell me what happened and get it off your chest, or sit here and wallow in it, see where that lands you. If you really wanted to die, you would've started with the vertical cut." She scoffs when I call her out. She knows I'm right.

"How would you know-"

"Roll up my sleeve," I snap, cutting her off.

"What-"

"Roll up my sleeve," I demand again.

Reluctantly, she begins to roll up my sleeve, keeping her gaze fixed ahead. The jagged vertical scar running down my wrist is an ugly reminder of a past I can't escape.

She gulps, her fingers lightly grazing the scar, her touch surprisingly gentle.

"I know because I didn't go for the horizontal cut," I whisper. "And guess what? It didn't make the pain go away. It changed nothing. My problems were still my own. So why don't you tell me what's wrong before you bleed out in the park-"

"I was raped," She sobs, my heart filling with pain. "He bruised my ribs, broke my collarbone, recorded all of it, and showed it to his fraternity." She moves her uninjured hand to her bleeding wrist. "I thought college would be my escape, and instead, I walked into a nightmare worse than the one I lived in here. I reported him, but his fraternity brothers destroyed the evidence, so all I could do was come back home to this hellhole. Everyone just thinks I'm psychotic and that I had some sort of mental breakdown."

"What's your name?"

"Eden. Won't take you long to figure out my last name in this town."

Holding her still, I take a shaky breath.

"I'll be seeing you at church, Eden," I whisper, her name rolling off my tongue and stirring something inside of me.

"I'm not-"

"You want a solution? Go to the church and let God give you a guardian angel."

"God's never helped me. I don't know why he'd start now."

I tighten my grip around her waist. "Then why am I here?" I ask, something about her pulling me in deeper that I can't explain. I guide her free hand to her open wound. "Put pressure on your wrist," I urge.

"Now tell me you'll go home. And you won't do that again." Maybe it's my calling to God, or just because I can feel her need to rebel against me, but having command over her choosing to live has me hanging on to her every word.

She shakes her head. "I'll go," she sobs. "But it won't change anything." I scoff, holding her steady.

"I promise you, Eden. This won't be the last time we meet."

Before she can get a good look at me, I release her and turn on my heels, lowering my head as I shove my bloodied hands into my pockets. I move quickly, slipping past the shrubbery to conceal myself from view. I make my way back to the streets, heading straight for my car. Sliding into the driver's seat, I lean back, watching through the window as she steps out onto the street, her arms hidden beneath her hoodie. She looks around, confused, but now wearing her cross again. A small sense of satisfaction settles in my chest.

I watch as she runs a hand through her hair, sighing in defeat. Even in her broken state, there's a striking beauty to her, something raw and real that pulls at me. I glance down at my hands, still smeared with her blood. The bright red nags at me, a reminder of the deep pain she's carrying.

Pain like that consumes you. It eats you alive.

Maybe another outlet could ease her suffering.

The thought slithers into my mind, and I tense my jaw, trying not to focus on the blood on my skin. But the need creeps in, unbidden—feral, insistent.

A need to see that blood again, but in a different context.

One from pleasure rather than pain.

Block it out.

You helped her. You brought her back to the church.

"Fuck."

I grab my phone, hating myself for what I'm about to do. Regretfully, I open social media, narrowing my search to Idlewood, and type her name into the search bar.

It doesn't take long to find her. I scroll through her page, seconds turning into minutes and want turn into need.

By the time I turned my phone off, only one name consumed my thoughts.

Eden Faulkner.

There's no harm in knowing her name... Right?

Philippians 4:19 (NKJV) "And my God shall supply all your need according to His riches in glory by Christ Jesus."

Chapter 14

EDEN

The strong smell of a roaring fire hits us in a cloud of smoke, forcing both Aiden and me to cough. The scent of weed and oak mixes in the air, the smoke dense and suffocating as it seems to follow us. Aiden hadn't pressed me further on what was going on between Father Briar and me, and our drive here was mostly quiet.

The mountains swallow the sun, casting the sky in rich, fading colors. I hitch my bag higher on my shoulder, wondering why I even bothered to bring a swimsuit. The chance of me letting anyone see my body is slim.

But I'd let Roman see my body. I'd let him do a lot more than just see it.

I push thoughts of Roman away as we reach The Overlook. A group of five is gathered around the fire. Someone strums on a guitar as the others chat idly. Seeing Zack's piece of shit car parked by the others, I shove down the nerves threatening to surface.

The fear I saw in Zack when I walked into the cathedral was both alarming and satisfying. But now, it feels like I have a target on my back after what Roman did to him.

Aiden suddenly stops and grabs my hand before the others notice us, his eyes scanning me with concern. "Are you sure you don't want to talk about what happened at the cathedral? Was Zack there? Did he say something to you?"

"No, nothing happened," I smile, hoping that it's convincing enough to get him to move on. "Spending time at the church feels like torture," I admit, not entirely lying.

Time alone with Roman is torture.

Torturous how much I want him to explore my body.

Exploring whatever is happening with Roman any further leads nowhere good. When I'm with him, it feels like I'm on top of the world, flirting with danger. But the moment I'm away, it all comes crashing down, leaving me alone with my vicious thoughts.

"We can come up with an excuse so you can skip your service hours," He suggests, smiling, trying to help with the little he knows.

"I appreciate it, Aiden," I reply, squeezing his hand. "But I'd rather Dad focus on what I'm doing right than what I'm doing wrong."

Aiden frowns, clearly displeased. "The last thing Dad deserves is for either of us to care about what he wants." He shakes his head, turning away from me as a familiar voice calls out to us,

"Aiden, Eden!" Zoey calls out, her dark curls bouncing as she waves us over, clutching a drink in one hand.

Luca stops strumming his guitar and looks our way, his eyes meeting mine with a smile, stirring a warmth in my chest.

This is someone I should be focused on.

This is someone safe.

Roman is dangerous. Forbidden. Fleeting. Nothing more than a test.

And one I've failed miserably.

As we walk up the hill, I see a few people passing a joint around, pausing as we approach, throwing us a welcoming smile. Everyone, that is, except Zack.

His hood is pulled low, hiding the bandage on his head, his eyes deliberately avoiding mine.

Cups filled with bright red liquid are passed around, and I notice two boxes of wine sitting on a log—the same kind used for Communion.

The irony isn't lost on me.

Luca sets his guitar aside and pats the spot next to him. I sit, tucking my hands into my pockets as his shoulder nudges against mine.

"Glad you made it," Luca says, his voice warm and welcoming. Zack and Nathan both lower their heads as Aiden joins us, the tension palpable.

I guess Aiden's been keeping his distance since everything went down.

"What the hell happened to you?" Aiden asks, taking the joint from one of the boys, his eyes narrowing at Zack.

"Zack managed to slip and hit his head on the holy water fountain," Zoey says, her tone dripping with sarcasm as she takes a long drink.

Zack glares at me, his expression a mix of anger and unease, as if he's waiting for me to challenge the lie he'd told the others.

I meet his gaze, my voice low and deliberate. "You should be more careful. It could've been a lot worse."

The tension hangs in the air, thick and heavy. There's an unspoken understanding between us—a threat wrapped in the guise of concern.

Zack shakes his head and takes a drink, his eyes fixed on me. "How were service hours with Father Briar, Eden?" Zack sneers. "Did you learn anything...useful?"

I shift uncomfortably, glaring at him.

"He seems like a real jackass," Luca says, staring into the fire. "Not that I've had many run-ins with the guy."

"Who's Father Briar?" One of Luca's friends asks, but Zack cuts me off before I can respond.

"Saint Michael's new priest. You should see him. He looks barely older than us. And has some fucked up looking tattoos," Zack snaps. "He seems to like Eden. Really like. You know, I'm way behind on my service hours, but not once has he taken a personal interest in me—"

"I told him about what you did," Aiden interrupts, his voice sharp. We turn to look at him.

"What the hell does he mean?" Luca puts his cup down, leaning his elbows on his knees, and stares at Zack.

"Go on, Zack," Aiden spits. "Since you're so eager to stir shit up, why don't you tell our new friend here how you ripped Eden's sweater off—"

"It's fine, Aiden," I whisper, cutting him off.

"Eden—"

"I said it's fine!" I snap, the group falling into an uneasy silence. I lock eyes with Zack, my voice low and dangerous. "Zack knows exactly what will happen if he's that fucking stupid again."

"Right," Zack mutters, nodding as he takes another drink. "Because I'm the one who needs to be careful, isn't that right, Eden?" He adds, his tone dripping with sarcasm.

"Jesus, you all sound fucking feral." Zoey rolls her eyes, hiccupping loudly as she fills her cup with more wine. Once she's finished, she walks to where we sit, nudging Luca aside, shoving her cup into my chest.

"Drink it. Trust me, I think you'll need it."

"Eden doesn't drink," Zack taunts. "She skips it every Communion. What's the reason for that, Eden?"

Zack's taunting words hang in the air, and I can feel the weight of everyone's eyes on me. For months, I've resisted—avoided alcohol like a plague. Not because I'm some devout saint but because I know what happens when I let my guard down.

But tonight, everything feels different. The tension, the pressure from Zack's relentless needling, the constant push and pull with Roman—all of it weighs on me like a suffocating blanket. The taste of rebellion, of doing something that everyone least expects, suddenly feels like a way to regain control.

I glance at the cup Zoey pushed into my hands, the red liquid sloshing dangerously close to the rim. A part of me knows this is a bad idea, that it's a step backward, but another part of me—the part that's tired, frayed, and desperate for a way out—wants to drown out the noise, if only for a little while.

Maybe it's the twisted need to defy Zack, to show him I'm not as predictable as he thinks. Or maybe it's the creeping realization that Roman has burrowed deeper into my psyche than I'd like to admit, and I just need something—anything—to push those thoughts away, even if it's temporary.

"Eden, you don't have to do that if you don't want to," Luca says softly, his voice a calm anchor in the storm that's raging inside me.

But even Luca's warmth, his gentle presence, isn't enough to stop me this time.

I give him a small, reassuring smile, but it feels hollow. My hand tightens around the cup, and I make my choice.

"The reason I don't drink, Zack," I hiss, lifting Zoey's cup to my lips and taking a defiant swig of the bitter red liquid. The taste is harsh, but I don't stop. I drink until the cup is empty, the red wine dribbling down the side of my mouth. I swipe it away with my sleeve, feeling the warmth settle uneasily in my stomach as I stand to refill the cup.

"Because the last time I did, I woke up in a hospital room," I say, my voice cold as I pour more wine into the cup. I stare at the red liquid, the memories it stirs, making my skin crawl. "And I was no longer a virgin," I mutter, glaring into the cup. The group is silent, their eyes fixed on me as I down the second cup without hesitation.

"The worst part," I say, my voice trembling, "is that the only thing I remember clearly... is the sound of my own screams."

I throw the cup into the roaring fire and shove my hands in my pockets. I glance at Aiden, his face pale, stricken.

"That night, I came home," I whisper, the words tasting like ash. "I ran away from the hospital before they could call Mom and Dad." My breath shudders as I continue. "Eric got away with all of it. And so did every other guy in that fraternity he let into the room with us."

The alcohol hits me hard, my empty stomach amplifying its effects. I grab the hem of my hoodie and pull it up, revealing the deep scratch marks Eric left, now mingled with the razor cuts I inflicted on myself afterward.

"My collarbone is still healing," I say softly, touching the still-discolored skin. "So are my ribs."

The healing nail marks sting as I run my fingers over them. "He grabbed me so hard when I tried to get away that he tore off some of his nails."

I turn to Zack, shaking my head in disgust.

"I started cutting the day after I got home," I whisper, biting down hard on my inner cheek to keep from breaking. "So there's your fucking story, Zack." My voice sharpens as I snatch a bottle of vodka from Nathan.

"Feel free to tell God," I say, popping the top off and raising the bottle in a mock toast. "I couldn't fucking care less what He thinks."

With that, I take a long, burning swig from the bottle and walk away, leaving the group in stunned silence. No one dares to say a word as they watch me go, the weight of what I've revealed hanging heavy in the air.

"Eden," Luca calls after me, his voice tinged with concern, but I keep moving, heading toward the water's edge.

A hand catches my arm, pulling me to a stop. I spin on my heels, ready to snap.

"Luca, I don't need you looking at me like some kicked puppy. That wasn't the point." I hiss, glaring at him. "I don't need any more religious pricks in my life pretending to care about me."

He closes his mouth, takes a breath, and then, to my surprise, steps closer.

"Who said I'm just another religious prick?" He asks, his voice steady. "And who says I don't care?" His hand reaches out, cupping my face, his thumbs gently brushing over my cheeks.

I grab his wrists, my eyes narrowing. "You don't know me," I whisper harshly. "Why the hell would you care?"

He shrugs, his gaze steady. "Look, we could spend weeks getting to know each other, building something, or you could just accept that sometimes, people care even after just one meeting," He says, his hands gently returning to my face. "Do you think I actually enjoy hanging around a bunch of potheads and dealing with Zoey's chaos?" He smiles slightly, shaking his head. "Aiden's cool, but I came here for you. To get to know you. Father Briar messed up our first shot, but he's not here now," He says, glancing around before looking back at me. "So, tell me to fuck off, or let me in and show me who the real Eden Faulkner is."

Before he can say another word, I close the distance between us, pressing my lips to his. He pulls me in, and I wrap my arms around his neck, leaning into the kiss. His lips are soft, but I need control—something real. I bite down on his bottom lip hard enough to draw blood. He gasps against my mouth, his tongue slipping past my lips as the kiss turns fierce and raw. The taste of his blood mixes with the wine on my tongue as he backs me into the nearest tree, the rough bark scraping my skin.

Pain is good.

Pain is needed.

"Shit," He breathes, pulling back slightly, a drop of blood on his lip. "I didn't mean to shove you that hard—"

Grabbing his collar, I pull him close.

"I'm not breakable, Luca," I hiss. "Don't treat me like I am."

His eyes widen, blood still on his lip. My mind flashes to Roman—

I drag my tongue across the blood on Luca's lower lip, and he stares at me in disbelief, the tension in his body unmistakable, his dick growing hard against me under his dark grey sweatpants.

I wait for him to take charge, to grab me, to do something—

"Maybe we should slow down," Luca says, his face flushed.

Fuck.

I screwed up.

Running my hand through my hair, I lean back against the tree.

"I'm sorry, Luca. I know that was a lot—"

"It's not that," He says, his voice softening as he looks into my eyes. "It's just... I want this to mean something, Eden. Not just for tonight, but for real. And right now, it feels like you're carrying a lot of weight on your shoulders. I don't want to be another thing you regret in the morning." He runs his hand down my arm, taking my hand. "Besides, I don't think Aiden needs another reason to be pissed off tonight," He adds with a gentle smile. Luca's kindness shines through, a light in all this darkness.

The problem is, I don't want the light.

I crave the dark.

I crave Roman.

But it's wrong.

It's all so wrong.

"Hey," Luca says softly, stopping me from biting my nails. "Can you look at me?" I hesitate but then meet his gaze.

"I don't regret anything that just happened. The blood thing was new," He admits, touching his lip nervously. "But it was far from a turn-off if that's what you're worried about. I just don't think touching you while you're drunk is the right thing to do."

God, this man is so kind.

Why the fuck am I dryer than the Sahara Desert right now?

"Right," I force a smile. "I guess I got a bit carried away."

"Apologize," Zoey demands, dragging Nathan and Zack over by their ears, with Aiden trailing behind her. Luca's friend follows, barely holding back his laughter.

Luca stands in front of me, looking pissed, while I lean back against the tree, trying to steady myself.

The boys stagger to a stop, both of them clearly embarrassed.

"Apologize, or I'll have someone hold you down while I kick you square in the dick," Zoey threatens, her voice sharp.

"Fine, alright—I'm sorry, Eden," Nathan mutters, shaking his head in defeat.

"Good," Zoey snaps. "Now you, Zack."

"It's fine," I interject, glancing at Zack's bandaged head. "Right, Zack?" I ask, my voice softer as I watch him closely.

"Water under the bridge, Faulkner," He says with a smile, though there's something unsettling in his tone. "So, where's this lake Zoey's been going on about?"

Chapter 15

EDEN

Walking with the group, I lag behind with Luca, our fingers intertwined as I lean on him for support. Up ahead, Zoey chatters nonstop at Aiden, nudging him until a genuine smile finally breaks through. Zack keeps glancing back at me, his gaze burning into me, but I keep my focus anywhere else.

The trail opens up to a small lake, its waters reflecting the vibrant colors of the setting sun. The scene is peaceful, almost surreal, as the forest surrounds us like a protective barrier. Luca, carrying both our bags on his back, gives me a reassuring nod.

"If you're worried about anyone seeing you, I can hold a towel up until you're in the water," He offers with a kind smile.

A buzz in my pocket breaks the moment between us. Tugging my phone free, my stomach drops when I see the contact name on my screen.

Roman.

Why the hell is he calling?

I can't answer this. Not here.

I hit decline and look around as the others begin to strip down and dive into the cool water.

"You go ahead," I grin at Luca, feeling my phone buzz again. "I've got to take this—it's my dad."

He nods, accepting the excuse, and does something unexpected. He leans in and kisses my cheek, a sweet, comforting gesture that catches me off guard.

I watch as he strips off his hoodie, his body a welcome sight. Meanwhile, the buzzing phone in my pocket starts to feel like it's burning a hole through my pants.

I answer the call, snapping. "What do you want?"

"Where are you?" Roman asks, ignoring my question entirely.

Zoey squeals as Aiden tries to dunk her under the water.

"None of your fucking b-business, Father," I slur, the alcohol blurring my thoughts.

"Have you been drinking?" Roman asks, disbelief lacing his voice.

I smile, feeling warmth spread in my stomach at the sound of his voice. "Maybe."

"Eden, what the hell are you doing—"

"Eden!" Luca shouts, waving from the water. "Get in! It feels fucking amazing!" The water clings to his perfectly sculpted body, every ripple highlighting his muscles, making the temptation nearly impossible to resist.

But it's Roman's voice that sends a fire scourging between my things.

"Is that the fucking coffee boy?" Roman's tone is thick with anger.

"It is," I sigh, unable to resist poking the bear. "Zack's here too. You really did a number on him, Father—"

"Eden, I'm not fucking around. Where are you—"

"Hey," Luca says, catching up to me as I lower the phone. "Everything okay?"

Instead of answering, I pull him into a kiss, making sure Roman can hear. Luca wraps his arms around me, his lips trailing down to my neck, each kiss sending a shiver through me that makes me giggle.

"I could get used to being greeted like that," Luca laughs, pulling back with a grin.

I lift the phone back to my ear, "I'm sorry, Dad, I'm kind of preoccupied right now—"

"You're at the reservoir. I'm coming," Roman says coldly before the line goes dead, leaving me staring at the black screen.

Whistling and cheering from the group fills the air as Luca and I kiss again, but my nerves are on edge.

"You ready?" Luca asks, completely unaware of the storm that's heading our way.

Tucking my phone back in my pocket, I stare at the water. "Of course," I smile, tearing off my clothes. I grab Luca's hand, and take off towards the water.

An hour later, drenched to the bone, we trudge back to our cars. Luca's hoodie is a comforting weight as I cling to his back, his hands brushing over my scarred skin with a casual intimacy that sends shivers down my spine.

Zoey is nearly out cold in Aiden's arms, her head lolling as he struggles to keep her upright.

"I'll drive Zoey home and bring her back for her car in the morning," Aiden says, adjusting her limp form.

"I'll take Eden," Luca offers, his smile warm. "And I'll help you with Zoey's car tomorrow if that's cool with you, Eden."

Aiden looks to me, waiting for my approval. I give a small nod, forcing a smile.

After we get Zoey settled into my car, I cross my arms and wait by Luca's truck, feeling the weight of a gaze on my back.

"So, who were you really on the phone with?" Zack's voice cuts through the night, low and unsettling.

"What do you mean?" I ask, turning to face him.

He leans against Luca's truck, his nod slow and deliberate, eyes fixed on mine with an intensity that makes my skin crawl.

"Your dad's out getting drinks with mine tonight. There's no way in hell he called you. So, who were you talking to that had you so flustered?" Zack asks, stepping closer, his voice dripping with suspicion.

"What are you insinuating, Zack?" I snap, narrowing my eyes at the arrogant bastard.

"Is there a problem?" Luca's voice cuts in, calm but firm, as he steps between us, his body shielding me from Zack, arms crossed in silent warning.

"No problem," Zack says with a smile that doesn't reach his eyes, raising his hands in mock surrender. "Have a good night." Zack saunters away, casually twirling his keys on his finger.

"You okay?" Luca asks, concern flickering in his eyes. Roman's angry voice from the call earlier still echoes in my mind, leaving me unsettled.

"Yeah," I smile, glancing at his truck. "Ready to go?"

He nods and opens the door, watching me as I slide into the passenger seat. As I look around, the inside of Luca's truck feels lived-in, far from the cold, immaculate interior of Roman's 4Runner. Sports gear is piled haphazardly on the floor, and scattered papers are shoved into the corners, a chaotic mix of school assignments and workout routines. The faint scent of sweat and cologne lingers in the air, mingling with the earthy smell of wet grass from our swim. It's messy, unpretentious, and entirely Luca.

He glances over at me, a smirk playing on his lips as he gently tucks a strand of hair behind my ear.

"Feeling any better?" He asks, his voice soft. My buzz has dulled, leaving me more clear-headed.

"If you're asking if I remember and whether I regret the kiss, yes, I remember," I whisper, leaning closer, closing the distance over the armrest. "And no, I don't regret it."

Luca's eyes drop to my lips, and he closes his eyes, letting out a groan of surrender.

"You're making it really hard to remember that you've been drinking," He murmurs, his cheeks flushing as a familiar strain presses against his sweats. He moves his hand to his lap to adjust himself, embarrassed.

"I didn't drink tonight to forget," I lie, replacing Luca's hand with my own. My fingers curl around his hardened length through his sweats, his eyes widening at the sudden contact.

"I did it to give myself the confidence for my little speech," I murmur, glancing down, "and for this."

Luca's head presses back against the headrest, a look of conflict in his eyes.

"Eden, after what you said—"

"Just watch," I whisper, sliding my hand up to his waistband, tugging it down just enough to reveal his boxers.

Before he can protest, I lower my head, silencing him with the touch of my lips against him, teasing him through the thin fabric of his boxers. A startled gasp of pleasure escapes him as I kiss up and down the length of his cock, tempting him with grazing the fabric covering his dick.

I wait for the familiar harsh tug on my hair, anticipating the roughness that usually follows.

Instead, his fingers thread softly through my hair, offering only tender touches.

Oh.

I scold myself for expecting anything other than his gentle touch, but I don't stop.

Grabbing the hem of his boxers with my teeth, I slowly start to tug the material down, his eyes widening in response—

"Eden," He interrupts, his hand gently grasping my chin, lifting my gaze to meet his. "Trust me, I want this," He murmurs, a sudden light approaching from behind us. "but you're still tipsy," He whispers, "and we have company."

I raise my head and glance outside, staring directly into the blinding lights of a car parked behind us. A car door slams shut, and Luca anxiously fidgets with his pants as we both watch a figure lean against his truck.

The darkness obscures the figure, and Luca, alarmed, reaches for the door handle.

"Wait," I whisper, blinking until the dark outline of a 4Runner comes into focus.

"Fuck," I mutter, feeling Luca's hand rub my back.

"Who is it—?"

"It's Father Briar," I hiss, seeing Luca's head shake in disbelief.

"Your fucking priest?" He asks, incredulous, as my mind scrambles for an explanation.

"My dad must've said something to him," I snap, lying effortlessly. "Aiden and I told him we were going to "Bible Study" with a group of friends tonight. My guess is that he called Father Briar since he knew I had service hours with him earlier today. He's extremely controlling."

"How did he find you?" Luca asks, genuinely puzzled.

"I don't know," I admit honestly. "I'm going to talk to him."

As I reach for the door handle, Luca grabs my hand.

"Maybe let me—"

"No," I cut him off, stopping him before he can insist. "I've got it."

I step out, shrinking deeper into Luca's hoodie as I approach Roman, who leans against the side of the truck, hood drawn, hands stuffed in his pockets.

"What the hell are you—"

He turns his head, revealing a bruised eye and wild hair.

"Jesus Christ—"

"Watch your mouth," Roman snaps, his voice edged with frustration. There's a heavy scent of alcohol on his breath.

His eyes trail down my body, narrowing at the sight of the oversized hoodie. "Is that... Luca's?" He mutters, his gaze shifting to the truck. "Is this his car?" He tugs at the hem of my hoodie, his eyes lingering on my bare legs.

"How the fuck did you find me?" I snap back, pressing my hand against his chest to keep him from closing the distance between us.

"Your dad might know people, Eden," he murmurs, leaning closer. "But so do I."

I shake my head, my voice low and sharp. "You're fucking unbelievable," I bite out, giving him a once-over. "You realize you're crossing into stalker territory, right?"

Roman scoffs, dismissing my words with a flick of his wrist. "Did he touch you?"

"What—"

"I asked, did he fucking touch you?"

"Yes!" I shout, locking eyes with him. "He kissed me without a hint of shame," I seethe, watching Roman's expression harden. "And just before you showed up, I had my head in his lap, kissing up the side of his cock, ready to—"

"Eden?" Luca's voice cuts through the tension. Roman and I turning to face him, our bodies inches apart. "What the hell is going on?" He asks, his tone filled with confusion as he fumbles with his clothes.

Roman's gaze remained fixed on Luca, his voice a deadly whisper. "Get back in your car and leave. Now."

"Roman—"

"No, it's fine, Eden," Luca says, his voice steady but laced with anger. "I think it's time for *you* to leave instead Father Briar. You're out here, stalking her like some creep—"

Roman lunges at Luca like a predator, grabbing his shirt and slamming him against the side of the truck. Roman's eyes burn with a wild fury, his grip unyielding.

"I said get back in your fucking car," Roman growls, his voice low and dangerous. "Before I rip your limp dick off and shove it down your throat." My hands pull at Roman's shirt, desperate to break his hold on Luca.

"Roman, leave him the hell alone!" I shout, but he doesn't even flinch.

"Fuck you, you crazy bastard!" Luca chokes out, struggling in Roman's grasp. Roman's hand coils around Luca's throat, his expression nothing short of madness.

"Last warning," Roman hisses, watching as Luca's face turns red and he gasps for air.

"Roman, stop!" I scream, hitting his back, my voice breaking with panic. "I'll go with you, just let him go!" I yell, my words finally cutting through the haze of rage in Roman's eyes. His body goes rigid, as if realizing that I'm still here.

Slowly, Roman releases Luca, who collapses to the ground, clutching his throat and coughing. I shove Roman aside, kneeling beside Luca, tears welling up in my eyes.

"Just go," I whisper, my voice trembling. "I'll be fine. Please, just go." I glare at Roman, the disappointment in my eyes sharper than any words could be. "Are you fucking happy now?"

As I help Luca to his feet, he tries to pull me with him, concern etched across his face.

"I have to go with him," I murmur, fabricating a lie on the spot. "Or else my dad will do something worse." The truth—that Roman might kill him if I stay—lodges like a stone in my throat.

Luca looks conflicted, his eyes flicking between me and Roman, who stands by his car, jaw clenched tight.

"Just go home, Luca, please. I'll be fine," I sigh, forcing my hands to unclench. "I should never have dragged you into my mess," I apologize, watching as he slowly nods, his expression a mix of hurt and confusion.

"Yeah," He whispers, his voice strained. "Maybe they were right about you."

His words hit me like a sucker punch, leaving me breathless as he turns and climbs into his truck. The engine roars to life, and he drives off, a cloud of dust swirling around me, thick and suffocating.

I turn back to Roman's car, anger simmering just below the surface of my skin.

If he wants to push his way into my life...

Fine.

Let's see how deep into the madness he's willing to go.

Chapter 16

EDEN

Roman slams his door shut, glancing out his driver's side window, his heater blasting to fight off the cold. Watching Luca's truck disappear into the night, his parting words still sting, my heart pounding in my chest.

"Have fun?" Roman sneers.

I scoff. "You're a fucking asshole," I whisper. "I'm not your property, Roman—"

"Tell me, were you thinking about me while you had those pretty lips on his worthless cock?" Roman growls, his knuckles white as he grips the steering wheel.

"Is that what this is about?" I snap, crossing my arms defensively. "You're mad because someone else touched me—"

"Or maybe you thought of me when he was kissing you," Roman interrupts, turning to face me. The bruising around his eye is stark, his knuckles bloodied, his entire demeanor rough and unhinged. "No, that can't be the case," He adds, sliding his hand under the hoodie and between my thighs. I can't help but open my legs for him as he moves to my waistline, the touch sending a spark through me.

He dips his fingers beneath my swimsuit bottoms, palming my pussy as he spreads my folds and swipes his middle finger over my clit. I gasp as he removes his hand as quickly as he'd put it there. "You're not even wet," He mutters, his voice laced with disdain. My mind scrambles, body reeling, but no words come.

I glance at his hand, noticing the absence of his ring. My breath catches.

Roman lifts his hand, studying his hand like it's something foreign. "You asked me in that church to make a decision," He says quietly, though the edge in his voice remains. "So I've made my decision. When I'm with you, I'm no longer the hand of God. You want to see it all, Eden? Fine. But know that ring held back monsters you can't even begin to understand," He warns. "That gentle touch you felt with me before? It took everything in me to give it to you."

"I never asked you to be gentle, Roman," I whisper, my voice trembling as I shift in the seat. "I never asked anyone to treat me like I'm some broken thing. But after tonight, I don't see that getting any better. I told them why I came home. I...I just needed to get it out." I pull my knees to my chest, feeling the weight of everything crashing down around me.

He says nothing, just watches me with a penetrating gaze, his expression unreadable.

My eyes catch on the bruising around his eye, the weariness etched into his face. He looks exhausted—worn down by whatever battle he's been fighting, both with himself and the world around him. And here I am, torn between wanting to reach out and touch him, to soothe the pain I see so clearly, and the anger simmering beneath my skin. Anger at him, at myself, at the whole damn situation we've found ourselves in.

Why does he have to look at me like that? Why does he have to be the one who's always in control, even when he's unraveling? It's maddening, the way he tries to protect me while keeping me at arm's length, as if that's supposed to make this any easier. As if that's supposed to make me feel less guilty for the mess I've become.

I want to hate him for the way he's made me feel, for the way he let his guard down just enough to draw me in, only to push me away again. But I can't. Instead, all I feel is this twisted knot of guilt and longing tangled so tightly around my heart that it's hard to breathe. It would be so much easier if I could just let go, if I could just walk away from this man who will never truly be mine, who belongs to something far greater than I could ever be.

Yet here I am, sitting beside him, feeling the pull of him like gravity. The weight of his exhaustion, his bruises, his burdens—it's all too much, and yet I can't tear my eyes away. I care for him more than I want to admit, and it terrifies me. Because I know that no matter how much I might want him, I'll never get all of him. I'll never be the one he chooses above everything else. I'll always be second to God, to his vows, to the life he's sworn to live.

And maybe that's what hurts the most. The knowledge that he'll always be just out of reach, that no matter how close we get, there will always be this barrier between us. I can feel the tension crackling between us, the unspoken words hanging heavy in the air. I want to reach out, to press my fingers to the bruise on his face, to show him that I care, even if I shouldn't. But I don't. Because I'm too afraid of what might happen if I do.

So instead, I sit here, waging this silent war within myself, torn between wanting him and hating myself for it. I can't help but wonder if he's fighting the same battle. If he feels the same pull, the same longing, the same guilt. Or if he's already made peace with it, resigned himself to the life he's chosen, even if it means leaving me behind.

The thought makes my chest tighten, the pain sharp and sudden.

I sigh, giving in to my desire to be closer to him. I reach over, my fingers brushing the bruise around his eye. He flinches slightly, grabbing my wrist with surprising force.

I glance down at his tight grasp but don't pull away. "How much did you drink tonight?"

"A lot," He admits, his voice softening. "After what happened in the church, it seemed... necessary."

He leans closer, his breath warm against my lips. "And what about you? I thought you gave up drinking?" He locks his eyes with mine, mouth parted slightly as he waits for me to respond.

"I did," I whisper back. "But it *also* seemed necessary after you had your tongue all over me earlier and then clearly regretted it the moment we were done. I couldn't deal with the shame I saw written all over your face, Roman." I was too tired to be anything but honest. I'm not sure how much more he could shut me out. I'd already begun to resign myself to the fact that this could never go any further.

Roman's expression hardens. "Is that why you let him touch you? You were trying to convince yourself that you'd be satisfied by anyone else?" His grip on my wrist loosens as he reaches to touch me again.

I stop him, catching his forearm in a firm grasp.

"Maybe I just wanted his cock in my mouth."

The moment those words leave my lips, I see the flicker of rage, quickly hardening into something more primitive and possessive.

"Fine," Roman whispers, his hand coiling in my hair, dragging my head closer to his lap. "You want to choke on something tonight?" His eyes glance down to the prominent bulge in his pants. "Then so be it. I'm done being gentle with you."

I try to lift my head, but his grip tightens, keeping me firmly in place.

"You were so eager to explore Luca," Roman hisses. "Afraid you won't be able to handle a real man?" He taunts, his voice laced with venom.

"Hardly," I whisper, daring to provoke him. "I'm just wondering if your pre-cum is as sweet as Luca's."

A rough, territorial snarl rips from deep in his throat. He tugs my hair so hard that a sharp yelp escapes me, my eyes watering from the pain.

"If I hear that bastard's name come out of your mouth again, you'll regret it." He glances down at his pants, the tension between us palpable. "Now, let me feel those pretty lips."

I glance at the thick strain beneath the fabric of his pants and swallow hard, feeling the grip of his hand ease slightly as I inch closer. I fumble with the button of his pants, tugging them down just enough to expose his boxers. My lips trail along his length, feeling the heat of him even through the fabric, lost in a heady, lust-filled haze as I listen to him groan. I let my tongue slide across his lower stomach, tasting the salt of his skin as I kiss my way up to the hard line of muscles on his lower abdomen.

Roman watches me, intrigued as I gather a bit of his skin between my teeth, sucking gently before nipping at him just enough to leave a small bruise.

"Fuck," Roman groans, his grip tightening in my hair as he pulls my head back. A devious smile curves my lips as he looks down at me.

"You think that's funny?"

I can't help but grin harder, but the moment he pushes his boxers down further, my smile falters at the sight before me. Roman wraps his hand around his length, stroking himself slowly and deliberately. My breath catches as I watch him, the reality of his size dawning on me.

He's bigger than any man I've ever messed around with, the kind of size that would normally make me pause, but with him, all I feel is a throbbing need pulse between my thighs that urges me to take him and make him mine.

"Come here, Angel," Roman whispers, gently pulling me back toward his lap.

My mouth waters. I part my lips and press a soft kiss to the tip of his cock. My tongue swirls around the head, tasting his salty pre-cum. Roman's eyes widen, his jaw clenching as I run my tongue down his length, trying to ready myself to take all of him in.

As I drag my tongue back up to the tip, I glance up at him, our eyes locking in a moment of shared understanding—this is just the beginning.

"Tell me you want it, Roman," I whisper. I gather the warm spit that's been pooling in my mouth behind my puckered lips, opening my mouth just enough to let a trail of moisture fall to the head of his cock.

He hisses, sucking in air between his teeth. He shakes his head, desire swirling in his blown-out pupils.

My lips stretch around his tip and I suck hard, my cheeks hallowing out before I release him, hearing a soft 'pop' as the suction breaks. "Tell me how much you're willing to sin just to hear me choke on your cock."

Without warning, Roman urges my head down. I open my mouth eagerly to take him in again as he thrusts hard, his tip hitting the back of my throat. I choke on the size of him, struggling to adjust, a rush of exhilaration coursing through me. Eyes half-closed, I savored the sensation, a mix of pain and pleasure, my body tingling with the thrill of it.

He guides my head in a bobbing motion, rolling his thumb over my cheek as spit escapes my mouth and drips to my chin. I curl my tongue around him with deliberate, sensual movements.

"There we go, Angel," He groans, letting me adjust as my tongue moves up and down his shaft, the wet messy sound of my mouth taking him in adding to the warm slickness in my underwear.

"Keep taking me," He challenges, tugging my hair. He slows his thrusts, driving his cock as far back as he can and holding it there as I gag again. Not ready to give up, I reach my hand to his base, stroking the part of him that won't fit in my mouth.

"Just like that, Angel," He groans, his head rolling back into the seat, the mix of alcohol and adrenaline sending a wave of courage through me.

Feeling a slight pulse in the base of his cock, I know he's close to release.

"You want to taste me, Eden?"

I simply nod, groaning against his dick. I move my mouth faster, meeting the movement of the frenzied thrust of his hips.

An explosion of sweet and salty liquid shoots down my throat. I swallow, guzzling down the taste of him like he's the only thing that can quench my thirst. He stifles a loud moan into the sleeve up his shirt, his eyes closed as I take every drop from him.

I release him after I've had my fill, sitting up, my torso still splayed over the middle console. As he opens his eyes, I drag my thumb over the wetness on my bottom lip before putting it in my mouth and licking it clean.

"Fucking Hell, Eden," He smirks, tugging up his boxers. "Do you realize how pretty you looked choking on my-"

Tearing off Luca's hoodie, I crawl over the console and into his lap, my wet pussy landing on his boxers, hungry for friction. I rock my hips, feeling him hardening again underneath me, my swollen clit trying to find relief as I move.

"Fuck, Roman-"

"Keep rocking those hips, beautiful," He commands, his lips pressed against my neck as he moves his hands further up my back to the tie holding my bathing suit top in place.

Removing my hands from his hair, I slowly move my arms backwards, untying it for him. As the material around my breasts loosens, I slip the top over my head, Roman completely still as he watches me.

"Touch me."

He leans into me, his lips landing on my nipple as he moves his hand to my other breast, cupping the fullness, massaging, and kneading. Watching as he takes his time feasting on me, I run my hands through his hair, tilting my head back as I give in to the pleasure coursing through me. I cry out his name again and again, reaching down between us, rubbing my clit as he nips at my nipple.

Rolling my hips, a sudden wave of nausea creeps in, cracking the dome of lust and euphoria that surrounds us.

"Fuck-" I hiss. Shoving Roman away from me, he keeps hold of my hips as I move my hand to the control on his door panel to roll the window down. I lean my head out of the window, releasing what feels like every drop of alcohol I drank tonight. As liquid continues pouring out of me, Roman coils his hand around my loose hair, holding it out of my face while I gag.

Embarrassment heats my skin as I lean my head down against the cool metal of his car door.

"I told you," Roman whispers. "Taking my cock like that will take some practice." He winks at me, and I know he's trying to let me know he's not judging me.

"Very funny."

Reaching into his glovebox, Roman pulls out a wet wipe, keeping me nestled in his lap, his hands gently preventing me from covering my breasts. He carefully wipes my mouth, ensuring no trace of vomit remains on my skin. He moves the loose hair that's fallen into my face behind my ear, and moves to brush his thumb along my jawline, the touch sending a shiver down my spine. My head feels heavy, my eyes struggle to stay open.

After wiping down the inside of his car with Luca's hoodie, he tosses it out the window, then rolls it up, sealing us off from the world. His gaze never leaves me as he runs a finger over my scars, his touch surprisingly tender despite the hunger in his eyes.

Slipping his hand down to my bathing suit bottoms, he finds the evidence of my desire still lingering as he glides his fingers through the wetness between my folds.

"Like I said, beautiful," He murmurs, his voice a low rumble. "I'm the only one who gets to touch you like this... the only one who'll make you feel this way."

He brings his fingers to his lips, licking them with a devious smirk. My body instinctively leans forward, collapsing into him as exhaustion takes over, my head coming to rest in the crook of his neck.

"I know I said I didn't want gentle," I whisper, barely able to keep my eyes open. "But can you please just—"

Without a word, Roman shifts me to the passenger seat, pulling off his hoodie and draping it over me. He props up the middle armrest and tugs me back toward him, resting my head in his lap. His fingers gently thread through my hair, lulling me closer to sleep.

I hear the sound of the car turn on, the hum of the engine coaxing me closer to unconsciousness.

"You're going to ruin me, Eden," Roman whispers, his fingers tapping the steering wheel. "And I fear I'm going to love every second of it."

That's the last thing I remember before I drift into nothingness.

1 Corinthians 13:4–8a "Love is patient and kind; love does not envy or boast; it is not arrogant or rude. It does not insist on its own way; it is not irritable or resentful; it does not rejoice at wrongdoing, but rejoices with the truth."

Chapter 17

ROMAN

Two Hours Prior

Despair is the only word that captures a bar at this hour.

Walking inside, the place is anything but classy. The bar reeks of stale beer and desperation, a suffocating mix that clings to your clothes the moment you step inside. The walls are stained with years of neglect, yellowed with cigarette smoke, despite the "NO SMOKING" sign hanging over the bar. Flickering neon signs, some letters burnt out, cast an eerie, uneven glow across the room, barely cutting through the dim lighting.

A few patrons—mostly men—are slumped over their drinks, lost in their own misery, while a couple of women dressed in too-tight clothes and heavy makeup hover nearby, their smiles tired and hollow. It's the kind of place where dreams come to die, where hope is a foreign concept, and where the darkness in a person's soul is reflected in every shadowed corner.

The cross around my neck feels like a weight, a constant re-minder of the moral battle I fought just to walk through the door. Thirty minutes—thirty agonizing minutes—spent in the car, staring at that damn "Open" sign, wondering if I should even be here. I could feel the cross pressing into my chest with every shallow breath, like it was trying to keep me anchored, to pull me back from the brink.

But it wasn't enough.

I was still reeling from what happened with Eden. The way she looked at me in the church, her eyes wide with a mix of desire and disappointment, as if she expected more from me, as if she thought I could be the man she needed me to be. And for a brief, blasphemous moment, I wanted to be. I wanted to forsake my vows, to let the world fall away and lose myself in her entirely. But then that familiar pang of guilt hit—God's reminder of the promise I made, the ring on my finger a shackle that binds me to a life I willingly chose.

When she left, I was paralyzed by the conflict between what I wanted and what I knew I couldn't have. I could still taste her on my lips and feel the ghost of her warmth in my hands. It was enough to drive a man mad. No prayer could silence the screaming thoughts, no scripture could drown out the memory of her skin against mine.

I sat there in the car, gripping the steering wheel until my knuckles turned white, torn between the man I am supposed to be and the man I felt myself becoming. This place—this grim, hollow dive—wasn't just a bar. It was a sanctuary for lost souls, a purgatory where men like me come to face their demons when the weight of the world becomes too much to bear.

No other encounter in my life has driven me back to a place as grim as this. The thought of Eden—how she looked at me, how she left me—was too much to bear. I needed to drown it out, to silence the incessant, pounding regret in my head, even if only for a few hours. The priest in me should have resisted, should have turned the car around and gone back to the rectory, but the man—the sinner—knew there was no turning back. Not tonight.

"Wanna drink, pretty boy?" The bartender's voice pulls me from my thoughts.

I didn't even realize I'd made my way to the bar.

"Scotch, on the rocks," I reply automatically, reaching for my ID.

"You're good," She smiles, eyeing me up and down. "You're the new priest, right? Took over for Kevin? I saw you at Mass."

Perfect. My bartender is also one of my parishioners.

I nod, handing her my card. She opens a tab and gets to work on my drink.

I take a seat, the weight of the day settling into my bones. Around me, the air hums with the low murmur of conversation, clinking glasses, and the occasional burst of raucous laughter. The women nearby hover just close enough to make their interest clear, their gazes lingering, assessing. Any other man might find their attention flattering, might indulge in the fantasy of losing himself in a stranger's touch for a night, but not me.

I'd kill to be attracted to one of them—to want them enough to let go, to drown in the heat of their bodies and forget everything else. But the thought of touching anyone who isn't Eden... it's revolting. It turns my stomach in ways I can't fully explain, as if my body rejects the idea before my mind even has the chance to consider it.

Eden has ruined me for anyone else. There's no other way to put it. Her memory clings to me, haunting every thought, every breath. The feel of her skin beneath my fingers, the taste of her on my lips—it's burned into my mind, seared into my soul. And nothing, no matter how tempting or convenient, could ever compare to the raw intensity of that connection. It's as if she's imprinted on me, leaving no room for anyone else.

I glance at the women around me, and all I feel is emptiness. They might as well be shadows, faceless and unremarkable, compared to the vivid, all-consuming presence of Eden in my mind.

And that's the problem. Eden is all I can think about, all I can feel. She's the one I want, the one I crave, and no amount of liquor or empty encounters can change that. The priest in me knows this obsession is dangerous, that it's leading me down a path I swore to avoid. But the man—the sinner—can't help but revel in it, drawn to the darkness like a moth to a flame.

All I want is to bend her pretty ass over my chair on the altar and pound into her until her voice is ringing through the church louder than any chorus could –

"You okay?"

I glance down, noticing the subtle shake, and set the drink back on the bar, trying to steady myself. Clearing my throat, I muster a faint smile. "It's been a long day. Even priests have those," I admit, the truth heavier than I'd like.

She leans against the bar, studying me with an air of seasoned wisdom. "In my experience, any man sitting at a bar this late on a Monday night has a head full of regrets, Father," She says, her tone direct but not unkind. "So, why not drown those thoughts in that glass and save the repentance for behind church doors?"

Her blunt honesty stings, but I can't help but appreciate it. I stare at the drink in front of me, the amber liquid reflecting the dim light.

"It's not a sin to drink, Father," She adds with a sigh. "You've already given your life to the Big Man upstairs," She continues, tapping the ring on my finger. "No need to punish yourself further by denying the few pleasures left to you, courtesy of Christ's sacrifice."

She starts to step away, her attention drawn to another customer waving her down. But something compels me to stop her.

"What's your name?"

"Renee," She nods. "You might know my daughter, Zoey."

I blink, surprised. The light, bubbly airhead who hovers around Eden before and after Mass seems a world apart from the woman standing in front of me. There's little of Zoey's grace in her mother's demeanor—Renee is rougher around the edges, the kind of woman who's seen life's harsher side.

"My husband remarried. Cheated, then found a pretty replacement," She says bluntly, a flicker of bitterness in her eyes. "So, I linger in the back of the church now. Seems I don't really fit in with the rest of the congregation anymore. Not that I care."

My thoughts drift to the front pews of Saint Michael's, always filled with Idlewood's wealthiest residents, their smiles polished but empty, their faith as much about appearances as it is about salvation.

Money and power—two forces that seem to hold sway even in the house of God.

A buzz in my pocket pulls me from my thoughts. I take a long drink from my glass before glancing at the screen. An unknown number flashes. I hesitate but answer anyway.

"Hello?" I say, the noise of distant chatter filling the line.

"Forget what I told you about Zack," Aiden's voice snaps, raw and shaking.

My grip on the glass tightens as I recall our brief, tense conversation—the one where Aiden spilled his guts about the vile things Zack and his friends had done to Eden. It had taken everything in me not to strangle the boy right then.

"Aiden, how did you get my number—"

"It was in my dad's phone," He hisses. "What the hell did you do to my sister in that church?" The accusation drips from his words like poison.

"Is Eden alright—"

"Alright?" Aiden scoffs, his disbelief sharp through the line. "She just fucking showed off the scars she gave herself to the whole damn group and then dropped a bomb on all of us – she told us why she came home from college. News flash, it's worse than I could've imagined," He vents, the words spilling out in a chaotic rush.

He must be high. Or drunk, maybe? Or both. Great.

"What did she say?" I press, a gnawing sense of dread creeping in. The little I know of her past before she moved back is just that—a little. But I remember what she'd said that night when I found her in the park.

She was raped.

"I'm not fucking telling you," Aiden snaps, his tone bristling with defensiveness. "But I do know she barely lets anyone get close to her, and now she's out there, pressed up against a tree, locking lips with Luca—"

Aiden's words hit me like a punch to the gut, igniting a fury that surges through my veins. The thought of Eden, *my* Eden, with another man—his hands on her, his lips claiming what should be mine—sends a wave of rage crashing over me. My fists clench, and my heart pounds, each beat fueling the jealousy that's quickly turning into something darker, something primal. How dare she let anyone else near her? The possessiveness I've tried to control now roars to life, demanding action. She belongs to me, and I'll be damned if I let anyone else touch her.

"Tell me where you are. Now." I interrupt, cutting off his rant.

"So you can tell my parents?" Aiden scoffs. "I thought confessing what happened with Zack might ease my conscience, not give you a reason to fucking pummel him. Whatever sick fantasy you have with my sister, it ends now," He threatens, the thought of her being taken from me turning my stomach.

"Is that right?" I respond, my gaze hardening as I glance over at Renee.

"Tread carefully, Father," Aiden warns, his tone venomous. "I'd hate for anyone to hear a rumor about just how personal you get with your altar servers behind closed doors."

The line goes dead, leaving me staring at my phone in disbelief, fury surging through my veins. I'm ready to wring his fucking neck.

"Renee," I call out, catching the bartender's attention just as she tops off someone's glass.

"Yea?" She asks, her eyes narrowing in curiosity.

"Where's your daughter tonight?" I ask, keeping my voice steady, though my mind is anything but that.

Her face twists in mild confusion. "Somewhere her daddy wouldn't approve of, that's for sure," She laughs, though there's no humor in my expression mirrored back at her. "Why?"

"One of my cousins is friends with her and mentioned they were going out tonight. I'm worried he might've had too much to drink, and I'm not sure where they are."

She shakes her head, amused. "You're a terrible liar, Father. But I have faith that when you do lie, it's for a good reason."

I sigh, shaking my head in frustration. "I need to know where Eden Faulkner is," I admit, watching as Renee's body stiffens.

"David Faulkner's girl?" She asks, saying his name like it leaves a bad taste in her mouth.

I nod, and her gaze hardens, something dark flickering in her eyes.

"You tight with the Faulkners?" She probes, her tone laced with suspicion.

"No," I reply, my voice firm. "But I need to find her before her father does."

She gives me a long, assessing look, a genuine smile slowly forming on her lips.

She sighs, glancing around the bar as if weighing her next words. "The reservoir. There's a sunset spot and a swimming hole. That's where Zoey said they were headed. But listen," She leans in, her voice low and serious. "Whatever ties you've got with the Faulkners, leave my girl out of it."

"What do you know about them?" I press, sensing there's more beneath her warning.

She shakes her head. Her eyes are hardened with icy contempt. "When I was married to Zoey's father, I saw the twisted shit David and his elitist buddies pulled right under the church's roof. I was ready to go to Father Kevin and the police," She whispers, her voice trembling. "Two days later, I got served divorce papers. Then, I was attacked at knifepoint by some masked thug after work. Lost my job too, courtesy of one of his wife's cronies. Zoey didn't speak to me for months. I nearly drank myself to death in this very bar. The only reason I go back to that damn church is to keep an eye on my girl. The Faulkner's are bad news. I'd stay away from them."

Her words sink in, and I stare at her, grappling with the weight of what she's just revealed.

"How do you know I'm not bad news?" I ask, my voice low, testing the waters.

She flips my left hand over, her fingers tracing the smooth skin. "You're not branded," She mutters, almost to herself. "Not yet anyway."

Without another word, she closes out my tab, her face unreadable as I drop a twenty into the tip jar.

"Look at the fucking body on that pretty thing," A drunken voice snarls beside me. I snap my head in his direction. My stomach churns as I spot my phone in the large man's hand.

On the screen was a picture of Eden. She stood by a fire, holding up her shirt, exposing her scarred skin. I could see her full breasts pressed tightly together in the same black lace bra she'd had on at the church. Beneath the image, Aiden's anger bleeds through in the caption:

This is your fucking fault!

I must have left my phone open after trying to search directions to the reservoir, and this nosey fuck had taken my phone when he'd seen the text come through.

The sight of Eden's skin, her pain, being devoured by this creep's hungry eyes makes me sick. I lunge for my phone. The thought of anyone but me seeing her like this is unbearable.

"This your pretty little plaything?" He sneers, leering at me as he holds the phone just out of reach. "Nice set of tits on that one," He grins, his hand grazing his filthy crotch. "Mind sharing?"

Shoving him hard in the chest, I swipe my phone back, watching with grim satisfaction as he stumbles into a nearby table. Shutting off the screen, I shove it into my pocket, downing the rest of my drink.

"I'm not in the fucking mood for bullshit."

His eyes flicker to the deep scar running down my wrist, then to the black ink snaking up and down my arm. For a moment, the bar is silent, patrons watching with bated breath. My cross, now untucked, gleams on my chest. I'm sure I could pass as some version of a Hell's angel.

"You're that pretty boy priest they just brought into Saint Michael's," The man slurs, sizing me up. "Tell me, where does it say in the Ten Commandments that you can keep a picture of a girl with tits like that in your phone—"

Before he can finish, I drive my fist into his jaw, relishing the crunch of bone against my knuckles. His head snaps back, and he slumps against a support beam, the room erupting in gasps as his friends scramble away from the pool table in the center of the room.

"Take it outside!" Renee yells, her voice cutting through the tension, trying to keep the bar from descending into chaos.

"Hey," One of the man's friends shouts, grabbing my shoulder, readying to throw a punch. "What the hell do you think you're doing—"

I twist his arm, forcing him forward and over my shoulder. He crashes to the floor with a thud, and I stomp down hard on his hand.

I hear the switchblade click open before I feel it. I sidestep just in time, the blade grazing my side. Curling my hand around the man's wrist, I slam his head against the bar counter, watching the light go out in his eyes as he collapses.

"Father," Renee's voice cuts through the chaos, pulling my attention to her. Her eyes are wide with fear. "Don't give David a reason to trail this back to Eden."

Fuck.

This whole town is incestuous. All it would take is this bastard on the ground opening his mouth, and David would be up my ass. And worse, he'd go after Eden.

Pain explodes in my face as the man who'd taken my phone clocks me right in the eye, the force sending me backward.

The man's companions lie unconscious on the floor, but he's still standing, holding his sore jaw and sneering at me. "You fucking religious fuck!" he yells. "I hope I see that pretty thing walking down these streets so I can make her pay for what you—"

I grab a beer bottle from the bar and smash it across his head. He crumples to the floor, ale splashing over both of us. With all three men out cold, I fumble for my wallet, slapping two hundred-dollar bills on the counter for Renee.

I glare at her as I back toward the door, the bar eerily silent now, the kind of quiet that ensures most of this will be swept under the rug.

"So long as I'm around, David isn't harming her or anyone else," I hiss, clutching my throbbing eye.

I nudge the door open and slip out into the night. Moments later, I'm in my car, punching the address for the reservoir into the console.

Chapter 18

EDEN

No one warns you how miserable your first hangover is after months of avoiding alcohol.

The pounding headache behind my eyes is relentless as I try to piece together the events of last night. My throat feels raw and swollen as if I've had strep for days. Touching my tender neck, the memories of what happened in Roman's car come rushing back.

I remember how it felt as he mercilessly thrust his cock down my throat, a mix of shame and arousal flooding my senses. But then the memory of vomiting all over myself and his car shatters that moment.

I sit up, opening my eyes to find I'm in an unfamiliar room. The room is bathed in the soft, golden light of a single lamp, the curtains drawn tight, barely letting in the morning sun. The space is impeccably clean, almost sterile, yet there's a warmth to it. The walls are a muted gray, adorned with minimalistic art, mostly religious iconography, but there's nothing ostentatious about it. A crucifix hangs above a small, dark wooden desk, the only clutter being a leather-bound Bible and a few scattered papers. Looking down, I realize I'm wearing nothing but a large shirt and my underwear, the smell of fresh laundry clinging to the fabric. Where the hell am I?

My phone sits on the nightstand, flooded with texts from Aiden and Luca, ranging from apologies to confusion about my whereabouts. Luca's texts, in particular, are a stream of remorseful apologies. I quickly reply that we need to talk, then text Aiden, telling him I decided to crash at Zoey's for some girl time.

Running a hand through my tangled hair, I cringe at the lingering scent of alcohol and vomit. Trying to piece together where I am, I quietly slip out of bed, noting the undisturbed sheets and pillow on the other side of the bed.

Creeping to the window, I pull back the curtain and blink past the pounding in my head. My heart drops when I see the church just a few yards away.

Oh fuck. I'm in Roman's house.

"Glad to see you're alive," Roman's voice cuts through the fog of my thoughts, and I spin around, choking on my words as I see him standing in the doorway.

He's wearing nothing but sweats, his tattooed, sculpted body on full display, making him almost impossible to resist. There's a large cut on his side, held together by a butterfly closure. He holds a cup of water, his gold ring catching the light as he moves. His face is stoic, as if unaffected by the chaos from last night.

"A-Am I in your house?" I stammer, my voice scratchy.

He glances around the room, then closes the curtain more and flips on a lamp, bathing the room in a soft, warm glow.

"I figured bringing you back here would be better than explaining to your parents why you were passed out in my arms, covered in vomit."

"Did we..." I trail off, glancing at his bed.

"No, and we won't," He warns, handing me the glass of water. "I almost hurt you. It took everything in me to hold back. The things I wanted to do to you...what do you think would happen if I lost control, Eden?" The feeling of him down my throat again was both exhilarating and nerve-racking.

"I was fine."

"Yeah?" He questions, his fingers grazing my throat with a light touch. "Is that why you can barely speak this morning? Because you're fine?" He scolds, tipping the glass of water towards me. "Now drink, Angel. You were messed up last night."

Not wanting to argue, I take the water and drink it down in one go. Just as I catch my breath, my phone buzzes, lighting up with messages from both Luca and Aiden.

Roman narrows his eyes and grabs the phone before I can react, his expression darkening as he reads the texts.

"How about I go to the Autumn Mass today? We can talk afterward," Roman mutters, reading Luca's message out loud. "Already making plans with pretty boy?"

I snatch the phone back from him, tossing it onto the bed, shaking my head in frustration.

"Would you rather me ignore him? After what you did last night? The last thing either of us needs is some rumor spreading that there's something going on between us, Father."

He looks like he's about to argue, but he stays silent, his gaze trailing over me with an intensity that makes my skin prickle.

"I like you in my shirt," He murmurs, a smile ghosting his lips as my cheeks heat up.

"Don't get used to it," I retort, brushing past him. "I reek of vomit, and it's nearly noon. I need to shower before Mass. It's a day of service for us both, Father," I add with a grin, pretending to gag as I stick a finger down my throat.

I stride toward the nearest door, my hand wrapping around the handle, only to find it won't budge.

"That's not the bathroom," Roman says, a smug grin spreading across his face as he nods towards the door beside it. "That one is."

I stare at the locked door, then at him. "What the hell is in there?"

"Nothing you're ready for," He scoffs, nudging open the bathroom door.

"I put your clothes in the wash. They should be dry by the time you're out of the shower."

I step into the space. The bathroom is immaculate, almost unnervingly so. White tiles gleam under the soft light, the air tinged with the crisp scent of soap and disinfectant. It's a space that reflects a need for order and control—everything is meticulously arranged, not a trace of personal clutter. The showerhead, polished to a shine, stands ready as if awaiting some unspoken command, and the neatly folded towels on the rack suggest a man who maintains rigid discipline in all aspects of his life.

Someone's a bit of a neat freak.

"I'll leave you to it. No need to dwell on last night," He mutters, retreating a step, though his eyes flicker with something he's trying hard to suppress.

"Right," I whisper, fighting the urge to lose myself in how damn good he looks, all controlled strength and simmering tension beneath that calm exterior.

I grasp the hem of his shirt, peeling it over my head, the cool air brushing against my bare skin. His jaw tightens, a muscle ticking as he forces his gaze to stay above my shoulders. I hand him the shirt, then slowly slide off my underwear, making sure to bend over deliberately, offering him a view he can't ignore. Running my fingers through my hair, I notice his eyes remain fixed on mine, his restraint fraying as I step closer.

When my hand grazes the front of his pants, I can feel the tension thrumming through him, barely contained beneath his composed exterior.

"Your lips say one thing, Roman," I murmur, leaning in just enough, "but your body tells me another."

His hand clamps down on the back of my neck, firm but not rough, like he's caught between his duties and his desires.

"Ah, ah, ah," I cut him off, my eyes dropping to the ring on his finger. "The ring's still on, Father."

I pry his hand off me, locking eyes with him, throwing down a challenge before stepping into the shower, leaving the door ajar. The steam from the hot water begins to fill the room, the heat matching the thrum of excitement in my veins. I wait, listening for any sign that he's going to tear down the walls he's hiding behind—or if he's going to retreat into the rigid safety of denial he seems to rely on to keep him safe from this thing that's growing between us. Seconds turn to minutes, and it seems he's made his choice.

As I lather soap through my hair, the events of last night dissolve, slipping away with the suds that spiral down the drain. The warm cascade of water from the oversized showerhead envelops me, a gentle embrace that soothes and cleanses. As I glide the bar of soap down my front, there's a sting from fresh cuts, and I hiss in pain.

I glance at the door, left just slightly ajar, to see if Roman would give in to the need I know he feels just as strong as I do. But he doesn't. My excitement, once bubbling under the surface of my skin, dwindles to nothing, extinguished as the water turns cold.

I shut off the water and reach for a towel, my thoughts a tangled web of uncertainty, replaying the hesitation in his eyes, the restraint in his movements.

This is so pointless.

He brought me here to keep me away from my parents.

As I step out of the bathroom, towel wrapped tightly around me, my breath catches at the sight before me. Roman's back muscles flex as he finishes a knot, the ropes on his bed taut and secure. The door to his mysterious room is slightly ajar, hinting at secrets kept just out of reach.

Two thick, braided ropes stretch taut from the corners of his headboard, their coarse fibers stark against the dark wood. Each rope ends in a pair of metal cuffs, their cold steel gleaming dully in the low light, hanging open as if waiting to snap shut. The cuffs sway ever so slightly, a silent promise of what could be, their weight pulling against the tension in the ropes.

A single blindfold, black as night and smooth as silk, rests atop the pillows. It lies there with an almost deliberate care, an invitation that teeters between seduction and surrender—or perhaps a test, a challenge for me to cross the threshold of his restraint.

The air in the room is cool, too cool, and it raises goosebumps on my skin. But it's not just the temperature that causes me to shiver. It's the sharp edge of anticipation that cuts through me, the electric undercurrent of tension that hums in the space between us, pulling tighter with every breath. I can feel it in the way the room seems to hold its breath, waiting as if the very walls are in on the secret we both refuse to speak aloud.

"Why so quiet?" Roman's voice cuts through the room, devoid of the playful tone he usually carries. His words hang heavy as if daring me to respond, to cross the line he's drawn.

Turning around, he places his ring on the nightstand, along with the cross he'd been wearing moments ago.

"Come here, Eden," He whispers, his voice a low, commanding hum that sends a shiver through me. He takes a seat on the edge of the bed, the bulge in his pants unmistakable even from where I stand. "Unless you're scared."

With a slow, deliberate step, I move closer, feeling the cool air brush against my skin as the towel loosens and drops to the floor, pooling around my ankles. The distance between us shrinks, and I can feel the heat radiating from his body as I stand before him. My breath hitches as I prepare to straddle his lap, already imagining the sensation of his lips on my skin.

Before I can settle into him, his hands are on me, not with tenderness, but with a roughness that catches me off guard. He shoves me onto the bed, his grip unyielding, his body pressing down against mine. The strain in his jeans is hard against my thigh, a stark reminder of the desire he's barely keeping in check.

His hand wraps around my throat, not enough to hurt but enough to hold me in place, his thumb brushing along my pulse. His tongue traces a slow, burning path down my neck, each kiss a brand that sears into my skin. When he reaches my ear, his breath is hot, sending a shiver straight down my spine.

"If you really want me, Eden," He whispers, his voice a rough rasp that vibrates against my earlobe before he nips it sharply, sending a jolt through my body. "We have to get that pretty pussy prepared for it so you're still able to walk once I'm done. I won't be gentle. Understand that now before we go any further."

His words shock me, a raw mixture of fear and excitement tangling in my chest. Before I can react, his hands move with practiced speed, fastening the cuffs around my wrists. The metal bites into my skin as he tightens them, my arms pulled above my head, leaving me exposed and vulnerable beneath him.

The ropes, once an abstract possibility, now bind me to the bed, the cold steel of the cuffs a stark contrast to the heat pooling in my core. His eyes cloud with intensity as he looks down at me, all traces of restraint gone, replaced by a hunger that both terrifies and thrills me.

I can feel the pulse of anticipation, the tension between us reaching a fever pitch, as Roman's control slips further away with every breath he takes. He's no longer the composed priest nor the man who brought me here to protect me from the

world outside. Here, in this moment, he's something else entirely—something primal, something I'm not sure I'm ready to face
but can't bring myself to resist.

"Roman—" I begin, but my words are cut off as his fingers
clamp down on my nipples, delivering sharp pinches that send
shockwaves of sensation through my body. My voice dissolves
into a gasp, any protest dying on my lips.

"No talking," He commands, his tone leaving no room for
defiance. He holds my legs firmly, his grip unyielding as he fastens
cuffs around my ankles, pulling them tight until I can feel the
strain in my leg muscles. He flips me onto my stomach, my
ankles drawn out so far apart that I'm left completely exposed
and vulnerable to him.

My ass is fully bared to him. My face presses into the softness
of his sheets, the scent of him surrounding me intoxicating and
overwhelming. The position is degrading, yet there's a thrill in
the helplessness of the way he's taken control, leaving me at his
mercy.

"What are you doing?" I manage to ask, my voice trembling
with a mix of nerves and excitement that courses through me like
a blazing fire. I can feel him behind me, his presence looming,
powerful. Though he still wears his pants, the weight of his body
presses down on me, his breath hot against my ear as he leans in
close.

"I'll stop once you've completed a Hail Mary," He murmurs,
his voice dark and full of promise.

"Stop what?" I ask, but before I can grasp what he means,
the blindfold from the pillow slides over my eyes, plunging me
into darkness. The loss of sight heightens my other sense, and I

feel the tension coil tighter within me, every sound, every touch magnified.

"You'll know," He whispers, his voice a tantalizing threat that sends a shiver down my spine. His hand glides over the curve of my ass, gentle at first, teasing. My body responds instinctively, my pussy beginning to throb with need, aching to be filled with his fingers, his cock, anything that's Roman's.

There's a moment of stillness, a pause that stretches into eternity, where I'm left teetering on the edge of something unknown, the tension between us a living thing, pulsating, waiting to break free. And in that silence, the only sound is the quickening beat of my heart, the ragged breaths I try to steady, and the promise of what's to come.

The sound reaches me before the sensation does—Roman's spit, a warm, slick liquid that lands between my folds. The warmth spreads, and then his fingers follow, gliding slowly over my yearning heat. I bite down on a moan, my teeth sinking into my lower lip as I strain against the binds that keep me helplessly in place. His fingers tease, tormenting me with every slow pass over my slick folds, never once dipping inside where I need him most.

"When I finally stretch this pretty pussy out, you're going to take every inch of me," He murmurs, his voice a low, possessive growl that sends shivers down my spine. "You'll feel me pounding into you, filling you up, claiming you..."

As he speaks, something cold and smooth touches my back, a startling contrast to the heat of his words. The object drags across my skin, leaving a trail of icy anticipation in its wake.

He presses it against my center. "What is that?" I manage to ask, my voice trembling with a mix of confusion and arousal, as his hand hovers at my entrance, the tip of the toy teasing my slick folds.

"A warm-up," He replies, the smugness in his tone almost palpable. "I'll stop once you're done with your prayer."

"Stop wha—"

Before I can finish, he slides the toy into me. The sensation overwhelms me, and a moan spills from my lips. My body arches instinctively from the sensation. The binds hold me firm, leaving me no choice but to take it, to revel in the mixture of pleasure and restraint.

A gasp escapes me as Roman begins to move the toy, dragging it out slowly, teasing my entrance before driving it back in, each thrust a deliberate, torturous stroke. "Fuck," I moan, my voice trembling with pleasure as his other hand finds my clit, the sensation sending jolts of ecstasy through my body.

Roman drives the toy in and out of me, his fingers skillfully circling my clit, sending sharp waves of pleasure coursing through my body. My legs tremble under the strain as he pushes the toy deeper, harder, faster, each thrust a deliberate assault on my senses.

"Will your tight little pussy enjoy my cock as much as this?" Roman's voice cuts through the fog of pleasure, painful desire lacing every word, his tone a possessive growl.

"W-Well, let's see, Father," I manage to smirk, though my voice quivers with the effort. "Will I finish my prayer or cum all over your little toy before you get the chance to feel me on your own cock?"

He drives the toy into me with a force that makes my entire body jerk. The slick sound of my own arousal echoes in the room, each wet thrust sending ripples of exhilaration through me.

"Start your prayer," He hisses, the command sharp and edged with something savage. "Or I'll make you choke on me while I drive this into your pretty cunt."

I can't take much more, my pride teetering on the brink as gasps and moans escape me with every breath. My body is aflame, every nerve ending alive.

"Hail Mary, full of grace—" I begin, the words tumbling out in a desperate attempt to comply, but they catch in my throat as he pumps the toy harder, faster, the rhythm relentless.

"Don't stop."

"The Lord is with thee. Blessed art thou amongst women—" My voice falters as he yanks the toy free, leaving me gasping, only for his fingers to plunge into me, working me even harder. His fingers curl inside me, hitting that spot I love so much with ruthless precision, sending shockwaves of pleasure through my core. When my moans replace the words, his hand strikes my ass, the sharp sting pulling me back from the edge.

"Keep going."

"And blessed is the fruit of thy womb, Jesus. Holy Mary, Mother of God, pray for us sinners—" The prayer is barely co-herent now, my voice trembling as I try to hold on to the last thread of control.

"Now, and at the hour of our d-death—" My words break off as he curls his fingers just right, and I bury my scream into his pillow, my release crashing through me with a force that leaves me breathless. My wetness gushes onto his hand, and before I can catch my breath, his mouth is on me, his tongue replacing his fingers, greedily lapping up every drop of my orgasm.

Even after I've finished, Roman continues to devour me, his tongue working me through every last tremor of pleasure until my body is spent, quivering beneath his touch. After a few more agonizing minutes, he finally relents, loosening the binds that have kept me tethered and vulnerable. My body slumps into the mattress, every muscle trembling, struggling to stop the shakes that ripple through me.

He pulls the blindfold from my eyes, and I blink against the light, my breath ragged as I lie panting on the sheets. I turn my head to look at him, catching sight of the toy resting on his nightstand, a stark reminder of the intensity we've just shared.

"That was a warm-up?" I ask, a smirk tugging at the corners of his lips as he meets my gaze.

"It was," He murmurs, his voice low and rough as he grabs my legs, dragging me toward him until I'm settled in his lap.

I can feel the strain of his desire pressing against me, the hard length of him igniting a fresh wave of heat in my core. Instinctively, I begin to roll my hips, savoring the friction as his hands clamp down on my thighs, holding me in place with a possessive grip.

"Afternoon Mass starts in thirty, and we both need to get ready," He sighs, though there's a reluctance in his voice that tells me he's fighting his own urges. "Besides, you're still not ready for all of me," He whispers, his words a tantalizing challenge.

My gaze drops to his lips, where a small trail of blood mars the perfection of his mouth. Without thinking, I reach up, wiping it clean with my thumb. But when I glance toward the toy on the nightstand, my heart skips a beat. A smear of blood marks its base, and embarrassment floods through me.

"Your body wasn't prepared for how hard I went," He whispers, his voice dark and steady. "And I'd be lying if I said what I would've done with my cock would have been any less bloody."

His words aren't meant to soothe; they're a warning, an attempt to scare me away, but I hold my ground, refusing to let fear take root.

"You don't scare me Roman," I whisper, leaning in, ready to claim his lips with my own.

"I wish I did, for your own sake," He snaps, his voice edged with frustration as he places his thumb on my lips, silencing me before I can kiss him. "You need a safe word. You tore from how hard I went, and you didn't stop me."

"I like the pain," I admit, a confession that sends a shiver of satisfaction through me, but he shakes his head, his expression serious.

"You say that now. Just think of a word..." His voice trails off as his gaze drops to my lips, his jaw clenching with the effort to maintain control.

"Want a taste of how sweet you were?" He asks, his thumbs slipping from my lips, leaving them tingling with the absence of his touch.

A smile spreads across my face as I lean in closer, my lips brushing against his as I whisper, "Yes, Father."

"If you're what sinning feels like, Eden, then I will gladly embrace the gates of Hell and beg for God's forgiveness for the rest of my life," Roman murmurs, his voice a low, fervent confession that sends a shiver down my spine.

His lips crash into mine, a collision of desperation and desire as if he's trying to consume every piece of me. His tongue traces the contours of my mouth, each movement deliberate, claiming. My hands weave into his hair, pulling him closer, savoring the taste of him, the heat of his breath mingling with mine. For a moment, time ceases to exist; it's just us, lost in the sinful pleasure of each other's touch.

But all too soon, the distant toll of church bells pierces the silence, a harsh reminder of the world outside this stolen, forbidden moment. Reluctantly, I feel him pull away, his breath mingling with mine one last time before he slips the ring back onto his finger—a cold band of gold that binds him to a vow he can never truly break.

No matter how intoxicating these fleeting moments are, he'll always be dedicated to a higher power. To him, I will always be nothing more than a sin, a temptation he's drawn to but can never fully embrace.

But the question that lingers, the one that gnaws at the edges of my mind, is this: What is he to me?

Luke 12:2: "There is nothing concealed that will not be disclosed, or hidden that will not be made known."

Chapter 19

EDEN

Wrapping my legs around his waist, I pull him closer as our lips meet in another heated kiss. His back hits the mattress with a soft thud, the ironed perfection of his black shirt now undone, revealing the chiseled contours of his torso beneath my hands.

I barely had time to slip on my bra and underwear before he began trailing kisses along my neck, his tie hanging loosely, forgotten in the wake of our mutual distraction of each other. The moment I turned to face him, the thought of getting ready for Mass was abandoned entirely.

"You," He murmurs against my neck, his voice thick with both desire and restraint, "need to get ready for service." His hand tangles in my hair, pulling just enough to stop me from kissing him, his impatience simmering beneath the surface. "Now."

"What's a few more minutes going to hurt?" I ask, my hands still splayed across his chest, feeling the steady beat of his heart beneath my fingers.

"My ring is on, Eden." Roman snaps, the warmth of the room cooling as he removes the ropes and handcuffs from the bed and the sex toy he'd used on me from the nightstand.

"I have nothing to wear," I admit, glancing at the dryer where my clothes are still tumbling.

He gently moves me off him, adjusting the strain in his pants before walking over to a drawer. He pulls out a pair of sweats and a faded t-shirt.

"You're lucky this shrunk," He smiles, tossing me the clothes.

I roll my eyes, starting to pull on the sweats, but he catches my wrists, stopping me mid-motion. "I'll do it," He whispers, his voice softening as he kneels before me, slowly pulling the sweats up my legs. His lips trace a tender path up my thighs, pausing to kiss each scar, lingering on the deeper ones as if offering silent absolution.

When he's finished, I grab his chin, forcing him to meet my gaze. "Why do you do that?" I ask, holding his face firmly in place. "Why do you act like all you know is darkness, yet touch me so gently?" My voice is quiet but insistent as I hold his face steady in my hand, refusing to let him look away.

He shrugs. "You were a good girl for me," He whispers, his eyes narrowing with intensity as he pulls the shirt over my head, his lips brushing against each breast with a soft, reverent kiss.

"Do as I say," He continues, his voice a low murmur that vibrates through me, "and you'll be rewarded." There's a note of quiet disappointment to see me fully clothed as he tugs the shirt down to meet my waist.

I help him button up his shirt, my fingers struggling slightly with the small buttons, but he doesn't stop me. He stands still, letting me tuck the shirt into his belt, his eyes watching me intently as I reach for his tie, the silence between us heavy.

"What are you thinking about?" I ask softly, watching as Roman's head begins to shake before I've even finished the question.

"You don't want to know."

"Try me," I whisper, my voice a delicate challenge as I loop his tie through with careful precision, drawing him closer in the process.

His eyes darken, the restraint he's been clinging to slipping away as he leans in, his breath hot against my ear. "I want to take this tie and wrap it around your throat while you're taking me—"

His confession sends a shock of arousal and fear racing through me, but before I can respond, the sharp sound of the doorbell slices through the air, reverberating through the house. We both freeze, flustered and caught off guard, the moment of raw honesty shattered. I notice his hand twitching as if fighting the urge to remove his ring, the symbol of a vow he can't bring himself to break.

In a flash, he pulls on the mask of a priest, the practiced expression of calm and piety that hides the turmoil beneath. "Stay here," He urges, his voice a hushed command as he heads for the door, leaving it slightly cracked behind him.

Curiosity gets the better of me, and I position myself in the sliver of the doorway, swiping my phone for distraction while I listen intently to the unwelcome interruption. My pulse quickens, a mixture of nerves and dread pooling in my stomach.

"Father Briar," Booms a voice I know all too well, the sound of it sending a chill down my spine.

"David, I—" Roman begins, his voice noticeably strained, but my father cuts him off with a genial tone that only deepens my unease.

"No, let me start. I apologize for intruding so close to Mass," My father says, his words accompanied by the sound of a hearty pat on Roman's back. I shrink back further into the shadows, pressing myself against the wall, heart hammering in my chest as I struggle to remain unseen.

What the fuck was my dad doing here?

"What can I do for you, David?" Roman asks, his voice carefully modulated to its usual affable tone, though I can sense the strain beneath it.

"I was wondering if you had a chance to go over the material I left with you, given our meeting is this Sunday—"

Meeting?

What fucking meeting?

"Yes, I did have a chance," Roman replies, his voice steady, but there's a slight hesitation. "I was a bit confused by the last page, given there was no photo—"

"Zoey," My father interjects smoothly. "She recently shared with her family her plans to break away from the Church once she goes back to college, and her father was eager to see that it doesn't happen. She's been marked as tainted and needs to be led back to God's righteous path. I think we've found someone eager to take on the task."

What was he talking about?

"How are your lessons with Eden going, by the way? Has she shown any signs of improvement?" My father's words cut through the fog of shock, twisting my stomach into knots.

My father asked Roman to instruct me.

And he accepted?

"It's been fine," Roman sighs, tugging at his tie in a gesture of discomfort. "I struggle to see some of the things you've described to me," He states, but I can hear the slight edge to his voice, the tension he's trying to mask.

"Trust me, Father, she has plenty of demons that need to be exorcised. Physical punishment seems to work best. But I'm sure you've found that out." My father's words hang in the air like a poisonous cloud, suffocating me with their cruelty.

My gaze flicks to Roman's bed, the memory of his forceful touch suddenly taking on a new, sinister light. Was this all part of some sick plan to break me, to make me submissive to my father's will?

The room feels like it's closing in on me, the walls too close, the air too thick. I glare at them through the narrow crack in the door, my heart pounding in my chest as I glance down at the time on my phone.

Fifteen minutes until Mass.

"You know, she didn't come home last night."

"I believe she was with Zoey. At least that's what she mentioned to me yesterday during her service hours." Roman lies smoothly, though I can see the way his fingers fidget with his ring, a telltale sign of his discomfort. "Although, given the circumstances, I'm not sure how much you'd want the two of them being around one another."

What in the hell are they talking about?

"It's best Zoey stays close to our family. Her mother is a hothead who's poisoned her mind with ideas of leaving the church.

The more time she spends with Eden is less time she spends with her heretic mother of hers." My father laughs, the sound grating on my nerves.

My gaze drifts around the room, searching for some clue to the cryptic conversation. My eyes land on a dark leather binder, half-hidden under a chair, its corner peeking out between a few miscellaneous books. The sight of it sends a surge of curiosity through me, a need to understand what kind of business Roman could possibly have with my father.

Creeping closer, I carefully tug the binder free from its hiding place, my fingers working the latch as my heart pounds in my chest.

What the hell could Roman be hiding?

Nothing could have prepared me for what I see when the binder slips from my grasp, spilling its contents onto the floor. I cover my mouth with a trembling hand, stifling the scream that threatens to break free. My eyes widen in horror as I stare down at the photos—blank, fearful faces of children, each one accompanied by a substantial price tag.

Panic seizes me, my stomach lurching as the reality of what I'm seeing crashes over me like a tidal wave.

All those children.

The numbers next to their names.

What the fuck is going on?

"Is someone else here, Father?" My dad's voice pierces through the haze of panic, his tone suddenly sharp and suspicious.

"Just—"

The door creaks open, and in a moment of sheer terror, I nudge the binder under Roman's bed, my heart racing as I look up to meet my father's perplexed expression. Our eyes lock, and for a moment, everything else fades away, leaving only the cold dread that grips me.

I quickly tuck my arms behind my back, hiding them from my father's view just as Roman's body barrels past him, positioning himself between us like a shield. The tension in the room thickens, crackling in the air like a live wire.

"Eden?" My father's voice is filled with genuine concern, his confusion evident as his eyes find mine. "What the hell are you doing here—"

"I told you to fucking stay silent and finish your prayer," Roman snaps, his voice harsh and cold, a jarring contrast to the man I thought I knew. He gets in my face, the fury in his eyes something I've never seen before, something that makes my blood run cold.

The slap comes out of nowhere, a sharp, stinging pain that explodes across my face. I don't even have time to process what's happening before I'm on the floor, my head spinning from the impact.

"Morning lessons," Roman explains, his voice icily calm as he glares at my father.

I dare to lift my head slightly, just enough to see the pleased expression on my father's face, the satisfaction in his eyes making my skin burn where Roman's hand struck me. The sting of betrayal runs deeper than the physical pain, cutting into me like a blade.

Crouching down to my level, my father's eyes rake over me, taking in my disheveled appearance, my arms hidden beneath my body. "I knew you were the right person for the task at hand

Father," He says with a twisted smile, his hand reaching out to tug at my hair, the gesture both condescending and cruel.

The realization hits me like a tidal wave, the full weight of the situation crashing down around me. The man I trusted, the man who held me with such tenderness only moments ago, has revealed himself as something entirely different—a stranger who's capable of unspeakable acts.

"You serve in ten minutes. Get your act together," My father hisses, his voice low and menacing. My eyes dart to Roman, whose gaze is locked in a cold, unreadable stare. "Maybe you should have been here last night instead of out sinning with your brother," My father continues, his lips brushing against my ear in a mockery of intimacy. "I sniffed out his bullshit lie in a second. Bible study with friends, right? Sadly, your brother was the one who had to pay for your dishonesty."

He shoves my head forward before straightening and offering Roman a handshake as if nothing had happened. "I'll leave you to it, Father," He smiles, patting Roman on the back with a camaraderie that made my skin crawl.

The moment the front door clicks shut behind my father, the cold mask Roman had been wearing shatters, replaced by a look of anguish. "Damnit, Eden, I'm so sorry," He begins, his voice filled with regret as he moves to help me up.

But I'm already standing, pulling away from him as I clutch my throbbing cheek. "Who the fuck are you?" I snap, my voice trembling with both anger and fear. "Who were those kids—"

"I had to do that," He interrupts, running a hand through his hair in frustration. "If Zoey's own parents are willing to put her up, what the hell do you think will happen if your dad thinks you're beyond saving? Do you think his focus will stay on Aiden forever—"

"Put her up?" I repeat, disbelief turning my voice sharp. "You mean she's in that binder? Are you telling me those children were *for sale*?"

"This whole town is fucking twisted, Eden," He says, desperation creeping into his tone as he tries to get closer to me, but I shove him away.

"And you're a part of it?" I scream, tears streaming down my face. "You fucking work with my dad for what? A goddamn religious child trafficking—"

Roman grabs my arms, forcing them down as he gets in my face. "I have taken no part in any of that twisted bastard's bullshit. Why the hell do you think I was so angry when Zack showed up yesterday? Your father had just given me that fucking binder, Eden!" His voice is strained, desperate. "I'm trying to protect you."

"You're just feeding me more of his lies," I yell back, my voice cracking as I get up in his face. "You fucking hit me—"

"What the fuck do you think he would have done if he didn't see me discipline you?" Roman shouts, his eyes wild with emotion. "He already hurt Aiden—"

Oh God.

Aiden.

Sadly, your brother was the one who had to pay for your dishonesty.

Roman tries to reach for my chin, but I pull away, fury and guilt warring within me. "Get your fucking hands off me," I hiss, stepping back. "You're just another one of my dad's sick fucking friends," I sob, watching the pain flash across Roman's face.

"Eden, I panicked—"

"Fuck you, Roman," I spit, lowering my gaze in disgust. "I will go to the fucking police, you sick bastard! Where are they? Where are the kids—"

"The police know, Eden," He whispers, his voice heavy with resignation as he readjusts his collar. "The police know, and they'll gladly defend the Church and drag you deeper into their bullshit for being suspicious," He warns.

"You agreed to fucking discipline me for my father?" I choke out.

The pain in my chest is overwhelming.

"To keep you safe," He mutters, his arms cautiously landing on mine. "To keep you away from him the only way I know how."

My mind reels, trying to process everything that's happened, the fearful faces of the children flashing before my eyes. "Where are they, Roman?" I ask again, my voice barely above a whisper. His mouth clamps shut, the truth too heavy to speak.

"I don't know," He finally admits, his voice breaking. "I won't know until that meeting on Sunday."

I try to hold back my sobs, but they come anyway, wracking my body as I struggle to stay composed. "And Aiden? Did you know bringing me back here would cause him to get hurt?" I ask, my voice shaking.

"I didn't know. But it was you or him. And I will choose you every time. You should know that by now," He whispers, his fingers grazing the material of his shirt above his wrist.

Guilt crashes over me, and I can't bear to be near him any longer. I push past him, my heart breaking.

"Don't fucking speak to me," I scream, swatting his hand away. "Don't fucking look at me. Stay the hell away from my brother and me," I hiss, my eyes burning with tears.

I nudge past his front door, giving it a hard slam behind me. The sound echoes in my ears, a final punctuation to the nightmare I'm living.

Finding the back way into Saint Michael's, I slip inside, my steps faltering as I make my way to the altar servers' changing room. When I finally see Aiden, our eyes meet, and the pain in his expression mirrors my own.

"Aiden, I'm sorry—" I begin, but the words are lost as he wraps his arms around me, pulling me into a tight embrace. The thought of my father laying a hand on him ignites a blood-hungry anger deep within me, a rage I can barely contain.

"Aiden, I didn't know—" I whisper, my voice thick with guilt and sorrow.

"It's my fault," He murmurs, pressing his head to my chest, seeking comfort. "I'm the one who told Roman where we were. Luca told me what Roman did. I should have known he was as unhinged as Dad—"

"This isn't your fault, Aiden," I say, my voice firm despite the tears threatening to spill out. "I will find a way out of this for both of us."

"There is no way out, Eden," He sobs, struggling to keep himself together. "Don't you see that? We're fucking trapped. I thought maybe Roman might be different—"

"I don't want to talk about Roman right now," I interrupt, trying to maintain some semblance of control. "I have to look at him all through Mass and hold it together."

Aiden stops, his tear-filled eyes scanning my face with confusion and concern. "What happened between you and Father Briar, Eden?" He asks, rubbing his bruised throat, his voice hoarse.

"Nothing that matters. It's over now," I whisper, brushing a tear from his cheek. "He was closer to Dad than I thought. There's no use in dwelling on that fact anymore."

"How bad did Dad hurt you last night?" I ask, my voice trembling as I search his eyes for the truth. He averts his gaze, the pain in his expression breaking my heart.

"I tried to fight back," He whispers, showing me his worn wrists, the skin raw and red. "He held me down. I thought I could stop him, but when he started touching me—"

"It's alright, Aiden. I'm here now," I whisper, my eyes scanning the room for a robe. "You stay in here until Mass."

I slip on my robe, tightening the rope around my waist as if it could somehow hold me together. With a determined stride, I shove open the door and make my way down the hall. The weight of Aiden's bruises and the fear in his eyes had ignited a fire within me. The thought of my father hurting him because of me is too much to bear. Anger sharpens into resolve, and without a second thought, I know what I have to do. I can't let my father get away with this—not when Aiden's safety is on the line. With each step toward the gathering space, my focus narrows, and by the time I spot my father, my decision is made: he will know I'm not afraid, and I won't let him hurt Aiden again.

As I step into the crowded gathering space, my eyes lock on my father, who's standing near the back, engaged in conversation with Zoey's stepmother. The anger simmering inside me boils over at the sight of him, the thought of Aiden pushing me forward.

He thinks he can get away with this?

Ignoring Zoey's voice as she calls my name, I stride purposefully toward my father, my hands clenched into fists. When I reach him, I grab his arm, my grip tight, my knuckles white.

He turns, surprised by my sudden presence, his eyes narrowing as he registers the anger in my expression. "What are you—"

"Don't you dare lay another hand on Aiden," I hiss, my voice low but laced with venom. My fingers dig into his arm as I lean in close so only he can hear me. "If you do, I swear to God—"

His eyes flash with anger, but he keeps his voice calm, his tone condescending. "Watch your tone, Eden," He warns, tugging his arm free from my grip. "You're already on thin ice after that stunt in Mass."

I glance around, noticing the people nearby beginning to take an interest in our conversation. I need to be careful. I force myself to take a breath, to rein in the fury that's threatening to explode. But I can't help myself from leaning in again, whispering harshly, "I'm not afraid of you anymore. If you ever touch him again, I'll make sure everyone knows who you really are."

My father's expression darkens, and I can see the tension in his jaw as he struggles to maintain his composure. "You need to calm down," He says, his voice dangerously soft. "We can talk about this outside."

He grabs my arm, his grip firm but not enough to draw attention. With a fake smile plastered on his face, he guides me toward the exit, his fingers digging into my skin just enough to make his point.

Once we're outside, away from the prying eyes of the congregation, he pulls me into a secluded corner of the parking lot. His face is a mask of barely contained rage.

"Do you have any idea what you've just done?" He snarls, his voice low and threatening. "You've made a fool of yourself and me."

I glare at him, refusing to back down, even though my heart is pounding in my chest. "I don't care what happens to me. But if you hurt Aiden again, I'll make sure you regret it."

That's when I see it—a flash of something cold and dangerous in his eyes. Before I can react, his hand lashes out, slapping me hard across the face. The force of the blow sends me stumbling, pain radiating through my cheek as I try to keep my balance.

"You will learn your place, Eden," He hisses, his voice seething with fury as he grabs my arm, yanking me back to him.

His grip tightens, and I feel the sharp edge of his car keys biting into my skin as he drags them across my wrist, leaving a stinging cut in their wake. I bite back a cry, tears stinging my eyes, but I refuse to let him see me break.

When he finally lets go, I stumble back, cradling my aching cheek and bleeding wrist. The world around me feels blurry and surreal as if I'm watching it all happen from a distance.

"You're going to sit in the car the rest of Mass," He orders, his voice cold and devoid of any emotion. "And when we get home, you're coming straight to my room."

I don't respond. I can't. All I can think about is Aiden and how I've failed to protect him. But as I turn to walk back toward the church, I catch a glimpse of Roman standing by the entrance, his eyes locked on mine. There's a look of fear in his expression, a silent plea that tells me he knows exactly what's happening but feels powerless to stop it.

After Mass ends, my father drags me to the car, his grip as tight as ever. "When we get home, up to my room," He whispers, and the dread in my stomach deepens.

But one thing is clear.

My father's focus was no longer on Aiden.

Aiden is safe.

And me?

Well, perhaps I was better off at college, far away from this hell.

Joshua 1:9: "This is My command: be strong and courageous. Never be afraid or discouraged because I am your God, the Eternal One, and I will remain with you wherever you go."

Chapter 20

ROMAN

I have it all planned out.

David Faulkner will die a slow, torturous death.

One so meticulously cruel that Ted Bundy himself would take notes.

It's been four days since David dragged her out of that church, leaving bruises on her skin that I can't get out of my mind. And what did I do? I just stood there, paralyzed by the fear of what everyone would see if I intervened—if they saw how much I care for her, how deep this runs. Eden is my greatest weakness, my one true vulnerability. If the congregation ever found out, I'd lose everything—my position, my calling, the life I've built. I'd be stripped of the collar, and everything I've worked for would crumble. But the worst part? I let him hurt her, and I did nothing.

These past four days, she's avoided the church entirely. I know because I've been watching, keeping tabs on her from a distance.

She's been lying to her father, telling him she's fulfilling her service hours, and I've been lying right along with her whenever he asks how her lessons are going. The thought of what would happen if he found out the truth makes my blood run cold.

And then there's Luca—hovering around her in the parking lot after her shifts, wrapping her in his arms, pressing ice against the bruise around her eye. Seeing him comfort her, knowing that bruise shouldn't even exist, fills me with a burning jealousy and regret. That should be me holding her, protecting her. But all I can do is watch from a distance, haunted by my own cowardice.

That should be me.

It's torture, this self-imposed exile from the one person I want to protect more than anything. Each day, I find myself drawn back to her, making excuses to pass by her workplace, to linger in the shadows where I can see. I watch her laugh with Aiden, the light in her eyes dimmed but still fighting to shine through the pain. And every time I see Luca's arm around her, that idiot's easy smile as he tries to comfort her, I feel a rage I can barely contain.

But what right do I have to feel anything? I'm the one who stood by as her father hurt her, who failed to protect her when she needed me most. I'm the one who's too terrified to show the world how much I care, to admit that she means more to me than anything else in this hollow existence I've carved out for myself.

Eden seeing that binder was the last thing I needed. She wasn't supposed to know, wasn't supposed to see the dark underbelly of this town. But now that she does, I can't stop thinking about it.

I roll my ring on the altar podium, the cool metal grounding me in this moment of helplessness. I glance at my watch—nine fifty p.m. Ten minutes until I have to stand before a congregation of people I can barely stand to look at, let alone preach to. They disgust me, every last one of them, but I play my part because it's what's expected of me.

Had David not made that agreement with me, had he not sworn to let me be the one to discipline Eden, I would've torn him apart the moment he laid a hand on her. But I had to hold back, I had to keep playing this twisted game to protect her. To figure out what the fuck was going on with those kids. The only reason he hasn't punished her further is that he still believes she's been fulfilling her service hours with me, and I've done everything in my power to keep that lie alive.

After he dragged her out of the church and hurt her in the parking lot, he had the nerve to apologize to me as if that could erase the damage he'd done. He swore he wouldn't touch her again, that he'd leave the punishment to me as if that somehow made it better.

So I slashed his car tires. It was the only thing I could do to release the anger boiling inside me, the only way I could make him pay without exposing everything. But it wasn't enough. Nothing I do feels like enough when I see the cuts on her arms, raw and jagged, a testament to the pain she's endured. And all I can think about is how I've failed her.

The minute I saw the blood on his car keys, I knew I had to walk away—I had to force myself to leave before my whole congregation bore witness to me killing the man in broad daylight.

The urge to tear him apart was almost unbearable, but I managed to resist, if only by a thread.

Since then, my phone has been silent. My sheets still carry the faint scent of her, a cruel reminder of what I've lost. Even now, as I sit here, I can't stop wondering just how much time Luca has spent with her, the itch to check on her growing stronger with each passing minute. I want to make sure she gets off her late shift safely, to know that she's okay, but I stay put, wrestling with my own demons.

Every night, I park near her house, keeping a careful distance. I watch, vigilant and ready to break in the moment I sense something is wrong. It's a sick sort of penance, this self-imposed watch, but it's the only thing that keeps me sane. Letting her get hurt in front of me feels worse than any sin I could commit. It's a betrayal of everything I swore to protect—worse than accepting the Devil himself.

Repenting does no good. The prayers that once brought solace now only make the guilt fester. In my life, I've made many mistakes, but none as great as what happened on Tuesday.

I glance down at the detailed plan in front of me, a blueprint for vengeance that I've been refining since the moment David Faulkner laid his filthy hands on her. The demons he unleashed within me prowl the very space I stand in, turning this cathedral into something far from holy. They whisper to me, urging me to do what needs to be done.

I want to watch them all burn. I want to see this place, this twisted cult, consumed by flames—with her at my side, free from the shackles that bind us both.

"Roman," Zoey's father beams, interrupting my dark reverie. My hand moves quickly, tucking the paper away as I give him a once-over, trying to suppress the disgust rising within me.

"I'm Seth. I don't think we've been properly introduced." He extends his hand toward me, his smile forced.

"Right," I mutter, scanning the cathedral for any sign of the other members of this godforsaken cult, hoping to find something—anything—to distract me from the bile rising in my throat.

"First meeting?" He asks, attempting to make small talk, his tone earnest but grating.

"Yeah, is it that obvious?" I reply with a tight smile, forcing out a laugh that sounds as hollow as it feels. He chuckles nervously in return, clearly unsettled by my demeanor.

Crossing his arms across his chest, he glances around the cathedral, then back at me. "It's a damn shame what happened on Tuesday with Faulkner's girl," He sighs, his eyes briefly meeting mine before looking away. "One more outburst from her, and David might consider swapping Zoey for Eden on that roster—"

Something snaps inside me, a thread pulled too tight for too long, finally breaking. Before I can stop myself, the words spill out, cold and deadly. "If you ever suggest that again, I'll kill you."

The air between us stills, Seth's voice stopping mid-sentence as his face drains of color. He stares at me, eyes wide, struggling to process what I've just said.

"Father, I—"

"Say her name one more fucking time, or even insinuate that any of you dirty bastards will lay a hand on her, and I'll crack your skull against this floor," I whisper, my voice low and deadly as I slowly turn my head his way.

Seth's confusion is palpable as he takes a step back, his bravado slipping away. "David said you were one of us—"

"Did he?" I tilt my head, letting the deep-rooted hatred within me claw its way to the surface. "Did he also tell you he molests his son and fucks your wife when you're not home?" The knowledge I've gathered on these people runs deep, far deeper than they could ever imagine.

They have their resources. I have mine.

"You're no fucking follower—"

"I'm not," I admit, following him down the steps with a deliberate slowness. "But David Faulkner has some deep ties to someone I care about more than anything, which is why you, Seth, are going to be my eyes and ears," I smile, reaching into the podium to retrieve the thick file I've prepared.

Seth shakes his head, lowering his gaze as if searching for an escape. "Why the fuck would I help you?" He mutters, his voice betraying the fear simmering beneath the surface.

I toss the papers toward him, watching as they flutter to the ground at his feet. "I have all of that on a drive, ready to go to a friend of mine closely tied to the FBI. David was smart—he tied your name to all the cars that transport the kids. Everything leads back to you, Seth. So you're going to help me create a clear paper trail leading straight to David, Kevin, and anyone else involved in this fucked up shit," I hiss, my words dripping with contempt.

"Lay a hand on Zoey, or even think about Eden, and I'll release all of it—and I'll kill you before DHS can even bust down your door," I grin, the threat hanging heavy in the air between us.

"Jesus Christ—" Seth's voice trembles, but I cut him off, closing the distance between us in an instant.

"No Jesus, Seth. Just me," I scold, watching him flinch as I drive the pointed end of a small letter opener just below his ribcage, the cold metal sinking into his flesh with ease. "One twist of my wrist, and it'll kill you before you can even make it to the hospital. A little trick I learned on my second tour overseas. But, as long as you make it through this meeting without opening your mouth, I'll gladly help you pull it out."

I adjust his suit jacket over the wound, the dark fabric hiding the evidence of our exchange.

"Now be a good disciple and shut your fucking mouth."

Grabbing the papers from him, I tuck them back into the folder on the podium, forcing a smile as the others begin to file into the space. Seth stands there, his face pale and drawn, but he stays silent.

David is the first to enter, his presence casting a shadow over the room. He pats Seth on the back, oblivious to the fear in the man's eyes. "Seth, how are you?" David asks, moving past me without a second glance. I keep my gaze locked on Seth, watching for any sign of betrayal.

Seth hesitates, most likely calculating his odds of survival, before forcing a smile. "Never better, David," He replies, his voice strained but passable. "Feeling lucky," He adds with a grin that doesn't reach his eyes.

David turns to me, dismissing Seth entirely, his focus now solely on the task at hand. There's something in the way Seth looks at him—a lingering stare that David, too self-absorbed, doesn't even notice.

They're all going to regret ever knowing David Faulkner.

"Father Briar?" David's voice breaks through my thoughts, his arrogance practically begging to be punished. "Ready to begin?"

I force a smile, adjusting my collar with practiced ease. "Absolutely."

Seated around the font of holy water, the scene before me looks like something out of a horror movie. Men and women pass around a roster sheet while shamelessly drinking the church's wine straight from the chalices used for Communion. There's no respect for the symbolism, no reverence for the blood of Christ they're indulging in like thirsty mosquitoes draining a vein. Their greedy mouths desecrate the sacred ritual, and the sight of it makes my skin crawl.

It doesn't take long to register that I'm the youngest person in this twisted group. Seth stays close to my side, his breath shallow and his face pale. I'm prepared to lean over and twist the letter opener I've hidden beneath his jacket at the slightest provocation.

I'm here for information.

I'm here to keep Eden safe.

The closer I get to all of this, the easier it will be to bring it all down.

Finding my phone in my pocket, I press the record button, positioning it so it can capture everything. I pray it's enough—pray I can gather enough evidence to expose them all.

"So, as you all know, Roman has replaced dear Father Kevin and was eager to fill the hole he left behind," David smiles, his expression smug as the others in the group raise their chalices in a drunken toast, their hands clapping in sloppy, welcoming applause.

Sick fucks.

I force a smile, leaning back in my chair with calculated ease. "I'm honored to have you all welcome me with such open arms," I grin, casting a glance at Seth, who struggles to hide his gasps of pain. His face contorts with the effort, and despite everything, I find his discomfort amusing.

"Father Briar holds a special tie to my family," David continues, playing the part of the concerned father. "As you all know, my Eden had another one of her psychotic breaks and nearly caused a scene—"

Hold it together, Roman.

I dig my nails into my thighs, grounding myself against the rage that threatens to consume me. I can't lose control now. Not here.

"Though Roman has been working hard to instill discipline in her, the line she walks with the Devil has been difficult for my whole family. My son has been my primary focus. My job as a father is to shield him from the dark—"

His words blur together, and it takes everything in me to maintain a calm facade. My mind races with every lie he's spinning, every twisted truth he's manipulating to paint himself as the victim and Eden as the monster. The same lies he uses to justify the horrific things he does to both of his children.

They'll all pay for what they've done.

And it starts with David Faulkner.

"But with Eden's persistent disregard for her faith, I'm especially grateful for the discipline Roman has been instilling in her," David says, his tone dripping with false gratitude. "She's needed someone to remind her of her place, and Roman's efforts to steer her back onto the righteous path haven't gone unnoticed." He smiles, raising his glass toward me. The air around us thickens with tension as he leans in, eyes glinting with malice.

"Which is why tonight, I ask you only one thing," He looks me over as if sizing up an opponent. "Show my daughter the fear of God. Give her a reason to be terrified of His strength," David warns, taking a deliberate sip from his glass. "Or, of course, I will have to do it myself."

Our eyes lock in a silent battle for dominance, the air between us crackling with unspoken threats.

"Are you questioning my effectiveness, David?" I ask, my tone light, almost amused, though there isn't a hint of humor on his face.

David's smile fades into something colder, more calculating. "I'm choosing to believe that you are truly punishing my daughter for her dalliance with the Devil. But if I were to catch wind that you were somehow walking a path of sin with her, well, our agreement would have to change," He says, his voice dripping with thinly veiled condescension. "I'm choosing to believe your outburst with Zack wasn't born out of a need to protect Eden," He adds, his eyes narrowing.

That fucking rat. Zack ran to David the moment I let my guard down. I'll have to deal with him later—God help him if we're ever alone again.

"You should know better than anyone, Father, women are a temptation. If you were to, say, care for my daughter in any way beyond instilling discipline and devotion, you'd deface the very nature of that ring around your finger."

"It sounds like you're throwing out quite a few accusations, David," I mutter, a smile finally creeping across his face. It's the smile of a man who thinks he's won, who thinks he has me cornered.

"I know my daughter, Father. She's not a clean woman," David whispers, leaning closer. "Consider this a friendly warning, man to man."

As he turns away, I see the truth for what it is. He has suspicions about Eden and me. This whole meeting—every word he's spoken—was just a way to tighten the leash around my neck.

The rest of the meeting becomes a dull hum of conversation in the background, their words cryptic, deliberately keeping me in the dark about where the kids are.

As the group shifts from business to banter, I catch Seth's eye, his expression guarded. "What does he want from Eden?" I ask, keeping my voice low.

"Complete submission," Seth shrugs, his eyes dropping as he mumbles the words.

I grip the sides of my chair, forcing myself to remain calm.

"She hasn't bled," I lie, speaking a little louder so the group can hear, feeding into the sick narrative David has constructed. I turn to him, my face indifferent. "You claim she carries sin, yet she's as innocent as our Mother Mary."

"A virgin?" David muses, his tone shifting as if he's seeing Eden in a new light, as if he's reassessing her value. He picks up on the conversation, eyes narrowing in thought.

"Yes," I say, standing slowly, the chair scraping against the floor. "I suppose the price tag doesn't quite fit the description for both her and Zoey—"

"Can you prove she still holds the light of Mary within her?" David asks, his voice a low rumble as the room falls silent. "Can you prove she is both submissive and untouched by a man?"

My mind races, searching for an answer that won't trap me further.

The thought of proving something so twisted turns my stomach, but I know I can't afford to show weakness here.

I tap my foot, stalling for time, shaking my head slowly as if pondering the impossibility of his request.

"If I can, she stays out of the bidding?" I ask, my voice steady, masking the storm brewing inside me. David's head tilts, his eyes narrowing as he considers my proposition.

"If you can prove it," David whispers, his voice dripping with skepticism. "Then yes. She has no place in the bidding."

I nod slowly, forcing a smile that doesn't reach my eyes.

This is all for show. He thinks I won't be able to prove it. He thinks he's already won.

"Deal," I say with a grin, extending my hand. "If I'm wrong, you may do as you please with her."

David hesitates, just for a heartbeat, before gripping my hand. His hold is firm, almost crushing, as he pulls me closer, his mouth brushing my ear. A cold shiver snakes down my spine as his words slither through the air.

"If I find out you are not one of us, and you're corrupting my daughter's soul with your heresies, I will make you watch her bidding and force you to witness the outcome. I can smell a heretic from a mile away, Roman, and your stench is unmistakable. I've sanctified my hands in this church's holy water, and I will gladly drown you in it if I discover you've been leading her astray."

He releases me, the threat hanging between us like a blade poised to strike. Then, as if flipping a switch, he slips back into his charming facade, excusing himself with a smile as the others begin to leave. But as the doors close behind him, the tension doesn't dissipate—it thickens, wrapping around me like a noose.

In my life, I've faced many demons. But I never thought I'd come face to face with the Devil himself.

A new resolve hardens within me, cold and unyielding. He's underestimated me. They all have. And that will be their downfall.

The room empties, leaving me alone with my thoughts. But there's no time to dwell. I can feel the clock ticking, each second a countdown to the moment when everything will come to a head.

The Devil might think he's won this round, but I've got my own cards to play.

I take a deep breath, steeling myself for what's to come. The final act is approaching, and when it does, I'll be ready.

Let him come. Let them all come. I'm going to bring the whole damn house down.

Chapter 21

EDEN

The cathedral looms ahead, its tall spires cutting into the dusk sky as I pull into the nearly deserted parking lot. It's been three weeks since everything started to unravel—since I confronted my father and cut Roman from my life. Three weeks of trying to keep my brother safe from our father's wrath. Three weeks of pretending Luca's presence in my life is anything more than a weak attempt at normalcy.

Roman's 4-Runner is parked near the entrance, the only other vehicle in sight. The sight of it is both comforting and unsettling, knowing what lies ahead. I step out of the car, the cool evening air brushing against my skin, sending a shiver down my spine. My hands tighten around the edges of Roman's flannel, pulling it closer as if it could shield me from the answers I came here for. The fabric still carries his scent, a bittersweet reminder of the man who's been both my savior and my tormentor.

I start toward the grand wooden doors of the cathedral, the click of my heels echoing in the stillness. At home, things have changed. Aiden has been quieter, more withdrawn. My father hasn't laid a hand on me since that day, but his attention has shifted—he's more focused on me now, leaving Aiden somewhat in the clear. But I know it's temporary. He's still in danger, just lurking under my father's radar for now.

Luca's been making an effort, inserting himself in my life more consistently after apologizing for how he treated me after Roman's outburst at the reservoir, and I've been pretending to forgive him. But it's not a relationship. It's a bandage over a wound that Roman left behind.

The cathedral's wooden doors are heavy, resisting as I push them open. Inside, the building feels more like a fortress than a sanctuary tonight. The dim light from a single lamp in the office down the hall casts long shadows, making the space seem even more oppressive. Each step I take toward that office feels heavier, like the air itself is thickening around me, weighed down by the questions that have been burning in my mind.

Why has Roman been lying to my father, telling him I've been completing service hours when we both know I haven't? What's his real connection to my father, and what does he know about the dark secrets buried in that binder I found? And why, after everything, can't I just let him go?

My heart pounds as I step inside, eyes locked on the chaos before me. The quiet click of the door closing behind me echoes in the stillness, and I know there's no turning back now. Roman's voice, low and weary, breaks the silence, pulling me out of my thoughts.

"Eden," He whispers, like he's saying my name for the first time.

I turn slowly, meeting his tired eyes. For a moment, the weight of everything unsaid hangs between us. The room feels too small, too confined for what's about to happen.

"I need answers, Roman," I say, my voice trembling with the weight of everything I'm about to ask. "I need to know what's really going on."

I pause my eye catching on his cluttered desk. Papers are strewn across it haphazardly, a chaotic mess that seems out of character for the man who usually exudes control. My gaze shifts downward, taking in the details—the faint scent of old leather, the worn edges of a thick binder, and a set of keys lying abandoned on top of a stack of documents.

I notice a notebook, its pages filled with scribbles and notes that are almost impossible to decipher from where I stand. There's a tension in the air, a palpable sense of something hidden just beneath the surface. My fingers twitch, a part of me wanting to reach out and flip through the pages to find the answers I came here seeking.

"What's all this?"

"My sorry attempt to find information on all the sick fucks in this congregation," He whispers, rifling through the papers. "That meeting on Sunday made it clear I need more leverage on all of them—"

"The meeting... about the kids in that binder I saw?" I ask, his body freezing.

"They don't trust me, Eden. They don't think I'm one of them because I'm not. I know you're convinced I'm a part of all this, but I promise you, the only thing I want is to get you and those children far away from this," He whispers, finally meeting my gaze.

"The deal you made with my father—"

"Was to keep you safe," He whispers, turning toward me. "He wanted to harm you, punish you. I wasn't going to allow it.

"And that's why you hit me?" I ask, rubbing my arms.

"He had to think I was willing to punish you the way he would, Angel," He whispers, taking a step closer. "But now one of those elitist cultist fucks has planted in his mind that our sessions weren't as cold-hearted as he'd like to believe."

I take a step back, shaking my head. "So now what? He thinks you're beating me into submission during our service hours? What kind of fucked-up logic is that?"

Roman's expression hardens, shadows deepening the intensity of his gaze. "He wants you to be as submissive as your mother," He says, his voice laced with bitterness. "He wants you to bow your head, accept your place without question, to be molded into the perfect image of obedience. He needs me to break your spirit, to make you pure in his eyes, cleansed of whatever he believes taints you."

The words send a chill through me, but I force myself to stand my ground. "And if you don't?" I challenge, stepping closer, needing to know just how far this will go.

Roman's eyes flicker with a dangerous mix of protectiveness and anger. "If I don't, Eden, then you won't want to know what he's capable of. But I won't let it get that far. You're not going to find out."

His hand reaches up to touch my face, but I jerk back, my spine hitting the edge of the desk. "Don't," I snap, my voice trembling with a mix of fear and anger. "Don't touch me like you care—"

Roman's hand hovers in the air, his eyes locking onto mine with a raw intensity. "I do care," He says, his voice rough and filled with something I can't quite decipher. "More than you realize, Eden. This—this need to protect you—it's tearing me apart."

His confession hits me like a wave, and for a moment, I can't find the words. The weight of what he's saying, of what he's feeling, presses down on me. "This isn't about you," I manage to say, my voice trembling. "This is about what my father wants, about the way he's trying to control my life—"

Roman steps closer, his gaze never leaving mine. "It is about me, Eden. It's about us. It's about everything that happened... Everything that started that day in the park."

I blink, thrown off balance by the sudden shift. "The park?" I ask, my voice barely above a whisper. "What does the park have to do with this?"

His eyes soften, and for the first time, I see a vulnerability in him that I hadn't noticed before. "That day in the park, when I saw you sitting alone on that bench... I didn't know what I was getting into. But I knew, even then, that I couldn't just walk away."

The memory stirs something deep within me, a fragment of a moment I had tried to bury. "You were there," I whisper, the realization dawning on me. "You were the one who stopped me."

Roman nods, his expression filled with a mixture of pain and resolve. "I couldn't let you go through with it, Eden. Not then, not now. I've been watching over you ever since, trying to protect you, trying to keep you safe—even if it meant lying, even if it meant going against everything I'm supposed to stand for."

His words hang in the air, heavy with meaning, and suddenly, everything starts to make sense—the way he's been acting, the way he's been covering for me, the intensity of his emotions. "Why didn't you tell me?" I ask, my voice breaking.

"I didn't know how," He admits, his voice rough. "I didn't know if you'd even want to hear it. But I couldn't stand by and let your father break you, Eden. I care about you too much to let that happen."

The sincerity in his voice pulls at something deep inside me, something I've tried to keep buried. I search his eyes, looking for any sign of deceit, but all I see is raw, unfiltered emotion. "You saved me," I whisper, the words barely audible. "That day in the park... you saved me."

Roman's hand finally moves, gently brushing a strand of hair away from my face. "And I'll keep saving you, Eden," He vows softly. "As long as it takes."

Roman's hand lingers on my cheek for a moment longer before he lets it fall to his side. The air between us shifts, the tension thickening, becoming something else entirely—something that crackles with a different kind of intensity.

I take a shaky breath, trying to steady myself, but the way he's looking at me now, with a mix of concern and something darker, makes it impossible to think clearly. His eyes drop, trailing over my body, taking in every detail.

"Eden," He says quietly, his voice low and filled with something that makes my heart skip a beat. "Why are you wearing my flannel?"

His question catches me off guard, and I instinctively wrap the fabric tighter around me as if that could shield me from the heat of his gaze. "I—I just grabbed something to wear," I stammer, but the lie is weak, even to my own ears.

Roman steps closer, his presence overwhelming. "Without a bra?" He murmurs, his tone holding a dangerous edge. He reaches out, his fingers brushing lightly against the fabric covering my chest. "Do you think anyone would miss the outline of those pretty breasts if they closely looked?"

His thumbs skim the curve of my breasts, the touch so light it sends shivers down my spine, and warmth pools between my legs. I can barely breathe, let alone respond. The space between us seems to disappear, the room narrowing down to just him, just us.

My mind is a haze of sensation and desire. The weight of his presence, the intoxicating scent of him clinging to the fabric I'm wearing—everything overwhelms me. "I wear it when I..." My voice falters, the words catching in my throat as his thumbs roll over my nipples, the cold metal of his ring contrasting sharply with the heat of his touch, making them even firmer.

"When you what, Eden?" He asks, his tone demanding and soft all at once, like a dark promise. His lips find the sensitive skin of my neck, and he gathers it between his teeth, barely sucking, just enough to make my body melt into his touch, every thought consumed by him. "Confess your sins to me, baby," He whispers, the words vibrating through me, making my knees weak.

"W-When I want to... touch myself," I finally admit, the confession slipping from my lips like a secret I've held onto for too long. His lips curl into a smile against my skin, a smile that's triumphant, like he's just won some unspoken game.

"There's no need to touch yourself, beautiful," He whispers, his teeth nipping at my earlobe, sending a jolt of pleasure straight through me. "Not when I'm here." His words are a command, a promise.

Roman's mouth hovers just inches from my skin, the warmth of his breath lingering as he pulls back slightly, his gaze intense and unyielding. My pulse pounds in my ears, matching the rapid rhythm of my heart. Every time his ring brushes against my skin, it feels like a branding iron, marking me as his.

"Roman—" I start, but my voice is breathless, weak.

"Keep saying my name, Eden," He whispers, his tone both commanding and desperate, as if he needs to hear it as much as I need to say it. His fingers fumble with the buttons of the flannel, each one coming undone with agonizing slowness. "Whisper it, shout it, scream it. Just let me fucking hear your pretty voice. I'll never get sick of it."

His words send a shiver down my spine, and I'm about to give in, to let the last button fall away, when a sudden surge of resolve tightens my grip on his hand, stopping him. I stare into his eyes, searching for the Roman I thought I knew beneath the burning desire that clouds his gaze.

"My father—" The words are a harsh reminder of the twisted reality that waits for us outside this moment.

"Wants me to prove to him that you're untouched, pure," Roman spits the word out like it burns his tongue. "He's convinced that if you were to—bleed—during some sick ritual, it would mean you're still untouched by sin."

"But I'm not—" I confess, my voice trembling.

"I know," Roman says through gritted teeth, his anger barely contained. "But he believes that if you bleed during a... I don't really know. A ritual or some kind of punishment, maybe? That it'll prove your innocence to him, that you're still...pure in his twisted mind."

The thought makes my stomach turn, the weight of what he's implying settling heavily on my chest. Roman's fingers hover over the last button of my flannel, his ring cold against my skin. Even as the tension between us thickens, he doesn't move to take off his ring, and the horrifying realization dawns on me.

"Then make me bleed, Roman," I say, my voice steely, even though fear tightens my throat.

He stops, his eyes searching mine, looking for any sign that I don't mean what I just said. The seconds drag on, and I can see the pain in his eyes, the desperation not to hurt me, even as he's caught in the web of my father's twisted demands.

"Eden..." His voice cracks, but I hold firm, knowing that whatever happens next is beyond just the two of us.

But I hold his gaze, unflinching, the words hanging between us like a challenge, a promise, and a surrender all at once. The decision is his now, and the room seems to hold its breath, waiting for what comes next.

"Or else I'm walking out of here to meet Zoey and Luca—"

Before I can finish, his lips are on mine, silencing the threat with a kiss so fierce it leaves me breathless. The last button of my flannel gives way under his force, the fabric slipping to the floor, forgotten. Wrapping my arms around his neck, he lifts me off the desk by the loops of my jeans, pressing me against him, his hard length digging into my thigh, sending a shiver of need through me.

As his hand moves toward his ring, a symbol of everything he's trying to hold on to, I slam his hand back down on the desk, refusing to let this moment be tainted by guilt.

"Don't—"

"Take it off," He hisses, eyes burning with intensity. "And put it on you," He seethes, his grip tightening on my chin. "I want my commitment to you to be equal to my commitment to God, Eden." Roman whispers, his voice trembling with raw emotion. He pries his finger free from the band, holding it in front of my outstretched hand. "I will kiss the ground you walk on, Eden Faulkner, so long as you can handle the demons that trail after me," He whispers, his breath hot against my skin. "Are you sure you can handle this?" He asks, his gaze locking onto mine, searching for any doubt.

"Slip on the damn ring, Roman," I snap, leaning in until our faces are inches apart.

Without hesitation, he slides the ring onto my finger; it feels foreign, heavy, and yet right. With a swift motion, he turns me around until my backside is flush against his chest, bending me over the desk. My pants are yanked down in one fluid motion, his hand wraps around my hair, pulling it tight.

Roman pauses, his eyes devouring the sight before him, the tension between us palpable, electric. His pants remain on, a symbol of the restraint he's barely clinging to.

"What are you—"

"I will not fuck you in the Lord's house," Roman whispers, his voice low, dangerous. "Not with my cock, at least." He reaches toward the bookshelf, his fingers curling around the marble cross, its base slender and smooth.

"Next lesson," He murmurs, glancing at the longer end of the cross. "Last time, it was six inches; this time, it's seven," He smirks, his eyes dark with desire. "Just two more inches till you're ready for me," He warns, his voice a tantalizing promise. He reaches for a small bottle on the shelf, holding it up for me to see—a vial of holy water.

With deliberate care, he pours the holy water over the cross, letting it trickle down my spine, the cool liquid running between my shoulder blades, down my back, and finally, onto my folds, where it mixes with the warmth already pooling there, my clit throbbing in anticipation.

"There," He whispers, his breath hot against my ear. "Now it's blessed," He mocks, dragging my underwear down, exposing me fully. His finger traces my warmth, slow and deliberate, teasing, his touch both a promise and a threat.

"I guess I didn't even need that, huh?" He murmurs, running the smooth end of the crucifix along my folds, teasing my entrance with its base.

"What's that safe word again, Angel?" He asks, my forehead pressed to the desk.

I bite the inside of my cheek, stifling a laugh.

"Repent, Father," I smirk, craning my head back toward him, his hand buried in my hair. "That's my safe word."

A soft sigh escapes him, a mixture of amusement and something darker, more primal. "We're going to need a whole lot of that after this."

With deliberate slowness, he slides the end of the crucifix inside me, and I let out an ungodly moan, the sound reverberating through the empty room. Roman's grip tightens, tugging my hair harder as he pushes deeper, the smooth marble stretching me in ways that make my toes curl. My body arches against the desk, my breasts pressing into the cold wood as I brace myself, feeling the solid weight of the cross fill me inch by inch.

When the horizontal crossbar hits, I gasp, the mix of pleasure and pain sending shockwaves through my body. All seven inches are buried inside me, and Roman pauses, letting me feel every inch of it before he slowly begins to drag it back out.

"Good fucking girl," Roman whispers, his voice thick with satisfaction as he watches me squirm beneath him. "Now, the fun part."

He thrusts the crucifix back into me with a force that has me crying out, my hands gripping the edges of the desk for dear life. Roman doesn't hold back, his movements quick and deliberate, driving the blessed object into me with an intensity that has my mind reeling, my body caught between heaven and hell.

"Roman," I gasp, the name falling from my lips like a prayer, my body trembling with every thrust.

"That's it, Angel," He growls, his free hand snaking around to cover my mouth, muffling my moans as he continues his relentless pace. "Take it. Take it all."

The sound of the marble sliding in and out of me, slick with my arousal, fills the room, the sensation overwhelming as Roman brings me to the brink of madness, pushing me to the very edge of what I can handle.

"Repent," I whisper against his palm, my voice barely a breath.

"Not yet," He hisses, his hand moving from my mouth to my throat, squeezing just enough to make me see stars. "Not until you scream for me."

The combination of his grip on my throat, the crucifix filling me completely, and the sheer force of his thrusts is too much. My vision blurs, the room spinning as pleasure and pain intertwine, pulling me under until I'm lost in it, my body writhing beneath his control.

"Roman!" I scream, the word ripped from my throat as the climax crashes over me, my body convulsing with the force of it, tears streaming down my face as I surrender completely to him.

"Good girl," He whispers, his voice rough with his own barely restrained desire as he slows his pace, easing the crucifix out of me inch by inch. The absence leaves me aching, empty, and yet so completely satisfied that I can hardly breathe.

Roman releases my throat, and I slump forward, my body spent, every muscle trembling from the intensity of what just happened. He takes a moment to admire his work, his hand trailing down my spine in a gesture that feels almost reverent.

"We're not done yet, Angel," He murmurs, his voice a promise of more to come as he pulls me up from the desk, turning me to face him.

Roman's eyes darken as he watches me, the challenge in my gaze daring him to push further. Without warning, he drives the crucifix back into me with a force that sends a jolt of pleasure straight through my core. I scream, the sound echoing through the room, my hands gripping the desk as the holy object moves within me, becoming slicker with each thrust. The desk rocks under the intensity, the wood creaking as Roman's pace quickens, his own gasps mixing with mine in the heated air.

"Eden," He whispers, his voice rough and filled with something raw. "God, such a pretty cunt."

He slides his fingers past my lips, and without hesitation, I bite down just enough to draw blood. The metallic taste spreads across my tongue, and the sight of his blood on my lips drives him wild. Roman's grip tightens, and he drives the crucifix into me harder, flipping me onto my back in one swift motion. My legs drape over his shoulders as he keeps the crucifix in place, my warmth wrapping around it as I writhe beneath him, completely at his mercy.

Sprawled over his desk, I stare up at him with a challenge in my eyes, my tongue slowly licking up the blood from my lips. The sight seems to ignite something darker in him, and he glances down at his nipped finger before glaring back at me, his expression a mix of lust and something more primal.

"Playing dirty?" He asks, his voice a low growl that sends shivers down my spine. My hands move toward my breasts, brushing over my nipples as I arch my back slightly, pressing myself against the desk in a way that makes his eyes narrow with hunger.

Roman's eyes darken with determination, a primal intensity that sends a shiver down my spine. He doesn't hesitate. Keeping my legs draped over his shoulders, he drives the crucifix into me with a force that steals the breath from my lungs, my back arching off the desk. The angle, with my legs elevated, brings a new, heightened pleasure, one that's as excruciating as it is ecstatic. My vision blurs with tears as the mix of pain and pleasure consumes me, my body trembling beneath his relentless grip.

"Touch yourself," Roman orders, his voice rough with command. "Touch yourself while you're getting fucked."

My hand shakes as it travels to my clit, fingers barely brushing against the sensitive nub, the small circles I draw sending shockwaves through my body. The pain grows sharper, each thrust pushing me closer to the edge, my screams echoing off the walls of the small office. Roman's free hand clamps down on my thighs, holding me in place as he continues to drive the crucifix into me, each movement bringing me closer to the breaking point.

"Roman—" I gasp, my voice faltering as my climax builds, an unstoppable force tightening low in my belly.

"Cum for me, Angel," Roman snaps, his tone leaving no room for disobedience. "Cum all over this crucifix so I can taste your pain."

The command breaks something inside me, and I let out a scream, the release crashing through me like a tidal wave. My muscles clamp down on the crucifix, my climax coating it, tears streaming down my face from the sheer intensity. Roman's hand stills, his eyes locking onto mine as he quickly pulls the crucifix free, both of us staring at the streaks of blood marring its surface.

Without a word, he brings the crucifix to his lips, licking up the mixture of blood and my release, his eyes never leaving mine. The sight sends another shiver down my spine, but there's no time to process it before Roman tosses the crucifix onto the desk, dropping to his knees between my legs. His hands drag me forward until I'm seated on the edge of the desk, his grip firm but not painful.

"Roman, what are you doing?" I whisper, my voice still shaky from the aftermath of my climax.

"Cleaning up the mess," He murmurs, his voice soft but laced with intent. "I told you, if you're good for me, you'll be rewarded."

He trails kisses up my inner thighs, his touch gentle now, a stark contrast to the roughness from before. His tongue traces a slow, deliberate path over my folds, licking up the mix of cum and blood. My hands tangle in his hair, pulling him closer as his tongue works its magic, the gentleness of his touch almost too much to bear after the brutal intensity of what came before.

Roman doesn't stop until he's cleaned every inch of me, his mouth warm and tender against my sensitive skin. When he finally stands, I'm left panting, my legs trembling with the aftershocks of pleasure. There's a smear of blood on his bottom lip, and before he can speak, I pull him toward me, licking the blood clean, my tongue tracing the curve of his lip.

He responds instantly, capturing my lips in a kiss that's as desperate as it is consuming. Our blood mingles together, a stark reminder of the brutal pleasure we've just shared. I wrap my legs around his waist, pulling him closer, needing the solid weight of him against me as I come down from the high.

Kissing until there's no air left between us, I finally pull back, my eyes flicking to the bloodied crucifix on the desk. "Will that be enough to convince him?" I ask, my voice barely above a whisper.

"I have no clue," He whispers, the weight of uncertainty heavy between us. Roman's expression darkens as he glances at the lit-up screen of my phone, several texts from Luca and Zoey coming through, breaking the momentary calm that had settled over us. His hand tightens on my hip as he shakes his head slowly.

His fingers glide over my phone, his eyes narrowing as he deletes the messages from Luca with a low growl. "What I do know is that little shit Luca is on thin ice. But, regrettably, he might prove to be useful."

"How so?" I ask, leaning closer, my nose brushing against his as I wait for his answer.

"Hard for your father to believe you're involved with me if you're dating Luca," He whispers, lifting me back onto the desk. His hands move with surprising tenderness as he helps me slip into the flannel, carefully buttoning it up over my chest.

"I'm not dating Luca—"

"I know that. I would have killed him if that were the case," Roman says, almost too casually, before his eyes meet mine, realization flickering across his face.

"Does that bother you?" He asks, his voice softening, his hands resting on my thighs. "I meant it."

"I know," I whisper, brushing his hair back. "Your darkness doesn't scare me, Roman. I've been surrounded by shadows my whole life—my father, this twisted version of the church, everything. I've learned to live with it, even find comfort in it. That's why I haven't let Luca get too close. I knew you'd react this way, and honestly? I've accepted that. You're not the only one who's willing to walk the line between light and dark."

Roman's eyes narrow, the anger and something deeper flickering within them. He tightens his grip on my thighs. "Has he touched you?" He asks, his voice low and dangerous.

"We've kissed," I murmur, feeling the tension in his fingers increase. "But, to make you feel better," I continue, slipping his ring back onto my finger, "he'll never get this."

Without giving him time to respond, I grab his shoulder and push him down into the office chair, his confusion evident as I turn away from him. I reach for his phone on the desk, pulling the flannel back over my head before straddling his lap, my back pressed against his chest. I drag his hands up to my breasts, urging him to cup them firmly.

"Eden—"

"Quiet, Roman," I whisper, opening the camera on his phone, my body shielding his face from the lens.

I snap several photos, capturing the way his hands touch me possessively, our faces hidden, but the intimacy of the moment is there.

Turning around to face him, I pull the flannel back on, my legs running across his lap as he holds me, his expression a mix of frustration and something else—something almost tender. I show him the photos, and to my surprise, a faint blush creeps over his cheeks.

"So the moment lasts longer," I whisper.

I tuck the phone into his pocket, my hand grazing over still-hard cock, feeling the heat of him through his pants. "I'm done with the lessons Roman," I hiss. "Next time, I want the real thing."

Sliding off his lap, I grab my pants and underwear, slipping them on while he watches, his face caught between confusion and disbelief.

"Where are you going?" He asks, his voice edged with something close to desperation.

"To a dinner date," I sigh, straightening my clothes, letting my eyes roam over him one last time.

"Not something we can do right now, but we should change that," I tease, throwing him a playful smirk.

"What? Go on a date?" He questions, his eyes narrowing with suspicion. "Priests don't date."

"Oh, really? Well, I guess you'll be the first," I warn, giving him a pointed look. "Otherwise, I'm fucking Luca."

His eyes widen in shock, his mouth dropping open as he stares at me.

"God bless you, Father," I mock, smirking as I head for the door. "Consider that payback for slapping the shit out of me."

I step out of the room, leaving him to think about the choice I've given him. Whatever he does next will tell me everything I need to know—how much of this is physical and how much of it is real.

I make my way to my car, my heart pounding in my chest. Once inside, I quickly send a text to Luca and Zoey, my fingers shaking from adrenaline.

Just as I'm about to start the engine, my phone buzzes with a new message.

R: My place. Tomorrow evening. Well, after the trick-or-treaters have gone to sleep. You want a proper date? Fine. You'll be staggering into November.

A smirk tugs at my lips as I pull up the calendar on my phone. Tomorrow is Halloween.

The Devil's Night.

Hebrews 12:28 (NIV): "Therefore, since we are receiving a kingdom that cannot be shaken, let us be thankful, and so worship God acceptably with reverence and awe."

Chapter 22

EDEN

"What the hell is that?" I ask, staring at the Halloween costume Zoey had picked out for me at Spirit Halloween.

"Oh God," Luca sighs, covering his face with his hands, while Aiden stops the slow rock of Zoey's chair to get a good look at the ensemble she's holding up.

"It's a sexy nun," Zoey says proudly, lifting the skimpy costume with a grin that makes me want to disappear into the floor.

"Aiden is going as Clyde, I'm going as Bonnie, and Luca can go as—"

"If you say a priest, Zo, I'm going to vomit," Luca interrupts, his hand resting on my thigh. My nails dig into my palm, resisting the urge to brush his hand away.

Roman's words echo in my mind. Play along with the idea that Luca and I are something close to exclusive, and it'll keep my father's suspicions at bay.

I give Luca's hand a small squeeze, ignoring the buzzing of my phone, undoubtedly more texts from Roman. After yesterday, I peered out my window before bed and saw Roman's 4-Runner parked outside, just as he promised. The sense of safety his presence gives me is something I can't shake, no matter how much I try to convince myself otherwise.

"So, where do your parents think you are tonight?" Zoey asks, as her mother laughs at a rerun of *Friends* in the background.

Roman called last night to explain Seth's involvement with my father, painting him as an even bigger monster than I could have imagined. When Zoey said she was staying with her mom tonight, I jumped at the chance to be away from home.

"Actually," Aiden says with a grin, "he thinks we're trick-or-treating with Luca." Zoey's nose wrinkles at that.

"Like, actually trick-or-treating? At our age?" She laughs, giving us all a once-over.

"He thinks we're handing out candy," Aiden adds, but his voice falters, and I catch the unease in his eyes. The mention of my father makes my stomach churn. It's not just about the lies we're telling him; it's about the darkness that lurks beneath every interaction with that man.

Zoey, ever oblivious to the weight hanging over us, just grins wider. "Well, it's one night to forget about all that, right? Let's just have fun and be stupid for once."

Fun. Stupid. I can't even remember what that feels like. But tonight, I'm supposed to pretend. I'm supposed to wear this ridiculous costume, sip cheap drinks, and laugh at dumb jokes. I'm supposed to act like Luca's hand on my thigh doesn't make my skin crawl because that's the role I've been cast in tonight.

I force a smile and take the costume from Zoey, holding it up in front of me. "You're evil, you know that?"

Zoey laughs, tossing her hair over her shoulder. "You'll thank me later when every guy at the party is drooling over you."

"Right," I mutter, though the idea of anyone other than Roman looking at me like that makes my stomach twist. I sneak a glance at my phone again, the notifications from Roman piling up. But I can't deal with that right now.

Luca leans in closer, his breath warm on my cheek. "You'll definitely turn some heads," He murmurs, his hand sliding a little higher on my thigh. The gesture should make me feel something—anything—but it only reminds me of how different his touch is from Roman's.

I shift away slightly, masking the movement as reaching for my phone. "I should probably let my mom know we're leaving soon," I lie, needing an excuse to break the tension building in the room. Luca's attention is starting to feel suffocating, and I don't want to deal with it right now.

Zoey, blissfully unaware, just nods. "Alright, but we need to leave in ten. I don't want to miss out on the good drinks before they're gone."

As I turn away to "text" my mom, I can't help but glance at the message notification that's still glowing on my phone. It's Roman, as I expected. But instead of opening it, I shove the phone back into my pocket. Tonight, I'll play the part Zoey's laid out for me. I'll be the sexy nun, the carefree teenager at a Halloween party.

But Roman's shadow looms large over everything I do, and I can't escape the feeling that this night is going to be anything but normal.

I close my eyes and count to ten, jerking my arm away from Luca when his fingers graze my scars.

"Sorry," I whisper instinctively, snapping my eyes open to his downcast expression. "I'm still getting used to... touch."

Your touch. I'm still getting used to your touch.

"You're fine, Eden," He murmurs, giving me a reassuring nudge, but the slight tremor in his voice betrays his hurt. It makes me want to reach out and smooth things over, but I just can't. Not right now.

"So, if we're not handing out candy, what are we really doing?" Aiden asks, his tone a mix of curiosity and apprehension.

Luca grins, a mischievous spark in his eyes as he reaches into his bag, pulling out two large flasks. The sight of them fills the room with an unexpected tension, a reminder that we're not kids anymore, that tonight is a step into something darker, something more dangerous.

"We're going to a party," He says, his voice laced with excitement. "And we're doing it in style."

Zoey cheers, grabbing one of the flasks from Luca's hand, her enthusiasm infectious but almost oblivious to the undercurrents in the room. "Finally, something fun!" She exclaims, already unscrewing the cap and taking a swig.

But I can't shake the unease that settles in my chest. The party, the costumes, the alcohol—it all feels like a distraction, a way to forget about everything weighing on my shoulders. But Roman's presence lingers in the back of my mind, and I know he wouldn't approve of this. Not the drinking, not the party, and definitely not the way Luca's hand seems to keep finding its way back to my thigh.

I force a smile as Luca passes me the other flask, the metal cool and heavy in my hand. "What's in it?" I ask, twisting the cap off and giving it a cautious sniff.

"Something strong enough to make you forget about everything," Luca winks, his tone playful, but there's something darker hidden beneath his words.

Forget everything. If only it were that easy.

"Here's to forgetting, then," I say, raising the flask in a mock toast before taking a small sip. The liquid burns its way down my throat, and I try to ignore the way my heart skips a beat at the taste of rebellion.

Aiden looks at me, concern flickering in his eyes, but he doesn't say anything. He's always been the one to look out for me, to worry when I do things that feel out of character. But tonight, he's letting it slide, maybe because he needs this escape just as much as I do.

"Come on," Zoey says, tugging on my arm with a grin. "Let's get out of here before your mom decides to call and check in on us."

I nod, sliding my phone back into my pocket, hoping the messages from Roman don't pop up while Luca or Aiden are watching. "Yeah, let's go," I say, my voice steadier than I feel.

As we head out, I can't help but glance back at the house, my stomach twisting in knots. The flask in my hand feels heavier with every step, the night ahead promising more than just a simple Halloween party. It's a night that could change every-thing—one way or another.

After hurriedly throwing together Luca's pirate costume and squeezing into Zoey's risqué nun outfit, the cold air brushes against my exposed skin. The thin white fabric barely covers my thighs, and the white fishnet stockings do little to keep me warm. My hair is curled, a white veil perched on my head, and my lips are painted in a deep red lipstick that matches the cross around my neck. Luca's eyes linger on my body, and I feel my cheeks flush with heat.

"Oh, stop it, Eden, you look sexy," Zoey smiles, her short black bob and white shirt the tamest parts of her outfit. Her push-up bra accentuates her already perfect figure, and her ripped black jeans show off her curves in all the right places.

"Can you imagine if our dad saw me like this?" I say, catching Aiden's gaze as he finally looks my way.

"I think he'd kill you, then kill me for letting you wear it," Aiden sighs, his outfit making him look like a young mobster. Zoey did a fantastic job styling his hair.

"He won't yell at you while I'm here," Luca says proudly, still unaware of the true extent of my father's wrath.

We pull up to the party house, the loud music already blaring through the neighborhood. The tall, pointed roof of the cathe-dral is visible just a few blocks away. The front lawn is scattered with people clutching red solo cups, some already sprawled out on the grass.

"This is fun?" I ask, the smell of alcohol and poor decisions hitting me like a wave.

"This is what normal is supposed to look like, Eden," Zoey says with excitement, linking her arm with mine. "One night of pretending we don't have the most insanely religious parents." She laughs, sliding out of the back seat. My phone buzzes again between my breasts, but I ignore it.

Aiden and Zoey are already making their way up the front lawn, eager to join the chaos.

"Whose place is this, anyway?" I ask Luca, who's still sitting in the driver's seat.

"One of my buddies from school. He didn't finish his last semester, so he's doing trade school locally. His parents are on vacation, so he's got the place to himself."

I watch as someone pukes over the railing of the deck and raise an eyebrow at Luca.

"Clearly, they made a good choice," I say sarcastically, my phone screen lighting up again.

"You're popular tonight," Luca smiles, but my heart sinks when I see three missed calls from Roman. That can't be good.

My thumb hovers over the screen, the temptation to call him back gnawing at me, but I tuck the phone under my thigh instead, forcing a smile at Luca.

"It's just my mom," I lie, tucking the phone under my thigh. "She's drunk," I add with a forced smile, but Luca's eyes stay fixed on my lips.

"So, are you ready to—"

Before I can finish, Luca suddenly leans over the center armrest, cups my face, and kisses me. His lips are warm, but the
lipstick smears, and I instinctively pull away, covering my mouth
with my hand.

"Luca, I'm sorry, I just—"

"What are we doing here, Eden?" He interrupts, his voice
tinged with frustration. He keeps his gaze forward, not looking
at me.

"What—"

"You drag me along to spend time with your parents and
friends, but every time we're alone, it's like you resent me touching you."

"I've explained it to you, Luca. A lot of messed up things
happened to me at school that I'm still trying to come to terms
with—"

"Are you sure none of it has to do with a certain priest?" He
challenges, Roman's name clearly hovering on the edge of his
words.

"Luca. I told you, what happened between you and Father
Briar was because of my dad," I whisper, reaching out to him in
an attempt to reassure him.

But he grabs my wrist, his eyes dark with something that
looked like obsessive anger. "I looked at your phone while you
were changing, Eden. Roman Briar has been trying to reach you
all night. Tell me why the hell he needs to talk to you when your
dad has no reason to worry about what you're doing," Luca says,
his grip tightening around my wrist, his voice trembling slightly.

"You looked at my phone?" I ask, dread tightening in my chest,
the image I sent Roman flashing in my mind.

"Only what was on the screen," Luca mutters, avoiding my eyes. "I even answered once. The line went dead silent when he heard my voice."

"What... what did he say?" I ask, the pit in my stomach growing deeper.

"He said your name. Then, when he heard my voice, he went quiet," Luca snaps, his jaw clenched tight with anger. "Is Father Briar manipulating you, Eden? Getting you to do things—"

I can't let him finish that sentence. Without thinking, I move over the center armrest, crawling into his lap, desperate to shut him up. My hands grasp his cheeks, and the skirt of my costume hikes up, leaving nothing but fishnets and my lace panties between us.

"This is what I want," I whisper urgently, my heart racing. "My dad asked Roman to keep a close eye on me. When he heard your voice, I'm sure he assumed I was doing something I shouldn't be," I lie, my stomach twisting as I feel Luca harden beneath me.

"So now, he's probably freaking out. He'll tell my dad you answered, and I'll deal with it later," I continue, my voice soft but firm. "So stop overthinking, and at least make the punishment I'll get when I get home worth it."

I press my lips to his, silencing him with a kiss that lingers longer than it should. His hands find my waist, pulling me closer, and his tongue slips into my mouth, tasting like toothpaste and vodka. His grip tightens, bruising my skin as he kisses me until I can't breathe.

"Luca, that hurts," I mumble against his lips, but he doesn't stop. His mouth trails down to my chest, and he clamps down on my breast with his teeth, muffling my scream with his hand.

"I thought you liked it rough, Eden." He growls, panic rising in my chest.

He's really fucking drunk.

Yanking me back toward him, he kisses me again, but I can't breathe. My side and breast throb, and I try to pull away.

Someone bangs on his truck, forcing him to stop, his too-tight grip finally ebbing from my sides.

"Get it, sister!"

He wipes the smudged lipstick off my face. "Fucking sexy as hell," He mutters, nudging me off his lap. "But not convincing enough."

I land back in the passenger seat, staring at him in disbelief as he slams the door shut and heads toward Zoey and Aiden.

Shaking, I try to process what just happened. My hands fumble for my phone as it lights up again. This time, I answer quickly, my voice trembling.

"Luca, you little fu—"

"Roman?" I whisper, fighting back sobs. "Are you home?"

"Eden?" Roman's voice cuts through, sharp and concerned. "What's going on?"

Words are lost to me as I try to suck in air but fail miserably.

"Is it Luca? What did he do?" Roman's voice is gentle, but edged with tension.

"I tried to convince him like you said," I sob, my words tumbling out. "And he grabbed me, wrapped his hand around my throat—"

"Where are you?" Roman's voice tightens, the sound of music growing louder in the background.

"Some fucking house party," I sniffle, glancing at Saint Michael's behind my shoulder. "I could walk to you and be there sooner—"

"No!" He exclaims, panic clear in his tone. "Stay where you are. Are you in a car?"

"Luca's," I sob. "But I don't know when he'll—"

"Lock the door, Angel. I'll come get you as soon as I'm done handling some things," He says, his voice cryptic and urgent.

"Roman, don't make a scene with Luca—"

"I'll handle him another time. Right now, my only focus is getting you safe," He says firmly. "Do you trust me, Eden?"

His question hangs in the air, and I bite my lip before whispering, "Yes."

"Then stay put, and I'll be there soon. Thirty minutes. Don't you dare leave. For the love of God, Eden, listen to me."

"Fine," I lie, trying to sound convincing. "I won't leave this truck."

He breathes a sigh of relief before clearing his throat. "Why are you even at that party?"

"Zoey made me. She bought this ridiculous costume, and half the party is puking on the lawn—"

A loud knock on his end cuts me off. "I have to go," Roman says abruptly, and the line goes dead.

My phone's screen darkens, leaving me alone with my thoughts. Before I can gather myself, Aiden's voice shouts my name, his hand banging on the window.

Opening the door, I meet Aiden's confused gaze. "What the hell are you still doing in here? Luca is pounding some drinks—"

His words trail off as his eyes take in my smudged makeup and tear-streaked face. "What... What's going on, Eden?" He asks again, but this time, a sob escapes my throat.

"Luca... he—"

Aiden doesn't wait for me to finish. His expression hardens as he turns on his heel, moving faster than he arrived.

Fuck. Fuck. Fuck.

I leap out of the truck, tucking my phone away as I sprint after Aiden. My heels slow me down, but I push through the crowd of drunken people, my heart pounding in my chest. I burst through the front door, shoving past people to try and get to my brother but it's too late.

"Get the fuck up!" Aiden's shout echoes through the living room.

Luca is slumped on the couch, a woman sitting next to him, her arm draped over his shoulder. My lipstick is still smeared across his face, a glaring reminder of what just happened. Zoey, who had been mid-throw in a game of beer pong, stops and looks at me with confusion.

"What's this about, Aiden—"

"I said get up," Aiden shouts, grabbing Luca by the front of his shirt and hauling him to his feet. "And apologize to my sister for fucking groping her in the car because you aren't man enough to try that shit in front of me."

Luca stumbles, his eyes widening in surprise as he looks between Aiden and me. "Grope her?" He scoffs, pushing Aiden's hands off him. "She came onto me. I was just trying to talk to her, and she started dry-humping my lap seconds later—"

"Bullshit," Aiden snaps, getting in Luca's face. "I wanted to believe all those rumors about you being a jackass were fake, but clearly," Aiden sneers, wiping my smeared lipstick off Luca's face with the back of his hand, "given you're coated in my sister's makeup and she's been crying, you're a fucking liar."

"Is that true, Luca?" One of the boys in the crowd of people asks, giving me a sideways glance. "Did he pull some shit with you—"

"Oh, don't fucking ask her," Luca snaps, his words slurring. "She's a fucking sneaky whore," he slurs, waving his finger up and down at me. "And clearly loves the attention."

The room goes silent, all eyes snapping to me. Aiden and Zoey look bewildered, and anger burns in my chest.

Ignoring the whispers, I take a step toward Luca, pushing Aiden gently to the side. Luca meets my gaze, his eyebrows raised in a taunt.

"Maybe I am a fucking whore," I hiss, my voice low and venomous. "Maybe I'm not. Either way—"

I drive my hand across his face. The slap echoes through the room, and Luca staggers back, crashing into the couch behind him.

Both Aiden and Zoey stare at me, wide-eyed, as the room erupts in shouts and whistles. Some of the men at the party pull out their phones to record, but Zoey is quick to make them put them down.

I take a step back, my heart racing, anger still coursing through my veins. I let the noise of the party fade into the background as

I turn on my heel and walk out of the house, my feet moving on autopilot.

As I step outside, the cold night air hits me, and I spot the tall, pointed roof of the cathedral in the distance. My mind is a whirlwind, but one thing is clear—I need to get away.

I drag a small, sharp rock across the side of Luca's truck as I pass by, the screech of metal on metal a small, satisfying revenge. I don't stop to look back as I make my way into the night, my mind already miles away from this place.

Chapter 23

Eden

Whoever invented heels clearly didn't consider how humiliating it is to walk down a dark sidewalk in the middle of the night, constantly pulling down your skirt as trick-or-treaters pass by.

My feet burn with each step, but I keep going, my phone turned off to prevent anyone from tracking me. Zoey and Aiden didn't have time to follow me, so the first block felt like a marathon, and now the final block feels like it's stretching on forever.

When I finally see Roman's house, candles flicker in the windows, casting a warm glow. Two cars are parked in the driveway—his 4Runner and a car I don't recognize.

The door is slightly ajar, which is odd because Roman is always so careful about locking up.

I step inside quietly, the candles providing the only light. The rich aroma of food fills the air, drawing my eyes to the dining table, which is set for two, fresh roses in the center, surrounded by candles. Food sits on the oven, some Chinese takeout from the looks of the to-go containers.

Is this for our date?

A smile tugs at my lips, but it quickly fades when I hear a loud thud, followed by Roman's angry voice.

"Wrong fucking answer," He hisses, followed by a deep, stifled groan of pain.

My heart races as I inch forward silently.

"Let's try this again," Roman's voice promises violence as he continues to speak. "What the fuck does David Faulkner know about Eden and me? And what should I know about that little shit Luca?"

Another scream tears through the air, and I freeze outside the door, steeling myself for what I'm about to see.

I push the door open slightly, and Seth's eyes lock onto mine. My hand flies to my mouth to stifle a scream.

Roman stands over Seth, a knife in his hand dripping with blood. Seth is sprawled on a plastic tarp, his hands bound and his mouth covered with tape, open wounds scattered over his flesh.

Jesus Christ.

Roman's ring and cross sit on a nearby desk, next to a glass of scotch, but it looks untouched.

"Did I say you could look away from me?" Roman snaps, grabbing Seth's chin and forcing him to look back at him. He's too focused on Seth to notice me yet.

"If I rip this tape off your mouth again, you better tell me everything you know, and next time I tell you to come over, you better not give me any fucking lip."

He rips the tape from Seth's mouth, and Seth gasps for air, his eyes pleading with me.

"Eden," Seth wheezes, his voice strained. "Please, call for help."

Roman finally notices me, his eyes widening as he takes in what I'm wearing. His gaze travels from my eyes to the teeth marks on my breast and back up to the smeared makeup on my face.

"Why are you here, Seth?" I ask, my voice cold and detached.

"Father Briar is insane, please, my sweet Eden—"

"Don't fucking call her that," Roman snaps, pressing his foot into Seth's chest, keeping him pinned down. "You nasty fucking pig."

"He's here," Roman starts, his voice laced with contempt, "to tell me about your father and that shit stain Luca."

"I don't know anything about the kid," Seth stammers, "and I've told you everything I know about David. I'll tell you more once I find out, but please, Eden, get him off me—"

Blinded by rage, I slam the heel of my stiletto into Seth's hand, twisting it into his palm as he screams. I grab the knife from Roman, and for a moment, he looks as shocked as I feel.

"That's for Zoey," I hiss, slashing a light, straight line down Seth's thigh. He winces, and I deliver a hard slap to his face.

Roman watches in silence as I step back from Seth, the knife trembling in my grip. I hand it back to Roman, but my heart is still pounding, a mixture of adrenaline and an unsettling shadow within me. The side of me that I've fought so hard to bury—the side that craves control, that hungers for vengeance—has broken through, shattering the carefully constructed façade I've maintained for so long.

The blade felt like an extension of my anger, a way to reclaim the control that was stolen from me. After what happened in college, after my father's suffocating grip on my life, this is the first time I've held power in my hands. It's intoxicating and terrifying, yet I can't deny the satisfaction that lingers in the aftermath.

But beneath it all, there's a wound that still festers, a deep need for justice, for retribution. I'm a woman scorned, and the rage that burns within me is far from quenched. It demands more, whispers that this small act of violence isn't enough to satisfy the storm inside me.

As I move away from Seth, a part of me wonders if I'll ever be able to put this side of myself back into the box where I've kept it hidden. But another part, the part that just tasted the thrill of control, isn't sure it wants to.

"Do what you will with him, Father," I whisper, leaning close to Roman's ear. "I'll be in the bedroom."

Without another word, I leave the room, nudging the door shut behind me as I make my way to Roman's bedroom.

After thirty minutes of waiting, I finally settled into Roman's bed, sprawling across the clean sheets with my heels still on, my stomach pressed to the soft mattress. I conceal my face with the veil, my sides aching from where Luca grabbed me too hard. I turn my phone on and toss it on the nightstand, listening to the sound of Seth's grunting as he moves down the hallway.

The front door slams, and I roll onto my elbows, peering at the door as Roman enters, his eyes devouring the sight of me in the raunchy costume. He adjusts the front of his pants, his stare both brooding and craving.

"Eden," He whispers, taking a step toward the bed. "I told you to wait there. I told you not to leave."

"I know," I challenge, pressing my stiletto to his chest, stopping him from coming any closer. "I didn't listen."

His hand trails up my fishnet stockings, stopping at my thighs. "What the hell are you wearing?" He asks, the virgin white of the attire almost comedic given the circumstances.

I arch an eyebrow, a sly smile playing on my lips. "A little something to test your faith, Father. Do you think you're strong enough to resist?" I taunt, pushing his hands away from my thighs as I sit up on my knees, much like I would during Mass.

"Tell me, Father, have you ever fucked a nun?" I tease, my hand grazing his hardened length, feeling his jaw clench.

"What the hell are you doing to me, Eden?" He mutters, genuinely seeking an answer as his hands graze my ass, pulling me closer until I'm leaning into his chest with my arms wrapped around his neck.

I lock eyes with him, watching his gaze drop to my breasts.

"Were you going to kill Seth?" I ask, his head shaking slowly.

"No," He whispers, gripping my chin. "Were you?"

"Maybe," I admit, my voice soft. "Depends on how angry he made me."

Roman's thumb and pointer finger move from my chin, trailing down my neck until they settle on the bite mark Luca left on my breast.

"Did he do that?" Roman asks, his voice laced with restrained fury.

"He wrapped his hands around me," I whisper, guiding Roman's hands down my sides. "Dug his fingers into my skin while he kissed me. Then he bit me. I called you right after."

"Lie down."

"Roman—"

"Lie down, Eden, before I leave this house and tear him apart. Just lie down and let me touch you."

Obeying his command, I let my back hit the mattress, watching as Roman slowly unbuttons his shirt, each flick of his fingers deliberate as he makes his way down.

"Tonight, Eden, another man touched you," Roman whispers, his eyes raking over the costume. "Another man felt you," He adds, tugging at his belt and dragging down his fly. He grabs one of the chairs in the corner of his room and sets it in the middle of the floor, and takes a seat. His cock strains against his underwear, and my eyes marvel at his gorgeous body.

"Strip off your clothes," He demands, pointing to the spot before him. "Now."

I hesitate, but the intensity in his eyes leaves no room for doubt. Slowly, I slide off the bed, standing before him as my fingers move to the veil on my head. I pull it off, letting it drop to the floor, feeling a strange mix of vulnerability and power under his gaze.

Next, I reach for the fishnet stockings, peeling them down my legs with deliberate slowness, savoring the way his eyes darken with each inch of skin revealed. The thin dress is the last to go, sliding off my shoulders and pooling at my feet, leaving me in nothing but my lace underwear.

Roman's breath hitches, his eyes roaming over my body, taking in every curve, every inch of exposed skin. There's something possessive in his gaze, something that makes my pulse quicken with both fear and anticipation.

"Turn around," He orders, his voice low and commanding.

I do as he says, turning my back to him, feeling the weight of his eyes on me. For a moment, there's nothing but silence, then I feel his hands on my waist, warm and firm, guiding me back onto the bed. He presses me down onto the mattress, his breath hot against my ear as he leans over me.

"Tonight, Eden," He whispers, "you're mine."

His hands move with a mixture of reverence and need as he explores my body, fingers tracing the lines of my spine, the curve of my hips. Every touch ignites a fire inside me, a reminder that in this moment, I belong to him, and only him.

His hands travel lower, pulling off the lace underwear and leaving me completely bare beneath him. I can feel the tension building between us, the anticipation hanging thick in the air.

"Do you trust me, Eden?" He murmurs, his lips brushing against my shoulder.

"Yes," I breathe, my voice trembling with the weight of the moment.

"Good," He replies, his voice a mix of promise and warning. "Because tonight, I'm going to show you just how much you mean to me."

His hands grip my hips, positioning me exactly where he wants me, his touch possessive and unyielding. There's no turning back now. No more room for doubt. It's just the two of us, lost in the heat of the moment, the rest of the world forgotten.

He takes his time, savoring every inch of me, every gasp and moan that escapes my lips. As the tension between us builds to a fever pitch, I realize that this moment is about more than just physical desire—it's about power, control, and the undeniable connection that binds us together.

"Look at me, Eden," He whispers, and I turn my head to meet his gaze, his eyes intense and focused, filled with something that feels dangerously close to worship.

"Whatever happens next," He says, his voice low and steady, "remember that you belong to me."

I slide off the bed, letting my legs drape off the side as I watch him, adrenaline coursing through my veins. "What are you going to do to me, Roman?" I ask, nerves sending goosebumps down my spine.

"I'm going to fuck you, Eden," He states, his gaze intense. "And you're going to take it like a good fucking girl."

Nodding his head, he motions me closer. "Now, come here, Angel."

My heels click against the floor as I cautiously approach him, my earlier boldness wavering. "And Seth?" I ask, now mere inches from him.

"He won't say a word, baby. Now, let me see it all."

Swallowing hard, I focus on Roman's steady gaze and his empty ring finger. I raise my leg, placing my stiletto on his thigh, and slowly slip it off, sliding my stocking off before moving to the other foot. I repeat the process, turning around and bending over to drag the other stocking and my underwear down in one smooth motion, offering Roman a view to test his restraint. When I turn back to face him, his hand is already fisting his cock through his underwear, his eyes consuming every inch of me.

"Should I keep going, Father?" I ask, my voice dripping with provocation.

"Keep going, Eden," He commands, his voice authoritative. "Do exactly as I say."

I inch closer, gripping the sides of the chair near his head. "How I see it, Roman, your cock is straining against your boxers, desperate to be buried inside me. So, Roman, tell me, who's really in control –"

My words are cut off as Roman grabs me, shoving me onto the bed, and slaps my ass. I gasp, a mix of pain and relief coursing through me as he undoes my bra, finally freeing my aching breasts. His hands are surprisingly gentle as he cups my sides, careful of the bruises, before flipping me onto my back. He kicks off his underwear, his gaze devouring me as if I were a feast laid out just for him.

His fingers slide between my legs, finding me already slick with need. He covers my mouth as he plunges two fingers deep inside me. The force of his thrusts makes my breasts bounce, and I bite down on his hand to stifle the moans that threaten to escape as he curls his fingers inside me.

"You like taking me like this, Angel?" He murmurs, his voice dark and intoxicating. "Or would you rather it be my cock that fills you up?" He taunts, his words sending shivers down my spine.

He pulls his fingers away, moving toward one of the candles lit on his dresser, the flames flickering in the dim light.

"I was going to treat you to dinner. Be a proper gentleman," He whispers, grabbing the candle. "But then you showed up wearing that, so full of violence... You've earned what I'm about to do to you."

Setting the candle on the nightstand, he flips me onto my stomach again, the sound of his pants dropping both thrilling and unnerving.

"Raise your hips for me, Angel," He mutters, guiding me onto my hands and knees. "If you scream, I'll drip this wax down your back and only go harder," He warns, his tip now running teasingly along my folds.

He rubs his tip against my entrance, and a needy whimper escapes me. Roman raises his brows, just as shocked at the noise as I am.

"Did you just whimper for my cock?"

"Yes, Father," I whisper.

I grip the sheets, biting back the moan of pleasure as he starts easing himself inside me.

"Three inches," He whispers, pushing his hips forward, sliding through the wetness, my pussy gripping him, urging him in deeper.

"Six," He pushes, the sensation of him filling me sending chills down my spine.

Holy hell, how much of this can I take?

He pauses, moaning next to my ear, the sound coaxing me to spread my legs wider for him.

"You're doing so good," He praises, pushing farther. "Seven, eight—" He continues, and my stomach feels like he's buried himself completely within me. "One more," He whispers, my teeth sinking into the sheets. He makes one final thrust, his lower stomach pressing against my ass as he buries himself fully inside me.

"Do you feel how well your pretty pussy is taking my—"

An uncontrolled scream of pleasure escapes me. He pauses.

Fuck.

"I told you what would happen if you screamed, Eden," He growls.

Hot wax drips down my spine, and I arch my back, hissing at the sharp, stinging sensation. Roman smacks my ass, and his hips thrust aggressively, driving into me so hard that the air is knocked from my chest. He winds my hair around his fist, forcing me upright as he grabs my wrists with his other hand, holding them behind my back. His cock pounds into me relentlessly, my legs on the verge of giving out.

Roman groans, my wetness dripping down my inner thighs, my voice reduced to breathy gasps. "Just like that, Eden. Take my cock like a good girl. This is what God desires, every sin, every surrender, give yourself to the pleasure He's ordained for you."

He releases my hair, and I slump forward, his hands still holding my wrists behind my back.

"Roman," I moan, my voice filled with desperate need.

"Louder, let everyone hear it."

"Fucking Roman," I scream, the pleasure mounting as I feel him hit deeper inside me.

"Who's fucking you, Eden?" He questions, the warmth in my stomach growing unbearable.

"You are," I gasp, looking back at him, my hair sticking to my lipstick.

"And whose pretty pussy is going to be filled with my cum?" he groans, the twitch of his cock igniting something deep inside me.

"Mine," I hiss. "Fucking mine—"

His release fills me, his hands clutching my hips as we both become a mess of inaudible moans. Roman continues to rock his hips, drawing out the sensation, until he slowly pulls out of me, letting me flip onto my back. His eyes devour the sight of me sprawled on his bed, his cum gently spilling from my center.

Roman runs a finger over my folds, marveling at his work before taking a seat on the bed. His hand moves to his still-hard cock.

"Roman—"

"You're not done, beautiful. Come get in my lap and ride me," He demands, his voice low and commanding.

I comply, dragging myself over to him, wrapping my arms around his neck as he carefully guides me onto his lap, his cock sliding back inside me. His hands push my hips down, making me take all of him in one quick motion.

"Just like that, Angel," He whispers, our foreheads pressed together. "Now keep rocking those hips—"

We're both startled as my phone's ringtone cuts through the air. I glance at the nightstand, seeing Zoey's face on the screen. Roman reaches over and grabs the phone, keeping himself buried in me.

When I move to get off him, he forces me back down, placing the phone in my hand.

"Answer it," He whispers. "And talk to her while you're riding my cock."

A million thoughts race through my mind, but I press the answer button and put the phone on speaker.

"H-Hello—" I stammer, trying to keep my voice steady as Roman rocks my hips for me. The restraint it takes to hold back my moan nearly drives me insane.

"Thank God, Eden. Aiden and I have been so worried. Fucking Luca vomited all over the lawn and was a sobbing mess. Where are you—"

"Is that Eden?" Luca yells in the background, his words slurring.

Roman's grasp tightens. His mouth gravitates toward my breasts.

"Get your fucking hands off my phone—"

"Eden?" Luca's voice is filled with regret and confusion, but I can barely focus on it as Roman's tongue swirls over my nipple and then sucks the delicate skin into his mouth.

"Mmm-mhm," I force out, my voice betraying a mix of a moan.

"Oh, Jesus, Eden, I'm sorry. I don't know what came over me when I touched you like that—"

Roman bites my nipple, and I let out a gasp, leaning into him as my legs shake uncontrollably.

"Keep going," Roman whispers, guiding my hips as he moves his mouth to the other breast, his hand massaging the one he'd bitten.

"You're a fucking a-asshole, Luca," I whisper, marveling at the sight of Roman dragging his tongue across my skin. "I don't need you—"

"Where are you, Eden—"

"Someplace I should have been all along," I whisper. "Lose my fucking number."

"Wait, Eden—" Luca's voice pleads, but I end the call and toss the phone to the floor. I grab Roman's chin, pulling him away from my breasts, and latch my lips to his, devouring him in a hungry kiss.

"Did you mean what you said?" He questions between kisses. "Do you feel like you should have been here with me all along?"

Pausing, I press my forehead to his, our breaths mingling.

"What does it mean if I say no?" I ask, his voice shaky.

"That this is... this is purely physical. Emotions aren't involved."

"And if I say yes?"

"Then things are much more complicated than I could have anticipated."

I stare into his eyes, the intensity between us palpable.

"Then things are complicated, Roman, and that's fine by me."

He says nothing, only cups my face and gives me hard, passionate kisses. I ride him until we're both convulsing from release once more.

As the evening fades into dusk, Roman pulls me into his arms, a sense of peace washing over me. In his embrace, I feel a rare safety, as if this is where I've always belonged—right here, where even God would smile upon us, knowing I've finally found my sanctuary.

Proverbs 5:19: "A loving doe, a graceful deer— may her breasts satisfy you always, may you ever be intoxicated with her love."

Chapter 24

EDEN

Reaching my arms out in a large stretch, I feel around for Roman, my fingers meeting only the cool, empty space next to me. Confused, I pry open my eyes, wincing at the soreness that radiates through my body. Last night's passion has left its mark, every muscle aching, my core throbbing as if it had been ripped apart and sewn back together.

I reach for my phone, still off from the night before, knowing that the countless messages from my brother and Zoey are waiting in my inbox. The early morning light filters through the room, painting the space in soft hues that remind me of the stained-glass windows in the church, the ones that catch the sun just right.

Sliding off Roman's bed, I wince slightly as my feet hit the floor, the soreness making every movement clumsy and torturous. I rummage through his drawer, finding one of his larger tees, the fabric soft and comforting against my skin as I slip it on. The familiar scent of him clings to the cotton, a mix of sandalwood and something darker that sends a shiver down my spine.

Nudging open the bathroom door, the remnants of his recent shower linger in the air, steam clings to the mirror like a memory. I wipe away the condensation with the back of my hand, my reflection coming into focus—disheveled, raw, my makeup smudged from the night's intensity. My eyes trace the faint bite marks along my neck and the way my hair falls in tangled waves over my shoulders. I look like a woman who's been thoroughly claimed, a thought that sends a flush of heat through me.

Peering down, I notice a new toothbrush resting on the counter, along with a bottle of face wash that I know costs more than two of my paychecks combined. Next to them, a note catches my eye. I pick it up, a smile tugging at my lips as I read the familiar scrawl.

Don't rush. You had a long night.

—R

"Oh, Roman," I murmur to myself, the smile growing wider despite the ache in my heart.

Don't make me fall for your good side too.

But as I stand there, wrapped in his shirt, surrounded by the scent and feel of him, I can't help but feel that something has shifted. What we shared last night—it wasn't just physical. It was a turning point, a moment where everything changed. And as much as I want to deny it, to push it away, I know that the line between us has blurred in ways that can't be undone.

With a deep breath, I turn to the sink, the cool water splashing onto my face, washing away the remnants of last night's makeup and some of the lingering doubts. But as I look up at my reflection again, I realize that what's left behind is something new—a woman who's seen another side of herself, of Roman, and who's not entirely sure what to do with that knowledge.

After washing my face and feeling somewhat more like myself, I step into the hallway, the rich smell of bacon drifting through the air. I take my time, pausing to study the few photos Roman has on the wall. My fingers brush lightly over a picture of him with his unit in the army—his face rugged, dusted with stubble and dirt. He's grinning widely, arms slung around the necks of his fellow soldiers, all of them beaming with a camaraderie that's palpable even through the photograph.

I move to the next photo, a stark contrast to the first. It's less exuberant, more tender. A beautiful woman with short hair covered by a pink bandana holds the hands of a young boy with jet-black hair, helping him walk. They're both laughing, a peacefulness in their expressions that suggests the moment is something that should be cherished.

I gently take the picture from the wall, unable to tear my eyes away as I make my way into the kitchen.

Roman stands at the stove, shirtless, his broad back facing me. A large mug of coffee sits on the counter, and the table is set for two, with a spread of breakfast items hot and ready. I can't help but notice the faint marks my nails left on his skin, a reminder of the intensity of the night before.

"Morning, Angel," He says with a warm smile, turning to face me. His gaze immediately drops to the frame in my hand.

"I—I'm sorry, I just loved the picture—" I begin, feeling a bit sheepish.

"She was a bright soul," He interrupts, turning off the stove before leaning against the counter. "You would have never known she had cancer."

"This is—" I start again, but he finishes the thought for me.

"My mom," He says softly, walking over to me.

He takes the frame from my hands, his fingers lingering over the image, especially on her bright, radiant smile. "She beat cancer more than once. I was always convinced my father's abuse is what kept her from overcoming it a third time," he sighs, his eyebrows furrowing as he gets lost in the memory.

"That's you?" I ask, tracing the image of the young boy in the photo with my finger.

"Surprised I was so cute?" He teases, placing the frame down on the counter.

Wrapping his arms around my waist, he pulls me close. I loop my arms around his neck, leaning into the warmth of his body. His lips brush lightly against mine in a tender kiss, soft and gentle, filled with a kind of sweetness that feels new between us.

"Do you miss her?" I ask, resting my forehead against his.

"All the time," He admits, his voice barely above a whisper. "It's why I chose to believe there was a Heaven to begin with and swore my life to find a way to meet her there one day." There's a vulnerability in his words, a glimpse into the heart of Roman Briar that I hadn't fully seen before.

"And how are you feeling, by the way?" He asks, a playful smirk tugging at the corners of his lips, shifting the mood.

The change is almost tangible, and I can't help but smile back, knowing exactly what he's referring to.

"Like we got in a fight rather than fucked," I admit, feeling the soreness in every muscle.

Roman grins and grabs my ass, lifting me onto the counter. His hands trail possessively under the shirt I borrowed, mapping out every inch of me.

"You'll have to get used to that feeling if you want to keep 'dating' me," He murmurs, though his expression twists slightly at the word "date."

"So we're dating now?" I tease. "You haven't even asked."

"Date is such a harsh word," He mutters, the weight of his faith still tugging at him. "But if anyone else touched you as I did, they'd quickly find out just how real God is," He growls, pressing his lips to my neck. I frown as I feel the cold metal of his ring brush against my skin.

"You put your ring back on," I whisper, disappointment lacing my tone.

"You sound upset," He replies, pulling back just enough to look at me, his hands still framing my hips.

"When you wear that ring, what does it mean to you?" I ask, placing my hands on his chest. "Could you walk out in public with it on and still hold my hand?" His jaw tightens.

"Eden, when I wear this ring, it signifies my commitment to something greater than myself. Here, in the privacy of my home, I can ask for forgiveness. But in the church, all I feel is the weight of judgment from above."

"So take it off and don't put it back on," I challenge. "Keep the ring off."

Roman steps back, shaking his head. "I can't do that, Eden," He sighs, rubbing his temple. "I can't abandon the one thing that's made me believe I deserve more than just suffering," He pleads, and I cross my arms over my chest, trying to mask the sting of his words.

"So you and me? What is this to you?" I ask, dreading his answer.

"You're not a sin, Eden," He whispers, his voice softening. "You're a blessing, something I never expected but can't bring myself to let go of. But even blessings come with their challenges. My commitment to God doesn't change, but that doesn't mean you're any less important to me."

His words bring a sense of warmth, but I push forward. "Is it impossible to see what we have as something more? Could it mean more than the oath you took with that ring?"

"That's the struggle," He whispers, his voice trembling. "I'm trying to find a way to honor both my faith and what I feel for you. As long as I wear the ring, it's a reminder that I can strive for both."

Watching his inner turmoil unfold, I struggle to find a way to comfort him. I pushed him into this, and now he's grappling with the consequences.

I jump down from the counter and pull him into a tight embrace, feeling a flicker of relief when he returns the hug just as firmly.

"We don't have to define anything right now, Roman. You've got me, ring or no ring. Wear it for as long as you need."

But what if he never takes it off?

What then?

Roman's hands cradle my face, pulling my gaze to meet his. The intensity in his eyes makes my breath hitch.

"I have never had anything in this life that has felt right after my mother died. I thought it was impossible to feel anything but pain until you walked into my life, and I realized keeping you safe meant more than anything else. You have sparked new life in me, Eden, and that's not something I take lightly—"

"Father Briar!" Zoey's shrill voice rings out, followed by the loud pounding on Roman's front door, cutting through the intimate moment like a knife. We both jump at the sudden intrusion.

Roman's expression shifts instantly, his usual guarded look returning as he releases me. "Did you tell her you were here?" He asks, his voice now cold and controlled.

"No," I whisper, stepping back from him. "But I have a feeling I know who did."

Zoey's voice grows more insistent, almost frantic as she pounds on the door again. "Eden, I swear, if you're in there open this door right now!"

Roman's eyes narrow as he processes the situation. "Your brother?" He asks, the tension in his voice unmistakable.

I nod reluctantly, feeling a mix of guilt and frustration. "He must have figured it out."

Before either of us can say more, the pounding on the door intensifies. Roman sighs, running a hand through his hair, clearly struggling to maintain his composure. "We'll talk about this later," He says, his tone firm but resigned.

I nod, turning toward the door. "I'll handle it," I whisper, giving him one last glance before reaching for the handle, bracing myself for whatever chaos awaits on the other side.

Trying to get ahead of me, Roman reaches for the door, but I'm just as quick, both of us clamoring to grab the handle first.

"She's my friend—" I start, but Roman cuts in.

"Your friend who is going to wonder why the hell you're here—"

We fumble for control, but Roman gets there first, nudging me behind the door as he swings it wide open. The realization that he's shirtless hits me a second too late, and I catch the faint sound of Zoey's audible gulp when her eyes land on him.

"Father Briar, I don't mean to interrupt, but..." Zoey pauses, frustration evident in her voice. "Aiden and I can't seem to find Eden, and we were wondering if she came to the church at all last night—"

Want to hide me, Roman? Then you'll have to tie me down.

"I'm right here, Zo," I announce, pushing Roman aside with a bit more force than necessary. His eyes widen slightly at my bluntness.

Clad only in Roman's oversized shirt, I see the wheels turning in Zoey's head as she draws her own conclusions.

"Holy shit, when Aiden said he thought you spent the night here, I thought he was joking," She whispers, accusations ready to spill from her lips.

"Luca pissed me off. Figured I'd get a good fuck in somewhere else," I say with a smirk, watching both Roman and Zoey freeze in shock.

"I'm kidding," I quickly add, rolling my eyes. "I was upset and lost last night and saw the church. Thankfully, Roman—Father Briar—was awake and let me stay rather than having to explain anything to my dad."

"Jesus. There you are," Aiden's voice cuts through, and I turn to see him making his way up the walkway. Roman steps further back, trying to avoid drawing attention to his shirtless state.

Looking around quickly, Roman snatches a shirt off the couch, narrowly avoiding Zoey's gaze as she attempts to peek inside, probably noticing the scratched-up state of his back.

"Are you hurt?" Aiden asks, concern lacing his voice as he steps inside, his eyes scanning me.

"Yes, please come in," Roman says dryly, doing his best to hide any evidence of what transpired last night.

"What the hell were you thinking, turning your phone off like that?" Aiden demands, shaking his head in disbelief. "And why the hell didn't you tell anyone where she was?" he snaps, directing his anger at Roman.

"She was fine, Aiden—" Roman begins, trying to keep his tone steady.

"You know, Father, it would be a real shame to find out you're preying on young, vulnerable women," Aiden spits, his voice sharp with accusation.

"Aiden," I snap, stepping between them, getting in my brother's face. "Roman didn't do anything—"

"Roman?" Aiden questions, his voice dropping to a whisper, careful not to let Zoey overhear. "I thought whatever was happening between you two was over?"

"Things have gotten complicated," I snap, my patience wearing thin. "Now, can we please fucking go before you make things even more awkward?"

I push Aiden back, my frustration boiling over as I usher him and Zoey out of the house. The tension in the air is palpable, and I can feel Roman's eyes on me, a storm of emotions barely contained behind his stoic expression.

As I reach the door, I glance back at Roman, my heart twisting with guilt. His eyes meet mine, and in that brief moment, I see the depth of his anger and the turmoil our relationship has stirred within him.

"I'll see you soon, Eden," He whispers, his voice strained, doing his best to hide the fury simmering beneath the surface. The intrusion by Aiden and Zoey has clearly hit a nerve, and I can sense the challenge that lies ahead in trying to navigate this complicated web we've woven.

Slamming the car door shut, I take a seat in the back, forcing on a pair of sweats Zoey had left in the car for after her shift at the brew.

Taking up the driver and passenger seat, the pair look back at me, waiting for me to say something.

"Well, don't both of you look delightful this morning-"

"Are you having sex with him, Eden?" Aiden questions, ripping the bandaid off as aggressively as he can.

So, we are having this conversation?

Great.

"I'm not having sex-"

"So he walks around shirtless cooking breakfast for all his altar servers that decide to spend the night?" Zoey questions, equally as off-put at my brother.

"Are you seriously both questioning me right now?" I prod, angered by their reactions.

"You ran off in the middle of a party and responded to no one for hours. Come to find out you spent the night with our priest who, news flash, you already admitted you had something going on with-"

"You told Zoey?" I snap, fully aware of how freely he is speaking in front of her.

"You think that's something I wanted to hold onto alone?" He questions. "My whole fucking life feels like one big lie just waiting to implode-"

Shaking my head, I kick Zoey's door.

"Eden-"

"I did fuck him Aiden," I hiss, both Zoey and him going deadpan. "And I loved every fucking minute of it. So you can run home, tell our dad, and see what the hell happens. Or, you can leave me the hell alone, and let me implode on my own."

Tugging up Roman's shirt, I show the pair the bruises Luca left.

"This was Luca, not Roman. If you want someone to send the witch hunt after, you're looking in the wrong place."

"Eden, that's not what we're saying," Zoey begins. "He's just... older and in a position of authority with our church. Priests are supposed to swear abstinence-"

"Well, this one didn't," I mutter. "So, are you both going to keep my secret, or tell the whole world my dirty sin?" I question, tapping my foot impatiently.

"And when he's tired of you? When the lust has worn off and he puts his faith over you? What then? Is that something you can deal with?"

It's the same question I've been asking myself repeatedly.

What happens when Roman chooses his faith over me?

"That's not your problem to figure out," I hiss, pulling up my dad's contact on my phone.

Slamming my phone down on the center arm rest, they both eye the device.

"Either call him or let it go."

Taking several seconds to look at the phone, Aiden and Zoey exchange a look.

"When this all comes crashing down Eden, don't say I didn't warn you."

That was the last thing Aiden said before starting the ignition, driving us away from the church and the night Roman and I shared.

Chapter 25

EDEN

Although I haven't had any alone time with Roman since Halloween, we've become masters at stealing moments whenever we can. Quiet exchanges in the altar server's room before Mass or brief touches in his office just before the service begins have become our sanctuary.

Roman convinced my dad to let me take on more service hours, and the facade is falling into place perfectly despite Luca's sudden absence. After what happened at the party, Luca has found himself at the bottom of my brother's shit list. Aiden's taken it upon himself to keep Luca as far away as possible—ignoring him during football and ending calls before I can even answer.

Though, I know if Roman ever saw Luca again, he'd probably kill him for what he did that night.

I used to think being close to someone as dark as Roman would be terrifying. I never imagined I'd crave it as much as I do now.

"Dark roast, one cream," Zoey shouts, placing the drink on the counter.

Pulling myself out of my mindless daze, I return to my station, pulling shots and frothing foam.

"So, the fall festival is coming up," Zoey grins, ignoring the wandering eyes of the man grabbing his drink. "Should I expect to see Roman there with you if you come?" She questions, using his first name so casually.

"You're asking me if a local festival will be where I decide to publicly flaunt my relationship with our priest?" I arch an eyebrow.

Grasping her chin, she pretends to ponder the thought. "Yes, I think that's exactly what I'm asking," she smiles.

"You're fucking delusional—"

"Who's delusional?" His deep voice cuts through the noise, making my heart skip a beat.

Looking up, I see Roman lingering at the register, his hair tucked away under a black baseball cap. He's wearing a large bomber jacket, clearly trying to stay concealed, avoiding prying eyes.

"Speak of the Devil," Zoey jokes, poking me in the back.

At least she's warming up to the idea of me and Roman.

"No one. Zoey was just suggesting that you join us for the fall festival at the fairgrounds," I say, offering him a smile. His eyes flicker toward Zoey.

"I'm sure no one would have an issue with that," He says sarcastically, and Zoey rolls her eyes.

"As long as you stay hands-off, Father, I see no harm."

Hands-off is nearly impossible for Roman.

"Do you mind making me a chai?" Roman asks Zoey, his voice casual but his eyes intense. She nods slowly, her usual grin in place.

"As long as you tip," She replies, getting to work on his drink.

As he slides a twenty across the counter, my eyes catch on his bare wedding finger.

"Where's—"

"Meet me in the bathroom in five minutes," He whispers, leaning over the counter, his lips barely brushing against my cheek. "I'm done waiting to fuck that pretty pussy."

He leaves the conversation at that, walking away with his hands tucked in his pockets.

"I'm taking twenty." Zoey doesn't even have time to question where I'm going; I'm already on my way, the air thick with the thrill of what's to come. My hand hovers over the door handle for just a moment, the reality of what I'm about to do washing over me in a wave of nervous excitement.

Roman's breath is hot against my neck as his lips trail upwards, each kiss sending shivers down my spine. "Look how easily you came crawling to me, pretty girl," He whispers, his voice low and rough, filled with dark satisfaction. The metal arm rail digs into my back, but the discomfort is lost in the heat pooling between my legs.

He takes his time, savoring every second as his canines graze my skin, sending a mix of pleasure and anticipation coursing through me. His hands fumble with the buttons of my blouse, slowly revealing the skin beneath, the fabric parting under his touch like a forbidden secret.

His free hand slips lower, rubbing me through the fabric of my leggings, the friction igniting sparks of pleasure that make my breath hitch. The smirk on his face grows with every small moan that escapes my lips, each sound a testament to the control he holds over me.

"Already so wet for me," He murmurs, his fingers pressing harder against my warmth, the pressure making me gasp. The strain in his pants is undeniable, a visible sign of his arousal that only fuels the fire inside me.

"Tell me, Eden," He says, his voice a dangerous mix of seduction and command. "Do you want me to pin you against this bathroom wall and fuck you?" He presses his hips against me, his hardness undeniable as he grinds against my leg.

I can barely form a coherent thought, let alone a response, as his fingers continue their slow, torturous movements. The teasing is maddening, pushing me closer to the edge with every passing second, and I can feel my resolve slipping away.

"Answer me," He demands, his voice a whisper against my ear, his fingers pausing their movements as he waits for my reply. The pause is deliberate, a calculated move to remind me who's in control.

"Yes, Father," I finally manage, my voice breathless, filled with need. The words are barely out of my mouth when his fingers move again, this time slipping under the waistband of my leggings, finding their way to my wetness.

He hums in approval, his lips brushing against my ear. "Good girl," He whispers, and just like that, the anticipation builds again, every nerve in my body screaming for more of him.

But this time, I want to be the one to take control.

Without a word, I gently push him back, sliding down to my knees before him. Roman's eyes widen, dark with desire, as he watches me, his breath hitching at the sight. The power shift between us is palpable, the air thick with tension as I undo his belt with deliberate slowness.

"Let me take care of you, Father," I murmur. The words drip with seduction. His fingers twitch at his sides, resisting the urge to touch me as I slide the belt free and unbutton his pants. His erection strains against the fabric, the anticipation in his eyes fueling my own desire.

With a flick of my wrist, I free him from his boxers, his cock springing to attention. I glance up, meeting his gaze, and the heat in his eyes sends a thrill through me. Slowly, I wrap my hand around his length, feeling the warmth and hardness in my grip.

Roman lets out a low groan, his control slipping as I begin to stroke him, my movements unhurried, savoring the feel of him. His hands finally come to rest on the back of my head, fingers threading through my hair as he watches me with a mix of hunger and restraint.

"You don't have to—" He begins, but I cut him off with a soft kiss to the tip of his cock, tasting the bead of pre-cum that has already formed.

"I want to," I whisper against him, and without waiting for a response, I take him into my mouth, slow and deep. The taste of him floods my senses, and I feel his grip tighten in my hair, his breath catching as I begin to move.

I take my time, setting a rhythm that drives him wild, my lips and tongue working in tandem to bring him closer to the edge. Roman's control slips further with every passing moment, his groans growing louder, more desperate as he fights to keep from thrusting into my mouth.

With Roman still catching his breath, I pull away slightly, keeping my eyes locked on his. A surge of defiance and raw desire bubbles up inside me, and before he can react, I tilt my head back slightly and spit onto his cock, the moisture glistening as it coats him.

Roman's eyes darken with a mix of surprise and intense arousal, his breath hitching as he watches me. The act is both a challenge and a declaration of power, a reminder that in this moment, I hold as much control as he does.

His hands grip my shoulders, his fingers digging in just enough to anchor himself as he watches me with a gaze that's both reverent and possessive. The room seems to hold its breath as I use my hand to spread the spit along his length, the slickness making each movement more deliberate, more intense.

"Eden..." He breathes, his voice a low growl filled with both warning and approval, the tension between us crackling like a live wire.

Without breaking eye contact, I lower my head again, taking him back into my mouth, the slickness from the spit making each glide smooth and intense. Roman's grip on my shoulders tightens, his breath coming out in ragged gasps as I work him with a deliberate rhythm, each movement a mix of devotion and defiance.

I feel his body tense beneath my touch, the control he usually holds over himself slipping away with every second that passes. His hand moves to the back of my head, guiding me as I hollow my cheeks, taking him deeper, wanting to draw every reaction from him that I can.

"Fuck, Eden..." Roman groans, his voice low and rough, filled with a hunger that sends a shiver down my spine. The sound of his voice and the way his body responds to me only urges me on. I pick up the pace, feeling the tension in him build to a breaking point.

His fingers tangle in my hair, his restraint hanging by a thread as he fights to keep from losing control completely. But I don't let up. I want him to lose control, to surrender to the pleasure coursing through him, just as I have so many times before. Just as I feel him tensing beneath me, his breath hitching in that familiar way that signals he's close, Roman suddenly pulls back, his hands gripping my shoulders as he steps away. The sudden loss of him leaves me gasping. My lips part in surprise as I look up at him, confused and frustrated.

Roman's eyes are dark, filled with a storm of emotions I can't quite read. He's breathing heavily, his chest rising and falling as he tries to regain control. His hands move to cup my face, his thumbs brushing over my cheeks, and for a moment, we just stare at each other, the air between us thick with unspoken words and unfulfilled desires.

"Why did you stop?" I whisper, my voice tinged with the desperation I can't quite hide.

"Stand up," He snaps, grabbing my elbows and pressing me against the cold tile.

He tugs at my leggings, forcing them down, underwear and all, giving me little warning as he aligns his tip to my slick warmth.

"Trying to get me to cum in your mouth?" He questions next to my ear, nipping at its top.

Bending me over, Roman forces my elbows to support my weight on the metal railing before driving himself into me just seconds later.

Pressing my forehead against the cold wall, I bite back a vicious moan the moment he buries himself fully inside me. My body, slick from anticipation, welcomes each powerful thrust, the motion made effortless by how wet I am. His hand coils in my hair, and with each pull, he amplifies the sensation, sending sharp jolts of pleasure and pain coursing through me.

"Fuck-"

"You like that pain, don't you?" He questions, reading me like a book.

The air feels like it's being knocked out of my lungs with each of his thrusts.

"Y-Yes-" I gasp, his cock driving in harder. "Fuck, yes." I whimper, struggling to support my weight on shaking legs.

"Beg for my cum, Eden," He whispers, mercilessly pounding into me. "Beg for me to fucking cum-"

"Please," I whisper, ready to collapse. "Please fill my pussy with your-" I beg, tears clouding my eyes.

Reaching his hand in front of me, he rolls his fingers over my swollen clit.

"Only if you cum on my cock first," He whispers.

Biting down on my shirt to stifle the screams threatening to escape, I feel Roman's fingers slowly rubbing over my clit, his touch deliberate and teasing even as he continues to drive into me. The warmth in my stomach builds, the sensation overwhelming as he brings me right to the edge.

"Fuck, Roman," I hiss, letting out a gasping, silent moan. "I fucking love this," I admit, feeling my climax surge. "I fucking love you—"

As if on cue, he releases my hair, his hand moving away from my clit as he grips my hips tightly, and I feel his release surge inside me. Both of us are left breathless, our bodies trembling as he quickly wipes away the evidence of our encounter before pulling my leggings back up.

The weight of what I've just said hits me like a ton of bricks. My head pressed against the wall. I'm too petrified to turn around and face him. Struggling to support myself, I lean heavily into the metal railing, the clarity of my post-orgasm haze settling in.

I just told Roman I loved him.

When I finally force my eyes open, I see, his hand nervously rubbing the back of his neck.

Is he embarrassed?

"Why do you look so unsettled?" I ask, watching him fumble with his belt, his movements hesitant.

"I'm not unsettled, Eden," He whispers, running a hand through his hair. But even as he says it, his eyes betray him. They're wide, searching, like he's trying to find solid ground beneath him but only feeling the earth crumble away.

"Look, Roman, what I said was stupid—"

"It's what made me finish," He interrupts, the confession hanging between us heavy with meaning. His cheeks flush, and there's a flicker of something in his eyes—something he's afraid to admit, even to himself. "I was close, but when you said that, it did something to me," He confesses, his voice barely above a whisper. "Did you mean it?" His eyes search mine, almost pleading for an answer.

Fuck.

What do I say?

I said it because I meant it.

I said it because I wanted him to know it.

"Or was it just the sex?" He asks, his voice tight with uncertainty, his expression a mask hiding a storm of emotions.

"People say things in the heat of the moment," I lie, the words tasting bitter on my tongue. "I'm sorry—"

"Your twenty minutes are almost up, Angel," He says, his tone distant, though I can hear the tension beneath it. "I don't want you to be late."

As he reaches for the door handle, I grab his hand, holding onto the connection that feels like it's slipping away.

"Did you want me to mean it, Roman?" I ask, seeing the conflict in his eyes, the war between his heart and the vow he's clinging to.

"People say things they don't mean, Eden," He whispers, his voice laden with disappointment I can't hide from. "Sometimes it stings."

He opens the door, and the hallway beyond seems to beckon him away from me, the distance between us growing with each passing second.

"Roman—"

"You need to get back to work. Don't let me stop you."

With a tense look, he slips his ring back onto his finger, the gold band catching the light—a stark reminder of the vow that holds him back. His face hardens as if the ring itself has the power to lock away the emotions he's so desperately trying to control.

"And how do you think I feel," I challenge, my voice trembling with emotion, "knowing that every time you put that ring on, it's like you're reminding yourself that I'm something forbidden? Like I'm a temptation you have to resist instead of someone you care about."

He turns back to me, his eyes filled with a tortured mix of emotions—fear, regret, and something deeper that he can't quite name. His voice is low, almost a whisper, as he says, "Probably like I just told you I love you, then looked like I was too scared to accept it."

His face softens, just for a moment, and I see the man behind the priest—the man who is terrified of what he feels for me, yet powerless to stop it.

Without another word, Roman turns away, his hands disappearing into his pockets, the unspoken truth hanging heavily in the air between us.

I fucked up.

I thought I was sparing his feelings. Turns out, I'd just shattered them.

Staggering back into the main part of the café, I see Roman collecting his drink from Zoey, his eyes deliberately avoiding mine as I move behind the counter. Tightening my apron, I take a stand beside Zoey, watching Roman retreat to one of the couches. His movements are tense, his demeanor closed off, and I can't shake the feeling of dread settling in my stomach.

"Why is he so pissy?" Zoey asks, frowning as she watches him. "He barely said a word once he grabbed his drink, and where did you two disappear to?"

"I think I messed up, Zo," I admit, my gaze fixated on Roman as he settles on the couch, the eyes of several women in the café drifting toward him, drawn to his presence.

He looks up, catching one of the women's gazes, and smiles—a gesture that ignites a surge of jealousy and anger within me.

When his eyes briefly flicker to mine, there's a defiant glint in them, challenging me, pushing me further into my own frustration.

No, scratch that. I definitely messed up.

"Well, go take an order," Zoey whispers urgently. "And try not to look like you just got fucked in the café bathroom," She adds, reading me like an open book.

Mortified, I duck my head, fumbling with the register screen, trying to gather my scattered thoughts.

"What can I get going for you?" I ask, my voice shaky as I focus on the task at hand.

"Eden?"

My heart stops.

All the anger that had been simmering in my veins instantly morphs into paralyzing fear.

I force myself to look up from the register, my breath catching in my throat as I take an involuntary step back, my body trembling uncontrollably.

Eric.

He found me.

He looks just like he always has—brown hair slicked back, his deep dark eyes locked onto mine with an intensity that sends shivers down my spine. The face that's haunted my nightmares for so long is standing right in front of me, and I can't breathe, can't think.

"Eden, are you okay?" Zoey's voice is distant, barely penetrating the fog of terror engulfing me.

"E-Eric—" The word stumbles from my lips, a broken echo of the name that has haunted me.

Memories crash over me—his hands pinning me down, the weight of his body suffocating me, my body being violated.

"E-Eric—"

The world spins, my vision blurs, and my body crumples to the ground. The last thing I hear is Zoey's panicked voice, calling my name, as everything fades into nothing.

1 Peter 5:8: "Be sober-minded; be watchful. Your adversary, the Devil, prowls around like a roaring lion, seeking someone to devour."

Chapter 26

ROMAN

There's no time for anyone to react as Eden collapses, her body crumpling toward the counter. The sickening thud of her head hitting the edge echoes through the café, freezing everyone in place. Zoey's eyes dart up to mine, wide with fear.

Moving without a second thought, I shove past the brunette man who's standing too close, who'd watched Eden fall with a disturbing lack of concern. I reach her side in an instant, kneeling beside her, my hands trembling as I grab a napkin to press against the wound on her forehead.

Zoey looks scared, her hands shaking as she clutches the rag in her hand. "I have no idea what happened. She was fine, then she started taking an order—"

"Give me a cold washcloth," The brunette man orders, trying to take control of the situation as he moves toward us with unsettling calmness.

He bends down, reaching for Eden as if he's going to take over, but the very sight of him touching her makes my blood boil.

"Get your fucking hands away from her," I snap, my voice sharp, louder than I intended.

Zoey blinks in confusion, clearly rattled, as she hands the man a rag. His expression hardens, his annoyance with me barely masked.

"She's my girlfriend," He snaps back, the words slicing through me like a blade, igniting a fire in my chest.

I know what this boy represents. At college, Eden was involved with someone—a boy who hurt her, who nearly pushed her to the brink of suicide that day in that park. A boy who left permanent scars, both physical and emotional. And now, here he is, acting like he has any right to be near her.

"She's not your girlfriend," Zoey interjects, her voice firm, cutting through the haze of my rage. "Why don't you get the hell away and let us handle this—"

"Roman," A familiar, grating voice cuts in.

David stands behind the counter, hands casually tucked in his pockets, his expression unreadable, as if Eden's collapse is nothing more than a minor inconvenience.

"Eric, step back and let them handle it. It's just a cut," David says, his tone dripping with indifference.

Eric obeys, stepping back like a well-trained dog, but not without throwing me a venomous glare.

Eden stirs, her eyelids fluttering as she mumbles in pain, her consciousness slowly returning.

"R-Roman, Eric—"

Before she can say more, I gently cover her mouth, trying to silence her before she says something that could make everything worse.

"You should've had some water before your shift, Eden," I lie smoothly, feeling David's cold gaze burning into me. "You're lucky I happened to be here."

Her focus shifts to Eric and her father, and the way she instinctively backs into me makes my heart ache with helplessness. Every fiber of my being screams to wrap her in my arms and eliminate the threat these men pose, but I know that any rash action could make things worse.

Her breathing grows rapid, her chest rising and falling with shallow, panicked breaths, her hands tremble in fear.

"Dad, why the hell is he here—"

"Eric is in town," David says, his voice dripping with false calm. "And from what I gather, you two left things on a rather sour note, Eden. I thought it would be best if you and Eric had some time to speak. I told him you were working today and that your shift would end soon. He was eager to see you. Though, I'm sure no one was expecting you to be this clumsy—"

The condescension in his tone makes my blood boil. The way Eden's entire body tenses against me tells me everything I need to know—she's terrified, and not just because of what happened in the past, but because of what these men are capable of doing now.

"I want nothing to do with him," Eden sobs, her voice breaking as some patrons begin to take notice of the unfolding scene. "I want nothing to do with you, Eric—"

"Well, Eden, you don't really have a choice now, do you?" David's voice cuts through her despair, his eyes narrowing as they land on me. "Does she, Father?" He adds, pushing my commitment to this whole fucking charade to the edge.

He wants to see if I'll crack under the pressure.

"I think it's best she comes by the church tomorrow," I say, forcing a steely edge into my voice. "She needs to remember the weight of her commitments; how much discipline is required from her."

David's gaze sharpens, a cold satisfaction flickering in his eyes. "Discipline, you say?"

"Indeed," I reply, letting a grim satisfaction settle in my tone. "And the church is the perfect place for her to confront her failures. She will be reminded of her place and her duties. It will serve her well."

Eric's scoff is filled with disbelief.

"You're the new priest at Saint Michael's?" He asks, his tone dripping with disdain.

"Correct," I hiss back, my hand gently running along Eden's back, hidden from everyone's view except Zoey's.

David's gaze remains fixed on me, his voice laced with a cold authority. "Get yourself up and get home, Eden," He says. His words are meant more for me than for her. "I'm sure Aiden and Eric can catch up while you collect yourself," He adds, still addressing me as though I'm the one being commanded.

Eden nods, too terrified to speak.

"Here, Eden, let's get you cleaned up," Zoey intervenes, her glare cutting through David's icy demeanor.

As Zoey leads Eden away, I rise to my feet, feeling the weight of the blood on my hands, both literal and metaphorical.

"Roman, can I talk to you outside for a second?" David's voice is deceptively calm, but I know better. This isn't a request—it's an order.

"Why the hell were you here?" David demands, his voice sharp with accusation.

Standing by the side of the building, I cross my arms, taking a step toward him. The night air feels colder as the tension rises.

"I was getting a coffee. Not very many places to do that around here—"

"Bullshit," David snaps, closing the gap between us. His proximity is menacing, his eyes narrowing with disdain.

"You think I'm oblivious to what's been going on?" He challenges, his words thick with unspoken threats.

"You'll have to be more specific, David," I reply, my voice steady despite the storm brewing inside me.

"She's seduced you, hasn't she?" David's question is laced with a false note of sympathy as if he pities my predicament.

"Seduced me?" I scoff, incredulous. "Do you have any idea what you're insinuating?"

"I know how the Devil operates, Roman. He creeps in when you least expect it. I fear he has ensnared you in his game. How much discipline is my daughter truly receiving—"

"You saw the cross, David," I retort, anger flaring as I recall the marble crucifix I had used with Eden. "You know I'm dedicated to teaching her genuine submission—"

"And none of what you've done has been driven by lust?" He presses, probing for an admission of guilt.

"Is that why you brought her ex back?" I counter, my voice sharp with frustration. "You think I'm compromised—"

"I didn't say that, Roman," He chides, shaking his head in mock disappointment. "I brought Eric here to remind Eden of her past. The life she led before college. Eric was a devout follower of faith with my daughter—"

A devout follower? That made *raping* her okay?

"You're already contributing greatly to our cause. Perhaps it's time I hand over the task of guiding Eden to someone who knows her better than you," David says, his tone condescending. "It was naive of me to expect you to manage her alone—"

"I can handle the time commitment. It's not an issue."

"You don't have to," David interrupts, his voice cold. "Eric is back for now. Maybe he can help my daughter find her way amid the darkness she's fallen into," David sneers, his disdain for Eden evident.

The urge to confront him violently is almost overwhelming.

"David," A voice cuts in, drawing me back from the brink.

Eric approaches, his head held high, a smug grin spreading across his face.

"Eric, I'm almost done—"

"I get what you're saying, David," I lie, forcing myself to stay calm. "But I've got it under control."

David's nod is far from reassuring, his skepticism evident.

"I hope you're right, Roman," David warns, his voice low and measured.

Brushing past me, David gives Eric's shoulder a reassuring squeeze, his smile disturbingly warm.

"You coming by for dinner?" David asks, his tone casual.

"Of course. Perhaps Father Briar would like to join us?" Eric's voice drips with malice as he raises an eyebrow.

"Roman?" David's voice snaps me from my thoughts.

"Of course," I reply with a forced grin. "Sounds great."

David seems satisfied with the response, nodding as he prepares to leave. "I'll see you both at my place around six?"

Both Eric and I nod in agreement.

Satisfied, David strides away, lingering by Eden's car, no doubt preparing to lecture her once Zoey escorts her outside.

As soon as David is out of sight, I retreat behind the building, hidden from view. My eyes lock onto Eric, who's observing Eden from a distance, an eerie resolve set into his expression.

"She's beautiful, isn't she?" Eric muses, his eyes following Eden's car as it drives away.

My grip tightens around my phone, my anger barely contained.

"Why are you here?" I demand, my voice cold.

Eric finally turns his gaze toward me, a smirk playing on his lips. "I heard through the grapevine that Eden found her way back home. I stopped by the Faulkner's place and learned she's been reconnecting with her faith. I thought it odd—Eden always hated church. Are you offering something other than guidance, Father Briar?"

"What the hell are you talking about?"

"I've been keeping an eye on you. You think I wouldn't look into where my girlfriend was and who she was spending her time with?" His gaze is cold, calculating.

"She's not your goddamn girlfriend."

"Careful, Father," Eric warns, his tone carrying a venomous edge. "Words like that are why it was so easy for David to believe you're driven by lust. As I see it, I'm back now. Eden will learn to forgive the past, so where do you fit into all of this?"

"Are you threatening me?" I growl, stepping closer, my anger barely contained. "Don't let my day job fool you; I would be glad to kick your ass."

"Look at how feral she's made you," Eric sneers, his gaze contemptuous. "This is why we had to break her.

Eric smirks, his eyes cold. "Eden's always been a temptation, a siren luring men into sin. Her presence alone is like a beacon for every dark impulse lurking inside them. We did what we did because she was a force of corruption—an embodiment of everything that leads men astray."

He leaned in closer, his voice dropping to a sinister whisper. "She needed to be punished for being a living temptation. If she was left unchecked, she'd only drag more souls into darkness."

I grab his shirt without a second thought.

Throwing him to the ground, I stomp on his chest before he can rise, slamming my foot over his hand and pressing my hand over his mouth to stifle his screams. Relishing the muffled noise against my hand, I wrap my hands around his throat, poised to crack his skull against the pavement, to watch his life drain from his eyes.

"I-I knew it," He chokes out, struggling for breath. "I knew you were fucking her. Tell me, how will David react when he learns you assaulted me?" Eric's grin is maddening. "You think he'll believe your word or mine?"

I release him, my mind consumed by Eden's suffering.

He hurt her.

Everything turns red.

He has desecrated what's mine.

"I dare you to try and take her from me." I hiss, my patience gone.

I drive my foot into his jaw, the lights flicker out for him. My phone buzzes in my pocket as satisfaction floods through me at the sight of him beneath me.

When I answer the call, I'm met with a trembling voice. "Roman—"

"How quickly can you pack a bag?" I demand, my thoughts darkening as I contemplate smashing Eric's head in further.

"Why—"

Zoey rounds the corner, her eyes locking onto the scene with a cold resolve.

"You asked me to choose, Eden. I've made my decision. Pack a bag for yourself and your brother. Tonight is the last night either of you will be in that house," I whisper, gripping Eric's head as he groans in pain.

Shuddering on the phone, Eden takes a deep breath.

"Okay. I'm trusting you, Roman."

After hanging up, Zoey gives me a puzzled look.

"They can stay with my mother and me until we sort this out," Zoey whispers, glancing at Eric with a mix of anger and concern. "But you better tell me right now what the hell is going on."

"Take your break, and I will," I reply, my tone clipped.

This is bound to be a very unpleasant conversation.

Chapter 27

EDEN

As we make our way downstairs, the sound of lively chatter bounces off the walls of the house. Both Aiden and I are tense as we approach the living room, where the back of Eric's head comes into view. I position myself behind Aiden, trying to stay out of sight.

"That's quite a tumble you took," My father jokes, his voice amused and jovial.

"What can I say," Eric's nauseating voice grates on my nerves, "I'm clumsy as hell."

"That you are," Roman chimes in, appearing from the kitchen with a glass of scotch in hand. His smile is as unsettling as it is calculated. "I'm glad I was there," Roman's gaze briefly flicks toward me before he moves closer to Eric and my dad, barely acknowledging my presence.

Finally noticing us, my dad's smile broadens with an unsettling warmth.

"Come here, kids," He grins, his invitation feeling more like an order.

Turning around, the sight of Eric's bruised face is disturbing. His eyes are wide, and the tension in the room is palpable.

"What the hell happened to you?" Aiden hisses, his anger barely masked by his attempt at neutrality.

"He fell going to his car," Roman explains smoothly, his tone dripping with insincerity. "Seems the elevation here didn't agree with him." Eric manages a nod in response.

I move toward the couch, my anxiety growing as Roman leans casually against its back.

"Well, I think dinner is almost ready—"

"Actually, David, there's something exciting I'd like to share with everyone," Roman interrupts with a grin that sends chills down my spine. My heart races, and anxiety grips my chest.

Roman takes center stage, his demeanor almost theatrical.

Roman's eyes, cold and calculating, sweep over the room. "As you're aware, Eden has been diligently fulfilling her service hours at the church," He begins, drawing nods from everyone in the room. "What you may not know is the extent of her commitment. Today, I had the opportunity to review some documents she entrusted to me."

With deliberate slowness, Roman retrieves papers from his jacket and places them on the coffee table, nudging them toward my father.

"This is a lease agreement," Roman declares, his voice smooth and confident. "Eden and Aiden will be moving into a new place in two days."

My father's confusion is palpable as he scans the papers. "Roman, this isn't what I intended when I asked you to guide my daughter. My children are not leaving this house."

Roman's gaze is steady, his voice smooth but laden with a gravity that commands attention. "David," He begins, "you must understand that the path to true devotion often requires more than mere ritual. It demands sacrifice, a renunciation of the familiar to embrace the sanctity of a higher calling."

He gestures toward the lease papers with a deliberate grace, his movements measured. "Eden and Aiden's decision to move into their own residence is not a mere change of address. It is a sacred act of faith, a tangible manifestation of their commitment to God's will."

My father's chair scrapes across the floor as he stands, his finger driving into Roman's chest.

"What the hell do you think you're doing-"

"You want her to know true discipline?" Roman questions. "Then throw her into the water and watch her come crawling back to you. Do you think she can make it with that job? Do you think she can make it without you? David, this is merely a test. Let me help you see it through."

As Roman continues to feed into my father's delusions of power, I see his face calm with realization.

"Fine. You want to leave Eden?" David stands in front of me, his eyes cold, a mocking half-smile twisting at his lips. "Fine. See how long you last without me."

The sting of his words leaves me reeling. I shake my head, trying to grasp the enormity of the situation.

"Leave your keys on the counter, and get the hell out of my house," He hisses, his voice a chilling whisper. "Both of you."

Roman's gaze meets mine, his eyes narrowing with an unspoken command. It's clear—run. Run now.

I grab Aiden's hand, the urgency propelling us through the front door. We stumble over the bags I'd packed for us earlier, grabbing them in haste. Outside, Zoey's car is parked, her hand frantically waving us toward it.

"Go," I whisper fiercely. "Go, go."

We scramble to shove our bags into the car, Zoey's face pale with shock, her breaths shallow and rapid.

"Zo—" I start, but she cuts me off.

"Roman told me everything," She murmurs, her voice quivering. "About my dad, my stepmom, the kids..."

The mention of "the kids" draws a confused look from Aiden. He's still piecing things together, uncertainty written on his face.

A sudden thud against the window makes us jump. A rock smashes into the glass, my father's furious shouts piercing the night.

Zoey slams her foot on the gas, and we lurch forward, the car speeding away. I glance back, catching Roman's smirk as he stands by the sidewalk. My phone buzzes with a new message—Roman's text with our new address.

The city lights blur as we drive into the night, the weight of our departure settling over us.

Roman

Staggering onto the lawn, Eric approaches his car, glancing back at me with a look of cautious curiosity.

There's only one more thing I need to do tonight.

I stroll over to him, my steps deliberate. With a tap on the hood of his car, I watch him slide into the driver's seat.

"I think we got off on the wrong foot—"

"How long do you think David will buy your lies?" Eric interrupts, his voice low and dangerous. "You think Eden leaving will change anything? I know you're the mole, and I'll make sure David finds out."

I clench my jaw, forcing myself to remain composed.

"How about this: come over for a drink at my place. Maybe you'll get a clearer picture of my role in all this," I offer.

Eric surveys me with a skeptical look, shaking his head.

"Why would I do that?"

Leaning on his open window, I take a deep breath, meeting his gaze.

"Perhaps I want to discuss Eden's true nature. You spoke about her being a temptation—well, I'd like to show you how I've been handling that particular 'temptation.' After all, if anyone should understand what drives a man to sin, it's someone like you," I say with a dark grin.

His expression shifts as he considers my words, finally allowing a thin smile to form. He glances at his watch, seemingly intrigued.

"I suppose I have time for a drink."

The room is dimly lit, the amber glow from the lamp casting long shadows on the walls. Eric lounges comfortably in an armchair, a smirk playing at the corners of his lips as he sips his drink, oblivious to the darkness that lingers just beyond the edge of the light.

I keep my gaze steady, though my mind churns with a storm of righteous fury. The air is thick with the scent of aged whiskey and incense, a dissonance that mirrors the turmoil within me. I sit across from him, the silence between us growing heavy, each tick of the clock a reminder of the divine justice I am about to enact.

"So, Eric," I begin, my voice low and deliberate, "you really believe Eden was a temptation sent by the Devil. Is that right?"

Eric chuckles, a dark, mirthless sound that cuts through the room. "You think too much, Roman. She's nothing but a sinner, like the rest of us."

I take a slow sip from my glass, letting the fiery liquid warm my throat. "A sinner," I echo, considering the gravity of the term. "The Devil's work is subtle, weaving through the innocent and corrupt alike. But sometimes, it needs a hand to guide its machinations."

Eric's eyes narrow, his amusement fading. "What are you saying?"

Leaning forward, I set my glass aside, my hand brushing over the worn Bible resting on the side table. The holy book feels heavy. Its weight is a tangible reminder of the sacred duty I bear.

"I believe the Lord has tested me," I say, my voice gaining a fervent edge. "He's shown me the corruption that festers in those who claim to be faithful while plotting sin in the dark."

Eric shifts uncomfortably, the realization dawning on him that this night holds more than idle conversation. "What the fuck are you talking about?"

"You spoke of Eden as a force of temptation, a means to corrupt," I continue, my voice now a whisper. "Yet, it's you who have allowed that temptation to fester, to poison you. It's you who's been an instrument of the Devil's will."

The Bible feels cold in my hand, but it grounds me. I open it slowly, turning to a passage that has become my guiding light in these troubled times: *"And if thy right hand offend thee, cut it off, and cast it from thee: for it is profitable for thee that one of thy members should perish, and not that thy whole body should be cast into hell."* (Matthew 5:30).

Eric's eyes widen, a flicker of fear crossing his features. "What are you doing?"

I stand, moving toward him with a calm, determined stride. The alcohol has done its work, loosening his inhibitions.

"You see, Eric," I say, my tone a dark melody of vengeance and faith, "sometimes the only way to cleanse the soul is to remove the source of corruption entirely."

Eric sneers, his bravado returning. "You think you're so noble, Roman? You're just another puppet in the Devil's game, trying to play savior."

The insult strikes a nerve. My grip tightens around my glass, the pressure of his words cracking through the veneer of my control. I shatter the glass in my hand, the shards cutting into my skin as I stare at him with fury ignited.

"You have no fucking clue who I am," I hiss, my voice trembling with righteous wrath.

Eric's laughter is cut short as I snatch a shard of glass from the broken pieces on the floor. His eyes widen in shock and fear as I approach, the edges of the glass catching the dim light.

"This is your final judgment," I declare, the words dripping with a grim sense of purpose.

With a swift motion, I press the glass shard into his neck, the blade slicing through flesh and muscle. Eric's eyes bulge, his mouth opening in a silent scream as he struggles against the inevitable. Blood pours from the wound, staining his clothes and the carpet beneath him.

As the life drains from him, I offer a silent prayer, my heart heavy with the gravity of my actions. "Forgive me, Lord, for I have acted as Your instrument. May this act purify the sin that sought to spread its darkness."

Eric's body falls limp. I step back, breathing heavily, the weight of divine retribution heavy on my shoulders.

The room is silent now, save for the faint whisper of prayers on my lips and the soft rustle of the Bible as I close it.

I stare at Eric's lifeless body, the remains of the shattered glass and blood painting a grim testament to my divine duty. The room still echoes with the weight of what's been done—Eric's challenge was met with the justice that only the righteous could deliver. I take a deep breath, feeling the fire of righteous anger cooling into cold resolve.

The phone rings, cutting through the silence. I pick it up, my fingers brushing over the edges of the device as though it's an instrument of fate.

"Seth," I say, my voice smooth but carrying the weight of an unspoken threat.

"Roman," Seth replies, his tone guarded.

"I trust everything's running smoothly on your end?"

"Pretty much. What's up?"

I let out a measured breath, keeping my tone even. "I've got a situation here. A bit of a mess that needs... handling."

Seth's pause is telling. "A mess? What kind of mess?"

"You know," I say, leaning against the wall, staring at Eric's body. "The kind that requires a certain level of discretion."

Seth's tone grows cautious. "You talking about something serious here?"

"Oh, it's serious alright," I reply, feeling a cold smile touch my lips. "But it's nothing you can't handle. And believe me, it's in your best interest to handle it well."

A moment of silence hangs between us, heavy with implications. "What's in it for me?" Seth asks, his voice wary but tinged with hope.

"I've been thinking," I say, pacing slowly around the room. "You've had some... complications with your name recently. You know, regarding certain church vehicles and their... activities."

Seth's breathing quickens, a mix of fear and relief. "Yeah?"

"I have a way to clear up those complications. It's a delicate matter, but with your cooperation, we can make sure your name is in the clear," I murmur, letting the words hang in the air.

Seth swallows hard. "What do you need me to do?"

"Just handle the situation here with the professionalism I know you're capable of," I reply smoothly. "In return, I'll make sure everything that's been tainting your name gets put right. We all have our roles to play, don't we?"

"Fine," Seth says, his voice steady now.

"Good," I say, the finality in my tone clear. "I'll be in touch with further details. Make sure you're ready."

As I hang up, I feel a grim satisfaction. The pieces are falling into place, each move aligning with the grand design I've set in motion. Tonight's work was necessary, and tomorrow, the path to cleansing the world of David Faulkner will be that much clearer.

Proverbs 15:18: "A hot-tempered man stirs up strife, but he who is slow to anger quiets contention."

Chapter 28

EDEN

"I didn't want to believe any of it," Zoey whispers, all of us huddled on the couch of the spacious apartment. My apartment.

Fully furnished, it was as if Roman had been planning for Aiden and me to come here for months.

"Then Roman showed me the file, and the names tethered to all of it..." Zoey trails off, sobbing in her hands. "My own father wanted to put me in that fucking auction, selling me off with the rest of those children that are God knows where," Zoey cries.

Aiden has remained quiet as he's taken all of this information in for the first time.

"The police-"

"They know," I answer before he can start. "Maybe not all of them, but the ones that are in power do. Our dad has been doing this for years, Aiden. Roman would have already gone to the FBI, but he was afraid they'd find out and move the kids. We still don't know where they're being held."

Aiden shakes his head. "Roman shouldn't have gotten involved. I know something more is going on between you two, but getting caught up in something like this could get you killed, Eden."

Running her hands through her curly hair, Zoey sniffles, the weight of what my brother thinks will happen to us, reminding her that we're all in very real danger.

"I won't leave Roman to deal with this alone, Aiden. He's tormented by the evil things going on in that church, and I don't know how far he's willing to go to put an end to all of it. I'm worried about him."

I'd called Roman seven times since we'd gotten to the apartment.

Each time, it went straight to voicemail.

Where the hell could he be?

Zoey's phone lights up, her teary eyes gravite toward the bright screen.

"It's from the correctional facility," She sniffles, all of us exchanging a look.

Tapping the answer button, she puts the call on speaker.

"You are receiving a call from an inmate in Idlewood County Jail. Press one to accept."

Tapping her screen, the person on the other line sounds frantic

"Zo-"

"Dad?".

"Zo, I messed up bad. I need you to come here so I can figure this all out," He gasps.

"Dad, I know everything. I know about the kids-"

"Zo, this isn't about that. I did something that is going to get me a lot of time. I need you to call your stepmom, and I need both of you to come in-"

"Fuck that stupid whore, and fuck you. I know what your plans were for me, Dad. I know who you really are-"

"Zoey damnit, just get your ass over here so I can get this figured out-"

"She and I will come," Aiden hisses. "And you can bet your sorry ass it's to say goodbye, not that you deserve it. "

Grabbing Zoey's phone, Aiden takes charge.

"Goodbye, Seth."

"Wait, Aiden, your sister-"

Hanging up, Aiden tosses the phone on the couch.

"Zoey, I'm so sorry," I whisper, rolling my thumb over her knuckles as I hold her hand.

"I'm sure whatever he's done, it'll be a well-deserved punishment," She says coldly.

Grabbing her phone and jacket, she swipes her keys from the table.

"Go. I'll leave you both to it. I'm still trying to get Roman to pick up the phone."

Still hesitant, Aiden trails behind Zoey.

"Call me if you need me. I'll be back soon."

Laying on the couch, I stare at my phone's screen, my nerves frayed with each passing minute. It's been four hours since I arrived at the apartment, an hour since Zoey and Aiden left, and still, the silence is oppressive.

Suddenly, the door rattles from frantic knocks. I jump, clutching my phone as if it might offer some solace.

"Eden," Roman's voice cuts through the stillness, a breathless whisper of relief. "Can you let me in?"

A surge of hope propels me to the door. I swing it open, my breath catching at the sight before me.

Roman stands there, a figure out of a nightmare, cloaked in a bloodstained hoodie. The dark hood shrouds most of his face, but the crimson splatter paints a grim picture of what lies beneath. His hands and face are streaked with dried blood, and he moves quickly inside, locking the door behind him.

"Roman—"

"He's gone," Roman snaps, pulling down his hood to reveal a face marred by the aftermath of violence.

My heart races, a mix of dread and relief. "W-who is gone, Roman? Are you hurt?" I reach out, hands trembling as I try to touch his face.

He grabs my wrists, his grip firm and unyielding. "Eric is gone," He murmurs, his eyes intense. "He can never hurt you again."

My gaze fixes on the blood that stains his clothes, the realization slowly dawning "Did you—did you hurt him, Roman?"

He doesn't answer immediately, but the intensity in his eyes and the grim satisfaction on his face speak volumes.

"Are you okay?" I press, desperation lacing my voice.

Roman nods, his expression hardening. "I've taken care of him. I made sure he paid for what he did to you. You're safe now."

"He can't hurt me again?"

"Nothing will hurt you, Eden Faulkner, so long as my heart is beating."

His words are a vow, a promise that envelops me as I wrap my arms around his neck, surrendering completely to his presence.

"Are you scared of me?" He asks, his breath warm against my ear. I shake my head, the fear of the night melting away in his embrace.

"This whole night, the scariest thing was you not answering your phone," I whisper, feeling his hands trace a path down my side. He lifts me effortlessly, my legs wrapping around his waist, drawing me closer.

"I can't think clearly when it comes to you, Eden," He breathes into my ear.

"Then don't think at all," I murmur, my lips brushing against his ear. "Show me how much you love me," I whisper, feeling his grip tighten. As I trail my tongue from his cheek to his lips, the metallic taste of Eric's blood lingers, an unsettling reminder of the night's violence. "Fuck me like you love me, Roman."

With a low growl, he tightens his hold and moves us without a word, carrying us to a part of the apartment I haven't yet explored. He opens the door to the master bedroom, but instead of stopping, he guides us into the adjoining bathroom.

He turns on the shower, letting the water heat before facing me again. His hands are swift, and I feel the heat of the water mix with the heat of his touch.

"I—"

"Shh," He interrupts, his voice a gentle command as he begins to pull my shirt over my head, his movements deliberate and unhurried. As he undresses himself, the blood staining his skin is a stark contrast to the raw need in his eyes. I try to ignore the prominent strain between his legs, focusing instead on the intimacy of the moment.

The steam from the shower starts to fill the room, the air thick with heat and anticipation. Roman's gaze is intense, his focus solely on me as he prepares to wash away the remnants of the night's violence, turning our shared space into a sanctuary of raw emotion.

"Roman-"

Shoving us into the shower, the warm water cascades down our bodies, his lips ferociously attacking mine, nipping and biting at my bottom lip every chance he gets. Running his hand down my front, he cups my center, letting his fingers slide into my wetness. Keeping me pressed against the wall, I gasp and moan every time his fingers move in and out of me, watching as the blood mixes with the water and trails down his skin. My breasts bounce as he pounds into me, his free hand wrapping around my neck for purchase.

"So fucking wet for me, pretty girl," He praises, pulling his fingers out of me, taking his time licking my slickness from their tips.

Turning me around, he presses my front to the tile wall, coiling his hand in my hair, spreading my legs as he runs his tip along my folds.

"Tell me how bad you want to feel my cock, Eden."

"So bad, Roman," I whisper, the water running down my body adding to the tendrils of anticipation creeping up my spine. "So fucking bad-"

I let out a gasp as he slides inside me. Keeping his hand wrapped around the back of my neck, he pounds into me mercilessly, passionately.

"Fuck, I love this," He groans, thrusting harder. "I love seeing you take me in like a good fucking girl," He whispers, using his hand to hold my hip in place.

Latching his teeth to the side of my neck, he releases his hold on my waist, driving harder and harder into me. He wraps his hand around the shower knob until his knuckles are white.

I glance down at my legs, looking at the light trail of blood slipping out of me and down my inner thigh.

My period.

Great.

Thrusting more aggressively, his lips brush the side of my ear.

"I love the way your blood looks on my cock," He whispers, slowing down his pace. "I want to be the only one to make you bleed, Eden."

He tugs my hair forcefully, the pain that stings my scalp sending me closer to release. His arm wraps around me as I moan, his cock twitching inside of me.

"You ready, baby?" He questions, holding me still. "How bad do you want it?" He taunts, keeping me at a tipping point.

"Please," I whimper.

Not needing much else, I feel his release implode inside of me, both of us letting out a vicious moan. Pulling himself from me, he moves in front of me, settling on his knees, my eyes wide with confusion as I struggle to support my weight on my shaking legs.

"What-"

Dragging his tongue up my lower thigh, he licks the blood that slipped out of me, letting it settle on his tongue, his hand gripping my thigh. Moving his tongue up my thigh and to my hip bone, he keeps moving up, sliding his tongue over my clit before working up my lower stomach. Moving up my body, his tongue takes its time going over my breasts before moving up my neck, finally settling on my lips.

Tasting a mix of blood and water, he kisses me as hard as he can, holding me until the water has washed away all of our sins.

Proverbs 25:25: "Like cold water to a thirsty soul."

Chapter 29

EDEN

Surrounded by the smell of sweet kettle corn and rich caramel, children run around the festival grounds with armfuls of tickets. Wearing a pair of shades and a beanie, Roman looks like any other hipster that I'd see in the coffee shop.

Wearing a cropped shirt and a black skirt, a lot of the skin on my arms and legs is exposed, making me more uncomfortable than I'd like to admit.

"There's a reason people say self-harm is done for attention," I whisper. "The stares you get when people see the scars is why."

"Fuck them," Roman smiles. "Today is a day to unwind. So what if a few people stare," Grabbing my wrists, he raises them to his mouth, gently kissing the skin. "I think you look kind of badass."

Smiling, I nudge his shoulder, fighting back the urge to lace my fingers with his as we walk.

"So, what are we doing first?" He questions, tugging down his sunglasses to get a good look at everything.

Focusing on the carnival games, he actually looks excited.

"Do you have a secret competitive side, Father?" I question, watching his shoulders shrug with embarrassment.

"I don't like losing. Even some rigged, carney game."

Looking around, I watch a couple throw darts into a wall of balloons. I grab his hand to drag him over to the game.

"Give us ten darts each," I exclaim. The booth attendant stares at my arms, taking his time to grab the darts.

"That will be twenty bucks-"

"Ten for not keeping your eyes to yourself," Roman says causally, sliding over a ten to the man. "Stare any longer, and you'll end up with one of these darts in your eye."

Taking several steps back, the both attendant fixes his collar, moving on to the next set of customers.

"Ready to get your ass whooped?" He questions, nudging me playfully.

"Depends. What does the winner get?" I question, balancing the darts in my palm.

"Hopefully to feel you tugging my hair while moaning my name," Roman whispers, my cheeks immediately heating.

Aiming at the balloons, he hits the first three dead on. Trying to mimic his movements, I miss the first two, getting the third by some miracle.

"Not bad," Roman jokes.

"You gotta aim like this," He smiles, taking a stand behind me.

Guiding my arms from behind, he bends down, resting his chin on my head.

"Drag your arm back and focus on where you want it to land."

Placing his hand atop my own, he guides my arm back, keeping his free hand on my waist.

"Which one do you want?"

"The pink one, up top," I grin.

Helping me aim, he moves his hand away from atop my own, landing a kiss on the side of my neck.

"Extra encouragement, Angel. Now let it fly."

Tossing the dart, it hits the balloon right in the center.

"See, you're a pro-"

"Father?" Someone calls, both of us looking away from the booth.

A trio of women from the church approaches, their eyes lingering on Roman's casual attire with an unsettling mixture of curiosity and admiration. Their gaze shifts to me, their disapproval thinly veiled.

"Ladies," Roman says, his voice betraying a hint of discomfort as he keeps close to me.

"I didn't think we'd see you at an event like this," The woman in front says, her grin wide and deliberately provocative as she loosens a few buttons on her blouse. Her flirtation is as blatant as it is unwelcome.

"Just taking Eden out to reward all her hard work at the church," Roman replies with a grin, his arm draped awkwardly around my shoulders in a gesture that feels more like ownership than affection.

"I didn't realize you took your servers out for such things. Am I too old to redo my altar server training?" She quips, her tone dripping with double entendre. "I'm sure I know a few things about getting the job done—"

Ignoring the comment, I snatch my remaining darts and hurl them at the balloons with a ferocity that matches the anger simmering within me. Each dart's sharp trajectory is a release of the frustration I feel, particularly the urge to make a scene in front of these women.

"Eden is doing just fine," Roman says, watching me with a mixture of concern and appreciation as I retrieve his darts from the ground.

"Well, if you ever need anything—" The woman continues, her gaze lingering on Roman with unwelcome intent.

"He doesn't," I cut her off, my voice sharp. "I'm sure your husband is looking for you somewhere that's not here."

The woman's head swivels towards me, her face a mask of shock and indignation.

"What—"

"I'm sorry," I snap, my tone icy. "Are we really going to stand here pretending you aren't staring at Father Briar's crotch?"

Her eyes widen in disbelief, the stares from the small crowd around us amplifying the tension. Roman's grip on my shoulder tightens, his own unease palpable as he takes in the unfolding confrontation.

The woman's face contorts with a mix of disbelief and irritation as she removes her glasses, her gaze now fixed on me with renewed sharpness. She tries to hide a smirk behind her hand, but it's clear she's riled.

"I know you're not speaking to me like that when your arms look—"

"What?" I cut her off, my voice cold and unwavering. "Like I cut? Newsflash: I do. Usually, it's to keep people like you at a distance. Are you going to keep pretending I'm wrong, or are you going to sulk away to the person you're flaunting that massive ring for?"

The woman's face pales as she looks at Roman, her shock evident.

"Eden, you're being incredibly disrespectful—"

"Yeah, Father?" I retort, the words dripping with intentional provocation. "You gonna do something about it, or are you going to keep standing there holding your—"

Roman's eyes widen, a look of genuine surprise crossing his face. He seems momentarily stunned by my audacity.

"Well, I've never—"

"Eden, come with me right now," Roman commands, his tone shifting to one of stern authority. He steps closer, his voice low but intense. "We are done playing games."

He grabs my wrist with a firm grip, pulling me away from the game with an almost palpable sense of urgency. A triumphant smirk tugs at the corners of my lips as we leave the gossiping crowd behind.

"No wonder David asked Father to get her in check," I hear someone whisper, their words laced with the lies Roman fed my father.

Roman leads me to a photo booth, away from prying eyes. As he slides the door open and nudges me inside, I lean back against the wall, my eyes locked on him with a smirk of defiance. He closes and locks the door, a decisive click echoing in the small space.

"What?" I ask, my tone taunting. "Can't I have a little fun?"

"Fun is exactly why we're here, Eden," Roman replies, his voice firm, almost reverent in its gravity. "Now, get on your knees for me."

I study him with a mixture of challenge and curiosity, my mind racing as I weigh my next move.

"What I did was entirely justified."

"You were angry because you saw the way those women were looking at me," He responds, stepping closer. "You were jealous. Jealous of their gaze, of their curiosity about what's in my pants. So why don't you show me just how much you value what you've been given?" His voice grows low, a hint of arousal unmistakable in his tone.

The heat between my legs intensifies, a shiver of anticipation running through me. I bite my bottom lip, the desire building.

"And if someone needs the booth?" I tease, a mischievous glint in my eyes.

"Guess they'll have to wait," Roman replies, his gaze darkening with promise. "Now show me."

I smile, pushing his chest firmly, watching him stagger back before catching himself, just stopping short of falling into the seat.

Guiding him to sit down, Roman's eyes flash with understanding as I look down at the bulge in his pants. He helps me with his belt, unfastening his zipper, his hardened length coming free. I drop to my knees before him, my tongue tracing up the base of his cock. I smile as his head tilts back, savoring the pleasure. I look up at him, my gaze innocent, as I swirl my tongue around the head of his erection.

"Mmm, Eden," He murmurs, a smirk playing on his lips. "Why don't you come up here and let me taste those pretty lips?"

Without hesitation, I shift to sit on his lap, wrapping my arms around his neck as his hands find my waist. He slides his hand up my thigh and moves aside my underwear with a deft touch. His fingers caress the lace that clings to me, his expression one of pleased satisfaction.

"Just for me?" He asks, a note of possessiveness in his voice.

"Always," I grin, feeling his head align with my entrance.

Connecting his lips with mine, I turn fully to straddle him, his mouth capturing my moan. His hands are on my hip, guiding me down until I'm fully seated on his cock, filling me up and stretching me to my limits.

He bites my lip hard, drawing blood, lapping it up hungrily as I rock my hips against him. He moves his tongue from my lower lip to my neck, coating my skin in a warm mix of his saliva and my blood. His hands slam me down hard onto his cock.

"Is this what you wanted, pretty girl?" He questions. "You wanted to feel my cock buried inside of you, reminding your pussy who it belongs to?" He questions. Rolling his fingers over my clit, he works me just right. I press my head to his chest, seconds away from release as his filthy words wash over me.

Tensing up around his dick, I latch my teeth to his shoulder, letting him feel the pain as my release coats him, catching us both off guard. Our breathless moans mix together, and I'm unsure which noises are coming from which of us. I pull myself off of his cock, lowering myself back to my knees before he can stop me. I wrap my mouth around him, licking up my sweet release from his length.

I savor the taste on my tongue, dragging back up his underwear once I'm finished. Wiping my lip clean, I readjust my clothes, watching as he does the same, his eyes glued to me.

I raise a brow at him as he pats his lap. "You think I'm not rewarding you after all of that, Angel?" He asks. "Sit down and let me take a few pictures with my girl."

Sitting on his lap, he throws a few dollar bills in the machine, clicking the **'take photo now'** button. Kissing my neck up and down, the camera flashes.

"I love you, Eden," He whispers, causing me to look him in the eyes.

Staring at him, another flash goes off.

"I love you too, Roman," I whisper. "So do one thing for me. Don't leave me."

He tugs at a chain around his neck, his gold band hanging from it.

"I told you I made my decision," He whispers. "I choose you."

Clouded with emotion, I press my lips to his once again, kissing him with a new hunger I've never felt before.

Flashing one last time, the camera captures something I'll remember for a lifetime.

The moment I knew I was truly in love with Roman Briar

1 Corinthians 13:8a: "Love bears all things, endures all things. Love never ends."

Idlewood
Fall Festival

Chapter 30

ROMAN

Swiping through the photos with quick, deliberate movements, I notice a couple approaching the photo booth, casting curious glances at Me and Eden as she staggers out. I interlace my fingers with hers, guiding her away from the booth. Her rosy cheeks, glowing with a mix of excitement and embarrassment, captivate me.

"I should piss you off more often," She says with a playful smile, our hands finally parting as we begin to mingle with the crowd.

"I kind of enjoyed seeing you so jealous," I grin, watching her eyes widen in surprise. "But you should know by now, my focus is solely on one woman."

"Look what the cat dragged in," Aiden's voice cuts through the moment.

Zoey approaches, her arms overflowing with fair treats and oversized lemonades, clearly having used Aiden as her personal shopping assistant all day.

"I told you they'd come," Zoey exclaims, rushing to hug Eden.

Zoey's gaze lingers on Eden, her expression shifting to concern. "Why are you so warm?" She asks, her voice tinged with worry. "Your skin is burning up."

"I'm fine, Zo," Eden reassures her, brushing off the obvious signs of the booth's activities.

I tuck the photos deep into my pocket, the memory of the moment etched vividly in my mind.

I love you too, Roman. So do one thing for me. Don't leave.

The way she looked at me when she said it was haunting. All her life, people had come and gone, leaving without a word. When I told Eden I loved her, it wasn't mere words; it was the essence of my being.

"I could really go for one of those," Eden says with a wide grin, eyeing the large lemonade.

I pull out a five and hand it to her, nudging toward the stand. "Go. You earned it," I joke, watching her cheeks flush with pleasure.

Zoey grabs her hand, leading her to the stand, leaving me and Aiden to converse alone.

"How long do you plan on playing the loving boyfriend act behind closed doors before you shatter my sister's heart?" Aiden asks, his gaze steady as he watches the girls.

"It's not an act. Once the kids are safe, I'm done with my priesthood," I say, meeting his gaze. "I'll take your sister far away from here. And if you and Zoey choose to come with us, you're welcome to."

Aiden raises his brows, confusion evident. "You dedicated so much to becoming a priest. Why give it up for my sister?"

"I love your sister, Aiden," I admit, his confusion deepening. "A life without her is a life I can't bear. If I'm to see Heaven's gates, I intend for her to be there with me. I once viewed our relationship as sinful, but now I see she's the reason I believe in an afterlife."

"You were skeptical?"

"I can don the clerical robes and preach to the masses, but the world's cruelty often makes it hard to believe in a loving God," I confess.

"I suppose that's why he gave us free will," Aiden muses. "The ability to sin—and to love."

"If loving Eden is a gift from Him, then I will cherish it."

"Are you not afraid of the repercussions of being so entangled with the church's secrets once they discover you're the mole?" Aiden asks.

Terrified. I'm fucking terrified.

"They won't know until it's too late," I sigh. "My priority today is ensuring your sister experiences a moment of joy."

Aiden's scoff catches my attention. "I used to think you were incapable of smiling, Father. Seems I was mistaken."

I touch the corner of my mouth, feeling the curve of my lips.

Eden Faulkner. Look at the life you've breathed into me.

Eden

"This is definitely going to make me piss myself," I joke, marveling at the oversized lemonade.

Between Roman's recent advances and this 32oz drink, I might as well be inviting a UTI to join the party.

"Isn't that part of the thrill?" Zoey laughs. "Walking around these fairs, always having to sprint across the grounds to find a bathroom?"

That, or riding my priest in the photo booth. I guess our ideas of thrill differ.

"You know, when he's with you, it's like he has a soul," Zoey smiles.

"What do you mean?" I ask, curious.

"When he's with you, Eden, he looks at you like you're the reason the Earth turns. It's as if your time together has changed his perspective on life."

As I reflect on Roman's earlier words about leaving his priesthood, a thought lingers. Did I give him a reason to see life differently, to see it as more than a battle?

"Though I have to admit, he's quite the looker," Zoey whispers. "Can't say I'm not curious about how he is in bed."

"Let's just say I need a day to recover after he's finished with me—"

"Hey there," A gravelly voice interrupts, causing both Zoey and me to turn toward a group of middle-aged men lingering near the cider station.

Ignoring them, we keep moving.

"Isn't that the girl from that asshole's phone?" One of the men says, raising immediate alarm bells in my mind.

Keep walking, Eden. Just keep walking.

But one of the men grabs my arm, yanking it painfully as my drink shatters on the ground.

His gaze lingers over my scars before settling on my face. "Couldn't see all those scars in the photo, but damn, you do have a pretty face—"

"Get your fucking hands off her!" Zoey yells, shoving the man away and wrapping her arms around me.

"Zoey, let's just go—"

But the other two men move in, blocking our path and encircling us like vultures.

"Yeah, that's definitely her. Same pretty eyes and pink lips," The man in front of me hisses, stepping closer. "Where's your boyfriend now? You look a lot more appealing when he isn't slamming my head into a wall," He sneers, a fresh scar on his forehead.

"Boyfriend?" I ask, horrified. "Did Roman hurt you?"

"He did a lot more than hurt me. He humiliated me and my friends," He snaps, nodding toward his companions.

The men behind us grab us, their fingers tightening around our waists as we struggle, causing a commotion that draws attention from bystanders who begin to record the scene.

"I think it's only fair we return the favor—"

Before I can react, Roman and Aiden burst into the scene. Roman's dark hair and Aiden's curly locks are visible as they drag the men away, beating them mercilessly. The crowd watches, many recording, as Roman pummels one of the men into unconsciousness and then turns to the next.

When Roman goes after the second man, Aiden steps in, trying to keep up with the fight. Roman, now focused on the man holding me, draws a switchblade. The man presses the knife against my lower back, his hand tightening around my throat.

"How does it feel to be so vulnerable, hm, Roman?" The man taunts, using the name I provided.

Roman hands Zoey off to Aiden and raises his hands in a gesture of surrender.

Fair security finally arrives, with Aiden briefing them as Roman tries to reason with the man.

"Grab that fucking gun, and I'll make sure she never walks again," The man threatens, gripping my throat tighter.

Roman's gaze is intense, clearly searching for a solution as the onlookers, including churchgoers, watch the standoff.

"Your issue is with me, not her. Surely you're man enough to put that knife to my back—"

"Why would I do that?" The man sneers, digging the knife deeper into my skin. "Her pain sounds so nice. Almost as nice as the look on your face."

The crowd watches, some recording, as Roman attempts to draw the man's attention away from me.

"Because it's me you're trying to get attention from, and it's worked—"

"I warned you. I warned you what would happen if I saw her—"

"Well, here I am," Roman exclaims, peeling off his flannel, ready to fight. "So why don't you man the fuck up and—"

Reaching behind me, I grab the knife, dragging it down my back until he has let go. I hiss in pain as I stomp on the man's foot, causing him to curse and loosen his grip.

Roman seizes the chance, pulling me away from the man despite the shouts from security. He drives his fist into the man's face repeatedly. Grabbing the knife from the ground, he thrashes at the man with the blade, continuing to threaten him even after security has intervened.

A medic presses a cloth to my back, applying pressure as they move me away from the chaos. Roman is eventually restrained by security but continues to struggle, trying to grab one of their guns.

Zoey and Aiden help me, with Aiden working to calm the security guards.

"Get the fuck off me," Roman snaps, breaking free from the security guards' hold, their attention divided between him and the three unconscious men.

"I've got it," Roman insists, taking over the medic's role, pressing the cloth to my back with a firmness that surprises me.

"Sir, I should really—"

"I said I got it," Roman interrupts, focusing solely on me.

He cups my face gently, his gaze full of concern. "Are you okay?"

"Can we go home?" I ask, my voice trembling.

"Absolutely," He replies, his jaw clenched with determination.

As I scan the crowd, I spot someone in a black hoodie lingering at the edge, their head down and a cross pendant hanging from their neck. They quickly tuck their phone away and turn, disappearing into the crowd.

Ignoring the onlookers, Roman keeps his hand on my lower back and guides us, along with Aiden and Zoey, back to the cars. As we drive away, Roman checks on me repeatedly, his worry palpable.

"That night I came to reservoir and you saw my face all banged up, I had a run-in with the guys who had you. He saw a picture of you on my phone—"

I grab his hand, stopping his spiraling thoughts. "Let's just go back to your place. I'm sure you can find a way to make it up to me."

Roman says nothing more as he puts the car in drive, the figure in the hoodie lingering in my mind.

Chapter 31

DAVID

"What am I looking at here?" I ask, my eyes fixed on the phone's screen.

"Just watch. One of our guys at the fair caught this on camera."

The video shows three men surrounding Eden and Zoey, both dressed in revealing outfits. The scene quickly escalates as the men grab the girls with aggressive intent.

"So what? My daughter probably mouthed off," I say dismissively.

"Just keep watching."

As the video progresses, Roman and Aiden appear, intervening with brutal force. The sight of Roman's dark tattoos confirms his identity. He's engaged in a fierce fight, trying to rescue Eden, who is being held hostage by the largest man.

"He won't do anything," I sneer. "He knows she deserves—"

Roman's relentless attacks on the men contradict my expectations. He focuses his fury on the attackers, pushing them to the ground. A medic attends to Eden's injuries until Roman takes over, his protective nature evident in his tender handling of her wounds.

"This next part is what you'll want to see," The assistant says, their tone serious.

I watch in disbelief as Roman gently cups Eden's face, his touch tender and concerned. The sight of their intimacy strikes me deeply.

"Roman Briar is not disciplining my daughter... He loves her," I hiss, my frustration palpable.

"Yes," the assistant confirms, nodding. "Roman Briar is a mole. His relationship with Eden is more than just a pretense. He's been playing Devil's advocate under the guise of bringing light."

I slam the phone on my desk, my anger rising. "How long until the bidders get a good look at the lot?"

"One month," They reply.

"And Roman still doesn't know the kids' location?" I demand.

"Unless he sees the remodel's construction plans, he won't find the basement anytime soon."

"There's something else," They add, their voice tense.

"Go on."

"Father Kevin called. Roman's been speaking to the Vatican about leaving the priesthood."

I'm enraged. Roman's influence over my daughter is evident. "What's next?"

"We need to give Roman a reason to submit, to back down. The town may be on lockdown, but Roman has resources. One wrong move and Homeland Security could intervene. We need a strategic approach."

"A threat won't be enough. We need to leverage his attachment to Eden," I plan, envisioning how this could work to our advantage.

"Let's put Eden in the lineup," They suggest, flipping through a portfolio of photos. They replace Zoey's picture with Eden's, emphasizing the new threat.

"Isn't that what I intended?" I question, a hint of satisfaction in my voice.

"It was a threat, but now it's a tactical move. Love clouds judgment. Roman's attachment to Eden could be our leverage."

Smiling, I savor the thought of Roman's shock when he sees the updated lineup. "Dangle his prized possession and watch him react."

"Yes. Eden's value to the bidders will be significant, especially given her resilience. This could drive Roman to act recklessly."

"And if Eden is out of the picture, Aiden will have to return home," I add, considering the implications.

"Precisely. It sets the stage for us to regain control."

My wife's voice interrupts, soft and obedient. "Dinner is ready."

"Prepare an extra plate for our guest," I instruct, turning back to the plan.

We toast to new beginnings, savoring the thought of Roman's downfall.

"To the end of Father Briar," We both agree, clinking glasses.

Chapter 32

EDEN

Roman tosses his keys onto the counter, his exhaustion palpable. His mind is a whirlpool of thoughts, each dragging him deeper into despair. His hands, bruised and stained with dried blood, speak of the violence he's endured.

"I should have known better than to trust those men," He murmurs, his voice heavy with regret. He runs a hand through his disheveled hair, his eyes reflecting the weight of his failures.

I reach out, gently clasping his hands to stop his spiraling thoughts. "Roman, you didn't know—"

"But I did," He interrupts, his voice sharp. "I knew they were low-life scum, and I should have confronted them. I walked away, Eden, and because of it, you got hurt."

"It's just a cut—"

"Not to me," He snaps, cupping my face with a desperate intensity. "I'm supposed to protect you, shield you from all the darkness in the world—"

"That's not living, Roman," I counter softly, my gaze filled with regret. "No one can be shielded from all the evils of the world. If you try, you'll only drive yourself mad."

His eyes drift to his shirt, still stained with Eric's blood. The grim reality of our situation hangs heavily between us.

"You've already risked so much by staying. Don't torment yourself over the fact that some people are beyond redemption," I comfort him.

"It's consuming me," He whispers, pressing his forehead to mine. "This longing, this overwhelming urge to keep you close, to make sure you're only mine—"

His gaze falls to the cut on my back, and I wince as he touches it gently.

"It angers me," He continues, his voice trembling with emotion. "It angers me that your pain brought no satisfaction. It angers me even more that I wish I were the one who inflicted it—"

"Roman," I interject softly, halting his distressing tirade. "I asked you to come here, not just to my house, for a reason. I know who you are, Roman Briar. So take the key, and—"

Before I can finish, he lifts me effortlessly over his shoulder, draping my upper body down his back. His hand rests possessively on my ass as he strides toward the bedroom.

"Remember, Eden, you asked for this," He growls, a predatory smile tugging at his lips.

"I know," I whisper, a smile of my own forming. "So don't disappoint me."

Coiling the rope around my wrists, he binds them above my head, keeping my body restrained on the bed. The closet door stands ajar, revealing a collection of torturous devices: nipple clamps, leg spreaders, vibrators—everything a mind could conceive. Roman has amassed it all.

"How many women have seen the inside of your closet?" I ask, watching him move away from my wrists.

"Just you," He replies, a hint of pride in his voice. "I thought collecting might curb the urge to use them. Clearly, that's not the case."

He pulls off my skirt, leaving me clad only in my crop top and underwear, my anticipation growing with every move he makes. Shirtless, his body in the dim light is a sight to behold. Tattoos snake up his arm and neck, ending at his hip, the intricate designs accentuating his muscular form. His dark sweats hang low, and he tugs at the drawstring, letting his hand brush over his growing length.

"So, Angel," He purrs, inching closer, "are you ready?"

"Depends," I retort with a sly smile, "how hard do you plan on going?"

"As hard as you can handle," He murmurs, his voice low and intense.

Roman retreats to the closet, emerging with a concealed object. With deliberate slowness, he pulls me to the end of the bed by one ankle, stretching me as far as my bound wrists allow, the strain adding a thrilling edge.

He yanks down my underwear and kneels at the foot of the bed. With my legs draped over his shoulders, he gains full access, the anticipation making my heart race. He retrieves a large silicone toy from behind his back, the same one he used to prepare me for his size.

"If you cum from this," He threatens, his voice a dark whisper, "I'll make sure you regret it. The only pleasure you get to have is from my cock."

He spits on my exposed warmth before dragging his tongue slowly down my folds, his touch deliberate and torturous. My breath hitches, small whimpers escaping as I close my eyes, losing myself in the sensation.

"Do you want it inside you?" He teases, nipping at my inner thighs, driving me to squirm.

I glance down at him, a smirk playing on my lips. "I want nothing more."

His eyes darken with a mix of desire and anger as he slides the toy into me, filling me completely. My hips buck, and my back arches in response, craving more.

"You like it, Eden?" He asks, his voice brooking no argument.

"I'd like your mouth even more," I whisper, my voice trembling. "Why don't you—"

He doesn't need further encouragement. His mouth lands on my swollen clit, his tongue working in tandem with the toy. He thrusts the toy into me with unrelenting force, his mouth teasing and tormenting, pushing me to the brink. I struggle against the bindings, desperate to free my hands, to push him away before the climax overwhelms me.

"What's the matter, pretty girl?" He asks, his grip firm on my thigh. "Are you going to cum on something that isn't my cock?" His tongue trails slowly over my clit, sending shivers through me.

Desperately trying to hold back, I meet his gaze. The sight of him working the toy in and out of me while lavishing attention on my clit is overwhelming.

I can't stop it.

The warmth surges through my lower stomach as I arch my back, letting out a guttural moan, my release coating the toy. Roman swiftly pulls it away, taking several measured breaths as he examines the toy, his tongue savoring the taste of my cum.

"That's not me," He hisses, his voice edged with frustration. "Bad girl, Eden."

Standing up, he sheds his sweats and retrieves something from the top of his dresser. My heart races as I catch sight of the gleaming knife, its sharp edge catching the light. Roman handles it with a dangerous calm, running his finger over the blade.

"I told you," He murmurs, "it angered me how he brought you pain. You will only bleed with me, Eden Faulkner."

He looms over me, pressing the knife's edge under my shirt, slicing upward until it's torn away, exposing my aching breasts. With my body on full display, he drags the knife's point gently down my chest to my lower stomach, tracing a path of tension and anticipation.

He makes a small cut, drawing a trickle of blood, my breath catching in a sharp hiss.

"Keep singing for me, Angel," He commands softly. "Keep fucking singing."

Tossing the knife onto the nightstand, he lets the blood trail down my hip bone, his tongue eagerly licking the blood from my skin. Dropping his underwear, he gives himself a few deliberate strokes before grabbing my legs, his eyes intense with a lingering emotion.

"I hope you're flexible, baby."

He grabs the backs of my thighs, pulling my knees to the sides of my head, stretching me as far as possible. Fully exposed, I bite my lip hard enough to draw blood, my anticipation mounting.

Spitting once more on my warmth for lubrication, he slides into me. The sensation of him is more intense compared to the toy. I let out a sound somewhere between a scream and a moan, wrapping around him, singing for him in the way he desires.

"There's my pretty girl," He groans, pulling back slowly before thrusting back into me. "God, you're so fucking beautiful," He praises, his movements growing more intense.

"Look at me fucking you, Eden," He hisses, his voice raw with desire. "Look at my cock driving into your perfect pussy."

Forcing my head down, I watch him as his cock slides in and out of me, hitting my g-spot perfectly due to the position he's put me in. Straining against the binds, I attempt to look away but am met with a sharp slap across my face.

"Did I tell you to stop fucking watching?" He demands, his anger palpable.

Defiantly, I meet his gaze. "Why don't you take off these binds and fuck me like a real man?"

The familiar look crosses his face. He grabs the knife from the nightstand, slicing through the binds with swift, practiced movements, and tosses the knife away.

He flips me onto my stomach with a decisive motion, the sting of his hand across my ass leaving me gasping. My hips instinctively lift toward him, a whimper escaping my lips.

With deliberate force, he lines himself up and drives into me, each thrust causing a reverberating ache in my hips. His rhythm is relentless, pushing me to the edge with every movement. I clutch the sheets, my moans mingling with the sound of our bodies colliding.

"Is this what you want, Eden?" He growls, his fingers digging into my hips. "You want me to make you feel every inch of me, to make you come apart for me?" His voice is rough, a stark contrast to the rising pitch of my moans.

I feel his intensity and my own pleasure blending into a heady mix. My fingers find their way to my clit, rubbing with urgency. He grips the back of my neck, pulling me closer so his lips can graze my neck, his free hand caressing one of my breasts. The dual sensation of his touch and the toy drives me wild.

"Cum for me, baby girl," He commands, his voice strained with desire. "Let go for me. Now."

The moment I surrender to my climax, he muffles my scream with his hand, our bodies entwining in a chaotic tangle of passion. We collapse onto the bed, breathless and spent.

He pulls me into his embrace, covering us both with a blanket. I rest my head on his chest, his heartbeat steady beneath me. He tilts my chin up, his kiss tender and reverent.

"You were perfect," He murmurs against my lips. "I love you."

"I love you too, Roman," I whisper, my voice soft but filled with affection.

He covers me with the blanket, his kisses gentle as he tends to the cut he made. "It will heal," He reassures me, his touch lingering.

"I don't mind," I smile, running my fingers through his hair. "It's a part of you."

His kisses trace up my body, returning to my lips. "You drive me mad, you know that?" He whispers, holding me close.

"I'll embrace every bit of it," I reply, a playful grin on my face.

"Once we're out of this mess, I'm taking you far away from Idlewood—anywhere you want."

"Anywhere?" I ask, my eyes lighting up.

"Just say the word," He promises.

"I've always wanted to see Scotland in the fall," I say, my smile widening.

"Then Scotland it is," He declares. "We'll explore the world together, making our own rules along the way," he adds with a teasing glint in his eye.

"Promise you'll stay with me?" I ask, my tone serious.

"Eden Faulkner, the moment we're free, I'm putting a ring on your finger and never letting you go."

"Eden Briar," I murmur. The name feels like a perfect fit.

"Almost as if God himself made it," He replies softly, holding me close.

Ecclesiastes 4:9: "Having someone to lean on through good and bad times is a sacred gift."

Chapter 33

Eden

"I look absolutely ridiculous," I seethe, glaring at the elf costume that clings to me.

"Don't worry, Eden," Zoey snaps with a forced cheerfulness. "The kids will love it."

The festive spirit is overwhelming, with twinkling lights and gaudy ornaments strewn about. A massive pine tree, cluttered with decorations, dominates the corner of the café, its presence a constant reminder of the season.

"I think Christmas has been tainted for me by the church," I sigh, feeling the weight of memories.

For me, Christmas was always about maintaining an image and avoiding greed. On the surface, my family's Christmas was perfect—glittering trees, golden lights, and endless presents.

No one would have suspected the truth: my father's violent rages, the angel on top of the tree serving as a symbol of his wrath, and the presents tossed into the fire when he'd had too much to drink.

"Holy shit," Aiden laughs as he enters the café, taking in the sight of us. "When you said they were making you dress up, I didn't expect this!" He pulls out his phone to snap a picture.

"Do that, and I'll grind your phone into coffee grounds," I hiss, swatting at him.

As I move, Roman's gold ring glints from under my shirt, catching the eyes of Aiden and Zoey.

"Is that—"

I quickly tuck the ring away before they can get a good look, returning to my work behind the counter. Their questioning looks are hard to ignore.

"Is that Roman's ring?" Zoey whispers, clearly intrigued. "He gave you his ring—"

"He's quitting his priesthood once this is all over," I whisper back, glancing around to ensure no one else is listening. "He gave it to me as a reminder that his role in the church is only temporary."

It's been four months since I met Roman and three since we became exclusive. Despite the short time, our bond feels deep and profound, as if we've known each other for years.

"Is that a priest's way of giving a promise ring?" Aiden jokes, unwittingly hitting closer to the truth than he realizes.

Roman was serious. His words from two weeks ago were no joke. Since then, his affection has only intensified—flowers in my apartment, spontaneous dates, and passionate intimacy. It's all been exhilarating.

"Maybe it is," I sigh. "But that doesn't change the fact that I'm stuck in this ridiculous costume serving coffee at nine in the morning," I add, handing a drink to a customer with a forced smile.

"Mass is tonight," Aiden whispers. "And Roman's meeting—"

"I know what tonight is, Aiden," I snap, my patience wearing thin. "I don't need a reminder."

"I just thought you might need some mental preparation. It's a lot," He says with genuine sympathy.

"It'll be okay," I say for what feels like the millionth time. "Roman will be okay."

The deeper my attachment to Roman grows, the more I worry about his well-being.

"I almost want to show up in this costume," Zoey says with a touch of defiance. "Elf hat and all, flipping off anyone who looks at me wrong."

"Have you talked to your father?" I ask, noticing her expression falter.

"No, not my stepmother either. My mom has added extra locks and alarms, and she even keeps a gun under her pillow. If my dad tries to reach out, she'll make sure to keep him at bay."

It's hard to see Zoey going to such lengths for her own safety. She puts on a brave front, but I can see the fear beneath.

We're all scared.

As the espresso flows into the cup, I fiddle with Roman's ring, counting to ten in my head.

It will all be over soon.

As I get dressed, I cinch the rope belt around my waist, pulling it tight.

The church is already alive with the festive cheer of Christmas, even though it's still early in the month.

I glance in the mirror, and for the first time in a while, my reflection doesn't look so weary. My eyes are bright with a new-found energy, something I've been missing for too long.

All thanks to Roman.

I hear the murmurs of people gathering in the waiting area as the doors to Mass prepare to open. Checking the time, I note that Roman still has twenty-five minutes left in confession.

Perhaps it's time for me to unburden myself of some sins.

In the dimly lit room, I look at the divider that separates Roman from his confessional. It casts an ominous shadow, adding gravity to the act of confessing one's deepest secrets. I shut the door with a deliberate noise to let him know I'd arrived.

"Take a seat, my child, and—"

"I've sinned terribly, Father," I interject, my voice smooth and teasing as I hear him shift behind the divider.

"Really?" He responds, his professional tone slipping into something more intimate. "What have you done Angel?" His question stirs a thrill within me.

"Let's see," I begin, sighing provocatively. "I can't seem to get my priest out of my mind. Sometimes, I wake up in the middle of the night, wondering what his touch would feel like."

A soft laugh escapes him as he continues.

"You want him to touch you?"

"Desperately," I reply, pushing further. "I'm consumed by sinful thoughts of his touch, his tongue exploring every inch of my body."

He shifts again, the tension palpable.

"I don't think I can help you from behind this divider," He murmurs. "What you need is some one-on-one prayer."

Smiling, I step past the divider and close it behind me. Roman leans casually in his chair, his eyes heavy with frustration and desire.

"You see what you've done?" He groans. "I have Mass in twenty-three minutes."

"What a pity," I smirk, leaning against the wall. "You still haven't helped me with my sinful thoughts."

"Come here," He commands, his voice edged with urgency. "I'll give you a reason to be on your knees."

I move closer, watching as he pulls up the hem of my robe, exposing my black dress underneath.

"Father Briar, what are you doing?" I ask, though my tone is more curious than concerned.

He meets my gaze with smoldering eyes filled with lust.

"Do you want to feel my touch?" He asks, his voice low and rough. I nod slowly. "Then ride me like the little slut you are."

I tear off his robe and fumble with his pants, finally revealing his underwear. I pull down my thong, letting it fall around my ankles, giving him a clear view. Pulling down his underwear, I quickly straddle him, aligning myself with him. The choir's music crescendos, masking the sounds of our encounter.

Roman guides me as I ride him, the choir's loud chorus covering my moans. His hand clamps over my mouth as I continue moving, the rosary I had brought from my pocket wrapped around his neck. The pressure of the rosary makes him even more intense.

"God, look at you. Is this what you wanted? Your priest's cock buried in your pretty little pussy?"

The door swings open suddenly, and we freeze, locked in our illicit act.

"Father, are you still here?" Comes Luca's voice.

Roman's grip tightens as he forces me down, his hand still over my mouth. The choir's music hides the sounds of our bodies.

"Of course," Roman says with restraint. "Take a seat."

I meet Roman's eyes, tightening around him as he tries to hide his groan.

"Father, I have so much to confess," Luca continues, his voice laced with tension.

"Speak," Roman snaps, his fingertips digging into my skin.

Leaning close, I whisper in his ear, "Forgive me, Father, for I have sinned."

Roman's eyes widen as I rip off the remainder of my robe and dress, revealing myself completely.

He devours the sight of me, his tongue tracing up my body, nipping at my nipples.

"I did something bad, Father," Luca says. "I hurt someone I cared about deeply. I wanted her so badly, I did things I'd never normally do—"

"I'm yours, right Father?" I whisper. "Are you going to let him say that?"

"I think you're better off without her," Roman grits out, covering my mouth as he thrusts into me.

The choir's music and Roman's loud voice drown out Luca's words.

"See, that's the thing. I want her—"

"You won't have her," Roman snaps, holding my hips tightly as I move. "You'll never have her."

I smile, taking off the rosary and kissing him passionately, biting his bottom lip until it bleeds.

"I don't think that's the case," Luca challenges. "She'll find a way to come back around—"

"No, she won't," Roman growls, his cock twitching inside me. "She's not yours anymore. The sooner you accept that, the better."

I squeeze his throat as I ride him, savoring the power I hold.

"You speak as though you're invested, Father—"

"Get out," Roman barks. "I'm done listening to you."

Luca's footsteps fade, the door slamming shut behind him.

"You're getting it tonight—"

"Why don't you shut your fucking mouth, Roman, and cum for me?"

With that encouragement, Roman's release fills me, and I moan, muffled by his hand. I ride him until I'm sore, then pull off, kneeling before him.

"Forgive me," I whisper, licking him clean. "I will never stop sinning with you."

Once I'm done, he pulls me up, helps me get dressed, and ties the rope belt around my waist. I settle back in his lap, kissing him gently, tasting the blood on my lips.

"I'm addicted to you, Eden," He confesses. "You're a drug to me."

"I love you, Roman Briar," I reply softly.

"Love barely covers how much you mean to me," He snaps. "Now, are you ready to get this Mass over with?"

I slide off his lap, and he takes my hand, guiding me past the divider.

He kisses the top of my head and nuzzles my neck, his voice soft in my ear.

"You were such a good girl for me. I can't wait to reward you when we're home."

It seems I finally have something to look forward to after Sunday Mass.

Chapter 34

ROMAN

I check the time as the other members of this nefarious club filter into the space, their movements synchronized with chilling precision. I instructed Eden to lock all doors and windows and stay confined in my room. The proximity of so many vile individuals to my home and to her unsettles me deeply.

It's almost over.

Just one more meeting to endure—

"Roman!" David's voice cuts through the tension as he strides over to me, an unusually bright grin on his face.

His cheerful demeanor is out of character.

I shake his grimy hand, forcing a smile. "David. How are things? How's the wife's mood swings been?"

"Could be better," He replies, dismissing the mention of his wife's declining mental health. "She's been insufferable since the kids left. But who cares about her feelings? She's nothing but a nuisance," He sneers, showing no remorse for belittling Aiden and Eden's mother.

"Ready for the last meeting?" David asks, glancing around the room.

"Last meeting?" I echo, puzzled.

"The last one before the bidding," He explains with a grin. "Everyone's coming in this Sunday. They're eager to see this year's lot." His tone hints at something more. "Millions are pouring in. I imagine you're looking forward to leaving Idlewood."

"Leaving Idlewood?" I narrow my eyes at him.

"Didn't Kevin tell you?" David continues, his smile widening. "He's finished scouting next year's lineup and decided to head home earlier than expected. Your time here will soon be up. By the end of next week, you won't be needed."

I meet David's gaze directly, raising my eyebrows. "I was unaware of my imminent departure."

"Are you really surprised, Roman?" David's eyes flicker past me, his gaze resting on the others in the room. "I'm aware of your little scene at the fair," He hisses, causing my heart to race. "I can't afford any leaks in this operation. I'm giving you a chance to leave Idlewood without my daughter by the end of next week. There will be no consequences if you do," David warns. "I'd hate for someone to get hurt because you can't rid yourself of your sinful ways."

I step back, adjusting my collar as David's words echo in my mind. The urgency of the situation intensifies—I have even less time to expose the horrors lurking behind these walls.

I click the record button, the small device hidden in my pocket. Taking a seat among the group, I cast a wary glance at Seth's vacant chair. Is he monitoring Eden and me from the outside?

"Hello, everyone, and welcome to one of our final meetings of the year before the big day," David announces with a forced cheer, eliciting applause and cheers from the crowd.

Brainwashed fools.

"As some of you know, this will be Father Briar's last meeting with us before our beloved Kevin returns home," David continues, his gaze sweeping over the assembly. All eyes turn to me.

Why hasn't David exposed me yet?

What is he holding back?

What's his game?

"Why is Kevin coming back so soon? Last year, it took him nine months—"

"After Seth's abrupt departure, Kevin felt the need to return sooner, to be here with all of you," David responds brightly, his focus locked on me. "I'm concerned that Seth wasn't working alone when he killed that poor boy Eric. I suspect we may have more traitors among us than I'd like to admit," David adds, his voice tinged with concern, causing murmurs to ripple through the group.

What does David want?

What is he trying to achieve with all this?

"In addition to announcing Father Briar's departure, I'm pleased to inform you that a new family is joining our organization," David announces. "They won't be present until the night of the bidding, but their financial contributions are a significant factor in our operations this year... and Father Briar," He says, finally locking eyes with me. "You are required to attend. Kevin wishes to see you off and to give you a glimpse of what you're leaving behind," David adds with a disconcerting smile, causing a shiver to run down my spine.

I swear to God, I will have this church raided before David can blink.

"How is the lineup looking?" Someone asks.

David, with his portfolio clutched under his arm, presents the catalog filled with children like a prized possession.

"I think there are some this year that will keep you at the edge of your seats," He boasts. "Remember, the bidders can't bid on what they can't see. If you favor any of the lots, make sure to keep it clean."

Rage boils within me. I imagine SWAT storming this place, tearing it apart from top to bottom. I grip the recorder tightly.

"Any questions?" David surveys the group.

"Let's see the updated portfolio," I demand, watching David's smile widen.

"Gladly, Father."

With a flourish, he places the portfolio in my lap. My eyes dart to the back of the folder, where my worst fears are confirmed. I swallow hard as bile rises in my throat.

Bright eyes stare back at me—Eden Faulkner, Bid #30, Active.

I hurl the portfolio to the ground, seizing David by the collar. My fury erupts.

"Why the hell is she in there?" I roar, shoving him against the edge of the holy water pool, ready to unleash my anger just as I did with Zack.

"You know damn well why she's in there," David hisses. "So better pay up, or she's going far away, and there's nothing you can do about it."

I slam my fist into his jaw. Gasps erupt around me, and some stand in alarm.

As his blood splatters, I keep my foot on his chest, catching my breath.

"If any of you lay a fucking hand on her, I swear to Christ I will kill all of you," I growl, revealing my true intentions.

I stomp on David's hand. He screams, his companions readying to pounce.

Prepared, I draw my Glock from my waistband, aiming it at David's head.

"I fucking did it to Eric, and I'll gladly do it to this piece of shit," I hiss. "If any of you try anything, I'll have DHS in here in minutes," I warn, hoping my bluff isn't too obvious.

"Do not fucking threaten me in this house," David sneers, glancing at the statue of Jesus above the altar.

"I'm taking Eden and Aiden, and we're getting the hell out of Idlewood," I declare, ready to put a bullet in every one of these fuckers' heads.

"You'll regret this, Roman," David spits.

"Yeah?" I retort. "Apparently you don't know who you're dealing with."

I aim for a femoral artery in David's leg and fire. The shot rings out with a sickening satisfaction. His scream echoes off the walls. I level the gun at anyone who tries to approach, my finger poised on the trigger.

"I'm leaving," I snap. "Call the cops, and you'll just make DHS more suspicious," I threaten.

Gun still in hand, I snatch the portfolio and shove past anyone in my way, heading for the doors.

"You'll fucking regret this!" David's voice, pained and desperate, follows me.

I turn, raise the gun, and fire again, hitting his hand with grim pleasure.

As he screams, I smile, bloodlust consuming me.

"I fucking quit," I growl. "All of you will burn in Hell."

Without another word, I exit, determined to get Eden far away from this nightmare.

"Roman, what's going on—"

"Grab your things, Eden. There's no time to explain. We're going to your place, then getting the hell out of here. Just until things blow over."

I toss a few essentials into a duffel bag, keeping the one thing most precious to me close at hand. Eden's eyes, heavy with sleep and confusion, follow my hurried movements.

"Roman, I need some answers—"

"They put you on the bidding list, baby," I snap, cupping her face in my hands. "They put you on the bidding, and I need to keep you safe. Please, listen to me. They're all here. We have to get out before they realize we're still around."

Finally, she nods in agreement, her fear palpable.

We exit the house and sprint to my car. I make sure Eden is secure before ripping the plates off the front and back, tossing them in the backseat. Starting the engine, I see people beginning to pour out of the church. I back out quickly, keeping the lights off, and make a break for it.

As we hit the main highway, my hands tremble with adrenaline.

"Roman—"

"Hand me my phone," I whisper, watching her reach for it. The screen is filled with missed calls from Kevin. My cover is blown.

"Call Echo," I command, trying to steady my breathing.

The phone rings several times before Echo picks up, his groggy voice laced with irritation.

"Jesus fucking Christ, Roman. It's like 3 a.m. my time—"

"Echo, shut the fuck up," I snap, my mind racing. "I need your help. This isn't the fucking time to ridicule my life choices. Do you still work for DHS?"

"Yeah—"

"I'm calling in my favor," I warn, hearing him shift in bed.

"Roman, what's going on? You've never called like this—"

"That church I took a job at? It's a fucking trafficking ring," I yell. "And they've got the woman I love caught up in it—"

"Woman you love?" Echo's surprise is evident. "Jesus, Roman, I didn't think Idlewood—"

"Echo, I'm begging you," I plead, my voice cracking. "I can't let anything happen to her. When was the last time I gave a shit about my own life? This woman has given me a reason to live. I almost lost her before I even had a chance. Help me, please."

"I can get on a plane with a few of my guys in a few hours," Echo says, his tone shifting. "How bad are we talking, Roman?"

"There's a whole fucking catalog of children," I sigh, glancing at the discarded portfolio. "My girl's in there too."

Silence hangs heavy before Echo speaks again.

"When's the drop?"

"Next Sunday. Here at the church. I don't know where they're keeping them—"

"I'll see you soon, brother," Echo replies firmly. "Glad to see you've found some fight again."

I end the call, a wave of relief washing over me. I reach for Eden's trembling hand, giving it a reassuring squeeze.

"Who was that?" She asks, her voice laced with fear.

"Echo. His real name is Elijah. We served together. He's been working for DHS since he got out. It was time to call in a favor."

As we approach her apartment building, I glance around. No one seems to be trailing us, no police in sight.

I park and turn off the car. Gathering Eden in my arms, I whisper, "I shot your dad. I couldn't keep pretending—"

"I don't want to be here anymore, Roman," She sobs, her voice breaking with genuine pain. "I don't want to be in danger—"

I hold her close, bracing for the uncertainty that lies ahead.

"I won't let them hurt you, Eden," I whisper, my voice steady despite the turmoil inside. "You need to stay with me at all times. Aiden too. I'll keep you both safe—"

"Aiden is at Zoey's mom's tonight," She cries, her voice trembling with urgency. "We need to go get him—"

"He's safer there tonight," I reassure her. "I'll get him first thing in the morning—"

She kisses me, holding on as if her life depended on it, and I respond with a fervor I've never shown before, kissing her as if it's the first time. My arms wrap around her with an intensity that makes me forget everything but her.

"Can we go inside?" She sobs. "And please, don't leave my side tonight."

I wipe her tears away, nodding solemnly.

"Only if you promise to do the same."

With little hesitation, I lift her into my arms, carrying her inside. I only release her once we're in the bedroom, gently laying her down on the bed.

Chapter 35

EDEN

Jolted awake by the relentless buzzing of my phone, I glance over at Roman, who sleeps peacefully beside me. It seems all he needs for a good night's rest is to exhaust every ounce of energy, leaving me sore and walking funny for days.

Wincing at the soreness, I carefully climb out of bed, pulling on a pair of Roman's sweats and a tee. I grab my phone and quietly slip into the living room, closing the door as gently as possible.

The contact on the screen makes my heart race: "Mom?"

It's 3 a.m. Why would she be calling at this hour?

Maybe I shouldn't answer. Maybe—

"Hello?" I whisper, trying to keep my voice low for Roman's sake.

"Eden?" My mom's voice is scratchy and raw, a clear sign she's been crying.

"Yeah, Mom. How did you get this number—"

"Eden, baby, listen carefully," She interrupts, her tone urgent.

She hasn't called me "baby" since I was a child.

"I need you and your brother to get out of Idlewood. Take Roman and Zoey with you. Do whatever you need to leave this town. But please, don't stay here—"

"Mom, what's happening? Are you okay?"

"I messed up, Eden," she sobs. "I messed up by staying in this marriage. I messed up by letting him hurt you kids. There's no way to undo what's happened, but I can try to make things right now—"

"Mom, what did he do?" I press, struggling to keep my voice steady.

"Eden, there's no time to explain everything. You and your brother need to leave town tonight," She cries. "And stay as far away as you can—"

"Who the hell are you talking to?!" My dad's voice erupts, cutting my mom off abruptly.

"I do love you and your brother, Eden," my mom's voice trembles through the phone. "I'm sorry I never said it when it mattered."

Suddenly, there's a loud noise, as if the phone was dropped and shoved under something heavy. My mom's sobs are now distant, muffled by the weight of whatever has been placed over the receiver.

"Who the hell were you talking to?" My dad's voice growls with increasing anger.

She shoved me under the couch.

"N-No one, David—"

The sound of a slap makes my body flinch. My mom's cries pierce through the line, raw and desperate.

Tears stream down my face, hot and blinding, as I tremble in fear.

"You fucking lying bitch," My dad hisses. "Where the hell is it? Where is the phone?"

"You aren't going to keep harming our kids, David!" My mom's voice rises, defiant despite the fear. "Look at what this church has done to you. Look at what it did to us. You want to preach about sin? Well, guess what, I'm looking the Devil in the face now, and it's fucking vile—"

"Shut your goddamn mouth!" He roars, his anger making her scream cut sharply through the line.

The sound of thudding and gasps for breath fills the call, my mom struggling to breathe.

"H-Help—"

"You hear that, you fucking sneaky bastard?" My dad's voice is cold and cruel, clearly unaware of who's on the other end. "You hear my wife calling out while my hands are wrapped around her throat? I bet you want to call the police. Go ahead, be my fucking guest. See what they say when you tell them something's happening at the Faulkner house—"

"D-David—"

"I've been wanting a new obedient wife for a while now."

A loud thud follows, the sound of something cracking making my stomach churn.

Taking shallow, shaky breaths, I can barely make out my dad's voice, cold and indifferent.

"Go ahead and enjoy listening to her final breaths. Rot in hell, you bitch."

The sound of my dad's footsteps retreating fills the line, and my mom's gasps pierce through the chaos.

"Mom?" I call out, my voice trembling with desperation.

"A-Aiden," She moans, barely coherent.

Aiden? Why is she mentioning Aiden now?

"Mom, what's wrong with Aiden? I need you to reach for your phone—"

"A-Aiden," she groans in agony.

She can't hear me. She doesn't realize I'm still on the line.

I text Aiden, but the messages turn green, failing to deliver.

Glancing at Roman, a moral dilemma churns in my mind.

I could wait for Roman to wake up—

"E-Eden," My mom pleads. "H-Help."

Frustration wells up inside me.

If I wake Roman, he'll go alone. What if my dad does something to him?

My dad needs me alive for the bid.

I need to know if Aiden is okay.

Quietly slipping away from the bed, I make my way to the kitchen, grabbing Roman's Glock and tucking it into my waistband.

I order an Uber, inputting my address with a sinking feeling of dread.

"It's for Aiden," I murmur to myself.

I glance back at the bedroom, torn by the urgency of the situation.

"Someone has to keep Roman safe too."

That's all it takes to propel me out the door and straight into the fire.

Thirty minutes later, after a nerve-wracking Uber ride and an agonizing wait on my lawn, I stare at the ajar front door of my house.

Quietly nudging the door open, I know calling the cops would be futile. They'd side with my father in an instant.

The hallway is strewn with broken glass and shattered photo frames. A disturbing smear of blood streaks across the wall, intensifying my dread. My hand stays clenched around the hilt of the gun tucked under my shirt, every sense alert.

A single light spills from my father's study, casting a red pool on the floor.

Mom.

Quickening my pace, I draw the gun, one bullet in the chamber, ready to fire if needed.

Peeking into the study, my heart sinks. There she is—her matted hair and lifeless body on the floor, a pool of blood forming around her head.

"Mom," I whisper, crouching beside her. I gently roll her onto her back.

"Mom, where's Aiden—"

I choke on my words, covering my mouth as I survey the horror. Her forehead is caved in, blood seeping from the wound, her eyes glazed over and unseeing. I tear the bottom of Roman's shirt, pressing the cloth to her head, and scramble for my phone.

I pray the paramedics will do their job despite the house's reputation.

"Mom?" I whisper, desperate for a response.

Nothing.

"Fuck," I murmur, tears streaming down my face. "What the fuck?" I dial 911.

"911, what's your emergency?"

"It's my mom," I sob. "She—"

"Hand me the phone, Eden," Hisses a voice that makes my blood run cold.

I turn to see my father standing in the doorway, his own gun shaking in his hand.

"Ma'am, are you still there?" The operator's voice crackles through the phone.

"Hand it to me, or I'll put a bullet in your leg," My father threatens.

I extend my arm towards him, keeping the gun concealed between my legs. He grabs the phone from me, his expression shifting to a falsely cheery mask.

"Hey there, sorry for the mix-up," He says, his voice smooth as he speaks into the receiver. "My kid dialed the wrong number by accident." He chuckles, the sound twisted and mocking.

"Thank you for understanding. You have a great night, Donna."

My father hangs up the call, dropping my phone on the ground and crushing it with his foot.

"You see what happened to your mother?" He barks, pressing the barrel of his gun against the back of my head. "All because you and Roman couldn't keep your filthy hands off each other."

"Is she dead?" I whisper, still pressing the cloth against her head.

"She's with God now," He sighs, "enjoying eternal life in Heaven."

His lack of remorse is chilling.

I let out a sob, trying to think clearly despite the overwhelming pain.

"If you do anything to me, Roman will come after you," I plead.

"I hope he does," My father snaps, pressing the gun harder into my skull. "Maybe then he'll learn not to mess around."

"You can't kill me," I hiss, forcing defiance into my voice. "You need me for the bid."

He pulls back the gun, holstering it with a grim nod.

"At least you understand that much," He whispers, his gaze icy as he looks me up and down. "Get up, Eden. It's time to get you prepared."

With shaking hands, I grab Roman's gun, rising to my feet. Coated in my mother's blood, I point the weapon at his head, struggling to steady my grip.

He raises his hands, a twisted smile spreading across his face.

"I see you came prepared."

"Take another step, and I'll put a bullet right between your eyes," I warn. "Now, where is Aiden?"

My father shakes his head, a mocking tone in his voice.

"Aiden isn't here. And you're not the only one who came prepared, Eden."

Before I can react, something hard and cold smashes into the back of my head, sending me crashing to the floor. Pain explodes through my skull and my vision blurs. I claw at the floor, trying to reach the gun, but it's kicked away. A strong hand grips my hair, yanking my face up from the ground.

"Knock her out. It's time to get her ready for the bid."

My face is forced down into the hardwood floor, darkness closing in.

If you can hear me, God, please don't let me die here.

Psalm 91:1: "Whoever goes to the LORD for safety, whoever remains under the protection of the Almighty, can say to him, "You are my defender and protector"

Chapter 36

ROMAN

Feeling around for Eden's warmth, I'm startled to find only empty space where she should be.

Sitting up, the faint light of dawn barely illuminates the room, offering little to go on.

"Eden?" I call out, my voice echoing unanswered. There's no sign of her in the bathroom.

I get out of bed and find the drawers where I keep my clothes in disarray, their contents scattered across the floor.

"Eden?" I try again, my voice rising with worry. I grab my phone, hoping for some clues.

No missed calls.

My eyes scan the room, and then it hits me: something else is missing.

I move toward the dresser, glancing at the top.

Where the hell is my Glock?

I swing open the bedroom door and fidget with the waistband of my sweats, heading toward the kitchen. My gaze locks with

Aiden's, who's sitting at the table with a spoon hanging from his mouth.

"Where's your sister?" I demand, noticing the bruises and scratches on my sides.

"Isn't she with you?" Aiden asks, looking disheveled and confused as if he had a rough night himself.

All our car keys are in their usual spot, untouched.

"I'm calling her," I snap, pulling out my phone.

I dial her number, but it goes straight to voicemail. I redial three more times, each unanswered call heightening my fear.

Zoey emerges from Aiden's room, rubbing sleep from her eyes.

"Hey guys—"

"Call Eden," I cut her off. "Something feels off."

Without a word, Zoey takes out her phone. Moments later, she looks at me with an expression I dread.

"Voicemail," Zoey mutters. "What's going on?"

I pull up "Find My iPhone," my heart sinking as I see the last location where Eden's phone was active.

"She was at your house this morning at 2 a.m.," I whisper, my eyes locking with Aiden's. "Her phone hasn't been on since, and my Glock is missing."

Setting down his cereal bowl, Aiden's face hardens, all traces of playfulness erased.

"Why the hell would she go there?" Aiden's voice trembles with unease.

"I don't fucking know," I growl, pulling on a hoodie and securing one of my pocket knives into my waistband. "But I'm not about to sit around and wait for answers."

I wrench open the front door, my breath catching at the sight of the visitor.

Echo stands there, his hand poised to knock, a large coffee in the other. Despite the years, his golden brown hair and rich dark eyes remain unchanged, though a deep scar runs like a river down his cheek—his only flaw.

"Jesus, if you were this excited to see me, I might have put on some ChapStick and given you a kiss—"

"Get the fuck out of my way, Echo," I snap, shoving past my old friend with a raw edge of desperation.

Echo's grip tightens on my arm, his eyes flashing with concern. "You and your girl are the ones who called me out here, Roman—"

"She's gone," I bite out, my tone hard as steel. "The last place she was is the last place she needs to be. Move aside, or I'll break your arm."

Aiden's voice cuts through the tension. "Roman, it's my dad," He says, his voice barely above a whisper.

I whip around to see David's name lighting up Aiden's phone screen, my heart hammering in my chest.

"Give that to me!" I bark, snatching the phone from Aiden's hand.

"David—"

"Put me on speaker, Roman. I'm assuming my son is there if you have his phone."

With a reluctant swipe, I hit the speaker button, allowing Echo to step inside, his presence a grim shadow in the doorway.

"Am I on speaker?" David's voice crackles through the line.

"Where the hell is she, David—"

"Watch your tone with me, Roman. I'd hate for anyone to get hurt because of your disrespect."

A piercing scream rends the air, Eden's cries distorted by muffling, her anguish slashing through me like a blade. My heart constricts with every sob, the raw pain palpable even through the phone.

"Eden—"

"Ready to listen?" David's voice is cold, detached, as Eden's sobs recede into the background.

"David, if you lay another hand on her—"

"You'll what?" His voice is a sneer, untroubled.

Echo, ever the professional, records the conversation, his gaze steely and focused.

"Here's the deal, Roman," David's voice purrs. "We play this game by my rules. You cooperate, and everyone gets what they want."

"What do you need from me?" My voice is a taut wire, every word laced with desperation.

My sole focus is keeping Eden alive, no matter the cost.

"What I need you to do is quite simple. Attend the bidding. Swear your oath to the church. Vow to keep its secrets buried deep, and then find your way out of Idlewood. Only when you leave town will Eden be free from the confines in which I've ensnared her."

I slam the mute button on the screen, my gaze snapping to Echo.

"There's no fucking way I can agree to that. He's asking me to trust he won't hurt her further."

"We need leverage," Echo insists. "Proof that this isn't just talk. If you can get me video footage from that church, I can bring in my team from the nearest city. Evidence is the only way we'll end this, Roman. I can rig a camera on you, funnel the live feed to myself. We're at a crossroads. We either act now and hope she's safe, or we don't and face the unknown."

Staring at Echo, it feels like a loaded gun is aimed not at me but directly at Eden.

"Roman? 5, 4, 3, 2—"

"I'm still here, David," I growl. "Fine. I'll agree to your terms, but I need confirmation that she's okay right now."

I hear him scoff, followed by the shuffling of movement.

"Speak up, bitch," David snarls.

Don't you fucking speak to her that way.

I swear to God, I'll kill David—

"Roman," Eden gasps.

Has she been screaming?

"Eden, are you okay—"

"Roman. I don't want to be here. Please—"

A harsh slap rings out, and she gasps. Gripping my phone with white-knuckled intensity, I fight to keep my composure.

"See what you've made me do, Roman?"

"Rot in hell, you bastard!" I roar, her muffled sobs making the situation even more unbearable.

David's laughter drifts through the line, followed by a clearing of his throat.

"There's someone else who would like to speak to you, Roman," David's voice takes on a mocking tone.

Another voice clears its throat, deep and authoritative.

"Quite a mess you've made, Roman."

Father Kevin.

"Says the man who deceived me about the true nature of my priesthood at this depraved church—"

"Now is not the time for moral high ground, Roman. At least I've never sullied an altar server and made the mistake of falling in love with her," He snaps. "I had grand plans for you. I thought you'd surpass those before you. But looking at your precious girl now, I understand why you faltered. She truly is delectable. See you soon, Roman."

"Wait—"

The screen goes black as the call ends. Trembling with adrenaline, I hurl Aiden's phone across the room, watching it shatter upon impact. My rage erupts in a scream, my only focus now on Eden.

"Roman, you need to calm down," Echo's voice is a calming force, his hand resting firmly on my shoulder.

"Calm down?" I explode, face-to-face with him. "The woman I love is being tortured, and I'm just standing here doing nothing—"

"You have an in," Echo snaps back. "I'll accompany you to the event. They can't stop me. We'll get her out, and all the other kids too. But until then, we have to be strategic. So, do your fucking job, keep a strong front, and when the time comes, help me expose all of this," Echo pleads.

Eden's screams and sobs echo in my mind, leaving me feeling nothing but defeat.

"So I'm supposed to just sit and wait, hoping for the best?" My question hangs in the air, met with silence from everyone around me.

"It's all we can do for now, Roman," Echo's voice is a soft plea.

Shaking my head, I grab my coat and head for the front door, ignoring the barrage of questions from the group.

"Roman—"

"I still have a job," I snap. "Or are we all pretending that everything is fine?"

The room falls silent, the weight of my words heavy.

"If anything happens to Eden, I will burn that church to the ground with everyone inside."

With that, I slam the door behind me, my hand gripping the knife in my pocket.

They want to wait? Fine.

No one said I had to follow along.

Given the afternoon light, it's far too early for anyone to be at the church on a Friday. As I touch my hand to fidget with my ring, a wave of nausea overtakes me when I realize its absence.

It's around Eden's neck.

I tuck my hands into my pockets, trying to steady my thoughts.

Approaching the office, I know the files within might be critical for Echo's efforts to expose this place sooner. Inside, the room appears unnervingly pristine, as though someone had recently swept through and tidied up.

I search for anything useful, but all the drawers are bare. The only item remaining on the shelf is a solitary Bible.

Sliding into the office chair, I attempt to power on the computer, only to find its wires severed.

They've already swept through here.

"Trying to find her?" Kevin's voice oozes from the doorway, his smugness palpable.

I turn slowly to face him. He stands there with a self-satisfied grin.

"I really thought you would have figured out where she was by now, given your military background in land navigation."

Land nav? That's all about paths and maps—maps.

The new construction plans. The renovations.

"Where did you put the blueprints?" I demand, my hand still clenched around the knife.

Kevin rises, a sneer playing on his lips. "You're putting it together too late, Roman. If I wanted you to see the blueprints, I would have left them where you could find them."

"She's in this church," I growl.

"Maybe. We had to transport all the items here for the big day on Sunday. Closing the church for a private event isn't simple. Everything must be perfect—"

I move swiftly, grabbing his collar. "Where is she, Kevin?" I narrow my eyes, my voice thick with anger.

"I would assume right now they're preparing her for the highest bidder. Though, she's quite a fighter. They'll need a lot of makeup to hide her bruises once we're done—"

I strike him hard, sending him crashing to the ground. I climb on top of him, drawing the knife from my pocket. Pressing it to his throat, he grins with a sickening delight.

"Where is my girl? Final fucking chance."

Coughing, Kevin shakes his head defiantly. "You think I fear death, Roman? There will always be another ready to take my place. God is watching you, and He's judging. Killing me won't solve anything—"

"No," I hiss, "I think it sends a message."

I slide the blade across his throat, and his shock is palpable. As his blood spills onto my face, I shift the knife to his chest, stabbing him repeatedly until his movements cease. Feeling around, I find the church keys and decide to lock him inside.

When this is all over, I'd gladly face any jail time if it means I'm one step closer to Eden.

I search for anything else of use, finding his phone and tucking it into my pocket. Stepping over his bloodied body, I remove my shoes and wipe my face with my jacket before draping it over him.

As I exit the office, I lock the door behind me. The phone buzzes in my pocket. Checking the screen, a flicker of hope ignites.

David Faulkner:

Everything is ready.

Eden is fine.

Bidders will arrive tonight.

Are we clear? Is the office cleared out?

I reply with a terse "yes," slipping the phone back into my pocket.

If God is watching me now, let's hope He still has some forgiveness left.

Colossians 3:13 "Bear with each other and forgive one another if any of you has a grievance against someone. Forgive as the Lord forgave you."

Chapter 37

EDEN

My head—it's like a drum pounding incessantly, the pain unbearable.

Why does it hurt so damn much?

I roll onto my back, gripping my throbbing head, desperately trying to piece together the fragments of my fractured memory. The phone call from my mother echoes in my mind, her voice quivering with fear.

And my father. He seized her. He hurt her.

My house. I rushed to my house.

I close my eyes, and the horrific image of my mother's lifeless body sprawled on the floor floods my mind. My hand reaches for Roman's gun before—

The impact. He struck me in the head.

Forcing my eyes open, I try to stand, only to be jolted by a sharp collision with cold metal. Blinking through the veil of darkness still clouding my vision, my eyes gradually adjust to the dim, oppressive gloom of the room.

I feel around, my hands encountering nothing but metal. The realization dawns on me: I am enclosed in a cage.

A dog cage.

What the hell is this?

I shake the bars, the rattling sound mingling with faint, sorrowful sobs nearby. The room is illuminated only by the flickering glow of candles, casting erratic shadows that dance across the walls. The air is thick with the musty scent of dampness and decay.

I hear the sobbing again and shake the bars harder, my fingers probing through the gaps in an attempt to grip them tightly.

"Is someone there?" I croak, surprised by how parched my throat feels.

Movement catches my eye a few feet away. Another metal cage shifts, and I realize that I am not alone.

"Yes," A young voice whispers, laden with despair. "There are about twenty others down here."

The children.

The fucking children.

I shake the gate of my cage with all my strength, desperate to find any give.

"It's okay, sweetie," I whisper, trying to sound reassuring despite the pounding in my head. "I'll find a way out of here—"

"You're Eden," The young girl's voice trembles. "They've been talking about bringing you down here for days."

"H-How long have you been down here?" I ask, my voice barely more than a rasp.

"I-I don't know," She replies, her voice muffled by tears. "They pump us with stuff from those clear bags," She gestures weakly, and I finally notice the IV drip attached to both her and my arm. "It makes everything confusing."

Ripping the IV from my arm, I clench the needle tightly, my mind racing. I need to get out, I need to—

"Take yours out," I whisper urgently. "All of you, take them out—"

"That only makes things worse," She hisses, fear evident in her voice. "Please, just stay quiet and listen—"

I glance down at myself and realize, with a shock of revulsion, that I am no longer in Roman's clothes. I'm wearing a white medical gown. My undergarments are gone.

What the hell is happening?

"The bid will happen soon," The girl sobs. "The men upstairs promise we'll go somewhere better than this. Maybe my new family will help me find my momma—"

"Upstairs?" I question, my voice trembling.

The girl falls silent, leaving me to listen to the muffled groans and sobs from the other girls in their cages. My focus shifts to the distant sound of a piano playing somewhere above us.

Jesus Christ.

We're in the church's basement.

Reaching for Roman's ring for solace, I discover it's been taken. They stripped me clean.

I jiggle the cage again, the lock sliding tantalizingly close but still just out of reach.

"Have any of you ever tried to get out?" I ask.

The girl's silence speaks volumes.

These cages were built for children, not for a grown woman.

Scooting on my rear, I press my feet against the gate's door, bracing myself for a desperate attempt to break free.

With every ounce of strength I can muster, I slam my feet against the gate. The loud rattling makes some of the other girls gasp.

"Don't—"

Ignoring her plea, I continue pounding the gate with my feet, shouting with each impact.

"Just," I yell. "Fucking," the lock rattles with each strike. "Open!"

The gate swings open with a creak, my heart pounding in my chest.

Still clutching the needle, I drag myself across the cold, grimy floor. I grab the first candle I can find and force myself upright, using the wall for support. The flickering light reveals the horrifying scene before me.

Dozens of cages surround me, some filled with multiple small children. They are dirtied and gaunt, their eyes pleading as they rub their faces with grimy hands.

All these children.

They've been here, hidden beneath this church, and no one had a clue.

Kneeling by the cage next to me, I unlock it, reaching inside before the girl can protest.

"No, no—"

I grab the girl's arms, making her focus on me.

"That IV is coming out, and then I'm finding us a way out of here," I whisper fiercely. "What they're putting in you won't help you get home to your mother. I need you to work with me here. What's your name?"

She hesitates but then meets my gaze.

"Hannah," She whispers, her voice trembling.

"Okay, Hannah, I'm going to take this out," I say, gently pulling the IV from her arm. She flinches, and I'm struck by the dark circles beneath her eyes.

How can a loving God allow this?

Where is my sign to have faith in Him?

I toss the IV aside, clutching the needle. I'm determined to drag Hannah out of this cage and find a way to escape.

"Okay, Hannah, we will get you and the other girls out of here—"

Suddenly, a door creaks open, and light spills down a staircase a few hundred feet away from us.

Hannah puts a finger to her lips, signaling me to be quiet and get back into my cage.

I shake my head, keeping her cage closed, and press myself into the shadows, hoping they conceal me well enough.

Two large figures descend the staircase, flashlights in hand, sweeping the cages furthest from us.

"All of them are here?" My father's voice questions, laced with menace.

Vile pig.

"Yup, all of them—"

Father Kevin.

"We should be able to get them all cleaned up tonight once they're out cold from the drips. Then, we show them off tomorrow and finally get our payday," Kevin's voice seethes with greed.

Vile men.

Their flashlights swing in my direction, and I press against the wall, my heart pounding as I watch Hannah's IV being reattached. Her fear is palpable.

"Wait," My father hisses. "Is... Is my daughter's cage open?"

I hold my breath, staring at the staircase. I could run. I could—

"Where the hell is she?" Kevin bellows, rattling Hannah's cage.

"I—I don't know—"

"Don't fucking lie to me!" My father roars, kicking the cage hard enough to make Hannah's head slam against the side.

"Don't you dare fucking lie to me right now—"

I charge toward my father, needles clenched in my fists. With all my strength, I slam them into his side, climbing onto his back and yanking them free before driving them back in. I scream with every ounce of breath in my lungs, kicking Kevin away and preparing to slam the needles down again.

"This is for my fucking mom!" I shout, seconds away from plunging these filthy needles into my father's jugular.

"And this is for all of these kids—"

Pain seizes me as my hair is yanked, and I'm slammed to the cold floor. The impact knocks the air from my lungs. Gasping, I feel something cold press against my forehead, forcing me down.

"You fucking bitch—"

"Shut up, David. My parents don't pay you to allow slip-ups like this."

A cold, metallic sensation presses against my forehead.

"L-Luca?" I whisper, recognizing the weight of the gun.

"Hello there, Angel," Luca hisses, his shadow looming over me.

My gaze falls on Roman's ring, dangling from Luca's neck, a taunting reminder of what's been stolen from me.

"Luca, what the hell are you doing—"

"Oh, come on, Eden. We can be honest with each other now," He says, his voice dripping with malice. "You fuck the priest. I try and give you an out by being mine. Clearly, you wanted the more nuclear option," He sneers, running his hand up my thigh. "Though, I don't think I've ever had to pay so much for a woman I want so bad," He snaps.

"Get your fucking hands—"

"Ah," Luca interrupts, pressing the gun harder into my head. "I'm sure you and the priest got up to some nasty stuff. Not that I'm one to kink shame, but there's a bullet in this chamber, Eden. I'm sure you're much less fun as a corpse," He says coldly. "So stay on the fucking ground and listen."

I remain motionless, my father now clutching his side, his face contorted with rage.

"Where is your brother, Eden?" My father demands, stepping closer with Kevin.

I spit on his shoes, a defiant grin spreading across my face.

"Fuck you—"

Luca uses the gun's barrel to strike my jaw, then grips my chin, his touch both painful and invasive.

"Come on, Eden, is it really that hard to cooperate?" He taunts, his hand moving further up my leg.

"Stop fucking touching me—"

"Then tell him where your brother is," Luca snaps. "And nothing else has to happen to you."

"Rot in hell," I hiss defiantly.

"Fine," Luca sighs with a sinister edge. "I should have assumed you'd prefer things to be painful."

He grabs one of the discarded needles and keeps me pinned with his legs, resting the gun above my heart. With brutal force, he drags the needle up my thigh. The searing pain makes me scream, my cries muffled by his hand clamped over my mouth.

"I'm sure Roman is with her brother," Luca whispers. "Call Aiden's new number. It's in my phone."

I shake my head, trying desperately to divert my father's attention elsewhere.

"Don't—"

"Shut your mouth," Luca snaps, his hand sliding dangerously close to an area I desperately want him to avoid. "Or I'll make sure your first time with me is on a cold basement floor."

I clamp my mouth shut as my father speaks to someone on the phone, putting it on speaker.

Luca leans in, his breath hot against my ear.

"Extra motivation for lover boy."

The terror is suffocating. Luca's fingers invade me, making the screams erupt from my throat, raw and unrestrained. His intrusion is a violation that amplifies my dread and helplessness.

I cry until I can't cry anymore, the agony relentless as his fingers continue their assault.

"He needs to hear her voice," Kevin whispers. "Stop what you're doing."

Luca's hand remains over my mouth as he reluctantly pulls his fingers away, my body trembling from the trauma.

"Speak up, bitch," My father demands, holding the phone near my mouth.

Luca removes his hand, pressing the gun to the side of my head, his fingers still tainted with my scent.

"R-Roman?" I choke out, staring up at the men looming over me.

"Eden?" His voice, a lifeline in the darkness, reaches me.

It's him.

It's really him.

"Are you okay—"

"Roman, I don't want to be here," I sob, my voice breaking. "Please—"

A sharp slap stings my face as my father strikes me, silencing my pleas.

"Time to go back to sleep," Luca hisses, his voice a cruel promise. "When you wake, you'll be mine, and there's nothing you can do about it."

As my father and Kevin walk away, taunting Roman on the phone, Luca forces me back into the cage. He jabs a syringe into my leg, pushing the plunger down with a cruel finality.

My vision blurs, dark spots clouding my sight, my body growing increasingly heavy and unresponsive.

"Goodnight, Angel," Luca scoffs. "That's the last time you're hearing Roman's voice."

Laying down, the pain throbs through me, each heartbeat a reminder of my helplessness. My eyes struggle to stay open as I cling to the fading echo of Roman's voice, my last tether to hope.

All light has dimmed.

God has once again rejected my prayers.

Chapter 38

EDEN

I always wondered how my mother felt, lying on that cold floor, a handful of xanax in her hand and a bottle of wine to wash it down.

Dazed and confused, I had always assumed she was trying to numb the pain.

Pain from her failed marriage.

Pain from her failure to be a mother to Aiden and me for most of our lives.

Pain was all she knew.

Every time she cracked open that pill bottle, she was giving herself a fleeting respite from feeling anything at all.

Now, with an IV in my arm, my thoughts muddled by the drugs, I understand her despair more intimately. The pain that once consumed her is now silenced by the same drugs coursing through my veins.

This is rock bottom.

And there's no fucking way out.

Masked women, clearly patrons of the church who might have watched me grow up, move around me. What do they think as they cleanse my skin and prop me up in this chair, forcing me to stay awake while the drugs weigh me down?

Do they see the washed-up girl, marred by the scars of her own tortured mind?

Or do they see the innocent girl who once roamed the church with a grin, too pure to be in this nightmare?

As they apply mascara and pull my hair into a sleek ponytail, I finally see what they see.

Merchandise.

Just as they are to their husbands.

A disposable woman.

One destined to be sold like a goddamn pig.

"I think she's ready," One of them whispers, removing the IV from my arm. "They double-dosed her after her little stunt."

Two women support my weight as they drag me in this tight red dress across the floor. My eyes lock with Hannah's among the young girls being prepped. The dread in her eyes is palpable.

I thought I would find a way out for both of us.

I thought I'd escape this hellish nightmare.

Now, I question if there will ever be an escape.

Has Roman given up on me?

Did Aiden flee?

God, I hope he did.

I've been hearing that name more in my mind.

God.

I was never much of a pray-er before all of this.

It always felt like something I did out of routine, not genuinely trying to reach out to the divine.

Now, all I feel capable of is praying.

Praying for a way out.

Praying for death.

Praying for any release from this torment.

In my past suicidal moments, I thought my pain was enough to make me want to reach the other side.

Now, I know it can always get worse.

"What happens after the night is over?" I ask in a sluggish tone as the women drag me past the double doors into the main cathedral, steering me toward the confession room.

"They'll put you on that altar and sell you off. What happens after that is up to God's goodwill," One of them whispers.

"Is that what happened to you?" I ask with a bitter grin. "Did you let yourself be sold and used by those men?" The women fall silent.

"That was the case for your mother," One of them snaps after a moment.

My father.

He bid on my mother.

"What—"

"You didn't know?" One of them scoffs, her tone dripping with superiority. "God, she really shielded you and Aiden from the truth. Maybe your father will find you a new stepmother tonight," She snickers.

Nausea churns in my stomach.

All those young wives circulating through the church.

I always thought it was a product of religious tradition.

Like how an army base is filled with young military wives seeking escape from their families.

I never imagined—

"Time to line up and wait with the others," One of the women snaps, shoving me into a crowded room filled with drugged-up children dressed to impress. "You're first on the lineup, Eden, so maybe crack a smile."

"Wait—"

The door slams shut behind me, and I bang my fists against the wood, jiggling the lock.

Fuck.

I sink to the ground, surrounded by dozens of pained expressions.

"Why are you here?" One of the little girls asks, her eyes filled with genuine sorrow.

"My dad is a bad man," I whisper. "And he hates me for loving a good one."

"Is the good man going to be here tonight?" The girl asks, a chuckle of defeat escaping my throat.

"If he is," I whisper, "then God has answered my prayers for the first time."

Chapter 39

ROMAN

"Like I said, I will be with you tonight in case anything goes south," Echo reiterates, adjusting his tie for what seems like the millionth time.

Underneath his suit, a wire nestles against his chest, transmitting every whispered conversation to his team in the van parked near the church.

He tucks a Glock at his waist, the suit completing his formidable appearance.

"And how do you plan on getting in?" I ask, raising an eyebrow. "They're not expecting you."

"I've played the pedo ring game before, Roman. This is not my first rodeo. Getting in is the easy part. Not killing every fucker inside is the hardest," He snaps, his gaze sharp. "Getting those kids out will always be the highlight of my job every single time," He says, a smile breaking through his stern demeanor.

I flatten my collar, allowing a smirk to creep onto my face.

"I'm sure nothing feels better than blowing their whole operation," I say.

"And now you too can be a part of it," Echo beams. "Faulkner," He snaps, turning to Aiden and Zoey. "What are the ground rules?"

Aiden and Zoey sit on the couch, rolling their eyes.

"We stay here and do nothing to help," Aiden reiterates.

"Perfect, glad we're all on the same page."

Tapping my foot anxiously, Eden's sobs echo in my mind.

I'm getting her back tonight.

I'm not leaving that damn church without her.

"And what is your role tonight, Roman?" Echo asks, ready to question me for what feels like the millionth time.

"We wait for them to confess on audio, then your guys swarm in and take them," I whisper.

"And what are we not going to do?" Echo presses.

My only response is silence.

"Exactly, we aren't going to just roll in and kill them," Echo says, his smile condescending as he slaps my back sympathetically.

Sometimes, his misplaced optimism drives me mad.

"I can't promise anything if I see Eden is hurt," I hiss.

"And I'm not asking you to," Echo warns. "But my protections for you start to wane if you kill these assholes before I have the proof I need. So do the opposite of what you would normally do, and everything will be fine."

This asshole.

He's lucky I have so much respect for him.

"My mom is still not answering the phone," Aiden says quietly, glancing at his phone. "Her phone has been at the house all night. She never goes anywhere without it."

"Maybe your father has made the night a no-technology event for the women in his family," Echo suggests with a sigh.

It's easy to question how David could raise children like Eden and Aiden.

It's a miracle they aren't psychopathic little brats.

"You ready?" Echo asks, surveying me.

I nod, unable to offer more than a simple affirmative.

Crossing my fingers won't suffice.

The last thing I can promise Echo is that I won't end the night in bloodshed.

Echo gathers his gear, leaving a pistol on the coffee table.

"Both of you, lock the doors once we leave. We'll update you once everything is said and done."

Zoey and Aiden lean back, nodding.

"Bring my sister home, Roman," Aiden says sternly.

I walk over to the couch, turning my back to Echo, and slyly grab the pistol, tucking it away where Echo can't see.

Not even blinking an eye, Aiden knows my true objective.

"It's my only goal."

Leaving it at that, Echo and I step out.

Time to burn this church to the ground.

Judges 6:23: "But the Lord said to him, 'Peace! Do not be afraid. You are not going to die.'"

Chapter 40

ROMAN

"**F**ucking hell. Isn't this quite the fucking setup," Echo whistles.

The venue is packed with expensive cars, all being parked by valet. We pull up to the front, greeted by a servant hired exclusively for this event.

"Your keys, sir," The valet says with a practiced smile.

I'm ready to drag this man out and beat him senseless in the car, but Echo answers for me.

"Roger that, bud."

Echo hands off the keys, his men stationed outside in tactical gear, poised to raid the place at Echo's command.

As we exit the car, other couples glide into the church, dressed in their finest for the evening.

Echo pats the valet on the shoulder, nudging me forward.

"You can't kill every single person involved in this. These workers probably think this is just a party," Echo murmurs. "Keep your fucking shit together, Roman."

We approach the front doors, greeted by another server.

"Name?" He asks, grinning as he scans the list on his clipboard.

"Roman Briar," I snap.

The server's eyes move to the top of the list, and he smiles.

"Ah, Father, welcome. And your guest's name?" He inquires.

What's Echo going to pull out of his ass for this one?

"Jacob Harkins," Echo lies smoothly.

The server looks down the list, nodding with approval.

"Welcome, Mr. Harkins."

He lets us both in, and I glance at Echo.

"He's tied up in the van right now. My guys grabbed him before he could make it to his car. I've got his I.D. in my pocket," Echo says, a satisfied grin on his face. "I told you, Roman, this isn't my first rodeo."

Inside, the space is crowded with dozens of people. New faces lock eyes with me, each one dressed to the nines.

The air is thick with the stench of money—Botox and facelifts, a testament to the wealth on display.

"Keep your head up, Roman. The night has barely begun," Echo whispers. "Now, I'm going to socialize. Try not to kill anyone."

He breaks off, finding himself in conversation with a nearby group.

Fat fucking chance I do that—

"Roman," A voice cuts through the din.

I peer through the crowd and spot his golden eyes—Luca.

He strides over, looking smug, dismissing the man and woman trailing behind him.

"What the fuck are you doing here—"

"I could ask you the same thing, Father. If you've come for Eden, I'm sorry to say she won't be up for bid very long. My parents have saved a great deal for tonight's event," He grins.

He fucking knew.

All this time, he knew what was going on.

"That's why you befriended Eden?" I hiss. "You knew about this bidding—"

"Had you not fucked what was mine, she wouldn't be in this bidding at all," He snaps, his rage stoking mine. "I was willing to keep her out of it, but I suppose she needs true discipline from someone who isn't you," He smirks, tugging at the necklace around his neck.

I recognize the chain. I step toward him, fists clenched.

"I doubt you want to make a scene here, Roman. We do have guards of our own," Luca smiles, nodding towards the men in suits watching the crowd.

"I couldn't allow Eden to go up for her bid wearing this ghastly thing," Luca says, pulling the chain from beneath his shirt. My gold band hangs from the end.

"Where the hell is my girl?" I demand, fury boiling over.

"An hour ago, she was on the floor, learning a little discipline from me," He grins, my stomach sinking. "She was so nervous, tight as hell. Perhaps you can still smell her on my fingers," He hisses, dragging his fingers towards my nose.

Grabbing his hand, I'm two seconds away from shattering his bones.

"You fucking hurt her?" I growl, finally seeing fear in his eyes.

"Maybe if she had taken it instead of screaming, I wouldn't have had to—"

I drag his hand down, squeezing until something breaks. I cover his mouth, pulling him into a corner away from the guards' wandering eyes. Sobbing, I pull the gun from my waistband, pointing it at his lower stomach.

"I could kill you and your parents before those guards even notice. There's a silencer on this pistol," I warn, glaring at him. "Now take me to my girl and those children, or so help me God, I will bring this church to the ground—"

"Roman," David's voice cuts in, breaking up Luca and me.

Walking with another member of their little cult, both men are dressed to the nines.

Perfect.

Glaring at Luca, I see he knows better than to speak.

"I didn't know if you'd make it. The bidding is just about to begin," David smiles, smug as ever.

"Perfect," I hiss. "I wouldn't miss it for the world."

Guided into the main cathedral, I see that most of the altar's usual decorations have been moved, revealing an unsettling display.

A red satin chair now dominates the altar, with a beautiful young woman standing beside it, holding a sign with bidding prices.

Forced to take a seat next to David, Luca hides his mangled hand, positioning himself toward the front of the room.

I scan the area for Echo, but he's nowhere in sight.

"If you try anything fucking stupid, I will make sure the guards put a bullet in your skull," David hisses, patting my thigh with feigned sympathy.

I check the guards; there are too many people between us. They wouldn't reach me before I could deal with David and his loyal follower.

Perfect.

"Ladies and Gentlemen, welcome to the 10th annual bidding," Announces the man who had been shadowing Luca. "I know you're all eager to see this year's lot, so I won't waste my breath on theatrics," He jokes, eliciting a few chuckles from the audience.

Do they think this is fucking funny?

The man smiles as he looks around. "I'm thrilled with the turnout this year. Your generous contributions keep our organization running. Happy bidding, and may God grace you all this evening."

As he takes his seat, the lights dim. My hand grazes the hilt of my pistol.

I could kill them both now. I could—

Jesus fucking Christ.

Bruised and worn, she stumbles onto the altar, her face red and swollen from what looks like countless slaps. Staggering, she needs two people to help her get to the satin chair.

Dragged, her heels scrape the floor. The red dress she wears is so sheer, it's nearly transparent under the harsh light.

Petrified, my heart sinks as her head remains bowed, refusing to meet the audience's gaze.

Eden.

My Angel.

"Isn't she quite the looker—"

Seizing the back of David's head, I force him down in what appears to be a grimly affectionate embrace. With the barrel pressed firmly against his chest, the layers of his clothing offer the necessary buffer to muffle the shot. My sole intent is to eliminate every soul around me. As the gun fires, David's body slumps, his hand instinctively clutching his chest before collapsing against me, almost as though he's nodding off in my embrace.

I catch David's follower's startled gaze. He barely has time to react before he too finds himself in a similar hold.

The crowd, transfixed by Eden, remains oblivious to the subtle disturbance unfolding around them.

"We will start the bidding at two million," The announcer's voice drifts through the air as signs rise around me, indicating the opening bid.

Fucking animals.

Another pull of the trigger, and the follower's eyes widen in shock. His body slumps onto my other shoulder, both men now bleeding from their wounds, gasping silently for breath.

The dimness of the room cloaks the blood seeping onto the floor.

"Slowly bleed out, you fucking pigs," I whisper. "And know the Devil waits for you."

I tuck the pistol back into my waistband. The bidding number climbs ever higher as Eden's head lifts just slightly before—

"Sold," The announcer declares, gesturing toward Luca's proudly raised sign.

Seeing him revel in his victory, I struggle to contain my fury.

"She will be waiting for you in the lobby. Bring in the next bid."

As Eden is dragged across the floor once more, her head finally lifts, her gaze scanning the crowd.

Her voice rises in desperate cries, her eyes locked on a young girl being brought in, lifeless and carried by a single woman.

"Fuck all of you!" Eden screams. "Hannah, wake up!" Her voice cracks as she reaches for the young girl, battling whatever they've injected into her.

I must act now.

I have to—

"Homeland Security! Everybody get down on the fucking ground!" A commanding voice pierces the chaos as gunshots erupt. Tactical officers storm every exit.

I shove David and his follower aside, allowing them to writhe in pain, and sprint toward the altar. Luca, faster than I, is already clutching Eden, trying to drag her away.

We collide with the red chair, my knuckles driving into his face. Anger blinds me as I feel nothing but a surge of red.

Eden's focus remains on the young girl. In our tangled struggle, Luca seizes my pistol from beneath my shirt. I fight to keep it from him, my grip tightening around his throat. Clawing at my hand, he fights until he gets the opportunity to toss the pistol away from the both of us. Fear encompasses my chest at the sound of the weapon sliding across the floor.

"There will always be more of us," He hisses through clenched teeth.

"And I will always find you—"

His words are silenced as a burst of blood splatters my face. A perfect hole forms on his forehead, steam rising from the wound.

Shakily, Eden picks up the scattered pistol, her gaze locking onto me with a mix of fear and disbelief. The young girl, still hidden behind her, trembles.

"Roman?" She whispers, her voice breaking as she lowers the weapon, tears streaming down her face.

Rising to my feet, it feels as though God Himself has finally graced me with His presence.

And she stands right before me.

I rush to her, enveloping her in my arms, kissing her with a fervent desperation. Her tears blend with mine as I hold her as close as I can, savoring the moment of our reunion.

Hearing the frantic shouts of Echo's men, my world narrows to Eden. Her body quakes in fear as her forehead rests against mine.

"You came for me," She whispers, her voice barely audible.

"It's all over, baby," I promise, trying to offer her solace. "It's all over—"

A gunshot echoes through the room. Eden's eyes widen, and a choked gasp escapes her throat.

"Eden?" I call out, desperate.

Her gaze drops to her hand, clutching her torso where crimson begins to seep through. Her body tilts backward, supported only by my desperate grip.

"No, no," I shout, turning my head to see David with a gun, a sinister smile curling his lips.

Echo's men respond with precision, taking David down with a fatal shot to the head. Others begin extracting children from the hidden spaces of the church.

Gasping, I refocus on Eden, my hands pressing firmly against her wound.

"I need help!" I cry out, watching her eyes flutter as her blood pools beneath her.

"Damnit, I need fucking help!" I shout again, seeing the distant flashing lights of the approaching medical vehicles.

A hand grips my shoulder, and I snap.

"I'm not fucking leaving her—"

"Roman," Echo's voice cuts through the chaos. "We've got medical services from town. EMTs are coming in," He hisses, and men and women with medical bags rush toward us.

"I'm not leaving her!" I shout again, feeling the one thing I never thought I would—tears—trail down my cheeks.

The last time I cried was when my mother died.

Who knew this moment could feel even more excruciating?

"Roman, they will help her, but I need you to let them work—"

"No, no—"

"Give it to me," Echo demands.

I watch in a daze as an EMT hands Echo a syringe.

"What are you—"

Before I can react, Echo plunges the needle into my neck. A cold rush of sedative overtakes me.

Collapsing onto the floor beside Eden, I see her motionless form being lifted onto a gurney. Struggling to stay conscious,

I reach out for her, turning onto my back. The stained glass windows above reflect the flashing lights of the service vehicles.

Perhaps God answered my prayers tonight.

Yet, I wonder, what would my life be without Eden Faulkner?

Perhaps He will grant me one last miracle.

Mark 9:23: "If you can? said Jesus. Everything is possible for one who believes."

Chapter 49

EDEN

Gasping, I force myself upright, instinctively preparing to strike the first person I see. My fist connects with a torso, eliciting a pained cry that seems eerily familiar.

"Ow," Aiden hisses. "I was just getting you pudding," He snaps, the chocolate desserts falling from his hands onto the floor.

Blinking in disbelief, I pinch my arm, hoping to confirm that this isn't a cruel dream.

Surveying my surroundings, I see medical equipment and an IV drip steadily working through my veins.

My first instinct is to rip out the IV, but Aiden's hand gently restrains me.

"You're in a hospital, Eden," He murmurs. "Echo's team took care of everything. All the kids are safe," He adds, a smile of relief softening his features.

All the kids? They made it out?

"W-What happened—" I start to ask but falter, clutching my side, struggling to draw a full breath.

"Easy, warrior," Aiden soothes. "You took a bullet."

"Dad—"

"Is dead," Aiden says firmly.

"Mom—"

"Also dead," He replies with a sigh. "I went to check on her. I found her..." His voice trails off, revealing the depth of his sorrow.

"Roman—"

"She's awake?" Roman's voice interrupts, his hands overflowing with flowers. The sight of him, a beacon of hope amidst my chaos, brings a wave of relief that catches in my throat.

Attempting to move, both Roman and Aiden gently restrain me.

"You need to stay put, baby," Roman urges softly. "You took a serious hit."

"W-What happened?" I ask, my voice a whisper as I try to piece together the fragments of memory.

"I'll leave you two alone," Aiden says with a warm smile. "But I'm not sure how long I can keep Zoey at bay."

He exits the room, and Roman moves closer, carefully settling me back onto the bed. He envelops me in his arms, his touch a grounding force amidst the whirlwind of emotions.

"Fucking hell. I never thought you could feel as good as you do right now," Roman sighs, pressing a tender kiss to the top of my head.

"Did I kill Luca?" I ask, the fragments of memory surfacing in hazy flashes.

"He's dead, baby. That's all you need to know," Roman whispers, his fingers gently tucking a stray lock of hair behind my ear.

Tears well up and breach the waterline of my eyes. I bury my face in Roman's chest, allowing his embrace to anchor me.

"It was terrifying, Roman," I sob. "What they did to those kids, what they did to me—"

"I'll never let anything happen to you again, Eden. I swear to God—"

God.

Had He finally heard my desperate prayers? Is that why Roman was here?

"He sent you to me," I whisper, lifting my gaze to Roman's. "I needed you, and He sent you to me."

"God has a funny way of working," He murmurs softly.

"Not just this time," I sniffle. "In the park, He sent you to me. You've always been there when I needed you," I continue, my voice breaking as his hands cradle my face.

"Those twenty-four hours without you were literal Hell, Eden. I never want to be apart from you again," Roman whispers, his lips finally finding mine.

He kisses me with a passion tempered by tenderness, careful not to be too aggressive. As I cling to him, my fingers reach for his ring, only to find it missing.

"Your ring—"

"I don't need it," He replies softly. "The only thing I need is right here."

A gentle knock interrupts us. "Ms. Faulkner?" A nurse calls from the doorway.

I'm eager to shed that last name.

"You have someone who's been eagerly waiting to see you. If you don't mind a bit of extra company," The nurse smiles, glancing at Roman, who is occupying the bed.

"Someone's here to see me?"

"Let me in!" A young voice demands, pushing past the nurse with a bright new energy.

Hannah.

She scrambles onto my bed, her excitement palpable, completely ignoring Roman's astonished gaze.

"You're alive!" She exclaims, grabbing my cheeks. "The stuff they put in these bags made me feel amazing. You took that bullet like a champ," She says with a grin.

In the light, I can see how many teeth she's missing. A new vitality seems to have been breathed into her.

"You seem to be feeling a lot better than I am," I joke, attempting to lighten the mood.

"Thanks to you," She beams. "They found my parents! I get to go home."

Hannah finally notices Roman, her gaze full of curiosity.

"Who's he?" She asks, examining him with intrigue. "Is he the man you talked about?"

"Yeah," I smile at Roman.

"Pleasure to meet you, Mr. Roman," She says, extending her hand. "Me and your wife here are pretty close—"

"Wife?" Roman's eyes widen with surprise.

"I might have insinuated we were serious. Her imagination must have run wild," I admit, a flush of embarrassment warming my cheeks.

"Pleasure to meet you..."

"Hannah," She replies.

"Hannah," Roman echoes, his tone warm. "It seems you've done a commendable job looking after my wife while I was away," he says, his acceptance of the label unflinching.

"I did pretty well," Hannah grins. "Though she never mentioned how handsome your face is."

I laugh softly, pulling Hannah into a tight embrace, savoring the comfort of her hug.

"Am I interrupting?" A man's voice inquires from the doorway, his arms laden with flowers comparable to Roman's.

Hannah springs from the bed, eagerly high fiving the newcomer. Roman and I watch with amusement as his eyes light up.

"I told you the medication would make you feel fantastic," The man says with a smile, casting a glance at the nurse who is equally pleased.

"I think it's time for Hannah to get ready to see her parents," He adds gently, attempting to usher Hannah out of the room.

Despite her protests, Hannah follows the nurse, waving goodbye with a radiant smile.

Once the flowers are set down, the man approaches me, extending his hand.

"Echo," He introduces himself with a grin. "I believe the last time we spoke was over the phone."

I grasp his hand with eagerness, finally matching the voice to the face.

"You're the one who got us all out," I say gratefully.

"I was just a part of it," Echo smiles. "The real heroes are both of you. Though, I must admit, I didn't think Roman was capable of such a broad smile."

Roman nudges Echo playfully, a genuine laugh escaping him.

"Now, you two," Echo says with a grin. "Are you ready to share everything you know?"

Roman

Letting Eden sleep peacefully, I hold her close, sharing a flask with Echo.

"Jesus, I didn't think it would be as bad as it was," Echo sighs, taking a generous swig from the flask.

My gaze remains fixed on Eden, my fingers lightly tracing her delicate features.

"You really do love her, don't you?" Echo observes, his smile warm as he watches us.

"I'm going to marry her the moment we're out of here," I reply, my lips gently brushing her forehead.

"I never thought I'd see your smile again," Echo chuckles, though he holds back a deeper sentiment.

"Out with it," I urge, sensing there's more he wants to say.

"You did well, Roman. What's the chance you'll consider joining my line of work?" Echo asks, his tone sincere yet probing.

"Are you inviting me into your world?" I counter, pointing at him with a hint of disbelief.

"You'd be able to keep Eden safe. Travel. Retire," He teases, nudging me. "You'd find a real purpose—"

"My purpose is Eden," I cut him off sharply. "Nothing else."

"Well," Echo says with a sigh. "You know where to find me. I'll be sticking around Idlewood for a while, keeping an eye on things. I have a feeling there's more to this town than meets the eye."

He hands me his card, his eyes gleaming with unspoken words.

"I'm only a call away. We could make a real difference together," He says, stepping back.

I glance at the card, then back at him.

"I'm not calling you," I say, a smirk pulling at his lips.

"I'll be hearing from you soon, brother."

With that, Echo slips away into the night.

As I sit by Eden's side, I reflect on the trials we've faced and the road ahead. I look to the heavens, finding solace in the promise of divine grace.

Chapter 42

EDEN

S*ix years Later*

"Tell me what you see, Mrs. Briar," He whispers, his breath warm against my ear.

Surveying the vast rolling hills of Scotland, I nestle closer to him on the picnic blanket, allowing the serenity to wash over me.

"Freedom," I whisper softly. "Absolute freedom."

For two years now, I've been happily married to Roman.

Never has life felt so blissful.

"Are you glad I finally took some time off work?" I ask, pressing my lips to his.

"Just as glad as you are that I did," He replies with a tender smile, his lips brushing my neck.

For the past year, I've been teaching photography at a local university in Spokehaven, a picturesque town far from Idlewood.

It's a place Aiden and Zoey eagerly embraced when we decided to leave.

Echo had spoken highly of this town, praising it as the perfect move.

Transitioning Roman into his new role was seamless with Echo's encouragement.

"Happy to finally spend some time with my girl," Roman grins, his kisses trailing down my neck.

"People could stumble upon us here at any moment, Roman," I tease, running my fingers through his hair.

"When has that ever stopped me?" he replies, his hands moving down my front.

Reaching the hem of my dress, he slides his hand up my thigh, finding the warmth he seeks.

"You seem quite ready for me."

He slips his fingers inside me, sending waves of pleasure through my body. I gasp and clutch his shoulders, my nails digging in.

"You keep singing for me, baby," He murmurs, his tongue tracing my neck. "I adore it."

I stop him by grabbing his wrist.

"What—"

"Roman, there's something I need to tell you," I whisper, my voice trembling. "I can't go on without you knowing."

His brow furrows in confusion.

"I'm sure I'll still want to be with you," He jokes, drawing me closer.

Resting between his legs, I reach into the picnic basket and pull out a small black box.

Nervously, I offer it to him. He takes it, his fingers grazing my arms.

"Why are you so nervous, baby?" he asks.

"You'll see," I reply. "Just open it."

With curiosity, he opens the box, and his eyes widen at the contents.

"Is that—"

I reveal the small copper IUD, which I had recently removed.

"You were talking so much about wanting a family," I say softly. "So, I decided to see my doctor—"

"Is that your IUD?" He asks, his eyes scanning the small device.

I nod, watching as he places it on the blanket and then takes a second look at the remaining item in the box.

Pulling out a pregnancy test, I show him the two red lines.

"I tested two days ago," I whisper. "I'm pregnant, Roman."

His gaze shifts from the test to me, his emotions a mix of disbelief and awe.

"You're pregnant?" He asks, his voice steady but filled with wonder.

I nod, overwhelmed with nerves.

"My baby is in there?" He repeats, placing his hand on my lower stomach.

Another nod from me.

"Look, I know it wasn't exactly planned—"

"We're going to be parents?" He grins widely. "You're going to be their momma?" His face is alight with pure joy.

"Are you upset?" I ask, my arms wrapping around his neck.

"Upset?" He replies, shaking his head vigorously. "God, no, Eden Briar. This is just more of you to love."

He kisses me deeply, and I laugh through my tears, feeling his hands explore my body with tender care.

"Well, since you're already pregnant, I guess you don't mind if I—"

"We didn't come out here just for a picnic, Father," I tease, feeling his hand give a playful smack to my rear.

"Careful, momma. You know what happens when you use that name," He whispers, his lips brushing up my neck.

"Yeah, I do," I reply, my voice low and inviting. "So, get to it, Father."

He trails his lips down to my lower stomach, kissing it reverently.

"I love you, Eden," He murmurs. "And I love you too," he adds, his grin wide. "Though, it might be a bumpy ride."

I gently hold his chin, my thumb brushing over his cheek.

"I love you endlessly, Roman," I say, my hand resting on my stomach. "Both of you."

Smiling like a man in a dream, he kisses me with a fervor that makes me feel alive and cherished. We continue to embrace, lost in our love and joy until the sun sets.

If this is what my life is, then God truly heard my prayers.

And he sent me Roman Briar.

The Universe
IS
EXPANDING

Welcome
to Spokenhaven

University

-For I have sinned.

Acknowledgements

Dark Romance? Who knew I would be dipping my toe in that field?

I want to express my heartfelt gratitude to my husband and my dad for their unwavering support throughout this journey. Your encouragement, patience, and belief in me have been the pillars upon which I've built this endeavor. I am endlessly grateful for your love and guidance.

To my best friend, Bekah, your constant presence and endless support have been invaluable. Your belief in my abilities has pushed me forward when doubt crept in. Thank you for being my rock and for always cheering me on. My girlies at Indie Forge, thank you for being my rocks through the highs and lows.

And to all the readers who have embraced my work, thank you for making this dream a reality. Your support and enthusiasm inspire me to keep writing and sharing my stories with the world.

Love you all,

-Katerina

ABOUT THE AUTHOR
Katerina St Clair

YOURLOCALWRITERZ

KATERINASTCLAIRAUTHOR

WWW.KATERINA
STCLAIR.COM

KATERINA ST CLAIR IS AN ACCOMPLISHED AUTHOR CURRENTLY PURSUING AN ACADEMIC PATH TOWARD BECOMING A CREATIVE WRITING INSTRUCTOR AT THE HIGHER EDUCATION LEVEL. RESIDING IN THE MIDWEST WITH HER PARTNER AND HER BELOVED LABRADOR SONS, SHE IS A DEDICATED PROFESSIONAL WITH A MULTIFACETED LIFESTYLE. WHEN NOT IMMERSED IN ORCHESTRATING HER NEXT LITERARY ENDEAVOR WHILE ENJOYING MUSIC, SHE FINDS SOLACE IN CULINARY PURSUITS OR INDULGES IN EXTENSIVE READING FROM HER EVER-EXPANDING TO-BE-READ LIST. HER LITERARY PREFERENCES GRAVITATE TOWARDS NARRATIVES CHARACTERIZED BY UNFORESEEN TWISTS, A QUALITY SHE ENDEAVORS TO INFUSE INTO EACH OF HER NOVELS.

Also by

KATERINA:

The Order Series

Made in the USA
Columbia, SC
10 October 2024

556d556e-5df6-4ce3-8093-6b2f091ddbb7R01